EVERY DOG

Richard C Katz

Red Wind Publishing

For Lynn

PART ONE

THE WINTER

1

"Happy friggin' New Year," said Billy. He pressed a finger against a nostril, blew snot into the snow, then wiped his nose on his sleeve. He leaned against a brick wall glazed with ice, folded his arms and looked down at his shoes.

Doc sat against the opposite wall, legs crossed like a yogi, a piece of cardboard pulled out of a dumpster under him. They were in an alley off Boylston Street between Tremont and Stuart, facing Boston Common. The entire block was deserted because of the weather and time of night.

Doc tapped a paradiddle on his legs, then pushed his glasses back up his nose. He wrapped a hand around the paper bag on his lap and leaned right to look around the corner into the street. The view was eastward down Boylston in the direction of The Improper Bostonian, a strip club he and Billy used to frequent. No people, no cars. Just snow.

He leaned back, checked the contents of the

bag, and rested his hands on his knees. Nothing had changed in the past three hours except more snow, which now dusted his and Billy's navy blue pea-coats and black wool ski caps. Leather gloves and heavy work boots completed their matching mugger's ensembles. Doc added a tan scarf and a thick wool sweater from Goodwill. He was glad he did.

There wasn't much of a moon. Feeble light from a distant streetlamp cast a jaundiced glow over the snow, reflecting Doc's mood.

Billy wrapped his arms around himself. "I hate the cold." He stretched, then punched and kicked the air to stay limber and warm. Neither man expected Teddy to put up much of a fight. It wasn't his money, after all.

Doc brought the paper bag to his lips and drank some of the wine. He rested the bag on the ground and rechecked the street. He looked up at Billy and shook his head.

Billy squinted at his watch and asked Doc for the fifth or fiftieth time, "Jesus, where is this guy?"

Doc shrugged and sighed, then regretted it as cold air poured into his lungs like wet cement. He coughed from the bottom of his chest, forcing something deep inside to rattle. He stood up and bent over to regain his breath.

Doc felt a gloved hand on his shoulder. "You sound like shit. You know that?" said Billy as he leaned on Doc to pick up the bag with the wine bottle. "When we get the money, you should forget about going to Arizona and come with me and Tiff to Maui." He gave Doc a knowing nod, took a swig from the bag, then handed it to Doc.

Doc and Billy worked for minimum wage at Bernstein's Shirts and Dresses, Doc pushing a broom and Billy loading boxes. Billy's advice meant nothing to Doc.

Doc held the bottle and drank deeply, washing down whatever foul thing he coughed up. The taste of the cheap wine wasn't much of an improvement. He adjusted his glasses and looked across to Boston Common for signs of life. Nothing.

"Sounds like you finally made up your mind," Doc said, baiting the younger man out of boredom. As long as Doc had known him, Billy was falling for one girl or another.

Billy shrugged. "I guess. Tiff, she's different. You never know, but...." He looked down at his shoes and rubbed at his nose with a gloved fist. "I mean, the past six weeks have just... it's been, like...." He shook his head, then looked at Doc with something like hope.

Doc felt pity for Billy but kept pushing. "Like what?"

"Like... she's not perfect. Life's been no bed of roses for her, too, y'know, but she says me and her are a good fit." He raised his gloved hand to show Doc. "Like a hand and a glove."

"You mean a hand *in* a glove," said Doc. From what he'd seen, Billy was more puppet than glove and Tiffany was pulling his strings.

"Whatever." Billy let the hand drop. "You like

her, don't you?"

"Sure, I do!" Doc made a sweeping gesture with his free hand. "She set this up for us, didn't she?" The two men laughed.

Doc coughed and cleared his throat. He checked the empty street again. The wind slapped his face, stinging his cheeks. Even his eyes felt cold. He looked back at Billy and shook his head. *Nada.* Nothing. Nobody. No Teddy. No homeless huddled in a doorway. Not even a stray dog would risk this weather. Doc felt they were a just couple of chumps wasting their time hiding in an alley instead of partying like everybody else on New Year's Eve.

Billy slipped off a glove and pulled a bent joint from a pocket. He held it up to Doc. "Want a hit? Warm us up."

Doc stretched his legs. "Not gonna help my cough much, y'think?"

"Well, maybe one or two tokes...?" Billy still held out the joint.

"And what the hell did I say about getting high while we're doing this thing?"

"Jeez, man," complained Billy. "It's no big deal." He slipped the joint back into his pocket and stared at the snow clinging to the brick wall behind Doc.

"Got to take a piss. Be right back," Billy said to the wall, then started down the alley.

Doc watched long enough to make sure Billy wasn't sneaking a toke, then turned away when Billy began to urinate against the wall. Doc settled back down on the cardboard and shifted his weight, trying to get comfortable, but was unable to ignore the block of ice that used to be his ass.

Still, as cold and miserable as the weather was, he preferred to be outside—sky overhead, fresh air—even if he could see his breath when he exhaled. Doc coughed hard into his handkerchief, examining the phlegm in the faint light. He was only 33 but looked and felt older. Years of potential had been stolen from him, years he was never going to get back. Physically he was strong, but deep inside somewhere, he felt weak. A paradox, he thought to himself and smiled. Doc's a paradox.

Doc lived his whole life in Boston. He was used to winter. But the last few years, since he got out of prison, the winter months seemed colder and to last forever. And this winter, Doc admitted to himself, is the worst. He felt the cold saturate his body, and rubbed his arms as if to warm his bones. In prison he dreamed of being free and walking on a sunny beach. Doc still had dreams, but he no longer believed in them.

A car horn honked "shave and a haircut" somewhere in the distance. Then it was quiet again. He closed his eyes. A gust of wind brushed up against his face. It felt cold, but good, reminding him of the cold ocean spray off the surf as it booms on Wollaston beach. His head dropped and he felt the tension dissolve from his neck. He lay back onto a scratchy blanket on the sand. "Tide's coming in," he heard a woman say. "Maybe we should move the blanket back." He slipped his arm around her waist and pulled her closer. She felt soft and warm. "Not yet, sugar," said Doc. "We got time."

"Hey, old man! Wake up." Billy stood over Doc. Billy kicked at the snow. "If you're going to grab a nap every time I go take a leak...."

Doc eased himself up as he worked through the stiffness. He straightened his glasses and looked around the corner.

"I don't know about you," said Billy, grabbing his crotch, "but my balls are freezing—"

Doc raised a hand. "Headlights...."

"Oh, crap! Anybody with him in the car?"

Tiffany told them Teddy usually walked up Boylston by himself to make the deposits, but they had a backup plan in case he drove or brought someone else along. Billy would act like a drunk and stumble out into the street, stepping in front of Teddy's car. As the car slowed down, Doc would sneak up on the passenger side and, drawing their guns, they would flank Teddy and any passenger. Doc still wasn't convinced he'd shoot if Teddy hit the gas and made a run for it.

"Hang on." Doc brought a hand to his mouth and smothered a cough. His voice was harsh. "It's not his car. It turned up Tremont." He kept watching.

"Shit. 'Piece of cake' my ass! He ain't coming tonight." Billy leaned against the wall next to Doc. "He's probably getting high and getting laid, like everybody else. This sucks."

Doc, still looking around the corner, waved an arm to get Billy's attention.

"What?" asked Billy.

Doc turned to Billy and whispered, "It's Teddy. Definitely him. He's walking. Alone."

2

"Teddy? Alone? You sure?" whispered Billy. When Doc didn't answer, Billy tapped him on the shoulder, but Doc ignored him.

"Better late than never," said Doc, mostly to himself. He patted down his pockets. "He's crossing Tremont."

"Alone?"

"That's what I said."

"I thought he'd drive."

"Yeah, well, maybe he needs the exercise. Like I already told you, it's less than two blocks, not worth losing a parking space."

"Yeah, but he's carrying fifteen grand, maybe a lot more!"

"Said he wasn't lazy, didn't say he wasn't stupid."

Doc took off his gloves and shoved them in his coat pockets. He rubbed his hands together then took off his glasses and slipped them into a sweater pocket for safe keeping. He looked at Billy just standing there, watching. "Snap out of it, kiddo. He's going to be here any second. Move!"

They rolled their ski caps down into ski masks that covered their faces. They checked their guns, the first guns each of them ever held. As an ex-con, Doc couldn't legally touch firearms, and neither man could afford one. Somehow, Tiffany had managed to get guns for tonight. Doc's was a black Tokarev, an old Russian-made semi-automatic, scratched and pitted with years of abuse. He flicked the safety off and on and returned the pistol to his coat pocket, silently praying tonight was not the night he'd shoot somebody for the first time. Billy held a shiny chrome .38 caliber Smith & Wesson revolver with a four-inch barrel and no manual safety. The gun looked big even in his hand.

"Remember," said Doc. "Bring it down on him hard, but don't overdo it. Impress him but don't kill him."

"Don't you forget to grab his gun before he does," said Billy.

Doc adjusted his mask as he spoke. "I know my part," he said. "You play yours."

"I'm cool. I'm cool."

Billy did not sound cool to Doc. He glanced at his watch—2:02 am—and felt a strange mixture of fatigue and adrenaline.

Both men pressed their backs against the brick wall. Suddenly Doc didn't feel the cold. Billy held his gun in his right hand. Doc could hear him breathing fast and turned to look at him, but Billy's mask hid whatever he was feeling. "Relax," whispered Doc. "Piece of cake."

Billy's eyes locked onto Doc's. Doc tapped his cheek below his eye twice with two fingers, a silent sign of caution he'd taught Billy for *two-ten*: with your two eyes, watch this guy's ten fingers. Doc learned the gesture his first week in prison.

Billy nodded in confirmation.

A moment later, Doc heard footsteps crunching through the snow.

Teddy walked past without so much as a glance toward the alley. He wore a leather car coat with the collar turned up and a Red Sox ball cap on his head.

His ears must be freezing, thought Doc.

The wind picked up, and a crow cried as Billy stepped behind Teddy, arm raised. The gun came down like a hammer.

Doc heard a *crack* and cringed as Teddy crumbled mid-step, almost falling to his knees. He lifted his right hand up to the back of his head. Expecting this, Billy grabbed his wrist and pulled it down and back. Doc stepped in front. Teddy looked into Doc's eyes behind the ill-fitting mask.

"What the fuck?" he said, balancing awkwardly on his toes and reaching into his coat with his free hand.

Doc grabbed the arm, but Teddy yanked free, so Doc jabbed hard at his solar plexus. The punch landed low, but connected and took the air out of

Teddy. He doubled over. Billy held on tight so Teddy wrenched his own shoulder, crying out in pain. Doc reached into Teddy's coat and from a leather shoulder holster removed a shiny Colt Commander, a compact beauty.

Billy released his grip, and Teddy stumbled forward. When he lifted his head what he saw was Doc pointing the barrel of the Colt at him.

"Shh..." Doc whispered as Billy jabbed the tip of the S&W against the back of Teddy's head. Teddy, gasping for breath let his arms drop in resignation.

That was quick, thought Doc. He was close enough to see that Teddy's pupils were pinpoints instead of being dilated from fear. Teddy was high. Might do something crazy.

The crow perched on the parking meter next to them, their only witness.

Billy shoved the barrel of the S&W into the back of Teddy's neck. "This way," he said and guided him into the alley. As Teddy rubbed his twisted wrist, Doc wrapped a nylon zip cable around both wrists and secured it with an audible rasp.

"Hey—" objected Teddy, his voice hoarse.

"Shut up. Keep walking," ordered Billy.

"You don't have to—"

Billy gave him a shove. "Shut up I said!"

"What the fuck d'you think—"

Billy shoved him hard. Teddy spun toward the street. "Help! Fire!" he yelled, but his voice was weak and his shouts didn't carry in the night air. "Rape! Rape!"

Doc leaned into the punch, hitting Teddy squarely in the mouth. Teddy's head whipped back. His ball cap flew off.

"You asshole!" he screeched.

Doc cocked his arm, ready to hit him again, but hesitated when he saw blood spilling from Teddy's split lip. Billy stepped in, striking the side of Teddy's head with the Smith & Wesson. Teddy howled, spraying drops of blood onto Doc's mask. Doc stepped back as Billy swept Teddy's leg with his foot. Teddy went down.

"Jesus," said Doc, wiping his mask with his sleeve.

"You whinny little bitch." Billy hovered over Teddy's sprawled body. "I told you twice to shut up. What's the matter with you? Try that again and I'll curb stomp that big mouth. Got that? You listening to me?"

Billy didn't wait for an answer. He grabbed the back of Teddy's collar and dragged him through the snow deeper into the alley, shouting over his shoulder at Doc. "Ain't you supposed to be doing something?"

Doc ran to the front of the alley to check for anyone who might be on the street. There was only the crow, still on the parking meter. It flapped its wings and flew off. Doc ran back and caught up with Billy who had let go of Teddy halfway down the alley.

"Sit up," Billy hissed. Teddy sat up and pushed the ground with his legs so he could lean against the wall. He spat red into the snow.

Doc jammed a red and green Christmas-themed knitted ski cap over Teddy's head and half-way down his face, covering his eyes.

"Hey, man," Teddy pleaded, looking in Billy's direction through the ski hat. His speech was distorted from his cut lip. "What do you want with me? Do I know you or something?"

Billy kicked him in the stomach. Teddy squealed like a child. He rolled onto his side and raised his knees to protect his groin. Billy bent over the crumpled form as Doc grabbed Teddy's legs, binding his ankles with another nylon tie.

"I know who you are," Billy whispered, "and I know what you do to the girls."

"What? What girls? What are you talking about?" Doc was looping another zip tie around Teddy's legs just below the knees. Teddy's denial sounded genuine, adding to Doc's suspicion that Tiffany's story about Teddy extorting sex for stage time was just that, a tale intended to rile up Billy.

"You got the wrong guy, man!" Teddy said up toward the sky from beneath the bloodied Christmas scene. "I don't know what—" Billy squatted next to Teddy and pressed the muzzle of his gun against the side of Teddy's nose. Teddy became very still.

"That's a good boy," said Billy. "Not another word."

Doc went through Teddy's two outside coat pockets and withdrew from each a blue bank deposit bag pregnant with cash. He stuffed the bags into his own coat pockets.

Teddy shivered. "Can you take the barrel off my nose, please? It's cold."

Billy accommodated him and poked it into his temple instead.

Tiffany was clear there should be at least a half dozen bags and to open Teddy's coat to check the inside pockets. Doc unzipped Teddy's coat and pulled it open. Teddy's body began to shake from the cold or fear, but Doc didn't care. He was staring at a brown canvas messenger bag that had been hidden under Teddy's coat, hanging by a strap around Teddy's neck.

"Jesus," whispered Doc.

He yanked the strap over Teddy's head and opened the bag.

"Jesus," he said again.

"What?" Billy's eyes were on Teddy.

The messenger bag was full of blue and maroon deposit bags, every one of them stuffed. Jackpot. Doc zipped the bag shut.

"We're good," he said.

He turned back to Teddy with a little more respect. What else was he hiding?

He rifled through Teddy's inside coat pockets, removing three more maroon deposit bags and transferring them to his own pockets. He pulled out keys and a cell phone from Teddy's jeans and tossed them over his shoulder into the snow. He rolled Teddy over and took the wallet from his back pocket, then rolled him back.

Doc took a moment to zip up Teddy's coat so he wouldn't freeze. It felt out-of-place, but right. Then, he stood and unbuttoned his own coat.

"What are you doing?" asked Billy.

Doc put the strap of the messenger bag over his head, just like Teddy had done, then buttoned his coat back up and shoved the loose deposit bags and the wallet into his own pockets. He kicked the snow to be sure he hadn't dropped or forgotten anything. He and Billy exchanged glances. Billy nodded. Time to go.

"Okay, listen to me good," Billy said to the ski hat covering Teddy's face. "We're leaving, but our buddy, Mario, is watching you from the street so keep your mouth shut and don't move. Count to yourself. When you get to 500, you can yell your head off or crawl out to the street. If you try anything before then, Mario will cut your balls off and stuff them in your mouth."

Billy tapped Teddy's groin with the barrel of his gun to emphasize the point. Teddy's body jerked back. Billy smiled.

Billy stood. "Let's go," he said to Doc.

Billy and Doc jogged toward the back of the alley. Billy turned to check on Teddy. He hadn't moved.

"Remember what I said!" walking backwards as he shouted. "Count to 500. Count slow."

Billy turned back but Doc was already gone. Billy picked up the pace and ran to the end of the alley. Rounding the corner, he was relieved to see Doc on Park Street trying to clean his glasses. Doc had already rolled up his mask back into a ski cap, reminding Billy to do the same.

Snow was coming down hard. But Billy didn't notice. All he thought about was Tiffany.

3

The storm was making a comeback, dumping snow on the city as if in revenge for some perceived slight. Park Street was a featureless landscape.

Fat snowflakes swirled onto Doc's glasses as fast as he brushed them off. A blurry Billy approaching caught his attention. He gave up on the glasses and slipped them back in his sweater pocket. What was the point anyway? There was nothing to see, just undefined shapes and edges all in white. A heavy, wet New England snow. He started walking. Billy would catch up.

A part of Doc felt calm, almost comfortable, now that he was walking—even if in a blizzard. Confined spaces could make him anxious. He had sweated, schemed and connived in prison for the daily privilege of pushing a cart to distribute mail, magazines and books to inmates locked in their own cramped cells so that he would have a few hours a day away from his. In spite of the wind and snow attacking his face, out in the open trumped being trapped for hours in the narrow alley.

Street signs and storefronts were obscured by clinging snow. Doc counted the intersections to confirm he was on the right block. He was struggling through a snowdrift when he saw headlights approaching from Washington St. He turned his face away as the car, like an igloo on wheels, crawled down the middle of the street. Doc thought about the driver entombed inside and picked up the pace.

Sweat trickled down his back. His throat was raw, his ears burned and his fingers were numb. His nose felt like it was about to break off like an icicle. Parts of his body were cold, others hot, and all of him was tired. He had no choice but to slog on and get to Tiffany's as fast as he could before he collapsed.

He turned right on Washington, slipping off the edge of the snow-covered curb. He stepped back up onto the sidewalk and patted his pockets to make sure he dropped nothing. He looked back over his shoulder to check on Billy, a large, dark shape barely visible about thirty feet behind. How the hell a guy so fit moved so slowly was a mystery.

He heard the clank of thick glass bottles before he saw her. A woman in an oversized coat, big hat and scarf bundled up like a babushka, was on his side of the street walking toward him. A white plastic bag from the 7-Eleven up the street swung from her hand. She must be desperate to go on a booze run in this storm, he thought. They passed each other, avoiding eye contact like good and proper Bostonians.

He let Billy catch up before cutting through the parking lot of the 7-Eleven. A few cars were parked in front, one with its lights on and engine running. Doc and Billy walked side-by-side past the large windows in the front and side and the loading dock in the rear. They turned down a narrow alley where the snow was only ankle deep, allowing them to make better time. Billy pointed out a black cat lit from behind, a silhouetted sentinel in a second-story window.

"Bad luck," Billy snorted. He was only joking, but Doc didn't like it and picked up the pace. They were that close.

They reached the service entrance in the rear of Tiffany's building. A security light with twin lamps flooded the space around the door with a brilliance that reflected off the snow on the ground and flakes in the air. It hurt their eyes.

Doc walked up to the door and peered through a small circular window. The thick glass was crosshatched with an iron security grate. The blazing security lights outside made it impossible to see anything inside other than it was dark. That had to be good enough for Doc. Hours earlier, Doc duct-taped the lock to keep it from engaging. He put a gloved hand on the doorknob, twisted it and pulled, but the door didn't budge.

"Billy, it's stuck," said Doc, loud enough to be heard. "Give me a hand."

Doc cleared away snow from the bottom edge of the door with his foot, while Billy, breathing hard, jerked the door open, an inch at a time. It took a few tries before the door opened wide enough for them to slip inside.

The stale air felt colder than outside, but the lack of wind and snow made it close to heaven.

Doc moved further into the room, casting a long shadow over discarded furniture, cardboard boxes and indistinguishable shapes under plastic tarps. Behind him, the wind shrieked past the doorway with a high-pitched whistle. The edge of the door scraped on the metal threshold as Billy pulled it shut, cutting off the wind, the light, and Doc's shadow. All that remained was a single tunnel of light from the window in the door, a crazy crosshatched projector beam that sliced through the dust and dark, leaving everything out of its path uncertain.

Doc put on his glasses, pushing them against his face with the back of his glove. They immediately fogged up. He sighed and put them back in his pocket, then felt his way to the stairs leading up to the apartments. The wood creaked from the cold as he put his weight on the first step. He stopped to watch the door at the top of the stairs, waiting to see if someone heard the noise. He was pretty sure no one did, but you couldn't be too careful. Miss something small and in a bat of an eye your plans, every risk, and all your dreams were for nothing.

He heard retching.

Billy was on his knees throwing up next to a tarp covered box. Doc waited for him to finish, then stood over him, not sure what to do.

Billy wiped his mouth on his sleeve and hung his head. Diagonal lines of light from the security grate crisscrossed his face.

"Sorry, man. I...I got dizzy all of a sudden. My heart feels like it's pounding out of my chest."

Doc held a hand out to Billy, more to get him moving than to help him up. He spoke to Billy in a whisper. "You got the jitters now that it's over, that's all. Take a deep breath. Come on. Let's go."

Billy nodded, but ignored Doc's hand. "Maybe it's the dust. I'm allergic to dust sometimes." Billy wiped his sleeve across his mouth again and sniffed at it.

"Whatever," said Doc. He had no time for this. Sunrise was only a few hours away. "Come on. Tiffany's waiting." Her name did the trick. Billy grabbed Doc's arm and stood.

Doc led the way as they climbed the three flights to Tiffany's floor and opened the door onto her corridor. For such a dump of a building, the narrow corridor was surprisingly bright. Voices and music filtered through one door, but the rest were silent on the way to apartment 29.

Doc knocked with restraint and waited. Nothing. He knocked again. No response. Billy started to say something, but Doc held up a hand to silence him. Doc began to sweat even more. He looked back toward the stairs, then at the elevator at the other end of the hall. They were alone, but that could change any second.

Doc thought again about screwing over Tiffany and taking off with the cash. She had the inside information and came up with a simple-enough plan. And the guns. All she needed was some muscle to take the risk. The deal seemed solid, but Doc never completely trusted her.

And then there was Billy. Billy never would go along with running out on Tiffany. Plus, Billy thought of Doc as a friend. Doc liked the kid, most of the time, and trusted him well enough. Pretty much.

Doc held his breath, put his ear to the door and listened. He heard muffled voices. They sounded serious. He pictured cops with guns drawn waiting on the other side of the door, watching the knob for movement.

Billy reached past Doc and pounded on the door. Doc gave him the stink eye.

"What?" whispered Billy. "Maybe she didn't hear is all I'm saying."

Before Doc could respond, he heard the sound of the deadbolt and the latch. The door opened, revealing Tiffany backlit by light from the TV.

"Sorry, guys," she said, pushing blonde bangs away from eyes puffy with sleep. "I dozed off watching a show." She looked up and ran her fingers through her hair. "My hair's such a mess."

"You look great to me, baby," said Billy.

On the TV behind her was a big man in a suit

and tie and a petite woman with short hair talking in a car. Doc recognized the show from years ago.

"How'd it go?" Her blue eyes shined at Billy like sunlight off the Pacific.

Billy stepped into her arms. She turned her head and he pressed his cheek against hers, rocking slightly.

"Oh, Christ, Billy!" she squealed. "Your breath!"

Doc wasn't waiting any longer. He slipped past them into the front hall of the apartment. The air inside was warm and dry. He flicked on the overhead light and turned off the TV.

"Billy, sweetie. You're fucking freezing!"

Doc turned around to see Tiffany stepping away from Billy and brushing invisible cold off her white blouse. She herded him away from the door, then peeked out into the corridor. Satisfied, she closed and double-locked the door.

Doc unbuttoned his coat. Tiffany's eyes zeroed in on the messenger bag hanging from Doc's neck.

Billy followed her gaze. "See what we found?" he said. "It's full of deposit bags, too."

"Yeah? Wow!" She looked at Billy with a warm smile and cool eyes. She didn't look surprised to Doc.

"Yeah," said Billy, pointing at Doc. "We checked all his pockets. Doc even got his wallet."

"You didn't tell us about the messenger bag, that he was carrying so many deposit bags." Doc wondered what else she didn't bother to share.

She didn't respond right away. Instead, she pulled out two backpacks from the front hall closet, and left them on the floor by the closet door.

"I didn't know. You're not complaining, are you?"

Her backpack was a bright blue and tan 36-liter Osprey, brand new and large enough for a weekend of camping. His was a faded green day pack, not much bigger than a student's book bag. Now her oversized bag made sense to Doc. Soon his pack would be stuffed with his third and the rest of the cash in hers.

"Did you use the guns?" she asked. "You shoot him?"

"Nah," said Billy. "Roughed him up though. Doc busted his lip. We warned him to quit hitting on the dancers. He won't bother you again."

Her voice gained an edge. "I told you not to mention my name."

"I didn't."

"Good," she said flatly. "Take off your coats and head for the living room, but give me the guns first." She made a gimme gesture with her fingers. "Doc, make sure yours has the safety on, but don't unload them. I gotta get them with the ammo back to the guy tomorrow or he'll charge me extra."

They handed her the S&W and Tokarev.

"I hate messing with these things," she said.

"Who is this guy?" asked Doc.

"Just a guy. You don't know him," she said.

She carried the guns into the kitchen. Billy and Doc stuffed their hats and gloves in their coat pockets and hung the coats on hooks in the closet.

Doc was exhausted. He left the messenger bag and loose deposit bags in a pile on the floor by the closet. When he looked up, he saw Tiffany standing in the entrance to the living room staring at the pile, playing with a small fire opal droplet that hung from a thin gold chain around her neck. She looked up and waved them in. "You guys must be freezing," she said, a distant lilt to her voice. "How about some hot coffee to warm you up?"

4

Billy wanted beer instead. Doc said to make it two. Tiffany pouted. "Jesus, I picked up a bag of ground beans from Dunkin just for you, Billy."

"Beer, baby. I'm stilled wired," he said. "Coffee later. When we get tired. Right now, Doc and me got to unwind. You know what I'm sayin'."

"Sure." The pout turned into a forced smile and she disappeared into the kitchen. She returned with a six-pack of Whale's Tale Pale, which she handed to Billy and went back to the kitchen. Billy wrestled two cans free and gave one to Doc.

Doc plopped down on the couch just as Tiffany re-appeared holding an orange-colored Gatorade and a clear plastic bag of rubber bands from Big Lots. Cradled in her other arm was a bag of pretzels and box of Oreos. Billy helped her with the snacks and rubber bands. She twisted the cap off her Gatorade. The three of them raised their drinks, but no one volunteered a toast. Billy dug into the Oreos.

He lobbed one to Doc who caught it undamaged in a cupped hand.

"I hope for your sake one of Tiffany's New Year resolutions is to learn to cook," said Doc.

"Hey, I heard that!" Tiffany gave Doc the finger. Billy laughed, pieces of cookies flying off his lips. Doc held out his cookie to Tiffany as a peace offering, but she waved him off. He took a small bite and a long drink of the ale.

"Thought you were ordering Chinese for us," Billy said.

"I did," she admitted. "It was delicious. Boston has great Chinese food. You should try it sometime."

"You finished it?" Billy sounded more impressed than angry. "By yourself?"

She set her Gatorade on the coffee table and walked over to the windows. "I guess I didn't order enough," she said, pulling the shades down all the way. "Don't blame me. You were late and I was hungry."

The men looked at each other. Doc shrugged. "What'd you order?"

She didn't have to think about it. "Shrimp and lobster sauce. Sweet and sour chicken. House fried rice. Egg rolls and barbecue pork strips."

"No wonton soup?"

She thought about it and seemed to like the idea. "Yeah, hot soup would have been good."

"And, you ate it all," Doc said. "All by yourself?" She didn't look big enough to have eaten a dinner for three.

"Not all at once!" She walked back to the table and for her Gatorade. "Come on! What is this? You were gone for like hours, so I picked at it and before I knew it, it was gone. Sorry." She didn't sound sorry. She took a drink of her Gatorade.

Doc gave a sad chuckle. "Who knew you had such big an appetite? What big teeth you have, Grandmother!"

"Huh?"

"Little Red Riding Hood," he said. "She tells the wolf just before he eats her, 'What big teeth—'"

"All right. I get it," she said. "So now I'm the big bad wolf with fucked up teeth? Screw you!"

She turned away from Doc and pulled a small strip of paper out of a pocket. She held it out to Billy. "Here's my fortune if you want to read it. It's a weird one."

Doc finished his Oreo.

Billy took the fortune and turned the paper over. "We could order something now," he said, ever hopeful.

"I already tried. They're not delivering any-more 'cause of the storm," she said.

"*Life does not get better by chance. It gets better by change*," Billy read. "What's that mean?"

She tilted her head, then shrugged her shoulders which made Billy smile. Everything she did seemed to make him smile.

Doc slapped a short drum roll on his legs, then stood up. "Excuse me. I need to use the facilities."

The bathroom was down a short corridor next to the bedroom. Doc flicked on the light and the exhaust fan sputtered to life. He lifted the lid on the toilet and took the longest pee in recent memory, then flushed, remembering to put the seat back down.

He splashed cold water on his face, letting the tap run as he checked himself out in the mirror. He looked like he felt: tired and old. His eyes were red from lack of sleep. He bent over and sipped water from the tap, gargled with it, then spit out the residue. He found the toothpaste and cleaned his teeth with a wet finger, then rinsed his hands and ran his wet fingers through his hair. Too much gray, he thought.

He lathered up and scrubbed his neck and dried off with a yellow towel, embarrassed by the dirt he'd left on it. The rough material smelled faintly of gardenias and mildew. He dropped it in the hamper.

He flicked off the light and heard the whir of a small electric motor before he entered the living room. They'd started without him. Good.

Billy and Tiffany sat on the floor at opposite ends of the coffee table. Tiffany was in a deep squat, her feet in white sneakers flat against the floor. A mess of loose bills filled the center of the table. The blue Osprey backpack was next to her, zipped open. Doc looked around but didn't see his backpack.

The zipper on each deposit bag was locked. Billy sliced through the thick canvas with a pair of electric scissors, cutting off one end of the bag, then dumping the money on the table. His tongue stuck out from a corner of his mouth as he focused on not cutting any bills or fingers.

Doc went through the living room and fetched his backpack still on the floor by the front door. When he sat down again, he noticed Tiffany was texting on her phone.

"Who you texting?" he asked, a little more than simple curiosity in his voice.

She turned the display off and put the phone on the floor. "Nobody," she said. "Just checking my messages." She pulled her hair back with a scrunchie and said "We'll put the counted cash in my pack because it's bigger. Once it's all counted, you can take out your share and load up your bag. That's okay, isn't it?" She flashed a million-dollar smile. "Simpler that way."

Doc nodded. She was right, of course. The sooner they sorted and counted, the sooner they could split the cash and be on their separate ways. Fair enough.

The whir of the power scissors ceased. Billy shook the bag. Bills fluttered out onto the table. His expression was flat, lost and content in his work. He checked the bag for stragglers. Finding none, he lobbed it overhand into the corner by an upholstered chair where it joined other empties. He fished a deposit slip off the pile of bills, crumpled it up, and dropped it on the floor.

Billy attacked the next bag as Doc and Tiffany

picked through the pile on the table collecting $100 bills. They worked quickly. Most of the bills were hundreds.

Their job was to collect bills of the same denomination—$20s, $50s and $100s—into stacks of a hundred bills each, secure each stack with an elastic band, and toss it into the backpack. Tiffany made a notation on an app on her phone every time another stack went into the pack.

Billy turned the messenger bag upside down and dumped out 24 more deposit bags then started in on them one by one with the scissors.

Tiffany turned the TV back on. An old episode of *Law and Order: Criminal Intent* was playing. They continued working while actors played lawyers, cops, civilians, and perps in the background.

By the time they sorted through the last bag, the beers were long gone and the Oreos and pretzels were down to crumbs. The Osprey was filled to the top. The remaining bills on the table consisted of ones and fives and higher denominations too few to make up their own stacks.

Doc sorted them into three piles of equal value while Billy joined Tiffany in the kitchen. Doc could smell coffee brewing. He couldn't hear them clearly, but Billy was doing most of the talking. They returned to the living room, each with a mug of coffee. Tiffany held hers out for Doc, steam rising, but he didn't take it. He was busy distributing bills, so he gestured with his head toward the side table under the corn plant.

"Almost done," he said.

After a moment, she put the cup down on the end table. "I slaved over a hot stove to make this," she joked. "Drink while it's hot. Don't let it get cold." She pointed at the cash on the table. "How much is left?"

"It's up to $1,913 a piece, but there's more."

"Walking-around money," she said. She stifled a yawn and picked up her phone. Doc glanced up and saw her check her messages. She noticed him watching and put the phone down. She smiled at him. "Force of habit. Let me and Billy help."

Billy took two loud, long sips of coffee, then he and Tiffany took up their spots on the floor.

Billy distributed the $5 bills. "Every dollar counts, right, guys? We earned it."

Tiffany took her time pulling out the $1 bills and moving them to each of the three piles. There weren't many. After only a minute, she stood up and picked up her pack by the handle, testing its weight. "Huh." She sounded surprised. "Not that heavy."

Doc nodded and said, "And it'll weigh even less when I have my share."

Billy finished his coffee and held his empty mug up. "More please," he said. She jumped up and took his cup.

Doc held out Teddy's wallet. "You better check this out," he said, "and add the cash. Best to get rid of the cards."

"Forgot about that," said Billy. He opened the wallet and distributed Teddy's cash, about $300, mostly in twenties, then shuffled through the credit cards and ID's.

"Anything we can use?" asked Tiffany.

Billy slipped the wallet into his back pocket. "He'll cancel the cards," he said, "but something might come in handy later. I'll hang onto it for later."

"Suit yourself," said Doc.

Tiffany leaned over and picked up Doc's mug. It was almost empty. She looked at him with approval. "I'll get you guys refills," she said and carried the empty cups into the kitchen.

Billy sorted through the bills in his pile. "God, I'm hungry. What good is all this cash if we can't get anything to eat?"

Doc leaned in close and spoke in a low voice over the T.V. "Billy, listen to me. I don't think you should drink anymore coffee"

"Huh? What?"

"Bill—"

"What?"

"Is everything okay?" Tiffany appeared and handed Billy his mug. "Drink up."

Billy rubbed his hands. "$2,860 apiece. Sweet!" He sat back. "That ain't too bad a piece of pocket cash!" He took the mug from her. "You sure this is mine? I don't want to get Doc's cold."

"I don't have a cold," said Doc. "It's my allergies."

Tiffany made a face at Billy. "I don't mix things up," she said. "I used to waitress."

"No kidding." Doc turned to Billy. Billy always said he had a thing for waitresses.

Tiffany nudged Doc's arm with his cup to get his attention. He took it and put it down on the end table by the corn plant.

"Drink," she ordered. She sounded a little angry.

"In a minute," he answered. His eyes moved from the piles of money on the table to her face. "What's the total?"

Tiffany worked the calculator app on her phone. Billy lit the joint he was carrying and handed it to her. She took a drag without taking her eyes from the phone.

She smiled before she spoke. "Boys, we grabbed the brass ring," she said, exhaling smoke as she formed the words.

"Huh?" Billy leaned forward, his leg jiggling. "C'mon, c'mon, c'mon! How much?"

She dragged it out, her voice just above a whisper. "Two million, eight hundred sixty-two thousand seven hundred and sixteen dollars."

Billy sat back and blew a wolf whistle. Tiffany let out a whoop. Billy held his hand up to high-five Doc. Doc responded without enthusiasm. He was thinking how much more money there was than he expected and that it was all in Tiffany's backpack.

5

Tiffany toked again and passed the joint to Doc. He took a cursory hit and handed it to Billy who bogarted it, producing a thick cloud of smoke. No one complained. Tiffany picked up the remote and turned off the TV. For all the excitement a moment ago, the room was uncomfortably quiet.

Doc shook his head. "Two-point-eight million dollars...." He looked at the others.

"Closer to two-point nine million." Tiffany pointed toward Billy. "And there's the walking-around money."

"How much is that each?" Billy sucked on the joint, but it had gone out. He sounded as tired as he looked.

She looked at her phone. "$954,238, give or take 33 cents." She turned to Doc, eyes glowing.

"So, Tiff, for you and me, that's..." Billy rubbed his head with his hands, "how much?"

Tiffany glanced at Doc's empty mug, then

at her phone. Her thumbs danced on the display. "$1,908,476 for you and me." She batted her eyes and blew him a kiss. "We did it, Billy-Baby! Maui, here we come."

"We could get our own bar," Billy half-whispered, more tired than dreamy. "In Hawaii."

Doc reached for his backpack and sat it on his lap. "I hope this is big enough for my share. You keep my 33 cents if it's not."

"What's your hurry?" she asked. "It's still snowing and you both are beat. You ain't going nowhere. We could all use some shut eye before starting out."

"Doc, think about it, man," said Billy. "The kind of setup all three of us could have if we combine our money... in fucking Maui! We're gonna buy a sailboat and sail around the islands. Who's got it better than us?"

"Well, we can't stay here in Boston, that's for sure, but stuck on an island is not my idea of paradise. I like big cities. Phoenix is warm and laid back. San Francisco's like Boston, lots of music and movies, things to do." Doc stood up, the backpack hanging from a strap in one hand. "Wherever I land, I'll buy a set of drums. Join a band. Play in clubs. Live the life."

"Yeah, but..."

Tiffany put her hand gently on Billy's. "Leave him alone. He'll figure out what he wants in his own time."

"Suit yourself," shrugged Billy. "But we're

gonna miss your sorry ass."

Doc nodded.

Tiffany heaved the Osprey onto the couch. "Whenever you're ready, Doc. Go ahead and take your share." She sat down next to Billy and put an arm around him. "Make it an even nine-hundred-fifty-five-thousand." She made every syllable sound like dessert. "You earned it."

She scooted her butt around to watch as Doc began to fill his pack.

"Don't worry," he half-joked. "I'll give you an honest count."

"Don't joke about it. You'll hurt our feelings." There was no humor in her voice. She stood up and collected their empty mugs. "We're partners. I trust you," she said, on her way to the kitchen.

"Tiff looks happy," said Billy, his eyes unfocused as he reached for the joint in the ashtray. "Last chance. You coming with us to Maui, right?"

Doc took the joint from Billy's fingers and dropped it back onto the ashtray. "It's dead," he said. He cleared his throat and slid down close to Billy. "Y'know, Billy, I'm clearing out, but I'm worried about you..." Billy was staring off toward the kitchen. "Billy! Bill! Hey man, listen to me," Doc said in a hoarse whisper.

Billy slowly turned his head toward Doc, but his gaze drifted. "What?"

"Does something seem... a little weird?"

"Huh? Nah. What're talking about? The money? You mean Tiff?" Billy dismissed the thought with a wave of his arm, then looked down at a bill in his hand. He shook his head. "She's... excited about the money... and going to Hawaii together."

Doc shook Billy's arm. "But the haul... it's almost three million?"

"Yeah, well, jackpot!"

"C'mon. You think it's luck?"

"Yeah, sure." Billy squinted, thinking hard. "Sure." He didn't sound sure.

"When have me or you been this lucky, ever? This was no accident."

"So what? You're overthinking things again, Doctor. Look at all this—"

"You know the kind of heat that will come from stealing this kind of cash? Who carries this kind of money in the middle of the night? I—"

Billy yanked his arm away. "Shit, man! What's your problem?" He looked at Doc as if he was ruining the moment. "If you don't like it, then fine. Me and Tiff will keep all of it." He picked up another bill from his pile.

Doc checked his anger and kept his voice down. "Jesus, man. That's not the point."

He knew he should just follow the plan and split, but he couldn't walk away without getting through to Billy. He glanced at the kitchen before continuing.

"Hear me out. Think about it.... Your girlfriend told us Teddy was carrying about fifteen grand, right? Fifteen grand! Don't you think the, ah, situation here is more than a little weird, like she might've known all along Teddy was carrying like three million dollars! And the way she's been checking her phone. What's that all about?"

"Chill out, Doc. She and me are tight. Things are working out good for everybody." Billy was back to examining the bill in his hand.

Something sounded wrong with Billy. Maybe it was the fatigue and beer and the smell of all this money. Maybe it was something else. Regardless, Doc kept at him. "Think, man! Use your head! Did you ever think that Tiffany might have known Teddy was carrying millions and didn't want to tell us, didn't want to scare us off? Then it wouldn't be luck, would it? It sounds more like a setup. I mean, it's like, I don't know, that bar could never take in that much in a night, not even on New Year's."

"You know what? Now you're sounding paranoid, man." Billy held a $100 bill in his hands. "Hey, did you ever wonder why Franklin is on a $100 bill?" His speech was breathy and low, like he was talking in his sleep.

Doc moved closer. "What's the matter with you?"

Billy rocked on his butt as he waved the $100 in front of Doc's face. He sounded angry. "You got to be president, you know what I mean, to get put on money."

"What the fuck are you talking about?" Doc shook his shoulder again. "You sound—"

"Here you go, guys!" Tiffany was back. "Fresh

brewed coffee!" Billy tried to plant a kiss as he took his mug, but she skillfully slipped away and gave him a peck on the top of his head. She settled not on the floor but on the ottoman to Doc's left and handed him his mug.

"Thanks." Doc wrapped his hands around his coffee mug. "I think our Billy-boy is fading on us."

"He's tired, like you should be," she said. "Drink your coffee. It'll help."

Doc looked her in the eyes. "You're not drinking coffee."

Tiffany forced a laugh, picked up her bottle of Gatorade and took a long drink.

Billy burped into his hand.

"Man," he said, sounding breathless like he'd run up ten flights of stairs. "I'm bushed. I think I'm ready for...."

They watched Billy open his mouth. He emitted no sound. His head wobbled on his neck like a bobblehead on promotion night at Fenway.

"Billy?" When he didn't respond, Doc asked, "What's going on, Billy? Billy!"

His head turned toward Doc, but his eyes didn't move. "How come Franklin's on... ah." Doc had the feeling Billy was looking right through him. "Oh, sh...,"

Billy's arm dropped and his mug fell to the floor. All three watched as the mug bounced but didn't break, splashing coffee on the rug. All of a sudden Billy collapsed. Crumbling from his middle, he tipped sideways and hit his head on the floor with a solid smack. He let out a soft grunt and then everything was quiet.

6

Doc got to his feet, turning to Tiffany for help. He slowly sat back down, his butt balanced on the edge of the couch.

Her blue eyes were wide and satisfied. Her smile broad enough to highlight tiny dimples on both cheeks. She had a mature confidence he'd never seen before. Relaxed and in-charge. God, she was good-looking.

She held the Tokarev in her lap. He saw the safety was off even before she raised the gun and pointed the business end at him. He flinched, then looked past the barrel at her eyes again.

"Thought you hated guns," he said.

"I'm improvising."

Doc nodded with respect and jerked his head toward Billy. "Reds?" he asked.

"Something like that." There was no mercy in her eyes, not a hint of concern in her voice.

Doc looked at Billy's still body with concern. "He all right?"

Billy adjusted a leg and let out a small fart.

Doc and Tiffany laughed. The moment felt good until the gun barrel dipped a little and pointed at Doc's groin.

"Men are dogs," said Tiffany.

"Some of us are housebroken," Doc responded.

Tiffany laughed alone. "Look at us," she said. "We shared a moment."

Doc didn't move. She seemed different.

"You haven't been drinking your coffee," she said. It was a fact not worth denying. "Where'd you dump it?" Then, with mock seriousness, "You better not have ruined the couch. I don't want to lose my deposit."

Doc snorted, and grabbed a glance at the gun. She pushed herself back a few inches, putting more distance between them. The gun was more than an arm's reach from him now. He slumped back into the couch.

"I'll tell you, but I got to know where all that extra money came from." When she didn't respond, he added, "Please."

"Then you'll drink your coffee."

He nodded in assent.

She sighed. "Okay, but you won't like it." She took a breath. "They expect big deposits for the bar on New Year's, St. Paddy's Day, Fourth of July, you know, the big holidays."

"It's still a lot of money to take in for that club."

"Yeah, but that's when it's, um... easier to hide the *extra* money being deposited."

"Yeah, but it still doesn't explain..." Doc squinted at her. "*Extra* money?" It began to sink in. "The extra money... the millions... it's not from the bar, is it?"

"There you go!" She nodded slowly. "I knew you were the smart one."

"Where... Who...?"

She leaned back and looked like she was enjoying herself. "The owner of the bar, Kyle Kelly, launders cash for people. He usually takes Teddy with him to ride shotgun when he makes the deposits, but for the past couple of months he's been going home early, hurt his leg or something. So, Teddy's been making the deposits himself, sometimes alone, sometimes on foot."

"Who's he laundering money for?"

"You'll love this," she smiled. "The money you stole belongs to some Russian mob. And Moe Weiss is the middle man. You know who Moe Weiss is?"

"Moe Weiss from the Washington Street Gang?"

She nodded.

Doc let out a nervous jab of a laugh. "He's what, laundering money for Russians like, ah, Russian oligarchs or Putin or...?"

She looked disappointed. She shook her head. The gun didn't waiver.

"Don't get dramatic, Doc. They're just thugs.

Local Russian gangsters. Load their guns one bullet at a time like everybody else. They have a lot of cash they want cleaned up before they spend it. That's where Kyle and the club come in."

Doc's eyes drifted to the floor as he absorbed it all in. "I'm impressed, Tiff. I never would have figured all this out." He looked up at her. "Was Teddy in on it?"

"No." She pressed her lips together and shook her head. "But he might as well have been. He bragged to me about a lot of things. I barely listened to him until he mentioned the deposits. Eventually he told me about Moe and the Russians. It wasn't hard to figure out the rest." She sat up straight and rotated the gun 90-degrees, holding it horizontally gangsta-style. "Hence, the Russian gun...." She tilted it back upright, pointing it at his chest. "...In case I have to use it. That's up to you, sport...."

"Oh."

"...In which case I'll wipe it down and leave it behind." She shook her head. "But we're getting ahead of ourselves. Let's not complicate things." She waved the gun at him. "Drink the coffee and I won't have to shoot you. That seems preferable, don't you think?"

For a moment, Doc wasn't thinking about the gun or the coffee. He understood that he had been over his head from the beginning. The room was getting smaller and he was trying to hide the fact that he was having trouble breathing. This was Mariana Trench deep. He needed time to think.

Doc's voice cracked along with his façade. "Wish I'd known these details before we pulled this off."

"I'm sure you do." She straightened up, done talking. "Come on, now. I told you what you wanted to know. Drink up so I can be on my way."

Doc blew across his mug, stalling.

"C'mon, you pussy. It ain't that hot." She motioned with the gun for him to hurry.

Doc spoke into the cup. "Moe's the big guy, blond, kind of bald, right? "

"You'll know him when he sees you," she said.

"Who's the tall brother always with him?"

"Russ Peart. Moe's bodyguard. Ex-cop and Navy SEAL. One scary dude. I'm feeling a little bad for you and Billy when that dude catches up with you two."

"Yeah?"

"No."

"What's going to prevent me and Billy from telling them who you are, that this whole thing was your plan?"

He knew his mistake as soon as the words left his mouth.

"Sweetie, you don't know a thing about me. Maybe my name isn't Tiffany. And maybe I'm not from Boise. You ever consider that?"

There was no bottom to this. He felt like a fool.

"No, didn't think so." She held the gun in both hands and pointed it at the center of his chest.

"Time's up. Make up your mind: the coffee or a bullet. Don't think for a minute I won't pull this trigger. It's New Year's Eve! Nobody in this shithole building's going to give a flying fuck about one more bang or one more dead—"

He sensed the word was coming before it left her lips. He saw her turn up her nose and the hate spoil her blue eyes before her lips and the tip of her tongue began to form the first sound. As desperate as his situation was, all he heard was that word. He was almost—almost—grateful to her for freeing him up. He forced an unconvincing smile. Some part of him wanted her to sense what was coming.

He bent forward and grinned, like a mischievous child. He shifted the mug to his left hand. Her eyes followed as he lifted it to his mouth, then stopped. "You asked where I dumped the coffee," he said from behind the cup. "Don't you want to know?"

Without waiting, he tilted his head left, gesturing with the mug at the corn plant next to him. Tiffany started to object, but her eyes shifted in that direction. She couldn't help it.

Doc's right hand was already in place.

7

She sensed the pressure before the pain. The left side of her neck felt like it was struck by a hammer. Agony spread to her face and shoulder and emptied into the entire left side of her body. The room flashed red, then darkened until it was the color of venous blood. All this happened in an instant.

She barely heard the sound of a gun but knew she hadn't pulled the trigger. Something smelled pungent in the air. Something tasted sharp on her tongue. The pounding of her pulse filled her ears.

The black redness receded, replaced by white light, pure and brilliant. Like sunshine, it was everywhere. It distracted her from the physical agony. It filled her with lightness and hope, then joy. Sweet Jesus! Her eyes filled with tears. So this is what it's like! She felt herself float up toward the light, higher and higher, until she recognized the familiar pattern of an old water stain on the ceiling. Then she knew she wasn't floating up to the Kingdom of

Heaven. She was on her back on the floor looking up at the ceiling light.

She remembered she'd been shot. She didn't have time for anger or regret.

Blood, thick and warm, filled her mouth and flowed down her throat into her lungs. She couldn't stop it. The muscles in her chest strained, but she could not breathe. The drum beat in her ears slowed and stopped. Her body rocked and she made a conscious effort to cough but her body seemed to forget how. The blood kept flowing, crushing her from the inside out. The light dimmed. She blinked once with great effort. Then the pressure in her chest disappeared and there was only silence and darkness as she and everything in her world faded. Then there was nothing.

8

Doc lay on the couch twisted on his right side. Everything was still as stone except for a haze of grey smoke floating up toward the ceiling. The barrel of Teddy's gun poked out from the crease between the couch cushions and his right leg.

Only Doc's eyes moved. The close-range gunshot still rang in his ears, but he listened anyway for voices or footsteps or a knock at the door. Nothing. He waited a while longer to be sure. He glanced at Billy on the floor. The kid hadn't moved an inch.

A sudden sense of urgency forced Doc to stand. He began to shake. Self-defense, he told himself, self-defense. As if that mattered—him a black man who just shot a young white woman. An ex-con convicted of attempted murder who beat and robbed a man hours earlier. Who cared if she threatened him with a gun? Who'd believe his story? He wouldn't.

He set Teddy's gun down on the coffee table

and looked at his hands. He folded them together as if he was praying but they still didn't stop shaking. Splattered blood covered the glass top and some of the cash. He searched himself and his clothes for blood, but found nothing.

Soft bubbling sounds forced him to look down at Tiffany. She was on her back, legs propped up mid-calf by the ottoman.

"Bleed out fast lying like that," he said to her. He was pretty sure she didn't hear him.

Her eyes and mouth were open, her head rested at a hideous angle. One side of her neck was a bloody mess of torn flesh; the big .45 caliber bullet severed her jugular and carotid. Doc stood frozen in place, panic rising as he watched blood squirt and flow from the massive wound in her neck. More dripped from her mouth and nose. Half of her white blouse was soaked red. Streams of blood fed a growing pool overtaking the rug. The stench was overwhelming. He couldn't decide what to do first. Then her arms jerked. He shuddered.

"C'mon!" he told himself. "Get busy. Do something!" Blood and God knows what else was about to seep through the floor to the ceiling of the apartment below.

Next to her left foot lay the spent shell from Teddy's Colt. Doc bent down to pick it up, but jumped back when Tiffany's legs kicked. Her right sneaker slipped off her foot and fell to the floor. Then she was still.

He left the shell on the floor—it didn't have

his prints on it—then used his foot to push her legs off the ottoman so she lay flat. The flow of blood slowed to a trickle. Doc went into the bathroom and returned with a stack of yellow towels. He dropped towels on and around her head and neck. The towels immediately turned an unnatural shade of orange but halted the spread of blood. There was nothing he could do about the stench.

He knelt next to Billy, shook his shoulder and called his name, but knew it was a waste of time. Billy wasn't waking up anytime soon. He was too heavy for Doc to carry or even drag. Doc looked up at the ceiling and cursed without making a sound. He was sorry he ever met him, that he ever thought of this kid as a friend. The big dumb ass dragged Doc into this mess, wouldn't listen to his advice, and now unbelievably was complicating his escape. He shoved Billy's hip with his shoe. Images of the type of animal whose money they stole assaulted his senses: their size, their sounds, their smells. He thought of torturous deaths they would design that made going back to prison for the rest of his life seem a viable alternative. Panic bubbled up in his throat. The course of his life was again out of control, a car speeding along a blind curve, wheels losing contact with the road. Doc always knew Billy thought with his balls, not his brains. "Never should have let you drag me into this," Doc said to the unconscious and dead in the room. "I should have seen this coming. I'm smarter than this."

He surveyed the room for anything that

might tie him to Tiffany or the robbery. He headed for Tiffany's bedroom. He'd give Billy at least that long to recover.

Doc rifled through a suitcase and a black twill weekender bag on the bed. Both were half-packed. He found nothing useful in either. Her laptop and keys were on the dresser along with two driver's licenses and a U.S. passport. He pocketed the keys to lock up the apartment when he left. He examined the licenses. The California license was current, but the Florida license had expired three years ago. Neither of the names were Tiffany's, but the pictures resembled her. The passport was recent and the photo looked exactly like her, right down to the defiant pout. The name matched the Florida license: Michele Cynthia Marcus. Funny, thought Doc, she doesn't look Jewish. He laughed in spite of himself.

He went through the oak dresser starting with the bottom drawer, everyone's favorite hiding place. There he found what looked to be a couple thousand in twenties under a worn flannel nightgown. The other drawers contained only clothes. In the closet he found a colorful Macy's shopping bag and dumped the contents on the floor. Two fat rolls of twenties and hundreds tumbled out with belts and scarves. He dropped the cash and the laptop into the shopping bag and left the bag in the living room. Then he gathered up the mugs and brought them into the kitchen where he washed them, which seemed important, then rubbed them dry with paper towels. Not sure what to do next, he tore the paper towels into small pieces and dropped them in the trash. He found a dish towel and carried it around the apartment, wiping down anything he might have touched. He tossed the dish towel into the shopping bag and checked his watch. Another hour or two of darkness, he thought to himself. That's all.

He considered taking the Osprey. After all, it was already packed with the cash. But its newness and brilliant blue made him uneasy. Too conspicuous. Doc went back to the bedroom and returned with the emptied black twill weekender. He stuffed all the cash into it and zipped it closed. There was a little lock attached to the zipper. Finding the key on Tiffany's keyring, he locked the bag. A useless gesture. It didn't make him feel better.

He tossed the deposit bags and guns into the shopping bag, and almost as an afterthought, crumpled up his backpack and stuffed it in as well.

A ringtone took Doc by surprise. It was coming from Tiffany's cellphone on the floor by a leg of the coffee table. The phone was locked, but the screen displayed the name, *JESSE*, and a phone number. The phone stopped after eight rings. The lighted display sequenced to *Missed Call*. At the bottom were two lines referencing Tiffany's last text: *Sent to: Jesse. 2.9 mil US$!!! CU 4 hrs.*

So now Jesse—probably Tiffany's boyfriend and partner in the double-cross—was checking on her. Doc took time to think it through. It would be too risky to take the cash through airport security so she would drive to meet him. *4 hrs* meant he wasn't local. New York was four hours away. From New York they could drive to Canada or take the time to conceal the cash and fly anywhere in the world. They had options. Millions of them.

It didn't matter where Jesse was and what their plans were. What mattered was the unanswered call would make Jesse suspicious. Doc turned off the cellphone so Jesse couldn't track the phone and dropped it into the shopping bag. He had to get moving before he ran out of time.

He put on his coat and shoved the Tokarev in his right pocket. He stood over Billy a moment, watching the kid's chest rise and fall. But he'd stalled long enough. Billy, he decided, wasn't going to make the trip. It was karma. He owed Doc and was going to buy Doc the time to get away.

Doc retrieved the Colt from the shopping bag. He cleaned his fingerprints off it with his shirtsleeve and slipped it under Billy's right hand. He stood and looked down at the two of them on the floor—Tiffany half-buried under blood-soaked towels and Billy curled up with the Colt in his hand. Doc felt something inside of him twist, like he got spun around in the storm. He suspected he was no longer moving in the right direction, but right now what mattered was that he kept moving. He checked his watch.

In less than two hours, he'd shot and killed a woman and framed the closest thing he'd had to a friend in years. Better you than me, he heard somebody say in his head, but it was not his voice. Doing what I have to do to survive, the voice continued. Taking care of myself. Plus, I'm a millionaire. I am free, the voice insisted. Free.

If that were true, his own voice asked, then how come I still feel trapped?

He put on his coat and cap, then checked the room one last time, avoiding looking at Billy and Tiffany. He pulled out the handle on the weekender, grabbed the shopping bag and walked to the door. He put his gloved hand on the doorknob, but didn't turn it. The feeling that he forgot something was particularly strong. He knew exactly what he was leaving behind. He opened the door and stepped out into the corridor. He closed the door, used Tiffany's key to lock it, then walked away from all of it.

Taking Tiffany's car was out of the question. It took him less than an hour to hike the two miles to his furnished room on Beacon Street. The snow had stopped falling, but streets were still deserted and full of snow. The snowplows hadn't even begun clearing the roads. The air felt as cold and hard and sharp as the ice crushing beneath his shoes. He dropped the laptop, the Tokarev and Billy's .38 off the B.U. Bridge into the Charles River, taking a moment to catch his breath as they sank into the water. A few blocks further, he shoved the deposit bags, the empty shopping bag, the towel and Tiffany's cellphone into a sewer by a curb at a deserted corner of Mass. Ave. He didn't bother to read the name of the cross street.

Once home, Doc washed up, grabbed a bite, and changed into fresh clothes. He tossed a few essentials into a duffle bag. For the first time in his life, he was grateful he did not own his own set of drums. Instead, he packed his three harmonicas and a tin whistle he bought on a whim. He left behind his favorite reading lamp, his linens, and the dishes he'd bought at Goodwill. On the way out, he slipped a note under the landlord's door. It said he was leaving for family reasons. He gave no forwarding address. He didn't have to worry about his job at Bernstein's Shirts & Blouses. No one would care if he didn't show up for work. No one expected two weeks' notice from the minimum wage earner who emptied trash, mopped floors and scrubbed toilets.

Doc walked two blocks toward Kenmore Square to Newbury Street. His '78 Mustang, white with red pinstripes, rusted chassis and dented passenger door, was parked under a blanket of snow at the back of the Publix lot. He threw the bags into the trunk and said a quick prayer before turning the key. He let the engine warm up while he brushed snow and scraped ice off the windshield and windows. He got back into the car just as it started snowing again.

He drove down Commonwealth Avenue toward the Mass Pike, driving slowly through the snow. Traffic was light but every car he saw made him sink little deeper into his seat. The sun was coming up, and he wanted to be out of town before the plows came out and other drivers reclaimed the roads. At the start, Doc had mapped routes to Phoenix and to San Francisco. But Tiffany may have told Jesse or someone else about his plans so he needed a new destination. He still wanted to be someplace on the west coast, but north of San Francisco was too cold for him. San Diego was good, but the music scene in Los Angeles was better. Somewhere in his head he knew it was always going to be L.A.

Since it was winter, he'd drive south for Harrisonburg, Virginia, then west for Nashville, Oklahoma City, Albuquerque and through Phoenix to Los Angeles. Major routes and big cities offered a lone black man driving an old car with out-of-state plates the most anonymity.

He allowed himself a moment to consider what life could be like in California carrying both the money and the weight of what he had done. It was not the future of his dreams. Doc thought about Billy and his misguided plan to go to Maui with Tiffany. Then Doc thought about Karma.

9

Billy sat on the bed talking to his parents on a landline, an old-fashioned yellow Princess telephone. He was telling them all about his new bedroom. He felt excited and happy. This was the first time he didn't have to share a bedroom, even though this particular bedroom was large enough for two or three beds.

The bed was big, a double with a blond maple headboard, and it had two pillows and a soft fluffy blue quilt that looked pretty new. The floor was wood, polished and waxed smooth. There was a large oval rug next to the bed. No more bare feet on a cold concrete floor when he got up in the morning. The ceiling was white, all painted, no cracks or stains and the walls were painted a light blue. Hung on a wall without windows was a picture of a lady in a white dress and red hat dancing closely with a bearded man in a straw hat. His face was inches from hers, but she turned her head away. She looked shy. They were outside in a park with trees and other people, and Billy wondered what music they were dancing to.

Daylight poured through two windows facing the backyard. There was a giant oak tree and a patch of green grass and flowers along a white picket fence. In the middle of the yard was an above-ground pool with a slide. Everybody knew how he loved to swim.

The bedroom had a door he could close for privacy. No lock, though. A light switch was by the door and had a tiny warm yellow nightlight. Next to the bed was a round table with a lamp, a phone, and a radio with an alarm that he was going to learn how to use. He even had his own flashlight in case he needed to find the bathroom at night.

Billy pictured his parents at the other end of the line, smiling and nodding in response. But when he listened, he heard nothing at all. The line was dead. Billy felt the bed tilt and himself sliding off, still holding onto the phone. He fell upside-down for a long time, never hitting the floor. When he looked up past his feet, he saw his parents looking down at him, watching his descent. He knew it was them, but he couldn't make out their faces. All he recognized were his father's glasses. Then he remembered he'd never met his mother, and the last time he saw his father was when he was five. The old man dropped him off in front of a church and told him to go in while he parked the car.

Billy reached for them, but it was too late; they were too far away to help or even to hear him.

The air surrounding him turned into sea water. Salt stung his eyes. Billy held his breath. Someone close by said his name and tried to pry the phone from his hand. Fingers grabbed his shoulder and shook him. He heard his name again as he fought to hold his breath, waiting to float to the surface.

"Billy, Billy."

Doc took the Colt from Billy's hand, then poured water from a glass onto his face. It surprised Doc how Billy woke with a start and grabbed for the gun without actually seeing it. Billy coughed and rubbed his eyes hard, then open them wide.

"Doc!" His voice sounded rough. "Doc. I thought... what happened? I was... we were... there. What time is it?"

Doc pocketed the Colt.

Billy tried to stand but fell back. Doc grabbed his arm and helped him sit up.

"Easy, pal. Rest for a second." He handed Billy the glass, half full of water, and squatted down next to him. Here, drink this. *Drink*." Doc held the glass to Billy's mouth.

Billy jerked his head back and pushed the glass away. "Naw, I'm...what happened? Where's...?"

"Drink it, Billy. Get that crap out of your system."

"What crap?" Billy looked around the room. "Tiffany," he called. Doc's expression was grim.

"It's bad, Billy."

"What's bad?"

"She drugged you, man. She tried—"

"Drugged?" He rubbed his face, ran his hands through his hair. "What? Oh God." His hands went to his head. "My head is killing me." Doc waited. Billy looked at Doc with suspicion. "Who?"

"Tiffany. She double-crossed us both. She—"

"What? No way." He tried to stand again, but gave up when his arms and legs shook. "Where's Tiff?"

"Tiff drugged you. Tried to drug me, too. She —"

"Shit, man. That don't make sense."

"Think, Billy. You passed out. From the coffee. She drugged the coffee."

"No she didn't. I passed out from the beer," Billy said, but his voice was flat and Doc knew he was working his way through to the truth. Billy got up on one knee, wobbled a bit, and dropped back onto the floor. "Tiff? Tiff!" he called out into the room. He looked at Doc. "What do you mean, drugged?"

"Drugged. Drugged is drugged. What'd ya think I mean? You got a headache from a couple of beers? Think about it. She drugged the coffee, man. I'm telling you. Reds or something. She told me she did it. She admitted it!"

Billy tilted his head and was quiet for a moment as if listening to another conversation. "What? No, she... no, she...." Billy looked around the room. "She wouldn't do something like that. We're going to Maui. I mean, why...?" His voice cracked. He squeezed his eyes shut and took a deep breath.

Doc gripped Billy's arm tighter. "Listen to me. You've been out for hours. We don't have time for questions. We're in a lot of trouble and we got to get out of here... You understand? You gotta trust me on this." Doc lifted Billy's chin and forced him to look him in the eyes. "Stay with me, man! I'm going to say it once." Billy jerked his head away. His eyes searched the room. Doc shook him by the shoulders until his eyes settled back on Doc.

"Leave me the fuck alone." Billy pushed and Doc fell back.

"Come on, man," Doc said from the floor. "She was playing us both. She drugged the coffee. I was trying to tell you that before you drank that second cup. That's why you passed out. She was going to take the money—all of it—and leave us behind to get taken apart by the mob." Doc waited while Billy processed what he just said.

Billy tried to look skeptical. "Why didn't you say something about it before... Wait a minute. Did you say the mob? What mob?" His eyes grew wide.

"The Washington Street Gang. You know, Moe Weiss and his guys. They were laundering the money for some Russians gangsters. That's whose money we stole. And Tiffany knew all about it."

Billy was quiet, thinking things over. "Washington Street? Moe Weiss?" he finally asked. Doc nodded. "Was... is that... did we just rip off Moe Weiss?"

Doc nodded. "And a bunch of Russians and the club owner, Kyle Kelly."

"You sure? How do you know that? Tiffany said—"

"She told me while you were out cold. She was crystal clear about it, clear as the gun she was pointing at me. She said maybe 'Tiffany' wasn't really her name and I found—"

"No. You're crazy. Her name *is* Tiffany and she and me are a thing! And what's Tiff got to do with Russians? Me and her, we're going to Maui, She wouldn't...." Billy brushed Doc's arm aside and started shouting, "I got to talk to her. Tiffany? Tiff!"

"Shut the fuck up, man! You want somebody to call the cops?"

Doc stood up and stepped back to give Billy room. The kid is still thinking with his balls. Why had he bothered to come back for him? He knew Billy would have a hard time accepting the truth about Tiffany. And now Billy was out of control.

Doc was sure he couldn't restrain Billy physically even if he wanted to, but he needed to take control or leave him behind. One or the other. And he needed to do it now.

"Listen to me, buddy, I could be halfway to the coast with all the money right now. But no, I'm here trying to save your ass. Your girl set us up as suckers, patsies. You and me. So grow a pair and own the fact, Billy. We gotta deal with this whole business now before the mob find us. Or the cops."

Billy stopped shouting and looked down at the floor.

Doc's voice grew softer, but the urgency remained. "When the cops get here, they'll take us in and claim we both murdered her. Worse, Moe's guys or the Russians may already be on the way. If they get here first, they'll tear us apart for taking their money.... You following me now?"

Billy's eyes focused. *"Murdered her*? Did you just say, 'murdered her'?"

Doc breathed out, deflated. "She's ah... Tiffany.... She's dead."

Billy sprung to his feet. "What do you mean?"

"I mean dead. Dead is dead. Jesus, man! You know what I'm saying."

"Dead... How ...? You're telling me somebody killed her? Who, you?" Billy took a step toward Doc. Suddenly his eyes went wide. He smells the blood, Doc thought. Billy pushed past Doc and saw Tiffany on the floor, head covered in orange towels. He dropped to his knees and rocked back and forth like a child.

"She drugged my coffee, too," Doc said, keeping his voice soft, his speech slow. "I told you she was acting funny the way she kept filling our cups and pushing it on us .... I thought she might be up to something and then you started getting dopey. The next thing I knew, you were out like a light on the floor and she had my gun. She was going to shoot me but I shot her first with Teddy's Colt." Doc looked to the floor in Tiffany's direction. "I swear I was fighting for my life, for both our lives."

"What did you do? What did you do?" Billy kept saying.

Doc wasn't sure if Billy was talking to him or Tiffany. A car passed by outside, its engine straining. Daylight crept around the edge of the blinds and he knew they were out of time.

Billy slowly got to his feet, turned and faced Doc, his expression flat. Doc's fingers found the Colt in his pocket.

"You shot her?"

"I had to. You understand what I'm telling you, what she was up to?"

Billy glanced at the body on the floor, shook his head, then looked at Doc. Doc wasn't sure what Billy was thinking or what he would do.

"Billy, do you understand what happened, what I had to do?"

Billy didn't respond.

"We good, Billy?" Doc waited as long as he could. "Billy, I gotta know right now, this second. Are we good? I could've...."

Billy balled his fists and rubbed his eyes, then slowly looked up at the ceiling as if for help from above. He took a deep breath and locked eyes with Doc.

Doc wrapped his hand around the Colt in his pocket. He couldn't shoot Billy, but if he had to protect himself, maybe he could scare him.

Billy's red eyes were cold sober. He opened his mouth and spoke.

"Where's the money?"

Billy didn't argue when Doc said they had to get out of Boston right now. He told him the money was in the weekender in the trunk of his car, parked down the block. When they were a safe distance away, they would make new plans and split the cash. Florida seemed the right destination for now. Doc's car could get there in three days. Plus, it was warm. Billy suggested Miami but Doc said Key West. It was as far south as you could get from Boston and still be in the U.S. They hoped it was far enough.

Doc felt bad about panicking and running out on Billy. He felt shame about setting him up with the gun, but he saw no advantage to telling Billy about it. After all, Doc rationalized, Billy was to blame for this mess. His mistake had been trusting Billy's judgment in the first place. Doc would never make that mistake again.

Once in the car, Doc described how he cleared the apartment of anything that might identify them, dumped the items down the sewer, then got his car and returned, all while giving Billy time to come to. It was mostly true and Billy bought it.

They drove to Billy's apartment to pick up some clothes and other essentials that Billy stuffed into his old beat-up suitcase. Like Doc, Billy owned little, but he would not leave his guitar—an old Yamaha six-string acoustic he bought for $100 from a guy at work. Scratched and dented, it was a source of comfort for Billy. The fact he could buy a thousand new Gibson guitars never entered his mind.

They hit the road as the good citizens of

Greater Boston drove to Dunkin' for their coffee and donuts. On the Mass Pike headed to I-95 South, they kept a steady pace with traffic and made good time. Doc drove while Billy slept, which was fine with Doc. He thought Billy would push the old wreck too hard too fast and then where would they be. In spite of all the cash in the trunk, buying a car now was not an option. They had to disappear quickly and without a trace.

They stopped for gas while still on the Pike. Billy pumped gas while Doc went around the back, wiped down the Colt and dropped it into a dumpster.

By the time they crossed into Pennsylvania, it began to snow again. Doc turned on the wipers and defroster. He tried the radio but the music, even old rock classics, brought him no comfort so he turned it off. For hours Doc drove to the monotonous sweep of the wipers, the heater fan blowing, tires cutting through slush. Billy was bundled up in his pea coat, curled against the door, snoring softly. Going back for him may have been the right call, Doc thought, but not necessarily the smart call.

10

"Your phone!" Katie's voice groaned like a trumpet missing a blue note. The phone chirped again, and this time she gave him a shove with her foot. Kyle opened his eyes. He was comfortable under the covers and hoped the call was a miss-dial and would stop on its own.

"Kyle!"

Now he had to answer. He picked up his phone, checked the time and shook his head—less than an hour's sleep. But any trace of sleep vanished when he checked the name on the call: *CJ*.

Six hours earlier, Kyle sat in his office at The Improper Bostonian stuffing the Russians' cash into deposit bags and filling out the deposit slips for his six accounts. He could have used twice as many accounts this time. It was by far the largest amount they had laundered since he and Moe started the operation six months ago. Close to three million, mostly in hundreds. They both knew they were pushing their luck and the limits of the scheme, but Moe was right. If they didn't do it, the Russians would look elsewhere for the service and Moe and Kyle would be out of a healthy taste of any future action.

Two months earlier, Kyle was skiing with his girlfriend, Katie, in Steamboat Springs when he fell, tearing his left MCL. After arthroscopic surgery and a month of physical therapy, occasionally his knee still would flare up. Tonight, the pain was particularly bad. After locking the deposit bags in the office safe, he left instructions with CJ and Teddy and headed home. Katie and he could relax in front of the TV while he rested his knee. She'd be disappointed but should understand. The next morning, they planned to spend two nights at Katie's condo in Wellfleet, about 20 minutes from P-town on the tip of the Cape. Katie wanted to do a lot of walking on the beach and shopping for antiques. Kyle needed to prepare.

He had told CJ to keep the club open until around 2:00 am. CJ had closed a hundred times before. And Teddy, who'd made the deposits for Kyle at least a dozen times, would do it again tonight. On his way out the door, Kyle had slipped Teddy $100 to pay one of the armed bouncers to ride with him on the deposit run. The three banks Kyle used were within five blocks of the club, but you never could be too careful with this much money, especially when it belonged to some heavy-duty Russians.

Thirty minutes after CJ's call, Kyle pulled up

in front of the club. He had his key out to unlock the entrance when two goons grabbed his arms. "Moe wants to see you," explained one as the other pulled a hood over his head. The hood smelled of stale cigarettes and other people's sweat.

Resistance wasn't an option. Other than his knee problem, Kyle was in excellent shape, but his days of beating back a pair of thugs were long over. They herded him to the curb and shoved him into the backseat of a car. "Push over," said the goon as he squeezed in next to Kyle while the other goon went around the car to sit on Kyle's opposite side, flanking him.

There wasn't much room, forcing Kyle to sit on his tailbone. He knew that was the idea. His back felt twisted like a corkscrew but he steeled himself for the ride. Sweat trickled down the small of his back. He craved a cigarette.

"Come on, guys," he said through the hood. "I need to talk to Teddy before I can tell Moe anything." Silence. "Look, there's no need for the hood. Let me—"

"Don't you fucking touch that," said the man on Kyle's right. "Moe said you wear the hood, you wear the hood. Now shut the fuck up if you don't want a punch in the face."

"Teddy's already taken care of," said the man on the left. "The boss will get to you next. Just shut the fuck up."

That was the last thing anyone said for the rest of the ride.

Kyle tried to make sense of what was happening. Teddy called CJ and CJ called Kyle, but CJ must have called Russ, too. The two had become friendly. And Russ reported to Moe.

Kyle thought he was solid with CJ, but CJ was ambitious and he couldn't blame him for that. The potential existed for CJ to make real money working for Moe. Kyle decided he had to be careful with CJ in the future, assuming there would be a future.

All Kyle could see through the weave in the hood's fibers were headlights of cars traveling in the opposite direction. Time, speed and the smoothness of the road led him to believe they were on the Expressway heading out of town, probably somewhere secluded where Moe could conduct business without interruption. Anyone would have every right to panic, but life taught Kyle how to push fear into a back corner and to stay focused on what's ahead.

A decade before the 9/11 attacks, weeks after completing his training at Ft. Knox, 17-year-old Kyle Kelly served as the loader in a four-man crew operating an Abrams A1A tank in the Battle of Medina Ridge, the largest tank battle of the Gulf War. Nine American tanks destroyed 28 Iraqi T72 tanks in 23 minutes. Leading up to the battle, Kyle rode on the turret, his upper body exposed, as he fired from the tank's M240 machine gun at troops and lighter vehicles attacking their flank. It was a lifetime ago, but his training, experience and the instincts he developed never left him. Kyle didn't let things get to him anymore.

He exhaled through his mouth as he closed his eyes, the tips of his eyelashes scraping the fabric of the hood. He let his arms go limp and placed the tip of his tongue against his upper gum ridge. He breathed in through his nose, then allowed his diaphragm to relax and let the air out through his mouth.

He repeated the process as he pictured the sun and felt the breeze on his face, his arm around Ana's shoulder, standing on a cliff overlooking a beach in Cascias. Waves rocked the Portuguese fishing boats moored just past the swimmers. It was the details that made the memories seem real: sunlight shimmering off the waves; the rough sand and smooth rocks beneath his feet; the softness of Ana's hands and cheek; the scent of her hair. He inhaled and smelled not sweat and cigarettes but frangipani, local flowers he still bought for the bar. He heard her laugh, the laugh that brought him joy and serenity —which was a miracle considering all he was going through back then.

Kyle returned to the present and focused on the mess he was in. He sensed they were driving south on I-93, going somewhere on the South Shore, maybe Nantasket where Moe kept his pride and joy, a 55-foot Asterion Power Mega Yacht. A one-way late-night cruise on the Atlantic was not how Kyle wanted to start and end the new year.

He still had time to think of a plan to offer Moe, if only as a cover to stall the inevitable. He knew that once Moe had the money back, Kyle's life would be forfeited for his error in spite of their history. It was just the way business was done.

Kyle needed to convince Moe he was in the best position to track down the men with their money and to do it quickly, especially if it was an inside job, which was the most likely scenario. He just needed a few days, a week tops. He'd start with hearing Teddy's account first-hand, a description of the guys who robbed him, maybe even an idea of who they were. Maybe a couple of days to sweat the staff to fill-in details and close-in on the guys. Whoever they were, they had the money close by. Then his only option to survive was to disappear with the cash before Moe had him killed.

After all, it was a lot of money and Moe was not the forgiving type.

Maybe he would go back to Cascias.

He had a plan.

The car slowed, interrupting Kyle's thoughts, and pulled off the highway onto a road that lifted him up and pressed him down into the seat. Hills, thought Kyle. So... not the beach. Kyle fell forward as the car decelerated without warning. No one tried to catch him, but Kyle was prepared when the car made a sharp left.

The car began to bounce and rock. It felt like this new road was unpaved. Kyle heard the crunch of frozen snow and gravel under the tires. Wherever they were going, they were close. Branches scraped the sides of the car. Somebody cracked a window and with the rush of fresh cold air came the familiar scent of pine. It all fell together.

They were on a secondary road in the Blue Hills. That's where I'd do this, he thought.

As a kid, Kyle hiked and explored the Hills and fished and swam in the lake. He tried but could not remember the name of the lake. Some rich guy's name from Colonial times. There was a campground nearby with a long Indian name he could never remember either. That's probably where they were taking him, the old campground by the lake, closed for business, deserted and barely accessible this time of year.

Not a one-way harbor cruise but a quiet place for a smack up, not a pleasant thing in of itself, but getting roughed-up tonight meant Moe would not kill him. Yet. Probably. At least not if Kyle made his case.

Crisp air crept up his coat sleeves and pant legs. He rubbed his wrists and wondered if it was clear enough to see stars. He thought about all the hours he spent training to navigate by the stars so he'd never get lost. He pictured Regulus in Leo, the Winter Constellation, and turned his hooded head up and to the left, no doubt making the thugs stare at him with confusion.

What if Teddy was already dead or had already led Moe to the money?

Christ, he thought, there will be pain, just a question of how much and how long. The car stopped. The door on his right opened and the cold night rushed in. One of the goons got out, grabbed Kyle's arm, and pulled. Kyle was slow to respond.

"Come on, old man. Let's go. It's friggin' freezing out here!" he said.

As soon as Kyle stepped out of the car, someone pushed him from behind. Kyle stumbled and fell to his knees in the snow. His hands burned with cold. Before he could stand up, someone ripped the hood off his head along with a few strands of hair and shined a flashlight in his face.

11

Someone caught Kyle under the arm and helped him stand up. Angry and embarrassed, he almost thanked the stranger out loud, but thought better of it.

"Watch your step, old-timer." More of an encouragement than an order. The light blinded him, but the voice was familiar.

"That you, Russ?"

One goon, likely the one that pushed him, kept the flashlight aimed at his eyes. Kyle used his hand to block the glare.

"Yeah, it's me, old man."

"Thanks," said Kyle. "And for the record, I may be older than you, but I can still kick your ass."

"*May* be older? Kick *my* ass?" Russ gave a snort and turned to the goon with the flashlight. "Turn that off, asshole." The light went out. "And what's with the hood? Who the fuck told you—"

"The boss said to—"

"Not this guy! The other guy. Outta my sight

before I let this old man beat your sorry ass."

The goon stepped away.

"Apologies, Kyle. Just a misunderstanding. This way," he said with a tilt of his head. "Unless you want me to get you a wheelchair."

"Up yours."

"Cranky, too. Come on. Moe's waiting."

They walked for about a minute along a narrow rocky trail. Someone stepped out from behind a large tree, waving yet another flashlight.

"Turn that off," said Russ. The light went out.

A pop echoed in the woods, the sound unmistakable. Kyle and Russ looked at each other.

"That-a-way." The goon pointed into the woods. Toward the gunshot.

They walked in silence until Kyle saw rays of light poking between the fir trees ahead. Russ touched Kyle's shoulder.

"Go ahead," said Russ. "I'm right behind you."

Kyle left the trail and walked into the woods, trying not to trip on snow-covered roots and rocks. He wove through birch and evergreens toward the light like a moth drawn to a flame. Men were talking but Kyle couldn't make out the words. Streams of cold sweat rolled down the small of his back. He stumbled on.

Moe and one of his bodyguards stood next to each other in a clearing, their backs to Kyle, looking at something on the ground about ten feet away. Kyle couldn't see around them, but he sensed what it might be. The bodyguard saw Kyle first and nudged Moe with his elbow.

Moe barely turned to look. "Do join us, Mr. Kelly," he said.

Kyle took a few hesitant steps forward and stopped.

Teddy was on his stomach in the snow, arms and legs splayed like he was skydiving. The snow was pink by his head.

Kyle prayed Teddy was simply knocked unconscious, but then he saw the shattered bits of bone and brain laying in the pink snow.

Russ took his place next to Moe and studied Teddy. Moe handed him something. That's when Kyle noticed the gun, a cheap revolver, a throwaway piece. Russ slipped it in his coat pocket.

"He say anything useful?" asked Russ.

It took Moe a moment to reply. "I think so." He turned and looked at Kyle. "Maybe. Thank you for coming, Mr. Kelly." Moe held out a hand. "We need to talk."

Kyle didn't move. He couldn't take his eyes off Teddy.

Moe put his hand on Kyle's shoulder. "Kyle, Kyle. You know the drill. This was necessary."

"But Moe—"

"Relax. I'm not going to shoot you, buddy."

Kyle wanted to believe him. "I needed to ask him—"

"All you need to do is correct the problem. Get the money back. Do it quickly and everything will be right as rain."

"Sure, but Teddy—

"You wanted to talk to Teddy?" Moe pointed. "Speak up. Maybe he'll hear you."

There wasn't much to see: a body in the snow, debris around the head. Teddy's face was turned away from them.

"You see, Kyle, it's thin ice we're walking on, eh? Both of us."

The name popped into Kyle head. "Houghton's Pond," he whispered.

"Excuse me?"

Kyle looked off through the trees. "We used to swim over there. Houghton's Pond. Sometimes we'd fish...."

"Yeah, we did." Moe glanced at his watch. "Listen to me, Kyle. My daughter and her husband are in Miami for the holiday. We've got their kids. In what, two hours, I'm supposed to be taking Ruthie and the grandkids for breakfast with her brother, Larry. Ever meet Larry?"

Kyle shook his head. "Haven't had the pleasure."

"There'd be no pleasure in it, trust me. Runs numbers for me. But right now, I'm freezing my ass off so, let's wrap this up."

Moe put an arm around Kyle's shoulder and led him close to Teddy. They walked around to look at his face. He looked surprised. His eyes and mouth were open. His eyes were black.

"What was his name," asked Moe, "his real name?"

Just a body. It wasn't a person anymore. "Teddy Hall..." he said finally. "Leonard Theodore Hall. He didn't like using Leonard."

Moe pulled Kyle a little closer. "Uh-huh. Well, take a good look at Lenny, Teddy, whatever the hell his name was, and understand this. It was quick only because I'm in a hurry. Merciful compared to what the Russians will do to you and to me God forbid if they learn we let somebody take their money. Got it? You with me here?"

Kyle nodded. He got it.

12

Moe released Kyle's shoulder. The lighter flashed as he lit a cigarette. "I'm supposed to stop all together, but...." He drew hard on the cigarette. The tip became bright throwing a reddish glow on Moe's face. Smoke leaked out of his nose and mouth as he spoke. "Hope this Teddy guy wasn't anything to you," he said.

Kyle didn't hesitate. "We were never that close."

Moe looked at Russ who qualified the claim with a nod.

Kyle explained. "My sister, Peggy...you met Peggy." Moe was noncommittal. Kyle sputtered on. "He lived with her for a while. She's why I gave him a job. He was all right but...."

"But what?"

Kyle shrugged. "No sense. Like last night, I gave him a hundred bucks for a bouncer to ride shotgun with him on the deposits. Did he say who—"

"He said he walked alone to the bank," said

Moe. "Must have pocketed the C-note."

"Son-of-a-bitch." Kyle said more out of disappointment than anger.

Moe glanced at the body. "No sense? Stabbed you in the back, Kyle, that's what he did. You should've seen this coming. You knew what kind of guy he was. This one's on you."

Kyle bowed his head and thought about it.

"So, he and Peggy still...?"

"Huh? No, God no." Kyle shook his head. "Not for years."

"That's good. That's very good. He got family in town? Anyone who might come asking for him?"

Kyle had to think about it. "He's... he grew up in Mattapan. Got a married sister in Boise, but no, no family in town. I'm sure of it."

"Where's he live?"

Kyle glanced up at the stars. "Uh. Newton Highlands with Carl, the floor manager." He turned to Moe. "You know Carl?" Kyle read distaste on his face. "I dropped him off there once. Small place."

"They like... a couple?"

"No, no. It's a two-bedroom condo, an investment for each of them. I don't know where he got the money, but now I'm worried about that, too."

Moe's voice took on an edge. "You got bigger problems."

Moe was right of course. "What did Teddy say happened?" Kyle asked.

"He said there were two of them, a short guy and a big guy. The big guy told him a third guy was watching from the street, but you know that was bullshit so they could get a head start. They wore masks but he could still see the short guy was black, the big guy white. They had guns, roughed him up, then tied him up with zip ties and went right for the money."

"They get the money in the messenger bag?"

"Like they knew."

"Fuck," whispered Kyle.

"The white guy told him something weird. 'Stop hassling the dancers,' but he said he never did that. He kept going on about it."

"That clinches it," said Kyle. "Wasn't some random mugging. These guys knew about the money from somebody inside."

Moe shook his head. "He kept moaning about them taking his wallet and his gun, like that was important. What can I say? He fucked us up and then his moaning got on my nerves." He took a final drag on his cigarette, then let it drop in the snow. "A black guy and a white guy. Mean anything to you?"

"What?" Kyle was thinking which dancers Teddy hung with. It was a long list.

"Jesus H.! Kyle! Keep up." Moe snapped his fingers three times. "You getting Old Timer's disease? I'm talking about the two guys that robbed your guy. He said the black guy was short and could throw a punch and the white guy was tall ... big, like he worked out at a gym. Ringing any bells?"

Cold and fatigue were numbing his brain. Or fear. Kyle pushed them away and focused. "Nobody on the staff jumps out, but maybe these two were regulars." He looked at Moe and put on an earnest face. "I'm on it, Moe. Look, I'll make this right. I wouldn't screw up a good thing like we got going."

"And yet, here we are." Moe raised his arms wide, then dropped them to his sides. "And the Russians' money is not. I'd call this the very definition of screwing up a good thing."

"I'll find the money, I swear," Kyle pleaded.

Moe's smile made Kyle think of a shark circling its prey.

"That's it, Kyle? I've got your word on it?" Moe shook his head and laughed to himself. "We went into this thing as partners against my better judgment, but you promised me you could handle your end. Sometimes you're like a brother to me, but considering the mess you created, we need an arrangement, a *modus vivendi* until you straighten this out. Know where I'm headed?"

Kyle graduated Boston Latin School. "Yeah, I get it," he said flatly.

Moe dropped the bomb.

"Here's what we do. I'm taking over The Bostonian. It's mine as of this moment."

Kyle opened his mouth to protest.

"Before you say anything, don't forget who you're talking to." Moe jabbed him in the chest. "I'll bring the papers around in a couple of days and you'll sign them. You find every penny of the 2.9 million, I tear up the papers and keep 15% of the club for the trouble you caused. You don't find the money and it'll be a totally different story. I'll sell off everything that's not nailed down, and that includes the girls. I'll rip out the copper pipes and sell that. Then I'll burn the place down for the insurance and if that's still not enough, I'll rip out your kidneys, lungs and liver and find buyers for them, too. There's a market for that stuff, y'know."

Kyle felt himself sinking into the ground.

Moe studied Kyle a moment then kicked Teddy's leg with his shoe and walked away from them both. "You got a week. One week," he said over his shoulder. "That's about as long as I can stall the Russians, if they don't get wind of this first. So get to work." Moe kept walking.

"Okay, Moe. I know—" said Kyle.

Moe kept walking and talking. "You really don't. I'll bring the papers to your office in two days. Can't get a fuckin' lawyer on a holiday. But you get to work on this now. Find these guys and the money and I'll do the rest."

Kyle shifted the weight off his bad knee.

"Russ, drop Kyle off at his car."

Reprieve.

Moe pointed back at Teddy. "Kevin, bag up that piece of shit and take him to the boat. Chop up the P.O.S. and spread him like chum in the ocean. Take Mick and Phil with you. You know where the boat keys are?"

Kevin patted a pocket. "Got 'em with me, boss." He glanced at Kyle. "Figured we might need the boat."

"Good man, Kev. I'm outta here. Got family waiting." Moe stopped and turned to look at Kyle. "I'll see you in two days. You better have something good for me then."

13

It was the second day of the new year and every-thing had changed. Russ was behind the wheel of a brand new, top-of-the-line black Escalade, Moe in the passenger seat. They turned onto Boylston Street a half a block from The Improper Bostonian when they saw it—a nondescript sedan parked under a sign that read, Loading Zone.

"Cop car," he said. "Right in front."

"Still got your cop eyes," Moe said with ap-proval. "Yeah, I see it, too. A Ford. What's that color? Green?"

"Might have started out that way."

"Go past them." He jabbed a finger at the other side of the street. "There's a space. Pull over there. Let's see who we're dealing with first."

Russ parked, blocking an alley, but left the motor running. They watched the cop car in the rearview and side mirrors. Russ chugged a can of Red Bull and slipped the empty under his seat. In less than a minute, two men in suits and overcoats walked out of the club into the street.

"Know them?" asked Moe.

Russ lifted his chin. "The older guy is Wertz. He was in Narcotics when I left. Started as a security cop at UMass Boston, I think, right out of the Air Force. Thought he'd be retired by now. The younger guy... must be after my time."

"You miss it, huh?" Moe grinned.

Russ raised his grin with a smirk. "That's why I became a cop. You make so many friends."

Wertz and his partner got into their faded gray cop car with cop plates and ancient twin antennae discretely tucked into the chrome trim. Russ waited for them to drive away, then backed the Escalade down the street and slipped into the vacated space in front of the club. "Don't forget the papers," said Moe as he stepped out onto the sidewalk. Russ killed the engine, grabbed a manila envelope off the back seat, and followed Moe to the entrance.

The doorman was new. He eyed the tall blond man and his fit black companion, but had the good sense to let them pass with only a nod. Once inside, they removed their gloves and opened their coats to let in the warm air while they adjusted to the dim light and the din. At first, it was all silhouettes and shadows, but shapes and details slowly resolved into a familiar scene. The din, however, remained.

Strings of tiny multi-colored LEDs lined walls painted flat black. Overhead spot lights projected faint reds and blues onto the customers, affording them the illusion of anonymity while camouflaging the dancers' stretch marks, pimples, cuts and bruises. The music was too loud, the bass thick and repetitive, and would have been annoying save for the half-naked women floating from table to table selling lap dances. The room smelled of beer, sweat and pancake makeup. To the customers, it was heaven.

About two-thirds of the seats were filled. "Decent for a weekday afternoon," said Moe.

Russ hooked a thumb in his belt and pointed a finger. "Here comes CJ," he said. A large man in a tuxedo jacket, white shirt with a black bow tie and black jeans approached and spoke loud enough to be heard over the music.

"Russ! Mr. W! How you gentlemen doing?"

"CJ," said Russ, extending a hand. "Haven't seen you at the range in a while." They shook hands. CJ snuck a glance at the envelope in Russ's other hand.

"Busy at home," CJ said. "Anything I can get for you, gentlemen? A drink or a table, maybe a seat in the VIP room?"

Moe shook his head. He put out a hand and CJ shook it. A firm grip. "Appreciate you calling Russ the other night. Smart move."

CJ smiled with delight. "Whatever I can do to help, sir." An image of Teddy flashed behind his eyes, but the smile never changed.

"Family doing well?" asked Moe. He had no idea if CJ was even married.

CJ beamed again. "Yeah, thanks for asking.

Monica's pregnant with our second. A girl this time."

Moe's smile was complete and genuine. "That's great news! Daughters are precious. Congratulations."

"Kids are what it's all about."

"Kyle in?" Russ asked.

"In his office all day. Want me to let him know —"

"Nah," said Russ. "He knows."

"Sure, sure. No problem," he said nodding enough to suggest there was a problem.

Russ looked around. "Lexi on yet?"

CJ looked at his watch. "Right about now. And hey, a couple of cops came through and went into the office to talk to Kyle. Thought you should know." Neither Moe nor Russ reacted. "Left right before you got here," CJ added.

Angry voices caught their attention. Two men were shouting at a waitress three tables deep.

"Shouldn't you be breaking some heads?" Russ said.

CJ took his cue and acknowledged Moe with a casual salute. "Good to see you again, Mr. W." He touched Russ on the arm, "Catch you later at the range, man." Then he slipped into the crowd.

Moe watched him go. "CJ... what kind of name is CJ?"

"Says everybody called him that since high school. It's Concepción Jesus Munoz."

"Nice accent. You half-Hispanic?" Moe smiled

to let Russ off the hook. He pointed in CJ's direction. "Looks like a good kid. Respectful. Smart, yeah?" Russ nodded. "Tough enough?" Russ nodded again. Moe considered this. "How do you know him? From here?"

"Saw him three years ago shooting a nine at paper targets at the Gun Gallery in Watertown. Good pair of eyes and rock steady hands, a totally dead shot with anything you hand him."

"You don't say?" Moe was interested.

"A combat vet. Afghanistan. We go for a drink now and then. Funny guy, clever, reads a lot. I met his wife a couple of times, a tiny gal, Monica. An accountant or something. Cute. Smarter than her husband."

"Ain't that always the case. An accountant, huh? We could always use—"

Russ shook his head. "I wouldn't go there, chief. She sounds like an honest girl."

"What about him?" Moe was always looking for new talent.

Russ smiled. "He's gold. Ambitious. Looking to move up, especially now with another kid on the way. And, yeah, he's good people. He opens and closes the club when Kyle's not here. Responsible, reliable. Discrete when it's required. Got a head on his shoulders. Seen him handle all sorts here, sometimes wrangle more than a couple of guys at a time all by himself. He's a good talker but good with his hands. His feet, too. Karate or something. But he keeps a cool head, listens to what you have to say, and is willing to do what you tell him. Next opportunity, I can give him a chance, see if he shapes up or not. I'll let you know."

"So, he wants in?"

Russ nodded. "Oh, yeah. He's hungry."

Moe watched as CJ and two other bouncers escort three customers out the front door. "Okay, do that."

"Okay then," said Russ.

"And tell him to drop that 'Mr. W' crap. "It's Mr. Weiss. Or Moe, if he works out."

"Will do, Mr. W."

Moe grinned as he turned around to view the action, seeing the place through the eyes of the new owner.

It was a good-sized room. Small tables crowded the floor, each surrounded by four high-back swivel chairs upholstered in a suede-like material that apparently defied cleaning. The chairs were wide and tilted back to accommodate lap dances and customers of any size. Bouncers in cheap tuxedo jackets leaned against the walls, arms folded, watching the customers watching the girls.

On the main stage, a dancer performed an inelegant striptease—if you could even call it that. These days dancers barely wore enough to strip. A couple of off-duty dancers threw singles and shouts of encouragement at her. Three more dancers shook and shuffled on small corner stages. The rest made money working the floor. The waitresses, most former dancers who got tired of that scene, wore crisp white blouses and short plaid skirts. The nod to parochial school uniforms was a nice touch.

Moe turned to study the moneymaker—a long bar that ended a few feet short of the stage. Three bartenders in a well-choreographed dance of their own supplied drinks, printed bills, and rang up payments. The bar stools were empty, the trick being to keep customers drinking at their tables for lap dances. That way, everybody made money.

Off the main stage, a narrow runway jutted into the room like the runway at a fashion show, except this model spun on a chrome-plated pole with its own spotlight—the brightest lit real estate in the room. Customers lined the broad ledge of the runway, leaning in to get a closeup view and wave tips at the pole dancer.

The music faded, and the DJ's booming voice commanded the audience to give it up for Lexi. They obliged. The hoots and whistles intensified as a barefoot strawberry blond with a semi-athletic build done up in a purple bustier and panties entered stage left. She had large blue eyes, the kind smile of a kindergarten teacher, and looked to be mid-twenties if you didn't look that hard.

Bouncing on her toes, she started her floor work with a cartwheel and ended by attacking the pole at a sprint, hanging on with her left hand and foot and using the momentum and her strength to swing counter-clockwise. As if by magic, she flipped upside down and, continuing to revolve around the pole, inverted back as quickly to an upright position. She hooked a leg around the pole as she reached up, spinning to the top, defying gravity as if to spit in Newton's face. Without warning, she dropped like a rock, stopping an inch from the floor, then climbed up halfway up to pose. Certain everyone was watching, she dipped, pirouetted, and spun some more. When she followed a fan kick with a twerk, the shouts of approval grew even louder. Every man and woman in the club fixed his or her eyes on Lexi's limbs as she swayed, swung and stripped more or less in time with the music.

Except Russ. He had seen her routine almost as often as he'd seen her dress up for dinner. Scanning the room out of boredom, he saw Carl, the floor manager, by the bar holding a drink (against regulations), staring at Lexi instead of keeping one eye on the crowd and the other on the bartenders.

A short, skinny dancer with curly dark hair surprised Carl with a kiss on the cheek. She snaked an arm around his waist, drawing him in closer, rubbing her thigh against his leg. Even from across the room it was obvious she was playing him. Russ saw her lips move. Carl leaned down, cocking his head to hear her.

She guided his head even closer so his ear was next to her mouth, blocking his view of the bar. Then she looked over his shoulder at a bartender with a shaved head who had been eyeing them all along. On cue, the bartender snatched a drink receipt and the cash—likely a handful of twenties— off a tray on the bar and stuffed them in the front pocket of his jeans. No money, no receipt, no record of anything. It happened that fast.

The music ended to shouts and applause. Russ watched as Lexi collected bills out of waving hands and off the stage floor, depositing double kisses on the cheeks of those who had been particularly generous, then running off with a beaming smile that Russ knew would vanish the minute she cornered the curtain.

"Show's over. Let's go," Moe said. They crossed the floor, catching Carl by surprise.

"Hey, Russ. Mr. Weiss. You here to see Kyle?"

"Hey, sweetheart," said Russ, ignoring Carl and bearing down on the dark-haired dancer with his best cop glare. "Business good for you and your skinhead bartender boyfriend?" She gave back a blank look, then spun on her heels, leaving without a word.

Russ and Moe stepped behind the bar to a locked metal door. Carl punched a code into the adjacent keypad and the electric lock clicked open. As he passed through, Russ thrust his upper body at Carl, who flinched and jumped back, letting go of the door.

Russ caught the door with his shoulder. "Stay on your toes, sport. You're costing us money," he said as he followed Moe into the back.

Carl waited till the door closed and the lock engaged before he got out his cell phone.

14

The door shut tight behind them, reducing the music to a muffled bass line. They walked down a narrow corridor with cheap wood paneling and a bare concrete floor. The air felt musty and cold, the low ceiling and paneling reminiscent of the interior of a plain pine box casket.

"You planning on keeping Carl around?" Russ asked, but Moe didn't seem to hear him. He'd stopped at the opened doorway to the dressing room and looked in. Lexi was retouching her eyeliner at one of the vanity stations. Her purple bustier was unlaced, exposing her breasts. Over by the racks of costumes, two other dancers, one short, the other tall, counted the bills in their hands as they talked and laughed, unaware of the men in the doorway.

"So, how'd you do?" the short one asked.

"$294. One guy gave me a $10 tip. You?"

"$250, more or less. Look at this!" She held up a $2 bill.

"Those are supposed to be bad luck," said the tall one.

"Really...? You want it?" The tall one reached for it. The short one whisked it back to her stack. "Too late," she teased. She turned toward Lexi. "Hey, Lexi. I danced a double with Jo."

"Who's she?" Lexi asked.

"You know. That little pixie blond."

"She's a freak. Whose idea was that?"

"I absolutely love this shit," Moe whispered over his shoulder to Russ.

"Some guy in a party of four. Somebody's birthday. One said he was a dentist—a loudmouth. He called Jo over after I got started. They all thought it was a big laugh except the birthday boy."

The tall one knit her brows. "Hang on. I think I danced at that table too. Big white guy, brown hair, bushy eyebrows and a big mustache?"

"Yeah," said the short one, brushing her hair. "He thought he was being funny."

"I know that guy." Lexi put down her eyeliner. "His friends call him *Robert*. Right? Not *Bob*, but *Robert*. CJ threw him out about a month ago because he wouldn't pay me for a dance. He's not supposed to come back here anymore."

"Didn't pay? said the short one. "Whoa! What happened?"

Lexi shrugged. "He was three sheets to the wind. I ask if he wants a dance, and he tells me to come back when the next song starts. It just started, like two seconds ago. And like I'm supposed to waste my time sitting with him waiting until the next song? Right! Give me an effin' break! I said I'd dance for the rest of the song—it had only started like five seconds before—and he could pay me if he wanted to. They always pay when you do that."

The other two nodded in unison like disciples at the feet of their master.

"Right! So, he says okay and I start dancing and he was into it. Hands on my ass. Couldn't be happier. Then the song ends and he looks all serious and says he'll pay me for the next song. Like it was a "two-for-one" sale and he was doing me a favor!" she barked a laugh. "Right, so I said that wasn't going to work for me. But he had to be a dick about it, so I gave CJ the sign and he threw the guy out."

"Threw him out on his ass?"

"Escorted him out," Lexi corrected herself. "Told him never to come back."

"CJ's so cool," said the short one.

"Nobody argues with CJ," said the tall one.

Lexi swiveled back to finish her makeup and saw Russ's reflection in the mirror. "Russ, baby! What a surprise." All three of the women turned toward the door. Lexi's smile grew wide and bright. "That for me?" she asked, pointing at the manila envelope in his hand.

"Hi, sweetheart," said Moe. He addressed the other two dancers. "Ladies."

"Hey, Moe. You and Russ here to see Kyle?" asked Lexi.

"Aren't you afraid of catching cold?" Moe

asked.

Lexi leaned forward. A small well-practiced hitch in her shoulders caused her breast to sway. Her eyes watched Moe's the whole time. "I'm touched by your concern, Mr. Weiss." She winked.

"I'll come back at closing and pick you up," said Russ. "We can grab a bite."

"Sure. Make it around 11:00."

"You're cute," the tall one said to Russ. She sat down at the vanity next to Lexi's. "You married?"

Lexi's voice cut like a knife. "You can forget about him." She smiled at Russ. "He's my brother."

"Your brother?" The tall one looked confused. She picked up a light green paddle brush and brushed her hair while watching Russ in the mirror. "Right," she whispered.

The short one sat down next to her and began recounting her money.

Moe nudged Russ, then cocked his head toward the end of the hall. They started toward Kyle's office without another word.

At the same time Moe and Russ were eavesdropping, Kyle was alone in the office, reviewing his options. He lit another cigarette as his cellphone rang, repeating the first two bars of "Sally Can't Dance." He checked the display before answering.

"Yeah, Carl. What is it?"

"Moe's on his way. I let him and Russ through.

Russ is carrying something in his hand, a manila envelope."

Kyle hung up and dialed Katie's cell.

"Hey," she answered.

"Where are you?" he asked, hopeful she was still at work.

"I'm home." Her voice became harsh. "You're not still in your office, are you?"

He took a breath. "Yeah, babe. Moe just got here. I thought he'd come earlier."

"Look, Kyle. I'm fucking sorry your work sucks for you, but you told me to make reservations for 6:00. Roberto and Leonora are probably already on their way—"

"You know I'm bummed about this, too. This'll just take a couple of hours and then we—"

"Yeah. Well, a couple hours won't cut it this time. I just wanted to have a normal evening with friends. Jesus, Kyle! You promised."

"I'll..." He wasn't sure what he would do, but he had to say something. "I'll pick up Chinese on the way home."

"What about Roberto and Leonora?"

"Call them and see if they'll come over the house for Chinese, maybe 8:00, maybe 9:00—"

The line went dead. A knock at the door, then the handle turned. Russ held the door open for Moe to enter.

Kyle waved and spun his chair so his back was to them. He still had the phone to his ear.

"Yeah. Gotta go. You're the best," Kyle said to

the dead line. He tried to sound convincing.

He spun back around and laid the phone on the desk. He looked up and saw Moe's shark smile for the second time in as many days.

15

"Trouble in paradise?" Moe dropped onto the couch like he already owned the place. "So, what'd those cops say? My name come up?"

"You saw? How about a drink first?"

Moe looked at his watch. "It'll just make me want a smoke."

"Russ?"

Russ shook his head. "I'm on the clock," he said, pointing a thumb at the door. "By the way, that curly haired skinny white girl out there, brown eyes —bad attitude. What's her name?"

"Natalie. Calls herself, Christina." Kyle cocked his head at Russ. "Been here four months maybe? Keeps to herself. Why? What'd she do?"

"She's got a racket going with that bald-headed bartender."

"Michael. Hired him around the same time. Why—what racket? Carl never mentioned anything."

"That's because Carl's an idiot. She cozies up to Carl to whisper in his ear, distracts him so Michael can grab cash and tickets off the waitress station."

What'd I just say? Cop eyes." Moe shook his head. "No wonder you're losing money."

"Looked pretty slick. It wasn't their first time," Russ said.

"Thanks," said Kyle. "I owe you one."

"That's two, now," smiled Russ. He turned to Moe. "If Moe wants, I could—"

"No." Kyle made a face. "I'll handle it. It's still my house, my responsibility."

"Speaking of which, give him the papers, Russ."

Russ dropped the manila envelope onto Kyle's desk, then leaned back against the door.

Kyle looked at the envelope, but didn't open it. He looked over at Moe without saying a word.

Moe pointed at Kyle. "Get yourself a pen, Kyle, and sign. You got no choice in the matter. Neither of us do."

They watched closely as Kyle opened a drawer, then settled back when he took out a pen.

"Open the envelope, read it and sign. It says I own the Bostonian until you repay the debt at which time, I retain 15% of the club and you and I are copacetic. *Capice*?" Moe was losing patience.

Kyle took the papers out of the envelope and started reading. "Three million? It was only 2.9."

"Consider the hundred grand the vig. You

probably got that much laying around."

Kyle shook his head. Deeper and deeper. "Leave me a little dignity. I won't have a pot to piss in."

"Not my concern. Motivating you, is. There're two copies. Sign them both and keep one. Give the other one to Russ. Simple enough."

Kyle flipped to the last page of the first copy, read it and signed. He read the second document, too, then signed it. Then he leaned back, his chair squeaking in protest, and tossed the pen on the desk.

Russ walked up to the desk and picked up Moe's copy. He slipped it into the envelope and carried it back with him to his spot by the door.

"So, what'd those two cops want?" Moe asked again.

"I think we just made progress." Kyle put his feet up on his desk, soles directed at Russ and the door. "A dancer," he said. "been here about four months, Tiffany... she didn't show up for work."

"Get your feet off my desk," said Moe. Kyle was slow to comply.

"So, she skipped work," said Russ. "Some of the people here don't exactly have good old Yankee work ethics."

"Actually, it is unusual. Dancers don't work, they don't get paid. And I want to talk to everybody working here, so I had Carl call her. He couldn't get hold of her—"

"So...?"

"So, I went to her place to see for myself, but I couldn't get in."

"You think she had something to do with our problem because she skipped work?" Moe made no effort to hide his incredulity. "That's all you got?"

"Well, here's the thing," said Kyle. "The door to her apartment was covered in yellow police tape."

Kyle let this sink in.

Moe nodded slowly. "These cops that were just here ...they weren't robbery, were they?"

"Homicide," Kyle said.

"Wertz finally made it," said Russ to no one in particular.

"Homicide," repeated Moe. He considered it for a while, then asked, "This girl, Tiffany? How—"

"Shot," said Kyle. "With a .45. Teddy's gun is a .45. You told me Teddy said they took his gun."

"I knew it! I knew he was in on it with one of those whores," shouted Moe, missing Russ's glare.

"You're missing the point," said Kyle enjoying the moment. "They took Teddy's gun from him and must have shot Tiffany with it."

"Was the gun registered?" asked Russ.

Kyle gave him a smirk and shook his head. "No."

Moe said, "What'd they say about the money? Tell me the cops don't have the money."

"They said nothing about money," said Kyle. "And I didn't ask."

"Didn't talk money?" Moe seemed to be trying to determine how good of a thing that was.

"Not a word."

"Then why'd they question you?"

Kyle finally felt in control. "Because she works for me, Einstein." Moe was too focused to take offense.

"They think you have something to do with it?"

"Sure they do," Kyle shrugged. "They're cops. They think everybody's full of shit."

Moe sat up. "So, what did you say to them?"

"The truth. She's been dancing here a couple months, never caused trouble, and that's it. We didn't hang out, weren't friends on Facebook or anywhere else." Moe waited for more. "That's it," said Kyle.

"They buy it?"

"How do I know? They ask the questions. They're going to keep asking questions for a while because it's a murder. She was a stripper. Sordid. Standard. Tonight, it'll be below the fold in *The Globe* and third page in *The Herald* and in a couple of days everybody will be talking about something else."

For a full ten seconds, the only sound in the room was the muffled bass line from the club.

"The cops will be back and talk to the staff, but they won't learn anything. Nobody except us knows about the money."

"CJ suspect anything?" asked Russ.

"Never asked a thing," said Kyle. "Does what

RICHARD C KATZ

he's told."

Moe stared at his shoes. He brushed something off the tip of one. He glanced over at Russ. "Think the cops found the money and kept it?"

Russ shook his head. "Nah. Not these guys."

Moe snorted. "Why, because you think these are the *honest* cops?"

"Christ, no," said Russ. He pushed himself off the door. "If they'd kept the money, that'd be the end of it. They wouldn't be talking to Kyle or anybody. They'd have stashed the cash and passed her off as a hooker or junkie in a transaction that gone bad. Anyway, the old cop, Wertz. He ain't bent. Not the way I remember him."

"Son of a bitch." Moe stood and started pacing. "Son of a bitch! I knew it was somebody inside. But how could she know about our business?" Moe stopped pacing and whipped around to Kyle. "You fucking her?"

"Fuck you!" said Kyle. "I don't dip my wick in the company inkwell."

"Lately," added Russ.

"Okay," said Moe. "Whose wick then? Teddy's?"

Russ said, "My money is on the late Teddy Bear himself. Was he close with any of the dancers?"

"Well, Kyle here says old Teddy Bear wasn't involved."

"What I said was he was too dumb to plan it and too smart to think he could pull it off. But Russell's got a point. The girls were always talking him

111

up. I figured it was about more stage time, but yeah, sure...."

"He was one dumb fuck," said Russ.

"And this Tiffany wasn't," said Moe. "A bad mix. I should've asked him...."

Kyle looked straight at Moe. "He could've given us more on the two guys after he thought about it. He might've recognized them from their voices and size, but that's not going to happen now!"

Moe ignored the remark, but Russ spoke up. "We'll make a note of it for the next time you fuck up. If these guys had any brains at all, they'd already have split town. They're gone like the wind."

"You sure Teddy wasn't lying?" said Moe. "To throw us off track?"

"No, I don't know for sure." Kyle fought to control his voice. "But my money is on him telling you the truth before you blew his head off."

"*Your* money?" Moe's eyes were cool and patient. "You mean *my* money," he said through his teeth.

"If Teddy was in on it, and his partners double-crossed him, he'd have given them up," Russ said to Moe. "I'm with Kyle on this one, boss."

"Something else to consider," Kyle said. "Tiffany wasn't friends with anybody here. In fact, she could be a first-class bitch. Wouldn't piss on you if you were on fire. I doubt Teddy and her got close enough to plan this, let alone trust each other enough to actually work it."

The room was silent. They were almost out of ideas.

"Wish I could shoot him again," said Moe. He turned to Russ. "Lexi know Tiffany?"

It was impossible to read Russ's expression. "No idea."

"Get her in here," said Moe. "Maybe she knows something that can help." He turned to Kyle. "You start asking the questions. I'll jump in when I'm ready."

16

Russ stepped out of the office and left the door ajar. Kyle broke the silence. "How'd it go with Ruthie and her bookie brother? Lenny? Larry? Which is it?"

"Larry. Good, good. Thanks," said Moe. "Larry and her are close. He's our youngest's godfather." Moe scratched his chin. "How's the hip?"

"It's the knee. Better, thanks."

"About the other night..."

"It is what it is."

They looked in opposite directions. Then Moe said, "For what it's worth—"

"Stop right there," said Kyle. "I don't want to hear you explain anything. My work, my bread and butter. I built this place from nothing."

"I know, I know...."

"You know what you're doing to me? I'm too old to start from scratch."

Moe leaned in, his voice reasonable. "Look. If we don't get the Russians their money, who owns what won't matter to either of us."

They remained silent until Russ returned with Lexi. She wore a short pink robe with a large multicolored embroidered unicorn covering the left side. She acknowledged Moe with a scrap of a curtsy as she stepped close to Kyle's desk. "I'm on the floor in a few. What's up?"

"This is important, Lex." Kyle tried to start slow. "How well did you know Tiffany?"

She picked up on it right away. "'How well *did* I know Tiffany? Why? She quit?"

Russ reached around and slipped a hand on her arm. "Lex, Tiffany was shot last night in her apartment."

She pulled her arm away and brought her hand to her mouth as she took two steps backwards. "Oh... my... God," she whispered. "Is she...?" Her eyes darted from Kyle to Moe to Russ. "She's dead, isn't she?"

Russ nodded.

"Wow!" she said and clutched her arms around herself. "Did they catch who did it? How did it happen? Was somebody stalking her? Was it, like, a customer?"

Russ stepped up and leaned into her ear. "The cops haven't arrested anybody yet, but we're sure no one else is in danger."

"You're sure?" Lexi turned to Kyle. "How come you're so sure?"

"It was a robbery. We're positive about that. We just want to find out if anyone working here or maybe a regular had anything to do with it."

"You don't think I did—"

"God, no, Lexi," said Kyle, soothing her like a child with his voice. "Nobody thinks that. But you can help—"

Kyle looked to Moe to add something, but it was Russ who spoke. "I know this is a shock, kiddo," he said. "Tiffany was into some bad shit with bad people and it backfired on her."

"Uh-huh." She didn't seem surprised. "So...a robbery. That's all.... You sure you're sure?"

"Look," Kyle said. "Here's the problem. The cops will find whoever did this, eventually, but we want to make sure they don't stick their noses into our business. We got to get ahead of this, so we're asking you for help. Tell us everything you know about Tiffany—friends and acquaintances here or outside. Anything you think could help. Think."

Lexi didn't need time to think about it. "All I can say is she didn't fit in, didn't give two-cents about anybody but herself. She was, you know, ego-tistical-like." She paused. "I mean, I don't want to speak ill of the dead but...." Her face grew into a sneer. "But she was kind of a bitch. Pretty much all of the time."

"How about the rest of the crew?" Kyle picked up a pack of cigarettes from his desk. "She tight with anybody?"

"She flirts, all right. I mean, I seen her put the moves on guys even when she wasn't dancing, sure, if she wanted something bad enough" said Lexi.

"When she wanted something, she could be real friendly to anyone."

"Wanted something," Moe repeated. "Like what?"

"Like more stage time, sometimes a ride. The usual."

"Ever borrow money, buy drugs, that kind of thing?" asked Moe.

Lexi shook her head.

"She flirt with Teddy?" he asked.

"No more than most."

Kyle offered her the pack of cigarettes, took one for himself and lit both. Moe was watching with intensity. "Moe?"

"Screw it. Who listens to doctors?" Moe took for one himself. Kyle lit it for him. He exhaled smoke at the ceiling. "So, anything else you can tell us? What about her regulars?"

Lexi bit her lip. "Yeah... what about them?"

"Any of them hang around for her shift to end?" asked Kyle.

She tilted her head and thought about it. "I saw this guy alone at the bar, nursing a beer, killing time. I remembered dancing for him maybe a couple of weeks before, but this time he turned me down. He sat there for about an hour, like he was waiting for somebody. Tiffany walks up and gives him a big mushy kiss, and then they leave together."

"When was this?" asked Russ.

"Um, maybe two months ago? Haven't seen him since."

"What'd he look like?"

"He was white, maybe twenty-five. Almost too cute for her. I remember that. Head full of wavy black hair. Pretty blue eyes. Tight shirt and jeans with big shoulders and huge muscular arms. He definitely worked out. Nice butt."

"You talk to him?" Moe asked.

"That time? No, just asked if he wanted a dance." Her eyes drifted over Kyle's head. "His friend wore glasses."

"His friend?" the three of them said almost in unison.

"Yeah. They were sitting together when I danced for the guy that one time before, so I figure they were friends."

"What was he like?" asked Moe.

Lexi looked confused. "The friend? Why?"

Moe's face became red.

Russ's voice was gentle but he spoke quickly. "Just answer Moe, honey. It's important."

The air in the room got hot all of a sudden.

"He was black, dark skin."

"Black guy, you sure?" asked Moe. "Not Latino?"

"No, he was black." Lexi looked certain.

"What else can you tell us about the black guy?" asked Kyle.

"Well, not much. He was quiet and I didn't dance for him so I didn't pay him much attention. Let me think.... He looked older than the first guy, like around 40 or older. Salt and pepper hair. With glasses, like I said. He was short. They were sitting, but I remember he was kind of small. Thin, too." She looked at Russ. "That's all I can think of. That help?"

The men exchanged glances. Moe spoke first. "Know these guys' names?"

"No, sorry. I don't know anything else about them. Haven't seen either of them since, but if it'll help, I can ask around."

"No, no." Moe's took it down a notch. "We're keeping this whole thing quiet. Don't want to scare everybody, you understand—"

"Sure. I get it."

"Just keep this conversation to yourself, sweetheart."

"Yeah. No. I won't say anything. Promise. You think they—"

Moe cut her off. "We'll take it from here."

"Thanks, Lexi," added Kyle. He stood up.

She got the hint. She leaned over the desk and stubbed out her cigarette.

"Remember what Moe told you," Russ said. "Nothing leaves this room."

"Sure. I understand completely."

"Wait a second, Lexi. Where are my manners?" Moe pulled out a roll and peeled off a couple of bills, stuffing them in a pocket on her robe. He smiled and tried to sound playful. "There you go. Go on. Get out of here."

She thanked Moe. Russ closed the door behind her.

Kyle lit another cigarette. "So, Tiffany had a

boyfriend who hung out with a black guy...."

"...a big white guy and a short black guy," added Moe.

Russ said, "Yeah. She was the inside man. Maybe Teddy was in on it, maybe he wasn't, but she had him on a leash. That's how she found out the routine and the schedule. She hired these two and they took the money and killed her to cover their tracks. These guys sound like serious players." He turned to Moe. "How come we don't know these guys? Do we know these guys?"

Moe shook his head, then exhaled a plume of smoke into the room. "Fuck if I know." He turned to Kyle. "How are *you* going to find them?"

There was a knock before the door cracked open. Lexi peered around the edge. "I was thinking," she said, slightly breathless like she had been running. "I seen Cristina dance for the cute guy before Tiffany started here. He could have been a regular of hers, maybe? She might know something, like his name and or maybe their names. You want me to ask her about it?"

PART TWO

THE SPRING

17

A flush washed across his face. His eyes rolled back and his head dropped. Vibration through the wheel shook his hands like a tap on the shoulder. His eyes snapped opened. He was mostly in his lane, the right two wheels rumbling on the shoulder. He swerved the car back on the road, then risked a glance at the clock on the dash. Maybe a minute had passed since the last time he'd checked. Jesus. How were they not in a ditch yet? He looked with envy at Billy leaning against the passenger door, sound asleep. Doc hadn't counted on Billy being unable to drive a stick.

This was the third (or fourth?) time Doc had fallen asleep at the wheel since the last pit stop an hour earlier. Hot, humid air blasted through the open windows, and despite his stiffness, had him swaddled in its warmth and wetness like a night sweat. He reached deep to shake off the fatigue and fear that had piled up over the twenty plus-hour drive.

But he came up empty. Doc was fried.

He twisted his neck back and forth and heard things deep inside crack. One hand on the wheel, he rummaged through the bouncing collection of empty water bottles by Billy's feet until he found one that promised a few drops. He wet his lips and tongue. It tasted like hot plastic.

The trees along that side of I-75 threw long shadows across the highway. From the west, a dark violet stain dominated a cloudless sky. Headlights from northbound traffic began to dance and merge. Blinking to clear his vision, his eyes wanted to stay shut.

Time to pull over.

A crisp blue road sign with white lettering announced a rest area in one mile. He turned off onto Exit 414, Lake City/High Springs, and eased the car east, putting the setting sun behind them. He passed a couple of gas stations, vowing to fill the tank. But not yet. Not yet. Rest. Sleep.

With difficulty, he navigated a series of signs to a narrow road leading to the rest stop. He slowed to a crawl, checking the place out. Functional enough. A new-looking information center with a pseudo-Spanish façade, racks of shopping guides. A sign that said INFORMATION OFFICE CLOSED. Vending machines and a little cubby sheltering a microwave. Another sign on a pole by the curb announced armed security patrolled 24 hours a day, most likely a bluff. Doc looked in all directions but saw no uniforms or marked cars. In the fading light, he could make out a grassy area with picnic tables and a few skinny young trees held up by wires, but otherwise unoccupied.

Beyond the picnic area the road emptied into a large parking lot. He counted three RVs before pulling into a space isolated at the end of the lot under the branches of an imposing oak. Without waking Billy, he pushed open the door and, barely able to stand, took a leak against the oak. When he dropped back down in the driver's seat, his need for sleep trumped his thirst. He pulled the door shut with a grunt, hit the lock with his elbow, and closed his eyes.

18

Birdsong startled Doc before he realized it was morning. He squinted in defense against the stabbing daylight and gave Billy a shake, then another. Billy woke with a start. "I'm up. I'm up," he mumbled in protest, rubbing his face and looking around. "What's happening? Where we at?"

"Rest stop. We should wash up and grab something to eat. Then gas up and get back on the road." Doc sounded confident and organized.

Billy struggled out of his coat. "Where are we?" He ventured a guess. "Georgia?"

"Florida," Doc answered. "Crossed the state line last night. Still got another ten hours to get to the Keys."

"It looks nice here." Billy turned around to take in the whole parking lot. "Warm. No snow."

Doc opened his door but didn't get out. "One of us has to stay in the car. I'll wash up first. They got vending machines with bottled water and food."

"Get me a cherry Danish," said Billy. "Hey, I

gotta take a leak."

Doc pointed. "Use the tree. I'll wait."

Doc took the keys out of the ignition and put them in his pocket. When Billy got back in, Doc stepped out. He rested his hand on the roof as he bent down to talk to Billy.

"Don't leave the car for any reason. Got it?"

"Yeah. Duh. What'd you think—I'm stupid?"

"Ask me something harder." Doc bit his lip. He didn't want to rile Billy up. Not now. They needed each other more than ever. But Billy responded with a good-natured laugh.

Doc stepped onto the asphalt and stretched. He rubbed his face, grimy with sweat and itchy with the coarse beginning of a beard. His nerves seemed to be waking up one at a time.

The early morning air felt cool and heavy. There was no wind. The drone of a thousand invisible bugs competed with the traffic rumbling along I-75, its rise and fall bringing to mind Mr. Marston's explanation of the Doppler Effect in high school science a thousand lifetimes ago. Doc shook himself fully awake and filled his lungs with the stink of rotting wood and gasoline. He spit. Tastes like Florida, he thought.

Doc scanned the lot. The RVs were gone. He hadn't even heard them leave. Three other cars were parked in the lot now. He'd pass them on his way to the vending machines and bathroom. He rotated his neck left and right, convinced the crackling sound wasn't going away anytime soon.

He studied the other cars from a distance, then leaned back into the car and asked Billy to hand him the map.

"What do we need a map for? I got my phone." Billy started fumbling in his pocket.

"Jesus! I told you not to use your phone."

"I know! I turned off the location setting like you said!"

"Just keep the phone off! Anybody's gonna call, you don't want to talk to them. Try not to be the one that fucks us up, okay?"

"Right, right" Billy said handing him the map from the glove box.

He sat on the trunk while he studied the map and figured they had about 500 miles to go before they reached the Seven Mile Bridge, gateway to the Keys. It would be only ten hours if he drove straight through, but he knew he'd have to stop at least twice for gas and to rest. He also knew he couldn't risk speeding. Florida was famous for speed traps, something a black man in an old car with out-of-state plates would do well to avoid.

He opened the trunk and fished out a change of clothes and his black leatherette Dopp kit from the duffle bag, then squeezed the sides of the week-ender to feel the money for reassurance. The money could mean the difference between freedom or prison or worse. Every decision he made from here on counted. It only takes one mistake.

He walked around the car to see how it was holding up. Doc's '78 Ford Mustang II was not a beautiful car to start with. It was oversized, under-powered and shared more parts with the Pinto than the original Ford Mustang. The car's exterior was dented and streaked with salt, mud, and a healthy swath of bug carcasses. My car looked like I feel, thought Doc. But the tires looked good. That was something.

He checked out the other cars with a side-ways glance as he passed them on his way to the restroom. A teenager with long greasy-looking hair was sound asleep behind the wheel of a brand-new Mercedes sedan. The kid didn't match the car. The owner should be old and rich and sleeping in a fancy hotel, not a rest stop. But Doc figured somebody hired the kid to transport the car—common enough—and the kid was saving money by sleeping in the car. That's what Doc would do.

The other two cars were empty and ordinary. A dark blue Buick with Michigan plates pulling a small white camper. A reddish-brown Saturn. Ot-tawa plates. Doc picked up the pace.

A man and woman sat at a picnic table while three little kids chased one another in the grass. Everyone wore t-shirts and shorts. The woman looked up and smiled at Doc as he walked by. He re-turned the smile and gave her a little wave. Voices echoed from inside the restroom as he approached the entrance. Two men exited, one exchanging a friendly nod as they walked by.

The restroom was a concrete box with sev-eral small screened openings at the top. Inside it was cool and smelled heavy with disinfectant. No showers. Sitting on the toilet, Doc studied the map again as if it might reveal an alternate route, but I-95 was the fastest, in spite of speed traps and the traffic. Standing at a sink, he removed his shirt and splashed water under his arms, a "birdbath" his mother used to call it. He dried off with wadded up paper towels from the dispenser. He was in a daze as he shaved with cold water and slipped on a clean shirt, feeling if not refreshed, at least revived enough to get back on the road.

The parents at the picnic table were deep in conversation. The kids, tired out, lay in the grass under the small tree. No one noticed Doc as he walked down the path and rounded the corner heading for the vending machines.

Sun dappled the area and warmed the top of his head masking a headache and lifting his spirits, until he stood in front of the vending machine. He took account of the sad assortment of plastic-wrapped muffins, sugary Danish, and candy bars on display behind the glass. Nothing substantial. The biggest surprise was a couple of hot dogs, $1.35 each. He peered through the glass for a closer look. Blue lines snaked through the dogs like varicose veins. He settled on a Danish, some muffins and a couple bottles of water.

Orange-brown splotches stained the interior of the microwave and the surface of the glass tray reminded him of a petri dish, but Doc brushed away the debris with a paper towel and used another towel to rest the muffins on. He wolfed down the Danish, a strange combination of dry and sticky, as the muffins slowly rode the revolving tray for their allotted thirty seconds. He finished off both muffins in less than a minute.

Doc still felt tired but now nausea replaced the hunger. He'd need something more substantial to eat if he was going to survive the next ten hours. An image popped into his head of a decent-looking motel that served a real breakfast. That would be their next stop. Someplace they could eat decent food and grab eight hours of sleep in real beds.

He yawned and his whole body stretched. It wasn't a fresh start yet, he thought, but it was a start.

19

They gassed up and continued south on I-75. Doc focused on the road as Billy followed up the Danish with blue icing with two of the three candy bars he'd bought, and then washed them down with a Diet Coke. Doc ate the remaining candy bar, a Three Musketeers, but the sugar high only made his headache worse.

The sign said "State Road 24/Gainesville/University of Florida." A big university town would offer accommodation and anonymity.

"I'm taking the next exit," Doc said. "We'll grab a decent meal and get a room with a shower and comfortable beds. We can sleep for a few hours, then get back on the road. What do you say?"

Billy responded with a hardy belch, then "Sounds good to me."

It took about a half hour to get to the center of town. Doc turned from Archer Road onto University Avenue and cruised by the main campus.

The University of Florida campus grounds

were a green paradise of manicured lawns and shade trees in the center of town. "Man, look at these kids," said Billy, pointing. "Shorts, tee shirts. In the middle of winter! Man, that's the life."

Doc was busy looking for a hotel. He planned to eat a good meal, clean up, and fall asleep watching a game on a big screen TV. They'd covered about twelve hundred miles, far enough to stop looking over their shoulders at least for a night.

They came upon a Hilton just past campus. Doc pulled into the parking lot in the front. Next door to the left was a small wooded swamp, complete with an observation deck, and to the right, the edge of a golf course that continued behind the hotel. Doc parked and got out of the car, not waiting for Billy.

A collision of bird songs filled the air. Doc conducted his ritual of securing the car while Billy headed to the observation deck. Doc followed. The deck was made of wood and wire and was less than three feet above the water. As they stepped onto the deck, one then a second alligator glided toward them, eyes just visible above the surface of the water. Neither man had seen an alligator up close before. Billy instinctively backed away when the sudden thunder of wings startled both men. They looked up to see a black cloud of birds launching from the trees toward the sky.

"Whoa, I've seen enough," Billy said, heading for the steps. "This is creeping me out, man. Plus, I'm starved. You starved?" As they crossed the parking lot, Billy asked, "What do they eat around here, hushpuppies?"

"No idea," Doc said. "Oranges. It's Florida. Seafood maybe. Snapper. Lobster...or what passes for lobster down here."

"Lobster for breakfast. Doesn't get much better than that." Billy said, quickening his pace.

A doorman, ridiculous in blue tails and gray top hat, opened one of a pair of tall glass double doors with the pomp and ceremony fit for a state visit. The lobby was small, but with an attempt at grandeur in its off-white walls, marble flooring, and brass chandeliers. Even the sunlight flooding through the forty-foot windows seemed excessive. Doc felt conspicuous and began to doubt his choice. The place seemed too empty for them to blend in —but hunger and the thought of a shower and sleep won out. And they were already here.

"Welcome to the Hilton. Checking in?" asked the millennial with short blond hair at the registration desk. He put down his newspaper and turned to his computer terminal. Doc shook his head. Fogged though his brain was, the idea that they'd have to show IDs to check-in surfaced.

"Restaurant?" he said. They could think about where to sleep later. Food was the key now.

The clerk pointed toward yet another set of giant glass doors at the far end of the lobby, then returned to his newspaper.

They entered the restaurant and walked up to a hostess in a bright yellow dress standing behind a small mahogany lectern. She was talking on a cell-phone and turned her back to them to continue her conversation uninterrupted. Doc and Billy waited while she nodded away to what was said on the other end of the line. Doc saw the restaurant was the size of a ballroom with expansive views of the swamp and a golf course. And nearly empty.

Doc pegged her as pretty with more pancake than personality. He waited for almost a minute before speaking up. He knocked twice on the lectern as if it were a door. She turned toward them.

"Two," Doc announced holding up two fingers in case she forgot why they all were there.

"A booth, please," added Billy.

"Hold on," she said. Doc wasn't sure if she was talking to him or to the person on the phone until she said, "I'll call you right back." She set the phone down and took two menus from a stack, then studied the seating chart like a general assessing troop movement, her black marker hovering over one empty table after another. Finally, she made her X, and sailed into the dining room, Doc and Billy in her wake.

"We don't have booths," she said, depositing two laminated menus at a table for four and snatching up the extra place settings. And then she was gone, back to her hostess stand like a Roomba returning to its charging station.

Billy examined the map of Florida on his plastic place mat as if he'd never seen a map before. He put a finger down roughly in the middle and looked up at Doc. "This is Gainesville, huh? Looks like we still have a way to go."

"Hi, I'm Brianna. I'll be your server today. What's your pleasure, gentlemen?" Her alto voice was smooth with a faint, but warm southern drawl. Doc saw strands of gold in her dark blond hair. Billy looked up. She met his gaze and smiled, revealing a slight overbite Billy apparently found mesmerizing. He cleared his throat and stared dumbly at the menu and back up at her. "Uh...."

"We're having breakfast," Doc said.

"Then you came to the right spot." The diamonds in her little gold lapel pin sparkled as she pointed her pen at the far wall. "We've got a buffet. Really good and only $19.95 per person, which includes coffee and dessert plus complimentary champagne."

"You got lobster?" Billy tugged his shirt down to smooth out the wrinkles.

"*Lobstah*? Oh, let me guess. You fellas from New York?"

"Boston," Billy blurted out. Doc cringed but no one noticed.

"Oh, cool! Sorry, no *lobstah* on the buffet."

"You making fun of the way I talk?" Billy was delighted and fully under her spell.

"No, sir. I would not do that." Her smile was genuine. "The customer's always right. *Lobstah* is officially the way to say it... at this table." She touched her lips with tip of her pen. "Tell you what. I can get you a side of lobster bits and you can mix them with your eggs from the buffet." Billy nodded enthusiastically. "They're frozen," she confided. "It'll take a couple of minutes for the kitchen to fix them up, but I'll bring 'em right out when they're ready. They are tasty." She put a hand on her hip. "Sound like a workable solution to you, Boston?"

"That'd be great. But no alligator. Hey, I've been meaning to ask somebody...." Billy pointed to the swamp, "Do people really eat those things?"

Doc rolled his eyes, but the waitress's friendly demeanor didn't crack.

"Gator? To me, it's like chicken gone slightly bad, and I grew up here. But some people love it. If you're feeling adventurous, we do have 'em, the Deep-Fried Gator Tots." She leaned into point to the item on Billy's menu. Something faint but flowery filled the air. Gardenias, Doc decided. When she glanced his way, he saw her eyes were Duffy blue, and he started empathizing with Billy.

Doc handed her his menu. "We'll have the buffet. And coffee and waters."

"And a plate of lobster tots," added Billy.

She rewarded him with a wink. "They'll take a few extra minutes. Meanwhile, you gentlemen help yourselves to the buffet."

Doc watched Billy watch her hips sway as she walked away from their table.

"You had to tell her we were from Boston?" he whispered to Billy.

Billy stayed on target. "She asked," he said. "I was just being nice."

Doc closed his eyes and let his shoulders slump. What was it about waitresses in polyester uniforms?

20

On the way to the buffet, Doc saw only two occupied tables. At one two middle-aged white guys were dressed for golf. The shorter of the two in a too-tight polo shirt was drinking beer with his breakfast and doing most of the talking while his much larger friend, head down, was forking in food. At the other table, two elderly women were toasting a fresh-faced teenager with generic champagne. What was it with alcohol for breakfast in Florida? Maybe the girl's grandmother and great-aunt were toasting the kid's graduation. Best of luck to you, Doc silently wished her. Hope your college experience turns out better than mine.

He and Billy carried a fair sampling from the buffet back to their table. Coffee and water were already waiting. They ate in silence, each bent over his plate. Doc focused on his food the whole time. It tasted that good to him. When his plate was empty, save for half a biscuit, he put his fork down and took a breath. Billy was eyeing the waitress, tracking her movements as she worked another table.

"Billy." No response. "Billy," repeated Doc, louder this time.

Billy looked at Doc. "What?" he snapped.

"What are you doing?" Doc said.

"Eating my food. What'd ya think I'm doing?"

"I mean with the waitress?"

"What'd ya mean? Nothing! We were just talking."

"Sure, you are. Try thinking with your brain. I'm begging you not to make trouble." Doc scanned the room again. "Maybe we better just eat and get back on the road."

"Relax. You said yourself we needed shut-eye."

Doc glared at Billy and forced himself upright.

Billy forked a sausage and held it at eye level. "One night. That's all each of us need."

Doc was too tired to argue. "Whatever. Yeah, maybe. One night. Separate rooms," Doc said to the sausage. Billy shoved it in his mouth and grinned.

Doc sighed. He turned the salt shaker over in his hand. The glass bottom, the chrome shaker top, it was all made of plastic——all of it phony.

Both men were tired and deep in thought so she caught them by surprise. "Here's your lobster." That smile and those eyes.

"Anything else I can get you?"

Doc tried to cockblock Billy and spoke for the both of them. "Nope, we're all set thanks," he said, then forked his half a biscuit.

"How about you?" he heard her ask Billy. "Is this enough *lobstah*?"

They laughed together. As their banter slid off into middle distance, Doc stared at his hand holding the fork as if it belonged to someone else, the biscuit growing heavier by the second. The thick aroma of maple syrup competed with ... what? Gardenias? He was drifting ... in a field of white flowers against a sea of green. He was about to fall face first into them when a new voice, loud and angry, jolted him back to the egg stain on his plate.

"Yo! Sweet cheeks! When you're done giggling with your boyfriends over there, I need another beer! Pronto."

Classic Jersey mook accent from the table with the two golfers. It was the smaller man. His short hair stood up like the fur on a scruffy dog. Brianna hurried over, but stood at safe distance. "Sorry, sir" she said. "I'm the only one on duty. What can I get you?"

"I *said* a refill." He smacked the bottle on the table and looked her up and down. "Move your ass, sugar tits. I ain't got all day."

Brianna squared her shoulders and reached for the empty bottle, but the man grabbed her wrist and pulled. She almost fell onto the table before he let her go.

Billy was there before Doc saw him get up.

"What the hell do you think you're doing?" Billy's voice was low key; his stance anything but.

The mook from New Jersey sat back in his chair with his mouth open as he registered Billy's posture and size. The big man across from him kept his head down and spread his hands flat on the table, signaling his friend was on his own.

Brianna broke up the Mexican stand-off, ripping a receipt from her pad and dropping it on the table. "See what you've done?" She cocked her head at Billy. "You pissed him off. I don't know what manners your mama taught you, but it's clear to me you weren't paying her any mind. Square up your tab and get out now or my boyfriend here will escort you out and you don't want that. And don't you ever think of coming back here again."

Brianna looked toward the hostess for assistance. She was watching but frozen, holding her phone a few inches from her ear. Brianna shook her head once and with a hand on her hip, turned back to her customer. He already had his wallet out and slapped three twenties on the table. With as much dignity as his unsteady gait afforded him, he wove his way past the empty tables to the entrance. His friend apologized and placed a couple more twenties on the table. "He shouldn't be drinking so early," he said.

The hostess lowered the phone and stepped to the side as the men passed, even though she was not in their way. The big man waited while his friend fumbled for a mint from the bowl and in a pitiful gesture, made a point of dropping the wrapper on the floor.

"Nice way to keep under the radar," Doc said when Billy sat back down.

Billy shrugged. "No choice," was all he said.

"She all right?" asked Doc.

"I guess." Billy shrugged. "She's seen worse, I bet. She's a waitress."

Brianna filled the water glasses for the women at the other table. They spoke to each other for over a minute before Brianna returned to thank Billy, rubbing a red splotch on her wrist. "Thanks," she said. "I could have managed, but I appreciate you stepping up."

"I'm sure you could of," Billy replied, "but I was happy to help."

"I think you scared him plenty. Man! I hate guys grabbing at me."

"I'll be sure to remember that," said Billy.

"Unless I ask them to."

"I'll remember that, too."

She flashed a grin. "You spooked that guy. Y'all cops or something?"

"Us? No." Billy laughed and pointed at himself and Doc. "We're a couple of angels."

She looked Billy up and down while waiting for him to elaborate. When he offered nothing further, she said, "Okay, then," and met his eyes.

The air felt thick and it wasn't just the humidity. Doc had enough. "I'm going for more food," he said. No one seemed to be listening. He headed for the buffet table and refilled his plate. When he returned, Billy was alone, sipping coffee. Doc sat down but didn't touch his food.

"So, what's the situation?" asked Doc.

"Her name's Brianna—"

"I know that. She told us."

"—and she's gonna meet me at the front desk —"

"Jesus!"

"Hang on! She gonna get the guy there to comp us a room for the night, her way of saying thanks for helping out, for the hotel."

"Oh," said Doc. "That's not—"

"And then I'm going to have a drink with her." He looked Doc squarely in the eyes. "She said to invite you." Billy's look said he wasn't going to.

"Don't bother," said Doc anyway, and accepted the inevitable. "I want to clean up and get some sleep before we head out. Get the check. Let's pay up, get our stuff from the car and check-in."

"She said she'd take care of the bill, too."

Doc left a $20 tip on the table, one of his own twenties and not from the robbery. On the way to the exit, they passed Brianna carrying food for new customers. She waved at them.

"See you in 20, Billy. You, too, Doc!"

Billy waved back. Doc put a hand on Billy's shoulder and spun him around.

"She knows my name?" Doc asked.

21

When they returned to the lobby with their bags, Brianna was already in her street clothes, showing her wrist to the blond guy at the desk.

Billy couldn't take his eyes off her. She wore a simple white silk blouse and light blue jeans that fit snug without a belt. On her feet were pink sneakers with white piping and gray low-cut socks. A red scrunchy held her hair back. The diamond stickpin sparkled from her right lapel. A tiny plain thin gold cross hung from a whisper of a chain around her neck. A little shadow and lipstick for good measure made her eyes and lips stand out.

Introductions were short. The name of the blond guy at the desk was Seth. He and Brianna started out together in the Reserves as 15R Apache helicopter repairers and they remained friends since. She helped him get his job at the hotel. He wasn't a fan of the golfer either, whom he said was named Livingston, "...an asshole from Orange, New

Jersey, who comes here to golf and who's an asshole even when he's sober."

Just as she promised, the room was comped by Seth. And as it turned out, they didn't have to show him any IDs to get the room.

"Ah, sweet! Here we go," Seth said, the contacts in his eyes reflecting light from the computer display. "I can comp you the big two-bedroom suite on the top floor for two nights."

"Awesome," said Brianna. "Mohammad Ali stayed there."

"Seriously?" asked Billy.

"It's booked for the afternoon after that so you have to be out by noon," Seth said, looking up from the screen. "Because this is a favor for Bri, it's under the table so don't charge meals or anything else to the room or we're all screwed. And you'll have to settle when you leave with cash for anything you take from the minibar. I can't help that. Oh, and be sure to tip the maids a few bucks each day. That way they keep this to themselves. Scratch our back, we scratch theirs. How's that sound?"

"No problem," said Doc. "Thanks, Seth."

Seth wrote the suite number on a small envelope, then slipped in the key cards. "Need help with your bags?"

"No, thanks." Doc's grip tightened on the handle of the weekender. He bent down and reached for his duffle.

"I'll take you guys up to your room," Brianna said. "Here, let me take the little one, Doc." Brianna grabbed the handle of the weekender. "That duffle looks heavy enough."

Not wanting to make a scene, Doc let go of the weekender. His voice was flat. "Thanks." Billy picked up his guitar case and raggedy-ass suitcase.

"Thanks, Seth. You're the best," Brianna said before heading for the elevators. "Come on, guys. This way. You'll love the suite. It's amazing!"

The suite was expansive. Billy put his suitcase down by the door. Brianna rested the weekender next to it. Doc immediately snatched up the weekender and followed Billy and Brianna into the living room.

Billy put down the guitar case on one of the oversized orange leather chairs and sat on the edge of the wrap-around sofa.

"Check out the size of this flat screen," Billy called out to everyone. He grabbed the remote off the bamboo and glass-top coffee table and started pushing buttons. The TV didn't turn on.

"Play with that later," said Brianna. "Let me show you the rest of this place. You're gonna love it."

She showed them the bedrooms, each with a king-sized bed, its own flat screen, and a bathroom with walk-in shower and jacuzzi. "I'll take this one," Doc announced, tossing his duffle on the bed, weekender still firmly in his grasp. "Gonna wash up and grab some shuteye. See you two later, maybe for dinner?" He thanked Brianna again and shut the door behind them.

In the living room, Brianna turned the TV on but left the sound off. Billy pulled a couple of Dos Equis from the mini-bar and handed her one.

"Don't forget Seth said you can't—"

"It's okay," said Billy. "I got it covered." He unlocked the guitar case, but she interrupted him before he opened it.

"Hey." Her voice grew soft. "I, ah, want to tell you again, thanks for standing up for me, back there," she said.

"Oh, you don't—"

"Yeah, I do. I really mean it. You didn't have to step up like that. I mean, that shows real character in my book."

Billy snorted and shook his head. "Well, what that guy did was just plain wrong in my book." His face became warm. He raised his voice to cover his embarrassment as he held up the guitar. "Like it?"

"Oh, you are a pretty one," Brianna said to the guitar. She reached for it and floated her hand down the neck. "How long have you had it?"

"Couple of years. Somebody owed me, so he sold me this at a discount. It was already pretty banged up when I got it."

"Can I play it?"

"I don't know. Can you?"

She let out a breath as she looked down at the guitar in her hands. Her thin gold cross dangled from her neck, catching the light in the room. She strummed three major chords, then played the same progression in a minor key, letting the strings ring and the wood resonate. It surprised him how good the guitar sounded. She licked her lips once, then finger-picked a bluegrass riff that sounded both new and familiar to him. When she was done, she passed the guitar back. The notes echoed in his head as he laid the guitar, more carefully this time, back in its case.

"It's all good," Brianna declared. She leaned back against the couch and dug deep in a front pocket of her jeans and produced a well-manicured joint.

"Let's have us a hootenanny," she said with a grin.

She explained it was "Gainesville Green," grown in her backyard. She lit it without asking, took a drag, then handed the joint to Billy. They smoked it down to a nub, talking only about the quality of the dope and the high it produced. When it was too small to handle, she pierced it with her diamond stickpin and handed it to Billy. He took a drag and studied the pin. Three rectangular diamonds that glowed unevenly.

"Nice," he said. Billy knew next to nothing about jewelry.

"Old miners cut. Kinda rare these days, I guess. It was my grandmother's." She took the last toke and then there was only paper and ash which she crushed between her fingers and scattered over the rug. She wiped the pin against the leg of her jeans, then stuck it back in her lapel.

"You play guitar really nice," he said. "What

was that tune?"

"Just something I used to play when I was trying out guitars in the music store to, you know... impress the guys," she admitted with a smile.

"Well, I'm impressed," Billy said.

Suddenly, it began to pour. Huge drops pelted the windows and furniture outside on the balcony, comforting in its steady drone.

"Listen," she whispered, picking up the remote and turning off the TV. "Does anything sound better?"

The sounds of the rain filled the room which in the darkness inside and outside took on soothing black and gray tones. Billy reached for her before his eyes had adjusted to the darkness. The rain stopped as suddenly as it had started and everything was quiet. Everything was soft—as soft as her lips when he kissed her.

"I'm going to need another one of those," she whispered.

"I'm going to need another thousand," he said.

"Jesus!" she laughed, and after a while, he lost count.

22

I t wasn't long before they moved into the bedroom. They undressed each other down to their underwear, then lay on the bed. Spooned together in darkness, Billy buried his face in the silky tangle of her hair.

"Look," Brianna whispered, the faint outline of her finger pointing at the sliding glass door. Billy shifted onto his elbow and saw a sky full of stars.

"Wow ... the Milky Way?"

"Yeah. We don't have all that light pollution you get in big cities." She stood up and tugged at his hand. "Come on," she said. "Let me show you!"

She led him out onto the balcony, no longer wet from the brief downpour earlier. The air was clear and cool, but thick with the smell of leaves, soil and the rain. The moon was a crescent, barely a sliver. She held him from behind and whispered in his ear about the stars.

"Look up there. That one? It always looks the brightest. You can find it any night unless it's cloudy. And over there...." She guided his arm with her hand on his. "You can see that one when it's extra clear, right after it rains. Like tonight." Billy could feel her warm, moist breath in his ear. "After looking for a while, your eyes adapt and you can see the colors."

"Colors?"

"Yeah! See that red one? Over there..." She pointed, but all he saw was white stars. "There! And see that blue one next to those yellow ones? You see lots of those. And that one...." She pointed high to their left. "That one is the coolest. It's kind of green. Ever see a green star before?"

He hadn't. And he didn't now. No colors, just points of sparkly white light. Diamonds in the sky, like you, thought Billy. Shimmering with light from the inside out... it was the biggest compliment he could think of.

Her fingers swept across the Milky Way. "There must be millions in that part of the sky. It's like, I don't know, a highway of stars and other things, too, like planets and their moons and asteroids and... maybe even people. Millions of other worlds. Wouldn't you like to...."

"Yeah. I would." He waited until she looked at him. "Right here, right under your stars," he whispered. He lifted her up and rested her with care on the chaise lounge. She reached up for him.

A door slammed somewhere out in the corridor, waking Billy. Brianna was curled beside him on the bed, asleep. Billy had no idea what time it was. After a moment, the indistinct voices of two men grew louder, then melted away as they passed the door and continued on down the corridor. He rolled onto his back and tried to focus on the soft rise and fall of Brianna's breath—but Tiffany's little white sneaker on the floor by the ottoman kept intruding. Tiffany smiling with tenderness while handing him a cup of coffee she drugged. Tears rolling down her cheeks as she lied to him about Teddy demanding sex from her. And him beating up the guy because of he believed her lie!

He tried to shake the thoughts out of his head. The image of blood-orange soaked towels covering her face persisted in the dark.

He felt conned, turned inside out. And her? Where was she now?

He took a deep breath, then another, and felt the anger and shame dry up into dust and blow away. Most of it. She was gone. She was not forgotten.

He sat up and stared hard at Brianna. She stretched and turned over. She opened her eyes and put her hand on his arm. "What is it? What's wrong?"

"I better check on Doc," said Billy. He got up.

"Wait … I heard him leave a while ago," Brianna said. "You were in the bathroom. I thought he told you."

"I'll be right back!" Billy rushed into Doc's room. The weekender was on the floor next to the bed. The money was still there.

When he came back to the bedroom, Brianna was sitting up. "Is everything okay?"

"Yeah, yeah. I, ah, was just feeling bad, like we were ignoring him. But he's fine, I'm sure."

"I thought he said he was going to sleep—"

Billy sat on the edge of the bed. "He has trouble sleeping. He must've went for a walk. He does that when he can't sleep."

"Say...," she said tentatively. "Billy. Billy what?"

"What do you mean, what?" He knew what she meant, but Doc warned him about telling others too much. He got up and slid the balcony door open breathing in the damp air. Stars still out. Smith, Jones... it doesn't sound right, he thought. She looks up to me. She listens to me. I don't want to lie to her, like Tiffany lied to me. I'm not like that. This lady deserves better.

Competing thoughts crowded Billy's head. Billy was tired of lying and being lied to, of running and hiding, of being afraid. Tiffany played him for a fool. But he wasn't a fool and he wasn't going to treat this lady like one.

The whole process took only an instant. He turned around. "Kaye," he said. "William Kaye. K-A-Y-E. I think it was something longer that got changed at Ellis Island."

"You think? Don't you know?"

"Nope. My mother died when I was little. My old man left me at the Park Street Church downtown and never came back. I was four."

The silence was deep but only lasted a second. "That's awful," she said.

He shrugged. "It is what it is."

"No middle name?"

He shook his head and said with a straight face, "No, I guess we were so poor, couldn't afford one."

She forced a grin. "No other family?"

"Not that I know of." He sounded like he'd answered that question a hundred times before. "Or want to know about," he added. He sat down next to her.

She smoothed his hair with her hands. "You got a girlfriend back home, Mr. Kaye?" she asked.

"What is this, a job interview?" he said a little too forcefully.

Her laughter slid right over his tone. "Well maybe...."

"Nah." He stifled a bitter laugh. "You?"

"Me? A girlfriend?" She smiled. "You'd like that, wouldn't you?"

"I could warm up to the idea."

Brianna looked down and pulled her hair back, the smile gone. "Had a husband for about three years, but that didn't work out." She let her hair slip from her fingers.

He nodded and waited.

"He was nice at first. And he was funny. But

then also a pig-headed S.O.B." It was her turn to look out at the balcony. "Dropped out of school. Never could hold a job, not even delivering sandwiches. High most of the time, which was okay because he was nice when he was high. His folks were rich, but he kept borrowing money from me, then just taking it. After a while, it was clear he wasn't ever going to be...." Her voice trailed off as she remembered.

"A mensch?"

She looked back at Billy. "Yeah, a mensch." She rested a hand on her leg.

"So, anyway, when I tried to get him to shape up, he got nasty and mean. Then I walked. Got a divorce. That was close to three years ago. I think he moved back to Texas."

"Texas," repeated Billy, as if was an explanation.

"How about you? Ever married?"

"Nope. Never came close."

She flopped back down on the bed. He lay down next to her, wrapping his arms around her from behind, spooning again. She placed her arms over his and wove their fingers together.

"We connected as soon as I saw you. You felt that, too, right?" she whispered.

"Yeah," he nodded. It felt insufficient.

"Billy Kaye, with an 'E'." It was barely a whisper.

He heard the wind in the trees shift and then the rain returned. The sound was everywhere, like some kind of energy saturating the air, filling him. A voice in the back of his head warned him don't get comfortable. Get the money, go find Doc and run. He told that voice to shut up. He heard another voice and recognized it as his own. It said *Life does not get better by chance. It gets better by change*. He decided it was time to change.

Later, naked and tangled up in bed, half under and half on the sheets, they talked about random things and listened to each other as if they were the only humans on the planet. They sat cross-legged and smoked another joint as Billy told her about his life growing up in foster homes. She told him she was fifth generation American and that her family had lived in north central Florida for almost 200 years. "My great-great-grandfather, Otto Steiner, came from Ansbach, Bavaria with his brother, Alois, and their wives, Sofia and Heidi, and settled near Micanopy. They weren't cut out to be farmers. Bad career choice. Nobody in the family in 200 years made anything of themselves. I'm the first of my family to go to college."

"College. Here in Gainesville?"

"Yep. The University. I wanted to be a veterinarian."

"Yeah?"

"Yeah. Well, I quit after three semesters and went back to waitressing"

Somehow this was a relief to Billy.

"So, then I joined the Reserves. I needed the steady income, plus I wanted to fly helicopters."

"Helicopters! That's cool...." Billy sounded uncertain.

"Didn't work out. Family curse. I trained as an AH-6 Apache Attack Helicopter repairer. I was really good at it. I got top reviews from my supervisor but he was more interested in my tits than my talent. I wouldn't go out with him so he never recommended me for pilot training."

"That... I'm sorry." And he was.

Her voice changed. "Sonny, you don't know the half of it." She took a deep breath and exhaled. "You grow thick skin. Then, after three years of that shit, I didn't re-enlist and went back to waitressing full-time trying to come up with something to do next. And that's where I'm at. I know I got something in my future. Just not sure what or where it is yet."

Her accent grew stronger as she told her story. He liked the way she talked, her voice, the expressions she used. To his Boston ears, it was almost poetry. It all felt comfortable and carefree. Everything did. Wherever she was from, however she talked, he thought, she was struggling to find her place in life, just like him. Different lives, sure, but here they were in the same place together. Chance. Change.

He ran his fingers through her hair. So soft. Her voice and laughter, smooth and textured at the same time, felt the way he thought clouds would feel up close.

The rain had stopped, but that same energy pulsed through him again. She held his wrists, unblinking as he stared at her. This is different, he thought. She wasn't like anyone he'd ever known. The con artists and cops, the strippers and waitresses, bartenders, bouncers, bullies and bosses of his world. People with power. People with angles and attitudes. She wasn't anything like that. She was pure. His old life was on some other planet revolving around some other star, the landscape filled with sharp, angular people half hidden in the dirt, poised to trip you up and cut you down. She wasn't like that. Brianna was this single flower standing tall in a garden, pointing him up toward the sun and new worlds.

He laughed at himself. She's turning me into a poet, he thought. With a tenderness he'd never known, he stroked her cheek with the back of his hand.

23

Doc took his time in the shower then went straight to bed. Clean sheets felt like heaven, but tired as he was, sleep failed him. His mind raced, reliving the past few days and reviewing his options. After a half-hour of losing the battle, he dressed, grabbed his keys and took the elevator down.

The hotel lobby was deserted and depressing. There was no doorman waiting when he stepped out into the night. Neither the parking lot nor the golf course was appealing, so Doc drove to the center of town. He parked on Archer Road and walked toward campus. On the way he noticed a man sitting in the doorway of a business that was closed. As Doc passed, the man asked for spare change. Doc ignored him, quickening his pace just a little until he entered the campus grounds.

The wide pathways winding past trees, manicured lawns and classic academic architecture had a familiar feel, reminding him of college back home.

He passed students carrying books and laptops, sitting on benches, checking cell phone messages. One woman sat under a tree reading an actual book by flashlight.

He searched their faces. No one looked back at him. He was invisible.

He slumped down on a concrete bench facing a large square three-story structure lit up from the front with floodlights. The front doors clanked open and a man and woman emerged, casting long shadows as they descended the granite steps. With his gray hair, glasses, rumpled sports coat and pressed jeans, the guy was clearly a professor, in-charge and in a hurry, or simply acting that way. The young woman trailing him wore an oversized t-shirt and cut-offs and carried a backpack. She was doing all the talking while sporadically tucking her long hair behind ears, and alternately looking down at the ground and up at the prof. By the time they reached the bottom of the steps, Doc heard enough to conclude she was angling for a better grade. It didn't seem to be working.

They rounded the Department of Psychology sign at the bottom of the steps and went on together, heading the way Doc had come. Doc waited a moment then stood, climbed the steps himself, and entered the building.

It looked abandoned. He could hear his footsteps echo as he walked down the corridor, past one empty classroom after another. At the far end, Doc slowed his pace. A broom and a mop sticking out of a cleaning cart brought to mind the life he'd left just days before. It was parked in front of the entrance to a lecture hall. He looked in, then stepped through the entryway.

It looked like the auditorium at UMass where he took Abnormal Psych. The floor was steeply sloped down toward the front where stood a standard lectern and behind that, a massive projection screen. Two aisles ran the length of the hall, separating a sea of seats into three sections.

He knew exactly where he was going. A third of the way down the left aisle, middle section, middle seat. He sat down and leaned back. He closed his eyes and the memories took over.

Winter. Late as usual. The lecture already begun. He searched up and down the aisles for an empty seat, and was about to give up and sit on the floor in the back when he caught sight of a vacant seat in the middle of a row next to a pair of slender legs in purple tights. He worked his way down the row, trying to avoiding heads and knees, and plopped into the seat next to those purple tights. Maria Kaitlin Chandler had long auburn hair, flawless skin and full red lips. Doc couldn't remember who said "hello" first, but he remembered the violet flecks in her emerald green eyes. And he remembered her voice—a soprano with a lovely lilt. He didn't want to stare but couldn't wait to look, and to hear her voice again.

They didn't pay attention to the lecture that day. Instead, they whispered wisecracks and passed drawings back and forth. They met in the same seats three more times over the next week and a half before he asked her to lunch. Over Diet Cokes and tuna subs, talking about the things 19-year-olds talk about, he was struck once again by how wonderfully random life was, how being late for a class had brought him to this beautiful and precious person. Life was twice as intense, a hundred times more fun, than it was just two weeks earlier. Five weeks to the day they met he moved in with her.

He recalled how she changed the cut and color of her hair every few months and still always looked great. He remembered walking on campus, hiking in Chapel Falls, standing together at the bar at Quicksilvers drinking beer and listening to the house band. He could see her curled up by the window in their first apartment reading another book by the afternoon light. He remembered the first time they made love. It was a Wednesday afternoon.

Staring at his arm on the armrest, he could feel the warmth of her arm against his, the gentle pressure of her hand in his. Her scent was in the air.

Doc looked around the empty lecture hall. It was Maria that had drawn him onto this campus, her face he'd been seeking. Something visceral pushed up from deep inside him. He felt the muscles of his eyes and jaw tense, and without making a sound, he cried.

He allowed himself the memory of their first night together and of their last—sitting next to each other in the pumped-up crowd at the stadium watching the UMass-UConn basketball game. He'd gotten up to get Diet Cokes and an order of fries to share. She'd have just two fries, but never failed to remind him to get the ketchup and mustard. And straws. She wouldn't drink from a can without a straw.

He'd been at the end of the line at the concession stand when the fight broke out in the crowd behind him. A blur of white and black arms and legs, punching and kicking, then rolling on the ground. He'd tried to step away but others moved closer, some to fight, others just to watch. Someone pushed him forward and down. He fell hard on the concrete floor, hitting his head and breaking his glasses. People stepped over him and then somebody kicked him. When he got up, someone grabbed his arms and held him while another punched him in the face and stomach. He was in a daze when the security cops dragged him away—to safety, he thought.

One of the white kids in the fight was badly hurt. He was from UConn and came from a prominent family. Someone stabbed him under his rib and he lost his spleen and a lot of blood, but survived. He and two of his friends testified at trial that Doc was the student who stabbed him after arguing about the game. They never recovered the knife, but that didn't seem to matter to anyone but Doc. Doc's attorney, a public defender confident the jury would acquit, did not present any witness to the assault. Maria took the stand to testify why Doc was waiting in line, but the prosecutor pointed out she didn't see the fight. The judge permitted only one character witness, Doc's mother, to testify. They convicted him of attempted murder in the second degree. Because of the severity of the victim's injuries, the viciousness of the attack in a school setting, and that a knife was used by the assailant, the judge accepted the recommendations of the prosecutor. Doc was sentenced to a total of 17 years.

Doc's mother collapsed in the courtroom the moment the judge cracked the gavel. Six days later, a prison chaplain appeared at Doc's cell and sat down next to him on his bunk to tell him his mother never regained consciousness. She had a stroke and died. Her funeral, he said, was yesterday.

At Walpole, time and numbers took on a new significance: sentence length, time served, time left, scheduled times, time of day, inmate identification number, and block and cell number. Maria visited him for seventeen 52-minute visits and one that only lasted five, the last. They spoke 21 times on the phone, each time for four minutes, and no more often than once a week. She wrote him twenty-eight letters, the longest, eleven pages, the shortest, one.

She wrote about school and her family and friends. He wrote about the bad food, avoiding fights in the yard, and working in the prison mailroom and the library. The first time she missed a visit, what he felt more than anything was relief. The visits, calls and letters became less frequent over time. All came to a stop after sixteen months. He didn't blame her.

He'd added up the elements of his life and it came to zero. He was nobody's son, nobody's brother, nobody's friend. He would never be a husband or a father. There was no longer a person for anyone to see. The man he always thought he was going to become never materialized.

He stopped thinking about his future and focused on the present. It wasn't that hard; it was all he had left. Each day he cared less about anything other than getting through whatever was in front of him. He changed into somebody he didn't know. He even had a new name. The other inmates called him "Doc" because he had gone to college. The name stuck.

During his third year behind bars, Doc learned from a local paper that Maria was married to a lieutenant in the Coast Guard and lived in Sandwich where she just gave birth to a boy, their second child. Doc traded his wallet-sized picture of Maria for a half-pack of cigarettes, then burned her letters.

Doc wiped his eyes and stood up in the empty hall. Though he didn't remember thinking about Maria in years, he knew a scrap of his former self still held on to the memory. The glow from that remnant provided him with a wisp of comfort, a distant emotional point of reference. But now, sitting here, reliving it in detail, he saw through the convenience he had created. It wasn't simply Maria he mourned. It was the death of the man he was to become, a person traveling through life with hope and love. Suddenly he had neither, and that lack of assurance and the support it provided, let the weight of the world crush him.

The train he thought he was riding left a long time ago without him. He knew that. But maybe now he had an opportunity to fix things, a second chance. The first day of prison may have been the worst day of his life, but this realization was the most terrifying and liberating of all.

"Here I am," he said out loud to no one. His voice was thin in the auditorium, an empty challenge. But his declaration had substance. When the greatest thing I cherish is memories, he thought to himself, it's no longer much of a life, is it? Doc had lived two lives—the college kid and the criminal. Neither worked out. Now he was ready to pick a new destination and start again.

Three's a charm. Three strikes and you're out. This was his last chance. This time he would not react with regret and despair, would not let life's random actions brush him aside to be swallowed whole. This time he had the money and motivation to follow his own direction forward. One lesson he learned in college and prison: life was movement and change; standing still was death.

The hell with hiding in the Keys. He was leaving for L.A. in the morning, with or without Billy.

24

Doc knocked on the bedroom door and waited, but got no response. He looked at his watch and knocked louder and longer, this time calling out.

"Bill! You up?"

"Yeah, yeah! I'm up now," said Billy through the door. "Jesus, what time is it?"

"Morning. We need to talk. You alone?"

"Yeah. I'm up. I'll be out in five minutes."

"Are you alone?"

It took Billy a couple of seconds. "Yeah, I said, yeah."

"There's hot coffee and Danish I brought up from the lobby."

"Super," said Billy without enthusiasm. "I'll be out in two."

Billy came out into the living room as promised in two minutes, in his underwear, face and hair wet, slits for eyes.

"Jesus! It's bright in here. Can you pull the

shades?" He shielded his eyes with a hand.

Doc pulled the drapes halfway. "Where's Brianna?"

Billy rubbed his face, then scratched his scalp with his fingers. "She headed to her place as soon as the sun came up. Where's my coffee?"

"Right in front of you."

Two large Styrofoam cups were in plain sight on the coffee table along with a pile of creamer containers and sugar packets.

"Oh," said Billy. "Thanks."

Billy opened the lid on one cup and added cream and sugar. He took a sip and set it back down on the coffee table, then dropped onto the couch.

Doc looked down on him. "You tell her about the money or anything?"

Billy picked up his cup and brought it close to his lips. "No, 'course not." He blew across the steam and drank.

"Okay. Listen. I got to tell you I need to get going...."

"You want to leave now, right now?" said Billy.

"Yeah, I do," answered Doc.

"I thought we were going to stay for a couple of days," said Billy. "Leaving today is not going to work for me. I'm sick of driving, and I'm starting to have a good time here." He looked into his cup. "I just kind of like it here."

Doc pointed at Billy's bedroom door.

"And Brianna?"

"Yeah, she's a peach."

"That's Georgia, Billy."

"Whatever." Billy sat up and made the pitch he practiced in his head. "I don't know about you, but this is far enough for me. I think we ought to stay. I mean...." He rubbed his hair again. "I studied the map—"

"You mean the one on the place mat at the restaurant?"

"Yeah. That one. Gainesville is a big city, bigger than Key West. And we're not trapped in a corner if they track us down."

"You got that from the map?"

"Yeah."

"This girl got anything to do with your decision?"

"No, man!" Billy sounded adamant, then dropped the act. "Well, yeah, of course. She and I clicked, you know? But I was thinking about this before, and I don't want to go to Key West—"

"I'm not going to Key West," said Doc. "I'm heading to California."

"Oh!" Billy considered that. "So, you changed your plans too?"

"Yeah. That's what I want to talk to you about."

"Well, I guess it's settled then," said Billy. "Pass me a Danish, will you?"

Doc handed Billy a cherry Danish. "I figured you might want to stay, so yeah, I made my own plans. What's best for me. What's best for you."

Billy had already taken a huge bite out of the Danish, but that didn't stop him from asking. "California. Where? L.A.?"

Doc nodded. "Always liked L.A. and I want to live by the ocean. I think I can pull it off now. And nobody's going to look there for us... for me."

"So, okay, when are you leaving?"

"Right after we split the cash." He jerked a thumb over his shoulder. "My clothes and stuff are already in the car."

Billy felt a mixture of relief and regret. "You've been talking about moving to Arizona as long as I've known you. The air or something...."

"Used to be that way, but now, the air can suck in Phoenix just like anywhere else. Lots of pollen just like every other landlocked city. The air quality in L.A. is a lot better than it's been, especially by the beach. There's the weather, the beach, the music scene...."

Both men were quiet, wondering what to say.

"You don't worry about earthquakes and global warming and those big forest fires?" asked Billy. It wasn't really what was on his mind.

Doc shrugged. "Sure, I do." He glanced at his bedroom door. "Look, we can talk while we split the money."

"Yeah, I guess."

"Get your duffle and bring it to my room."

Doc slipped the *Do Not Disturb* sign around the outside handle then double-locked the door to the corridor. He put his coffee cup on top of the dresser, then dumped the money from the weekender onto the bed. He and Billy stood in silence on the same side of the bed. It was only the second time they saw the cash that changed their lives.

"I got questions for you," Billy finally said. Then he took a sip of coffee.

Doc bent over and began sorting the stacks of cash into two piles. "Go ahead," he said. "Ask. We can do this and talk."

Billy took a step back to get out of Doc's way. "What are you going to do about work?" he asked Doc. "I mean, we don't need to work, but we got to find jobs anyway, right? For appearances, right?"

"Yeah. Absolutely. Don't bring on attention and make trouble for yourself. Find something easy or fun to do. Part-time is okay, but you got to get a job."

"But...." Billy's face was a combination of concern and confusion. "If we're hiding, we can't use our real names, right?"

Doc turned to Billy. "Not for a couple of weeks, just to be on the safe side, but after that, we got no choice. It'll be okay."

"You think so?"

"Definitely," Doc went back to sorting the stacks. "They don't know our names, and even if they manage to figure them out, there are probably thousands of other guys with the same names."

"Yeah, but—"

"It's not like in the movies, Billy. If you want to change your name, you got to do it legally. You have to change the name on your social security number, which you need to get a job, pay taxes, put money in a bank, that sort of thing. You can't make a change like that without leaving public records for anyone to look up and see. We'll keep a lower profile if we just leave things the way they are."

"Tiffany knew our names."

"And that might mean her partner, Jesse, could know, too, but he doesn't know where we are. It's a gamble, but a better risk to hide among all the other people with the same names than to change our names and attract attention from somebody running a search. Better to be lost in the crowd. I mean, this guy, Jesse, and Moe and his gang... they don't have our social security numbers, our fingerprints or DNA, right? They don't even know what we look like. So what's a couple of ordinary names going to do for them as long as we stay out of their way?

"So, what are you going to do?"

"Like I said, pay everything with cash as long as I can. When I get to L.A., I'll find a place to live, get a job at a music store—"

"That's when you'll start using your real name?"

"Yeah, sure. Then I'll buy a drum kit and get into a band."

"So, you'll work at the music store so people

don't ask questions...."

"Right, and because it'll be fun. Better than our old jobs. I'll use the cash when I can—groceries, clothes, movies, restaurants... a lot of Ma and Pa operations are happy when you pay cash anyway so they can skip paying taxes."

"What about hiding the rest of the cash?"

Doc stopped sorting and sat on the bed. He took a breath. "Split it up. Put some in a checking account, some in a savings account, no more than five grand each time and usually less if you can wait. You don't want them to think it's drug money or something like that. Somebody will notice all that cash."

"Five grand? Is that because of the IRS?"

"Right. If it's over ten grand the bank will report you to the IRS, and you don't want that kind of trouble. Store most of the cash in a couple of safe deposit boxes in one or two banks. And every few weeks, take a little out and add to your accounts, a little bit at a time. You get the idea."

"Makes sense."

"After a while, invest some of the savings in something totally safe, like CD's, Certificates of Deposits."

"I know about those."

"We don't need to risk losing any of it. Put some cash into CDs to hide the money in plain sight and get a little interest to boot. If there's too much sitting in your savings account, the bank will get all nosey over it, so it's better to invest it in CDs."

"Thanks. I'll do that. Ah...." Billy scratched

his head and looked puzzled.

"What?" asked Doc. "What's the matter?"

"I want to know... how'd you figure all this out? I mean, about not changing our names and the things about the bank? Did you read about it or something?"

"Walpole," said Doc. "Hours of talking to cons who had the same kind of problems. It's something I've been going over in my head since we got into this mess."

"Yeah," smiled Billy. "I guess you would."

Doc went back to sorting cash. "So, what are you going to do for work?"

"Um, not sure, yet." Billy grinned. "Maybe deliver stuff? I like to be outdoors in this weather."

There were two equal piles of almost $1.5 million on the bed.

Doc picked up his coffee cup from the dresser. The coffee had cooled, but he drank it anyway. "That should work, but be careful." He gestured at the two piles. "This kind of money attracts attention. We're dead if anybody catches us or even catches on to what we got. The guys looking for us are animals, but people in general go and do crazy things for money like this." He gestured at the two piles on the bed. "Best if nobody outside of this room know about this."

"Yeah, I get it," said Billy. He tapped his cheek with two fingers like Doc taught him.

Doc returned the gesture, then rubbed his hands together. "Okay. Which pile do you want?" he asked. Billy studied each and pointed to the further one.

Doc repacked his half into the overnighter. Billy stuffed his into his duffle bag, already half filled with clothes. He made a mental note to buy his own backpack later.

"Where are you thinking about hiding your money until you find a bank?" asked Doc. He looked around the room. "You can't stay here much longer. Seth said two nights."

Billy thought for a moment. "I can get a safe deposit box, like you said. There was a Bank of America in town. Or a storage locker."

"I'd go with the safe deposit box. Whatever you do, tell nobody about it, and that includes this woman or anybody else you meet."

He paused, waiting for Billy to acknowledge he understood.

"Yeah, I won't. Don't worry about me."

"I mean it, Billy. Lie if you have to, but don't say a single word about what we did or the money or where it's hidden," warned Doc. "That's how you get caught."

"Yeah. Okay. I got it."

"Once one person knows, everybody will know."

"Yup, yup. I know."

"If you slip up, tell them another lie. Don't admit—"

"I said don't worry about it!" Billy looked at the door and back at Doc.

Doc took a breath. "Sorry," he said. "I just want you to be careful. It's my ass, too."

"What time you leaving?" Billy looked at the digital clock by the bed. It was 10:38 am. "Brianna's getting off at noon today. She'll want to say good-bye."

"You tell her I had to get on the road early. Tell her I said thanks for the room and all." He thought of something else. "Don't tell her I'm going to California. If you got to say something, tell her I wasn't sure where I was headed and that I'll be in touch."

"Will you?"

"Will I what?"

"Be in touch? We don't have new cellphones or email addresses yet. How are we—"

"Look. Better if we don't know about each other for a while, just to be on the safe side. You know what I'm talking about?"

Billy was motionless, then said, "I guess... if you think so."

"They catch you or me, the first thing they're going to do is check our phone calls and contacts looking for the other guy and the rest of the money. It'll be best if we don't contact each other for a few months."

Billy said, "Yeah, I guess so," but didn't sound confident.

"And a word of advice," interrupted Doc. "When you get a cellphone, don't let them publish your name and number in a directory. Opt out to make it harder for them to find you. In fact, get somebody else to buy the—"

"Jesus, Doc! Stop it. You're making me nuts!" He caught his breath. "I'll handle it."

"Okay. Just be careful." He smiled. "I worry about you."

"So, how am I going to find you then if I don't have your number. You know, if I'm out that way? I mean, L.A. is a big place."

"I'll be on the west side. Remember that. I'll be as close to the ocean as I can live and work, maybe Santa Monica."

"But that's still a lot of territory to cover."

Doc looked serious. This was his plan. "Check out the music stores. I'll be working in one. With any luck, I'll be playing in a band, too, blues or old rock and roll." He shrugged. "I'm too old for the new stuff." He laughed, then said, "How many blues joints can there be in that part of town?"

Billy looked unconvinced.

"Come on! It's not that big a place. Venice, Santa Monica or West L.A. That's where I'll be working and living." He patted the overnighter. "I don't think even this is enough to rent for long in Malibu or the Palisades. You can work with that, can't you?"

"I guess." Billy looked down at his feet. He hadn't put on his shoes yet.

"Walk me to the door." Doc grabbed the handle of the overnighter and lifted it off the bed.

They walked together out to the living room. Doc started to reach for the door handle, but offered his hand to Billy instead.

"It's the journey, Billy, my man, not the destination that counts. Not what I expected, but I'm glad we shared this part of the road together."

Billy shook Doc's hand, then gave Doc a brief hug.

"Venice, Santa Monica, West L.A., music stores, blues or rock bands," Billy repeated, getting used to the idea. "Okay, I can do that."

"Wherever I live, it'll be small but there'll be a couch for you to crash on, Bill. Brianna, too, if...." Doc grinned. "Just bring your share. It's expensive out there and I ain't going keep buying you coffee and Danish." The grin disappeared. He looked Billy straight in the eyes. "Be careful, man. Careful what you say and do. And who you say things to. Trust no one and nobody." He doubled-tapped under his eye and was gone.

The door closed and locked by itself. Billy was on his own.

25

Billy considered moving in with Brianna, but she hadn't offered. He knew from experience it was better to wait for the woman to ask. But looking for a place seemed such a hassle, especially without a car, so when Seth offered a discounted rate for a regular hotel guest room for the month, Billy jumped on it.

The next day he opened an account at a bank and rented a safe deposit box. He waited two more days before he returned and stored his share of the money in the box.

He hung out with Brianna practically every free moment for a month. They ate and slept together, walked to the movies, and went to concerts. They drove to Jacksonville and bet on jai-alai and explored Micanopy and Cedar Key. They spent four days on the beach in St. Pete's and a long weekend at the Seacrest in Clearwater. They worked out daily at the hotel's health club. Billy's old life in Boston, the cold and trouble he ran away from, was mostly behind him.

Brianna left her laptop with Billy for him to search online for an apartment, a car and a job. He ended up as a part-time courier for a law firm. Prescott & McNeil, Attorneys-At-Law, were two low-rent lawyers who specialized in DUI's. Billy had seen their late-night TV commercial, "If we don't win, you don't pay." He met with the younger partner, Malcolm McNeil, who hired Billy as a private contractor, paying by the job with no benefits. The work provided the illusion of employment and was interesting enough to hold off boredom. Billy needed a car for the job, so he bought a used Honda Civic for cash from a UF student about to default on his loan.

Things were starting to go his way, but Billy remained cautious about the trouble he left behind. He googled The Improper Bostonian and read online news articles and public police reports. To his relief, there was no mention of the robbery. There was, though, a short article in *The Boston Herald* about Tiffany's death. The police concluded the murder resulted from a drug deal turned bad. There were no suspects.

It took a month for Brianna to ask Billy to move in. Her apartment was on the ground floor of a two-story hundred-year old Victorian-style house. The place had old world charm with large rooms and a porch. Four ancient oak trees provided shade for the front yard which was wide and deep, setting the house back from the street. Someone had hung a tire swing from a tree limb.

Billy loved how convenient the weather was, as opposed to Boston. Here, he could always count on changes in the weather to be on time. This time of the year, a downpour started like clockwork every day at 5:00 p.m., clearing the air of heat, humidity, and bugs. The refreshed air, infused with ozone, energized him for hours into the night.

They were lying naked in bed enjoying the sound of the late afternoon rain just outside the open window. A Curtis Mayfield song played through a small Bluetooth speaker on the nightstand by the bed. Brianna lay on her stomach. He kissed the small of her back, dipping into the shallow pool of sweat, tasting salt and soap. She made a low sound that made his whole body grin. He hugged her hips, resting the side of his face on the thin cushion of her perfect butt. A welcome breeze caressed them both, cooling down their skin. Billy could not suppress a smile. Less than six months ago he was broke and trudging through snow. Now this. Sex, drugs, and rock & roll was once again the life.

Brianna rolled over and propped herself on an elbow. It had been on her mind for a while and this was as good a time as any.

"Billy," she said, "don't you think I deserve to know what kind of trouble you and Doc got into in Boston? If we're really being honest with each other, I should know, don't you think?"

He had already let it slip that Doc was somewhere in Los Angeles, but Billy didn't know exactly where because Doc felt it was safer for the both of them. "I take it you guys were doing something illegal and it backfired on you, and I can deal with that, but I need to know what I'm getting into if you expect me to hang in there for you. You understand?"

It took Billy an uncomfortable moment before he responded. "I ah, we...what happened was.... Listen, did you ever do anything really bad, something you never thought you'd do but you were so desperate for money you did it anyway?"

The air was steadily cooling from the rain. She pulled the sheet up to cover herself, holding it up between her arms and body. "How do you mean, desperate for money? Like... like what?"

"Something illegal, like steal something."

"Is that what you did, steal something?"

"You first," Billy said.

She flashed both eyebrows, then dropped her gaze. "Yeah." He waited for her to elaborate. "When I tended bar... sometimes a customer would leave a twenty or a ten on the bar to cover his bill and split, and I'd slip it in my pocket and not ring it up."

"That the worst thing?"

She looked at him. "Yeah, I think so. It's something I'm ashamed that I did, but it's not like I physically hurt somebody."

"Did you do it more than once?"

"Yeah."

"Well, I did this thing just one time."

"What was it?"

He took a deep breath before starting. "I got talked into robbing this lowlife guy of money he was carrying to the bank. I swear I never did anything like that before or since. I was scared, but that's what I did."

"You mean like a break-in, a burglary?" There was a little hope in her voice.

"No, worse," he said. "More like we mugged him. Ambushed him on the street at night."

"Jesus!" She sat up. "Did anybody get hurt? Tell me the truth."

"No. No. We didn't hurt anybody," lied Billy for the first time to her. It didn't feel good to him and he knew there would be more lying.

"So, what happened?"

He sat up. "We scared him, that's all. Shook him up, so we could take his money. It was a stupid thing to do, but we got tricked into doing it."

Her voice was steady and low. "You got tricked into it?"

"It was a stupid thing to do. I was stupid, and desperate."

"Did Doc talk you into it?"

"No, it was more the other way around."

"Then how did you get tricked?"

"Someone we both knew," he said, "worked there and had it all figured out, the who and where and when. And, it turned out the uh, the money belonged to some bad people. Organized crime-types. We didn't know."

"You saying you stole money from... from... organized crime people? By mistake?"

"Yeah," he answered. "It was a lot of money." He was still proud of how much, but careful not to mention it. "The guy was making the bank deposits from a strip club, but the mob money was in there, too." Then, after a pause, he added, "The guy, he really was a piece of shit—harassing the women who worked there, at the club, for sex." It had been Billy's motivation for treating Teddy so savagely, but now Billy suspected it was just another one of Tiffany's lies.

"But you robbed him. With a gun?"

Billy nodded and almost smiled.

"You didn't shoot anybody, did you?"

"No, no." Billy sat up, looked her in the eyes. "Nothing like that. We hit him a couple of times —Doc did—that's all. But only after he tried to get away, but we didn't hurt him, not really."

"That's crazy, Billy. How'd you get tricked into doing that?"

"Look, I said I know it was stupid. We didn't know what we were getting into. I was broke. We were broke. And she said he'd be carrying all this money—"

"She?"

"Yeah," he confessed. "She worked at the club as a dancer. She figured it all out and told us what to do, then tried to double-cross me and Doc. She was going to take the money and leave us hanging out to dry with the criminal-types after us. So, me and Doc split." He looked down at the floor. "And that's all there's to it." He prayed she didn't ask more about Tiffany or the money.

"The criminals, they're like the Mafia?"

"Something like that. Yeah."

"Jeez!" She studied his face. "How much did you end up with?"

"I don't want to talk about it now."

"What happened to her, to the dancer?"

"I don't want to talk about that either. Maybe later." Never, he thought.

"You didn't hurt her, did you?"

"Me? God, no. I, we wouldn't do that. God, no."

He was ready for her to ask more about the money, but instead she asked about him. "But you're okay, now? I mean, you don't seem like.... You never did that before and you're not going to do that again, right?"

"Right." He stroked her shoulder and smiled to reassure them both. "My head's in a totally different place, now. It's like, I don't know how that was me. Like it wasn't me, it was just life happening to me, circumstances and stuff... and this woman... look, it'll never happen again, I swear." It was his turn to look down. "I'm embarrassed to even talk about it to you."

She took a big breath and let it out slowly. "I wasn't expecting this. I mean, I don't know what I was thinking happened, but not this. I can understand being low and broke and doing something stupid, but you're better than that. Billy, you're a good person." She folded her arms across her chest. "As long as you're safe now and are honest with me...." Something seemed to cross her mind. She looked at the clock on the night stand. "We'll finish this later. I got to get ready for work. I'm leaving in a couple of minutes."

Billy felt like he just dodged a bullet.

She moved quickly and rolled toward the night stand. She opened the baggie on the top of the night stand and stuffed a pinch of grass into the tiny, tarnished brass bowl of a hash pipe. She leaned back against the headboard and lit up. She passed him the pipe and he drew a long toke. His head swirled with the fragrance of her hair and the stench of burning marijuana.

Getting ready for work. Now he knew what she meant.

Billy jumped, startled by a short flash of light and a burst of thunder coming through the window from the outside world. The tension dissolved as he watched the window curtains dance in the breeze to Curtis's falsetto and horns and drums mingled with the rhythm of rain playing against the side of the house and the distant swish of tires pushing through water flooding the road. He felt okay. He was stoned.

"What do you want to do this weekend?" he asked, desperate to turn the conversation away from Boston. "Let's do something new," he said, trying to hold in the smoke.

"Ah, okay," she said with anticipation.

He exhaled. "I mean when we've smoked all the dope—"

"Not in Gainesville, honey."

"—heard every local Tom Petty-wannabe band, eaten takeout from all six Chinese places, which by the way suck, every one of them. Let's see... we drove for hours to see the ocean, and lost money betting on jai-alai. What else can we do here for fun?"

"Already getting bored with me, huh?" They both smiled. She took a healthy toke, only exhaling after he took the pipe from her. It was dead. She got up and he watched as she put on a pair of faded blue panties and slipped into a pair of jeans draped over the back of the chair. She retrieved a pocket knife with a three-inch blade from her front pocket and held her hand out toward Billy. "Toss me the pipe," she said.

She cleaned out the pipe with the blade of the knife, then shook the charred contents of the bowl into the pot of a red and green leafed plant on the bureau. The sweat shimmered on her collarbone and breasts. Billy saw it all and thought, yes, I could stay with this woman forever, but instead pointed at the knife. "What a good scout you are. You do come prepared."

"What? This thing?" She held up the knife. "Every good old boy or girl carries a pocket knife. You don't have a one?"

He shook his head.

She wiped the blade on the leg of her jeans.

"Here," she said, snapping the knife shut and tossing it to him in a smooth underhanded arc. "My gift to you."

Billy caught it in his left hand. "Don't you need it?"

"I've got another two or three of them," she said, "but this one's the best... the more suitable for a gift."

He admired the small brown textured handle, worn along the edges but intact. It felt warm in his hand. "Thanks," he said, placing knife on the bed stand. "My first pocket knife."

"Really?"

"Yeah. I'll take care of it."

She put a pinch of grass in the bowl and lit it. She sat on the bed and passed him the bowl, the contents still glowing.

"Hey, tough guy... I know what we haven't done yet?"

"Yeah? What?" He was interested.

"Let's go shooting?"

She had shown him the gun she kept in her top bureau drawer for protection, a Sig Sauer like the one she used while in the Reserves. "Yeah, sure. Maybe." He took a drag. The grass was dry and harsh. He coughed once and suppressed a second. "Eh, shooting at what? I don't hunt." He handed her the pipe.

She took a long toke and smoke-puffed out her words. "I don't hunt either. I meant shooting at targets. But maybe you don't have the energy.

Maybe you'd prefer being bored in bed with me all weekend."

He reached over and smoothed one of her eyebrows with his thumb. "Nothing says we can't do both."

"At the same time?" she joked. "Hey, that's messed up."

"That's not what I meant," he laughed, "but let me try to picture it." She raised an eyebrow. He pointed at the pipe. "It's out."

She set it carefully on the nightstand. "I got to go. Seriously."

"I saw the gun in the drawer. You got another gun so we can both shoot?"

"Oh, the Sig? Yeah, I got a bunch. An old .44 Colt that's got to be close to 100 years old, but I don't shoot that one anymore. It's a collectable, and I don't want to wear it out. I got a 9mm Beretta 92FS I bought when I was in the Reserve, too, but that sucks. I'm looking to get rid of it. I got a couple little pistols and an M4 I got for cash at a show, and an old Winchester 94 my Daddy bought me as a kid to teach me to shoot. I keep that for sentimental reasons."

"An M4? That's like an M16, right?"

"Jeeze, I really, really got to get going," she said, looking at the clock on the nightstand. She got up and looked through blouses hanging in her closet. "Um, yeah, an M4 is like an M16 but better, 'specially for me. Shorter muzzle. Lighter. Most soldiers use them now." She pulled a silk Tommy

Bahama blouse with blue and green flowers off a hanger and slipped it on. "The military version is automatic but you can only buy the semi-automatic version. But a buddy of mine—you'll meet Earl at the range—sold me the parts and showed me how to convert it to automatic."

"Oh, cool," he said, even though he did not think it was cool or cared to meet this friend. "Where do you keep the guns? Here? I only saw the one."

She pointed at the closet with her chin as she adjusted her collar. "I keep the handguns in a gym bag right there, each one wrapped in a towel to keep them from getting banged up. The M4 is in there, too, but I got a nice hard case for that." She looked at herself in the full-length mirror. "I'll show them to you when I get back if you want. They're not loaded but wait for me to show them to you first. Okay?"

"Sure. Yeah, I'll wait." He had to ask. "You said you made the M4 into an automatic? What do you need an automatic for?" He gave a little snort. "You planning to rob a bank or something?"

She was brushing her hair but stopped to answer. "Well, it's my gun and I like tweaking it. Same as I liked working on chain guns on the Apaches in the Reserves."

He fired up the pipe again. The grass crackled like a brushfire. He took a drag and held it. The smoke thickened and curled, hanging in the air and stinging his eyes. He blinked to clear them, then waved his hand in the air to scatter the smoke.

She smiled. "I guess I like the way machines work, guns included. I like how this one's designed one way and another gets the same results but in a different way. Like the way they design cameras or helicopters to work, depending on what you need them to do." She bent down to get a clear view of the minute hand on the clock. "Jesus, I-am-outta-here!"

She kissed Billy on the mouth. "Sugar, you still have that new car smell."

"It's the dope," he said and kissed her again. She patted his cheek, grabbed her wallet and keys, and kept talking as she hurried from the bedroom into the hall. "I got friends from the Reserves who bought land outside of town. They built a camp with a shooting range. It's private, very cool setup. We can go there to shoot, even the M4 on auto."

"Sure. When?"

"This Sunday?"

"Cool. Sunday. But not too early."

"Yeah, I'll let John know we're coming. I'm sure the boys will want to meet you." She did a little spin in the doorway and struck a pose. "How do I look?"

"Gorgeous," beamed Billy.

26

The outside world was a blind spot. The sea was without dimension, devoid of light, depth and movement. Clouds the color of coal blocked the stars and shrouded the moon. It was impossible to see the surface of the water a few feet beyond the deck.

Moe wore his tan Burberry with the winter lining, but he had lost his hat. His ears didn't feel cold, though, and he no longer noticed the wind. He sat on a padded bench in the stern. Behind him, the sound of the engine slowed to a near idle and the boat began to rock. He listened to the three voices at the bow speaking Russian.

Moe thought about everything he had done and everything he would never get to do.

"Moishe, you are cold?"

Moe looked up and saw Georgy Vadimovich Ragulin, Yuri to those close to him.

"You are cold," declared Yuri. "Here."

Moe took the silver flask from Yuri's hand.

"It's good Mamont. The best vodka from the oldest distillery in Russia, in the Altai mountains. The cleanest of water there is. Where they found the remains of a wooly mammoth years ago. You know about this wooly mammoth?"

Moe held his breath and swallowed about a half-cup's worth. He didn't care about wooly mammoths. He handed the flask back to Yuri who slipped it into his coat pocket.

"It's good. Thank you, Yuri," said Moe. "I thought you told me Beluga was the best."

A playful grimace crossed Yuri's face as he tilted his head. "A truckload of Mamont came into our possession. I like it better now." He reached into a pocket. "Cigarette?"

Moe shook his head. "Do something for me?"

"Anything, Morris. Anything within my power." Yuri sat down on the bench and patted Moe's knee twice.

Moe didn't bother asking Yuri to let him go. He knew that was out of the question.

"I worry about my family. I know you understand or I wouldn't ask, but—"

"Take comfort in this: Ruthy and your children are safe, Moishe. You have my word we will not harm them." Yuri put his bear paw of a hand on Moe's shoulder. "You've done well, my friend, and acquired many valuable things. You gave to us your properties, your territory, your business. After tonight we consider your debt paid." He pointed a fat finger toward the bow. "Such a beautiful boat you acquired. A shame to sell it." He shook his head and sighed. "There is only one more thing I must collect. This is unfortunate, but business dictates it. You understand. Yes?"

Moe did not respond.

"Yes, of course you understand. You would do the same. No?"

Moe bowed his head. He did not trust his voice.

"Yes, yes, you have done the same." Yuri stood up. He gestured with a hand. "Come on. Stand up and see how beautiful the moon looks tonight."

Moe stood and looked Yuri in the eyes. Yuri's eyes were kind, his smile, certain. Moe looked up at the sky.

"Look, look." Yuri pointed up and behind Moe. "The moon comes out."

Moe hesitated, then turned.

Fast moving clouds shredded, revealing a nearly full moon. Moe closed his eyes and remembered a prayer he learned as a child.

"This is the same moon I watched in Russia, a cold, beautiful, pale mistress. I know her well." Yuri put a warm hand on Moe's back and rubbed gently, as if reassuring a child. "She is like a lover, no? Someone you may have been with many times, but see? She plays with you, hiding behind a veil of clouds. Not so familiar. Mysterious, yes? Then she lets the veil float away. And now, now she stands before you, naked. Look! Look!" Yuri clapped Moe's shoulder and said, "Here, let us drink a toast to her, a toast to mysterious love. With Mamont, the best Russian vodka." He reached in a hip pocket.

Moe continued to stare at the moon. His lips moved as he silently prayed.

It was beautiful face, pale and cold, shining down on him. He could almost make out the eyes.

Yuri drew a gun from his pocket.

27

It was a straight shot out of the city, east on University Avenue to Route 24. They tried to beat the heat by leaving early, but Sunday started out hot and humid, the sun promising to burn without pity. Billy's Civic was less reliable than hoped so she drove her Jeep even though the AC wasn't working. The top was up for shade and the windows down for a breeze, but the wind provided no relief. Brianna said it would toughen them up for being out on the range all day.

They stopped at a drive-thru for breakfast. Billy fell asleep to houses and malls as the Wrangler headed east by southeast. When he woke an hour later, they were driving past forests of sad-looking trees drooping from the heat, separated by an occasional meadow or swamp.

"Looks like we're in the sticks," he said, interrupting the silence. "How much further?"

"Coming up on the left," she said, slowing the jeep, and turning into an almost nonexistent break in the trees. A rutted dirt road hid in the shadows of a stretch of unending pines. He felt the temperature drop 20 degrees and smelled the musty sweetness of pine bark and rotting wood.

They bumped along over hills and holes, Billy thankful that he'd left the Honda behind. He slipped off his shades and enjoyed the cooler air, thinking about a cold beer. "How long—"

"Any sec now." She pointed straight ahead. "Look there. You can see the gate."

They came out into an area cleared of trees and exposed to sunlight and heat. Billy put his shades back on and squinted, but could make nothing out from the glare. The ground was rocky and dry. Brianna slowed to a crawl. About 20 yards ahead, Billy saw glints of sunlight which resolved into an eight-foot-high silver chain-link fence topped by rows of barbed wire. He could make out buildings including some sort of wooden tower behind the fence.

The jeep stopped about ten feet in front of the fence. The cloud of dust kicked up by the tires floated past them in silence and on through the links in the fence. There didn't seem to be a gate. Without warning, he heard the whirring sound of an electric motor and metal creaking. A section of the fence slid to the left, opening wide enough for the Jeep to pass through.

Oh, this doesn't look good, thought Billy.

Brianna sat immobile, staring straight ahead with both hands on the wheel.

"What are we waiting for?" asked Billy.

"Them," said Brianna, pointing ahead then behind.

Two men converged on the jeep. The tall and skinny one emerging from the woods approached the jeep from behind. The barrel-chested one sauntered toward them from behind the fence. Both wore baseball caps, light brown shirts, jeans, and heavy, dust-covered black boots. Sunglasses covered their eyes and kerchiefs the lower halves of their faces. Billy hoped the masks were to protect against the dust. Each held an assault rifle angled toward the ground.

"They recognized the jeep," she said, turning to Billy. "If we were in your car, they'd be... like paranoid."

"This isn't paranoid?"

Brianna rested her hands on top of the steering wheel as she leaned out the window. "How y'all doing?" she shouted.

The skinny one removed his red ball cap and stuck it under one arm. He pulled down the white kerchief to reveal a youthful grin. He looked like a teenager. He quickened his pace to join up with the other man already at the driver's window.

"How ya doing, Earl?" Brianna asked, beaming at the half-hidden face, then nodded at the kid. "Tyler, you stuck on perimeter duty in this heat? When is Earl here gonna cut you some slack?"

The brim of the Earl's black and white cap was frayed. He pulled his blue plaid kerchief down. He had a thick close-cropped beard and yellow teeth. He spat onto the ground before speaking.

"Hey Brianna," but he was looking at Billy. "What you doing?"

"We're fixin' to do some target practice. I called John. He said it'd be okay." She looked around. "Why? Something goin' on today?"

Earl looked her in the eyes and smiled. "Hell, sugar! Don't get your panties in a twist. You know you're welcome anytime. Just John didn't say nothin' about you bringing somebody. A heads-up would've been good." He casually pointed the business end of his rifle toward Billy. "So, tell me, who here's your friend?"

28

The Jeep crawled over the hard-rutted ground. Earl and Tyler had gone on ahead into the camp. Brianna sounded enthusiastic. "Did you notice the flash suppressor on Earl's gun? Man! He built it from instructions he got off the internet, and that green dot laser scope? He scored that off Amazon Prime. Cost him only about sixty bucks. Free shipping." Brianna drove past the gate and turned right. She parked between a shiny new pickup and a black VW Beetle, a well-kept relic with a split rear window.

Billy remained quiet. Online bargains weren't on his mind. Guns were.

"You know, the government wouldn't even spring for those holographic scopes for the troops in Operation Freedom, even though the company that made them offered them at cost."

"Yeah?" said Billy, wondering how Doc was doing.

She stopped the engine. They both got out.

Billy stretched, then craned his neck to take in the guard tower. Empty. He cocked his head and listened to the fading clicks and creaks of the jeep engine as it cooled down. Insects buzzed in the air. Birds called out warnings. Otherwise, silence.

Brianna walked around to the back of the jeep. She removed the canvas bag with her pistols and two sets of military-style ear plugs.

"Did you see the gun in Earl's holster? A P320, the same Sig model I used in the Reserves." She waited, then looked him in the eye. "I know what you're going to say. We're going shooting, that's all." she said. "I guess I should have told you more."

"Yeah, a little heads-up would have been nice." He kept his volume low in an attempt to control his anger and conceal his fear. "Armed guards? Masks, fences, a fucking watch tower! The fucking guy pointed a rifle at me! What kind of friends do that?"

"Calm down. They're not masks." She started laying out the bag of guns on the hood of the jeep. "They're for the dust, is all." She stood tall and looked hard at Billy. "Hey, look it's not what you think."

"No?"

"No! Well, it is and it isn't."

"Thanks for clearing that up."

"They're Preppers, playing soldier, that's all." She started arranging the guns, but Billy expected more. "Okay. They act like it's a militia camp," she admitted.

"Act like a militia?"

She lifted her chin. "They're not serious... well, sometimes Earl and Tyler and maybe John for sure..."

"Brianna—"

"Look. Let's not make a thing out of this. It's nothing new. This friend of mine from Georgia, but living out here, she was a door gunner on a CH-146 Griffon. Marilyn was one of the first female gunners. Me and her were hanging out at a bar, drinking and dancing to meet guys. She was pretty and real funny and like I said—"

"This going anywhere?"

"Yeah. So, one night we meet Earl. He buys us drinks and introduces us to John. They both like to dance, seemed nice guys, and fun. Turns out they both served and they like to shoot, too. Okay?"

"And this?" Billy gestured at the camp. "...all this?"

"That didn't come up until later." She squinted at him. "Look. I'm not into this survivalist crap. You know that, right? I mean, you know me. Everybody's equal, regardless."

"What's equality have to do with it?"

"Well...." She took her time which only worried him more. "Sometimes they mouth off about the government, about immigrants, that kind of thing. You know. But I tell them, hey, my ancestors were immigrants! Everybody..." Her voice trailed off. "What I'm trying to say is I had some fun with these guys and this is a great place to shoot for free. I just don't buy into their politics and shit. You know that, right?"

Billy shook his head as if to shake off a thought. "Sure. Yeah...."

She sighed and dropped her shoulders. "Look at me. Me and them, we never talk politics. Never! That's like a rule. I advise you to do the same and we'll all get along fine. I've known these guys now a long while, and they are harmless."

Billy nodded. "Uh-huh."

"We all like to shoot, that's all, so they let me come up and that's the extent of it. Okay? That's the whole picture."

Billy flapped his arms. "Okay, Bri. Whatever you say."

She waited and then added, "They're Preppers, that's all. Not violent. If I thought they were, we wouldn't be friends. Period. I'd have nothing to do with them or this place. You know that, don't you?"

"Sure I do. It's just... kind of weird."

"Come on, Billy! Earl likes to think he's some sort of survivalist, but he's so dumb he could throw himself on the ground and miss." She smiled wide and he felt himself give a little. "Tyler... he's a sweetheart. A kid who wants to be a cowboy, practices tossing a rope and quick drawing his pistol. He still lives with his mom for crying out loud. He doesn't have a father so he looks up to Earl and John. He's kind of a nerd, more comfortable with computers than girls, and if you hadn't noticed, has a crush on me."

"Yeah. Subtle he ain't."

"And John..." She searched for words. "John can be serious as a snake bite. I'll give you that. He's a believer, or maybe it's part of an act. I don't know. He set all this up."

"A believer?"

"He's a talker, is what I'm saying."

"About what?"

"Well, independent living, for sure. He hates the federal government, the whole shebang, right down to the mailman. Nothing wrong with wanting to be self-sufficient." She shrugged. "Within reason," she added and looked up at the clear sky, blue as the ocean, then at Billy. "We don't have to join up or take an oath or be blood brothers or anything." She raised her right hand and smiled. "Promise."

"Sure."

"It's such a great place to shoot out here." Then, with a playful edge, "I didn't think this would bother you."

He didn't like seeing disappointment forming in her eyes and around her mouth. Our first argument, he thought. He pulled back, took a deep breath and sucked it in.

"Okay, Bri," he flashed a one-sided grin. "Sorry I freaked. I'll be cool." He picked up the bag of ammunition out of the jeep. "Lead the way," he said, squaring the brim of his cap.

"You okay, then?"

He picked up the bag with their water bottles

and snacks. "Yeah-yeah. Come on, woman. Let's do this." She searched his eyes without reacting, then turned and led the way into the camp.

Billy followed.

29

They walked toward the center of an open area. Brianna said they called it the parade ground. Earl and Tyler, rifles slung over their shoulders, stood under a flagpole, the base surrounded by a circle of smooth round rocks painted white. Above them, a flag slumped against the top of a tall pole, its identity hidden but for a white field and red markings. Billy was pretty sure it wasn't Old Glory or even the Stars and Bars.

"Hay." The kid offered his free hand and a friendly smile to Billy. "I'm Tyler."

"Hey, Tyler. I'm Billy."

"This here's Earl. Me and him work at Earl's recycling station in Ocala."

Billy shook hands and perked up. "Recycling?"

"Junkyard," offered Brianna. Everyone but Billy laughed.

"It's a different kind of recycling," said Earl. "A refuse dump, but there's profit in most everything people throw out if you're looking hard enough." He pointed at Tyler. "Picked Tyler up there, didn't I?" He and Tyler found that pretty funny. "Drove up Friday after work in the double-cab over there." He pointed toward the truck parked next to the jeep. Earl waited until Billy realized he was supposed to turn and look. He did.

"Nice truck," said Billy.

"John here?" Brianna asked altogether too brightly.

"In the office," Earl said, "working on his speech for the barbeque coming up end of the month." He turned to Billy. "It's a recruitment party. We usually get around fifty or more, mostly guys but more and more chicks, too." He glanced at Brianna. "Free burgers and beer, show some videos, you know, movies and documentaries that John finds. The music's good, too. Tyler, what's the name of that band?"

Tyler looked at Billy. "You ever hear of *Double-H*?"

Billy shook his head. His smile was empty.

Tyler looked dumbfounded. "Never *heard* of em? Well, they're damn good and they're playing again outside right here." He pointed at the flag pole. "You guys should come." He looked from Billy to Brianna.

Billy's expression gave away nothing.

"Tyler, go tell John Brianna and her friend are here," said Earl.

"Right!" Tyler took off in a trot toward the

closest building, a log cabin.

"Every three or four months, John has a Meet and Greet," Earl said to Billy. "We're looking for folks interested in helping us stand up to protect the Constitution and our First and Second Amendment rights. Like Tyler said, you're invited." He looked at Brianna. "Both of you."

Billy nodded solemnly, doing his best to look agreeable.

"I've been to one," Brianna added. "The guys outnumber the girls like ten-to-one."

"This is nice, out here." Billy made a thing of looking around. "So, what do you call this place, all of it?" Billy didn't care, but thought it best to move the topic along.

Earl looked up at the limp flag. "We are the O.R.M., the Ocala Regional Militia."

Billy turned toward Brianna, but she spoke before he asked. "I never joined. Never my thing. Earl knows I'm not into politics and speeches. I'm just here to shoot with my friends." She patted Earl on the arm.

Earl winked at her. "Long as you're not shooting at your friends."

I'm a long way from Fenway, thought Billy.

A screen door slammed shut. Tyler walked behind a taller man coming toward them from the cabin. "Come on," said Brianna, taking Billy's hand. "Let's go meet John."

Billy realized he was holding his breath. He let it out quietly. He braced for introductions.

"Brianna!" called John as he closed in on them, arms outstretched. He wore same kind of brown shirt and jeans uniform as Earl and Tyler, but without the cap. He looked to be in his mid-thirties with a military bearing and body to match, except his hair and beard needed a trim.

"Good to see you. You look great." He held her shoulders, kissed her on the cheek and they embraced in a brief hug.

He extended his hand to Billy and flashed a wide smile revealing unnaturally white teeth. His eyes were a disarmingly pale shade of blue.

"John Gates, Commandant of The Ocala Regional Militia. Welcome to The Compound."

"Billy Kaye." Billy match the strength of John's grip.

"Billy's my friend. I brought him up here to shoot with me," explained Brianna. "You said it wouldn't be a problem."

Amazingly, John's smile widened all the more. "Hell, no problem, Bri. My bad. I must have misunderstood." He smiled at Billy, then returned to Brianna. "We're happy to see you, that's all. You haven't dropped by in a while. And I'm happy to meet your friends. Say, how is Marilyn? You hear from her these days?"

"We kind of lost touch."

"Ah, too bad." John exchanged a glance with Earl and turned back to Billy. "William *Kaye*, huh...." He scrunched up his face as if testing the water. "That British? Irish?"

"Maybe, on my Dad's side," he said. "I guess."

"You should check that out. It's important for a person to know where he came from, respect his heritage."

"Uh, huh."

"Come on, John," laughed Brianna. "Don't start! We're up here for some shooting, that's all."

"You any good?"

Billy shrugged and smiled without conviction.

"Well, we got a sweet outdoor range," John continued. "Four hundred meters for rifle and sniper practice with ten stations. Over on the one side we got a 50-meter stretch for pistols that can accommodate twenty shooters. And next to that there's a range for the littlest kids learning to shoot .22 pistols and rifles, part of our Weekend Warriors program. That one accommodates twelve, plus a supervisor for each kid. We feel one-on-one mentoring is important to the development of little minds."

Get them when their young, thought Billy. "Yeah," he said. "I get that."

"It's the future of our kids we're fighting for. Here, let me carry that." John took Brianna's canvas bag over her protest, then said over his shoulder to Billy, "Come on. Let me give you a quick tour of the compound on your way to the range." He stared pointedly at Earl.

Earl stepped up. "Brianna? You got a minute? I need to talk. Nothing crucial."

"Yeah. Sure thing," she said. "See you at the

range, Billy."

Great, Billy thought. This is just great.

As they walked down a path past a couple of single-story buildings, John explained he'd bought the lot at a bankruptcy auction. "Thirty acres of woods and swamp. Sold off all but six and used the funds from the sale to build these buildings, the fence, and tower. We put up the flagpole and the shooting ranges ourselves."

He proudly pointed out two identical prefab buildings with flat roofs and faux wood siding, one for a bunkhouse and the other for meetings and storage, he said, with space for more as new members joined. He pointed over his shoulder with his thumb back the way they came. "Tyler built the cabin himself. A genuine log cabin from an expensive kit. The kid is special, I'll grant him that." A gray dish antenna with "DIRECT TV" printed on it stuck out from the cabin's peaked roof.

Under a sun that seemed too bright, John pointed out the propane tanks and blue water tanks that sat next to each building. An array of black solar panels and various antennas covered the roofs, and beyond them, a modest-sized windmill creaked slowly at the top of a narrow metal tower. John explained it pumped water from a well that filled the blue tanks.

"Impressive," said Billy. "Is it just you and Earl and Tyler now, or...?"

"We have thirty-three members officially as of today. They all come out for Battle Assembly over a weekend every three months. We're going to move that up to every other month. And then once a year we have a week of Annual Training exercise, also mandatory. Other than that, we man the Compound with as little as two, although membership is going up and things are changing fast"

"And Earl and Tyler, are they—"

"Earl's my Second-In-Command and Tyler's his recruit. Come on." John turned onto a small trail. "You'll love this firing range."

30

On automatic, the M4 was loud and hard to control. All Billy hit was air and dirt. Anything more than 25 feet from him was a waste of ammunition. Brianna fired controlled three-shot bursts at 60 feet and shredded the targets. Firing single shots, she hit the target every time at 130 feet. Switching to a left-handed stance, she hit the bull's eye nine out of ten times.

"Ambidextrous," she said as she flicked on the safety.

"Yeah, I noticed," said Billy with a smile.

They'd been alone on the shooting range for over two hours before Billy called it quits. At first, he hadn't wanted to let Brianna down so put up a front, but after a while he began to relax and enjoy himself. They dropped their ear protection in the bag, and he rubbed his sore arm and shoulder as she showed him how to break down the M-4. He was crossing the parade ground, carrying the bag of ammunition back to the jeep, when Tyler shouted his name.

"Billy! Hey, man! Wait up!" Tyler clapped him on the shoulder. "You're not leaving already, are you? How'd you do?"

"Not too good with the M4. Not too bad with the Ruger," Billy said. He didn't tell Tyler the target was ten feet from him when he was shooting the handgun. He glanced at the pistol holstered on Tyler's right hip and the M16 slung over his left shoulder. "I'd have better luck throwing rocks."

"I guess you ain't shoot much before, huh?"

"No, not much."

Tyler drew the pistol in a flash. By the time Billy reacted, Tyler was already spinning it in his hand. "Well, I'll be happy to give you a few pointers, when we both got the time." Tyler holstered the gun. If he saw Billy flinch, he didn't let on.

"Yeah, thanks. Sure. I'd like that."

Tyler looked down at his boots and sighed. "Yeah, takes practice." He squinted at Billy and put a hand around the M16 and slung it front and center. "Listen. Why don't you come back with me to the office? John wants to say, goodbye."

Billy knew his plan to slip away quietly was finished. He looked over his shoulder toward his escape, and saw Brianna standing by the jeep talking to Earl. He turned back to Tyler, still waiting, still grinning. "I think Brianna wants to get going," he tried.

Tyler shook his head, the grin never changing. "Naw, you got time." He cocked his chin at the jeep.

"Earl's talking her damn head off. You got a good ten minutes afore he comes up for air. Anyway, we got cold draft. Who the hell would say no to free cold draft, huh?" He let go of the M16 and gestured with his hand. "Come on. John's waiting and the beer's getting warm."

Billy squared his shoulders. His voice was flat. "Yeah, a cold draft sounds good right now." He took the initiative, heading straight for the office without waiting for Tyler, fighting the urge to look back at the jeep and Brianna.

31

"**S**orry we're out of draft." John's voice echoed from the kitchen. "We had four kegs, but they drank them dry at the last Meet n' Greet. I got a Cornelius Keg in the kitchen—Tyler brews light ale. It's good, but that's gone, too. Coors is all I got left."

A portable CD player shared a table stacked with books and pamphlets. From the speakers, Merle Haggard crooned something sad about a father buying his daughter a gift. Billy knew the song, but by Dwight Yoakam. He liked this version better.

"Coors is fine," Billy called out. One beer. That's all, then get the hell out.

John returned with two cans of Coors Light and handed one to Billy. The metal was cold and frosted.

John gestured toward the couch by the window. "Take a load off." Billy sank into the old brown couch, placing the bag of ammo next to him.

Looking satisfied, John dropped into the recliner opposite the couch. The recliner creaked as John leaned back and popped the can open. "You know this tune? Sure, you do. People knew what it was all about back then. Am I right?"

In the middle of a swallow, Billy nodded as though he had any idea what John meant. He stole a glance out the window. Tyler was headed toward Earl and Brianna. Three cans of beer dangled from the plastic six-pack rings hanging from his hand.

"So, what do you think of our setup?"

Billy considered the vaulted ceiling, the fireplace, exposed beams, and mismatched furniture and thought of the home decorating shows Tiffany used to watch. "Well," he said, setting his beer on the floor, "Pretty comfortable." He pointed to a laptop next to the stacks of books on the table behind John. The lid was closed. "Is that a PC or a Mac on the desk there?" Just making conversation.

John chuckled politely. "A PC. Tyler's the computer geek around here. He knows spreadsheets and programming. He made our webpage. You wouldn't think to look at him—just a kid—but he's got a head on his shoulders. Gets a lot done for us. Me? I can bang out an email, but I still like the printed word best. Books still matter. Actual books you can hold in your hand. I sell these."

"Uh-huh." Billy walked up to the table and squinted at the titles. *The Confessions of Nat Turner, My Awakening, The Protocols of the Elders, Debating the Holocaust, The Myth of Extermination....*

"See anything you like?"

Billy walked over and picked up a copy of *Mein Kampf*.

"You got a soft spot for the classics," John said shaking his finger at the book. "That is one slow but steady seller. Everybody's heard of it so it always sells out at the Meets n' Greets. Once a fellow came up the road looking for a copy." He finished his beer in three swallows. "Selling books helps pay off the rest of our little piece of heaven on earth. That plus dues and donations."

Billy tried to keep it light and kill time. "How much do you get for it?" he asked.

"You can buy *Mein Kampf* in any language for your Kindle off Amazon right now for 99-cents, but I get $20 for that book you're holding there, no sales tax." He grinned. "Had somebody ask me if I had an autographed copy by the author."

Billy had to laugh. "What did you do?"

"Told him I would sell him my copy and said to wait. I went into the bedroom and wrote 'Adolf Hitler' myself on the title page, then sold him the book. He went away happy."

Billy nodded with his mouth open, feeling like an idiot. "Nice," he said, knowing there was nothing nice about any of this.

"That there in your hand is the best damn English translation *Mein Kampf* you can find. I'll give you a special family discount since you're a friend of Brianna's. And it's going toward a good cause. Ten dollars."

Billy put the book back down like it was crawling with ants. "Right. Thanks, but I'm fine. Thanks though," Billy said thinking maybe he should have played along and bought it. He glanced out the window.

"Relax, Bill." John pointed at the couch. "We're talking, that's all. Give me five minutes."

Billy sat down slowly. Go with the flow, he told himself. Just float along.

"I came down here from Des Moines. Too cold for me in the winter. You live in Boston your whole life?"

"How'd you know I'm from Boston?"

"Your accent. Hard to miss. Me, I'm from Shafer, Minnesota, the St. Croix Valley." John fixed his pale eyes on Billy. "You ever been there?"

Billy shook his head.

John maintained his gaze. "So, why'd you leave Boston?"

Billy stared right back into them. "The weather."

"Ever been to Lexington and Concord?"

"As a kid on a school trip. What about them?"

"1775 and 'the shot heard around the world.' Well, the more things change, the more they stay the same. Waco, remember that? That was our new 'shot heard around the world.' We're still obliged to refresh the tree of liberty with the blood of patriots. But I'd prefer if it wasn't our blood we used, if you catch my drift."

"Uh huh..." Billy said.

"The Waco folks—little kids, too—fought, gave their lives to defend their right to live free, and the American government killed them for it. Right? Burned them up." He grimaced and shook his head. "We still need real patriots to defend our independence and faith against an overbearing and intrusive government that no longer represents us."

Billy scratched his head, watching John watch him, thinking he smelled something burning. He picked up his half-empty can of beer, finished it off and grabbed the bag of ammo.

"Hey, John. My ears are still ringing from the shooting and I'm pretty worn out. We got a long drive ahead of us." He stood. "Thanks for the beer and letting us shoot here. I enjoyed talking," he said with all the fake enthusiasm he could muster.

"That's all right." John said, rising slowly from the recliner. "Hope to continue our conversation soon."

"Looking forward to it the next time," said Billy, eyeing the door.

"You should think about coming to the barbeque. Bring Brianna with you, too."

"Sure."

Billy let John lead him to the door. "Be safe," he said, holding the screen door open for Billy. "And do me a favor. Think about what we talked about."

Billy felt like he was in John's crosshairs all the way to the jeep. He slipped into the passenger seat and set the bag on floor. Brianna hugged Tyler and Earl, then hopped in the driver's side.

Billy watched them walk away. "Drive," he said. "Let's get out of here."

"You were in there for a while," she smiled. "What did you guys—"

"Drive. Get me the fuck out of here."

The smile disappeared. "Okey-dokey." She started the jeep. Neither spoke until they were on the highway when Billy asked what she had been talking about with Earl and Tyler.

"Just talk, that's all. They asked how we met, where you're from, the usual stuff." She looked at him. "Did something happen in there with John?"

"Yeah. Something weird. Tell me what you said to them."

"I don't know. Stuff. I told them how we met at the hotel—"

"What makes them so interested in me?"

"'cause they're friends of mine. Jesus, Billy. What's the problem?"

"Did you tell them about Doc, about robbing that guy?"

"No, of course not. I wouldn't do that."

"What did they want to know?"

"Just stuff. They were being friendly, asking what kind of work you did, why you came to Gainesville—"

"What'd you say?"

"Nothing! Jeeze! I said you worked on a loading dock and was sick of the cold." She glanced over at him. "What's got you so riled up?"

"Oh, I don't know. My girlfriend is buddies

with a bunch of white nationalists who are toting guns and insisting I spend time with the Commandant of their paramilitary compound! He tried to sell me a copy of *Mein Kampf,* for Christ's sake. It doesn't bother you—this stuff? Christ, Brianna—"

"I told you they never talk about that crap with me. I didn't think John would.... Look, Billy. I'm sorry."

"What the hell else did you think he'd be talking to me about, just him and me, alone, in command central?"

She slowed the jeep and pulled off the road. She faced Billy and left the engine running. "Billy, baby, I am so sorry. I didn't think all that much about it." Her voice began to shake. "I-I never thought John would lay that on you. They know I'm not into it. I thought you and me would have fun shooting, that's all. That's all I ever do there. I guess..." She banged a fist on the steering wheel. "Damn. I'm so goddam dumb."

Billy leaned his head back into the headrest and closed his eyes. He sounded tired. "Yup. That was not pleasant."

"I thought you were starting to get bored and, I... I wanted to try something different with you. God! I didn't think it through. I wasn't thinking, didn't think—"

"Yeah. I get that." He wanted this behind them. "Hey," he said opening his eyes and looking at her. "I understand, I really do. It's all right, Bri. I'm good, now. We're still good. I feel better that we're out of there. Come on, drive. Let's put some miles between us and them and go home."

She pulled back on the road. They drove in silence for miles before she said, "I'm not hanging out with them anymore. We'll find another place for us to shoot, okay?"

He didn't answer. He was thinking about California.

32

Brianna followed Billy into the kitchen and dropped her keys on the table. Billy opened the refrigerator and took out a carton of 2%. He hesitated, glanced in her direction, then took a glass from the cupboard and poured.

"You want some?" he asked. She shook her head and hugged herself.

She waited in silence while Billy drank the milk and rinsed the glass in the sink. The refrigerator motor kicked in, sounding louder than usual. Brianna came over to him. They held each other for a long time.

They never went back to the Compound to shoot. Instead, Billy bought a couple's membership at the Gator Gun Club, an indoor range on the east end of the city. Brianna was a good teacher. He enjoyed shooting with her and figured improving his skill with a gun wasn't a bad idea, given his situation. After shooting, they'd go out for drinks and appetizers at the Lion's Den Bar.

Life with Brianna was good. Resolving their conflict at the Compound brought them closer. Brianna taught him to cook pasta and rice dishes and Billy taught her how to play pool at the Lion's Den. He slept better than he had in years. Occasionally, he thought about Doc and wondered what his friend was up to.

Brianna was working late on a Tuesday night when Billy came back from playing pool. The apartment was dark, which was odd because she usually left a light on. He unlocked the door and tried the hall light, but it was out. As he stood in the dark, he caught a whiff of something stale, something not theirs. He moved to the kitchen, felt for the wall switch, and flicked the light on.

What felt like a bolt of lightning jerked him upright, stiff as a board. For an instant he thought the electric shock came from some fault in the light switch, but the pain and paralysis continued. He made noises but could not speak. His legs buckled. He collapsed to the floor in a heap. He remembered nothing after that.

33

Weekday afternoons were usually slow, but ever since the Russians took over The Improper Bostonian, business during the day was dead. CJ and Lexi sat by themselves at the bar watching the Sox at Yankee Stadium. Top of the eighth, two runs behind with two outs and a man on third. A batter they'd moved up from the minors hit a line drive past the pitcher. The ball bounced over the second baseman's head into centerfield. The crowd drowned out the announcer's shouts. CJ shot his arms in the air and screamed, "GO!"

Without breaking his stride, the centerfielder scooped up the ball and fired it home. The ball and the runner from third converged on the catcher at home plate just as the front door to the club opened. Sunlight reflected off the TV screen, obscuring the play. CJ and Lexi shouted a unified protest and whipped around toward the door.

There was Russ gesturing from the street. Lexi

slipped off her stool, but Russ shook his head and pointed at CJ. Russ didn't enter. Instead he let the door swing shut. The club was dark again.

Lexi and CJ exchanged glances. CJ shrugged. "Guess I'm up."

"Better see what he wants," said Lexi who turned back to the TV.

"Let me know what happens," said CJ slipping off the barstool.

"You, too," she said, eyes back on the game.

CJ headed for the door, his mind already on a different kind of score. Something was happening. He could smell the potential. Outside in the too bright sun, he brushed at the lint on his cheap black velvet jacket to little effect. Russ was over by the alley entrance. They walked together about halfway down and Russ offered him a cigarette. CJ waived it off. Russ lit it, took a drag and blew the smoke off to the side.

"How's biz?" asked Russ.

"Things suck since they gave Kyle the boot. These Russians don't know shit about running a club. Their friends all drink for free and don't tip the girls. They cut my hours so my take-home's less. Nobody's happy." He took a deep breath. "Bummer about Moe. How you holding up?"

"Kyle got a lead and we're trying to put something together," said Russ. "You told me you were in the Army,"

"Army Reserves." CJ liked how this was starting. "Afghanistan."

"What did you do there?"

"Infantry, like I told you before."

Russ hummed approval. "You saw action, right?"

"On patrol sometimes, yeah. Home inspections, checkpoints or hunting for T-men."

"What else?"

CJ shrugged. "Drove a truck for eight months."

"Hauling what?"

"Anything they loaded—equipment, weapons, ammo, explosives, rations." He gave a short laugh. "Didn't seem to matter to the Taliban. They shot at us anyway–and ambushed us once."

"Where?"

"Panjwai District. Why?"

"You take anybody down?" Russ's expression was oddly hopeful.

"I told you about it before, already."

"Tell me again... this time, in detail."

CJ hesitated for effect. "They hit a truck with an IED—not my truck, but one right ahead of us. The fuckers strapped it on a donkey or something and waited for us. Killed the driver and blocked the road, then came at us from both sides." He waited but Russ didn't react. "We held off about 30 Taliban until two Apache's arrived. I'm pretty sure I shot three or four of the motherfuckers." After a beat, he added, "I have a feeling this is about more than my military service."

"You're right." Russ flicked his cigarette off to the side. "I need somebody to watch my back, someone who won't screw up. Somebody willing to do what's necessary if the shit hits the fan."

"We both know I can do whatever you need."

"I don't know if I know that. Convince me."

"What's the gig?"

"It's out of town. Will that be a problem? I know your old lady's due soon."

"This isn't our first. She'll call if she needs to. Where's the job?"

"Florida. You used to live there, right?"

"Big state, Russ. Where in Florida?"

"North central, outside of Gainesville."

"That's where I went to school for a semester on the MGIB." CJ's smile was huge. "I know the area pretty good."

"MGIB?"

"That's what they call the GI Bill now. It ain't free no more."

Russ looked CJ in the eyes. "This may be nothing but a milk run or it might be a shit storm. We won't know until we get there."

CJ took a breath. "Kyle know you're talking to me about this?"

"Kyle's financing the trip. We're working it together."

"So, what's the gig?"

Russ looked CJ up and down. "We're making an exchange."

"How much?"

"We give them ten grand, they hand over—"

"I mean how much you paying me?"

Russ smiled in admiration. "Twenty-five grand, if all goes according to plan. That's for one day's work and four days' travel. I'll pick up the expenses along the way, supply the equipment, and show you where to park your ass and tell you what to do."

Now it was CJ's turn to smile. "Details."

"It's sounds simple enough. We meet them at their camp—"

"Camp? Like a, a summer camp?"

"I don't know. He mentioned we'd see a perimeter fence and some cabins. It's about 40 minutes out of Gainesville, somewhere in the freakin' woods. I got the GPS coordinates," said Russ. "They give us Billy and we give them the payment."

"Billy, Who the fuck is Billy?"

"One of the two assholes that robbed Teddy. He was Tiffany's boyfriend."

"No shit! So, she *was* in on it. I heard...." C.J. looked up sharply. "You found the money!"

Russ took in a deep breath. "We're hoping he's got it or can lead us to it."

"Billy. Like Billy the Kid. How did you find—"

"Wasn't hard. One of the dancers—Christina? You know who I'm talking about. The guys who rolled Teddy were her regulars months before Tiffany met them. She knew the one guy's first name, Billy. He called the other guy, Doc."

CJ considered the names. "Don't ring any bells. Guess they never caused any trouble before. How did you find out this one guy, Billy, was in

Gainesville?"

Russ lit another cigarette, then continued. "That part dropped in our lap. Kyle got a call from some redneck from there calling himself Tyler. Kyle said he sounded maybe 18, polite, and nervous enough to probably be on the level. He wanted to hand Billy over to us for—get this—100 G's. Kyle talked him down to ten. Told him we don't have that kind of money anymore. Which isn't far from the truth."

CJ shoved his hand in his pocket and pulled out a stick of gum, unwrapping it slowly as Russ explained that Kyle thought Tyler didn't know about the money. "If he did, he never would have bothered with us."

"But how'd he know to call Kyle?"

Russ shook his head. "He wouldn't say, but I'm guessing Billy the Kid couldn't keep his mouth shut. Maybe this cracker heard enough from him to look online, read *The Herald* or *Globe*, and put it all together. I mean, what isn't on the internet these days?" Russ grinned and nodded. "I kind of admire the kid's initiative."

"So how do we find the money?"

"We collect Billy and ask him. If he's got it hidden, I guarantee he'll tell us where. If he only has half, which ain't bad, or his partner ripped him off for the whole thing, either way he'll help us find the partner and the rest of the money. It's not that difficult once you find the guy."

"Sounds straight forward enough."

"Well, he's the rub." Russ took a long drag. "We don't know this Florida kid from a hole in the wall. He may sound legit to Kyle, but we're going to be in his backyard and I'm sure he's surrounded by his redneck friends looking for a piece of the action. So, you're the insurance, in case things go to shit."

"So, how exactly...." CJ rephrased his question. "What's my part in this?"

"You'll be hiding nearby with a sniper rifle watching my back while I'm out in the open making the exchange. I know you're a good shot."

"I am, but—"

"They'll have a home team advantage and know the ground better than us. We get there a day or two early and recon the area, but I'm sure on the day of the meet he'll have a shooter of his own watching from some vantage point."

"You know all this... how?"

Russ grinned. "Trust me."

"I want in, but sounds like it calls for a telescopic lens. I don't own a sniper rifle."

"But you shot one...."

"I shot with a few of them."

"Don't worry about the rifle. I said I'll supply everything. I saw you shoot an AK-47 at the Gun Gallery. You were dead on with it."

"Thanks."

"I got an AK-74, full auto, with a scope. It's a ghost. We'll dump it afterwards if there's trouble. Otherwise, you can keep it with my thanks."

CJ nodded with approval. This was getting

better and better.

"I'm asking you instead of one of Moe's guys because you've been in firefights, so I'm counting on you to keep your head."

"I can handle it."

Russ took a drag, then studied CJ's face for a full five seconds before he blew the smoke out his nose. "Here it is in plain English. You watch my back. Shoot to kill without hesitating if any son-of-bitch so much as looks at me cross-eyed. Just don't shoot Billy under any circumstances."

"How will I know—"

"I'll put my cuffs on him. I want to be clear on that point. Don't shoot Billy. We need him talking."

"Noted."

"My ass will be exposed to these good old boys. I'm counting on you to be cool and quick and shoot straight. So, I want to hear you convince me."

To CJ, the future looked bright. His reply was immediate. "Fuck, yeah. I'm your man. If anything happens, I'll finish them off before they touch a trigger. When do we leave?"

34

Ten minutes later, they were in Russ's Corvette driving to the Gun Gallery. The two men talked about sports and music, but in the back of his mind, CJ was busy sorting out truth from fiction.

True—his days of wrangling drunks were coming to a middle. A couple more gigs like this and he could move on, move up, and make more money. He had a growing family, a responsibility to provide for them.

Also true—he was superb at shooting silhouettes printed on paper targets. He'd spent thousands of hours shooting enemies both foreign and intergalactic on his X-Box.

And true, he served on checkpoint duty for a week before he was assigned to driving trucks. Driving a truck in an active war zone was dangerous and required nerve, but most of his tour was unusually quiet. As things turned out, he never shot at a human being.

The story he told Russ about the ambush and firefight was true. At least, that's what a buddy told him. But it didn't happen to CJ. Battling dehydration and giant desert spiders were CJ's most significant experiences, but he knew that would not impress Russ.

They drove to the Gun Gallery in Canton. Russ parked next to the only other car in the parking lot, a late model dark blue Lincoln Town Car. CJ recognized it as belonging to Sam, the manager.

"They look closed," he said as Russ switched off the engine and got out. CJ followed.

"Sam's letting us use the range by ourselves for a couple of hours," Russ said over the roof of the car. "We need privacy so you can try the automatic."

Russ looked around to make sure they were alone, then pressed a button on the car's remote. The trunk of the Lincoln popped open.

"Go ahead," Russ said. "Look."

CJ looked. On the floor of the trunk was a long narrow gun case and a black tote bag.

CJ pointed. "That my gun?"

"We're looking at a mandatory ten-year sentence in Massachusetts just for standing here." Russ looked pleased with himself. "Be my guest. Open it."

CJ unlatched the locks and opened the case, revealing an AK sniper rifle. He recognized the model right away—an AK-74M, a lighter, modernized variant of the AK-74 made in Russia, itself an improved version of the classic AK-47. CJ had shot AK's in the past.

"Sweet," he said.

"Go ahead. Pick it up."

The rifle was seamlessly mated with a new Russian Army scope. The barrel was flat black, the body and stock green camouflage. Other than adjusting the scope and getting comfortable with the trigger, there wasn't much for CJ to do.

"You'll need this," said Russ. He opened the black tote to reveal twenty-five 30-round magazines of 5.45x39mm cartridges.

CJ stared at the ammunition. He felt he had crossed a point of no-return.

"Okay, show's over," said Russ. "Put the AK back in the case." He lifted the ammo bag out of the trunk. "I'll take this. You carry the case. Let's do some shooting."

"With pleasure," said CJ. Russ closed the trunk. CJ almost felt giddy walking into the Gun Gallery. This gun was a serious nail-driver, and CJ was ready to do some hammering.

35

The air was so humid it was hard moving through it. He was running and stumbling up a hill through grass almost up to his waist. Something or someone chasing him was closing in. He pushed harder, but fatigue and the pain in his gut were winning. The thick air pressed against his face. The tall grass snarled around his legs and his feet. Sweat clouded his eyes. One more step, then another, became his mantra. We'll get over the top and then it'll be downhill on the other side. Hell, I'll roll downhill if I have to. But the top got no closer.

The sun was already below the horizon where the sky glowed blood red. Out of nowhere, Felix, the Johnson's black cat, ran by Billy's feet and disappeared. He hadn't seen that cat since he was eleven and in foster care with the Johnsons. Billy cut his hands as he parted the sharp blades of grass, searching for Felix. He didn't call out his name, afraid his voice would alert whoever was chasing him. Billy was responsible for Felix, who was old for a cat, at least 18 years old, and almost blind. He wouldn't survive out here on his own. Billy had to find Felix and save them both.

The last of the light melted away. A cold wind kicked up. His fingertips brushed against Felix's fur. He grabbed the cat. It dug its claws into Billy's arms. Billy didn't mind. Then the ground shook and he bounced onto his side in the wind-whipped grass. He held on tight to Felix, clutching his fur. High-pitch snapping-sounds like ten thousand static electricity shocks cracked behind him. Then his body exploded with pain and everything disappeared.

Billy woke with a start. He was lying in a fetal position on his right side. Felix... he hadn't thought about old Felix in years. What the hell time was it? When had he gone to bed? And why was he still in his clothes? The room was stifling.

Pain radiated down his neck and spread out through his arms and down the small of his back to the balls of his feet. His whole body began to shake. He whimpered, rolled onto his back, and realized his mouth was taped shut. He took a deep breath through his nose to try to calm himself. The smell of gasoline was overpowering. Everything was black except for a defined line of light above him. The floor shook. He bounced, smacking the back of his head. Metal things rattled in the blackness. It all came together at once.

He was jammed into the trunk of his Honda.

Then another bump, as if to emphasize the point, and panic rushed in. His wrists were handcuffed behind his back. He grew light-headed and rolled onto his side, breathed through his nose, and waited for the panic to subside, but nothing changed. The mob had him. Maybe headed for I-95 to take him back to Boston. He'd never survive the trip. Sweat stung his eyes. He shook his head from side to side but it only made him dizzy.

He remembered the pocket knife Brianna gave him. He rolled onto his back again and bent his knees but could feel nothing in any pocket—keys, wallet, knife, even the new cell phone—gone.

He struggled to loosen the tape on his ankles while he tried to remember what led up to his abduction. The car made a sharp left and he rolled and crashed into the wheel well. It felt like they'd turned off onto a dirt road. The car slowed to a crawl. There was a scraping noise as the car bottomed out, then sped up again and stopped with a jerk. There was the whir of an electric motor and more scraping sounds. The car advanced for less than a minute and then the engine went silent. There was a faint sound of birds. And the smell of dust. Billy knew where he was.

36

The driver's door creaked open, and Billy heard what sounded like one side of a cell phone conversation. "Yeah. I'm early. Get here as soon as you can." Billy recognized the voice, but felt no relief.

Key in the lock and the trunk flooded with cool morning air and dappled sunlight. Billy squinted hard and saw a silhouette towering over him, one arm resting on the lid, the other pointing a small handgun at him.

"Rise and shine, Billy-boy," said Earl. Billy looked from the gun up to Earl's face. Earl took in the damp air with a deep, audible breath. "Lovely morning, ain't it? Whatever you paid for this crap car, you got took. I bet I end up giving away the parts." He gestured with his free hand. "C'mon. Let me help you up out of there. But I'm warning you boy, and just this once, don't try nothing. I don't need much of an excuse to deliver you banged up and bloody. You catch my drift?"

Earl waited a moment for Billy to respond. When he didn't, he grabbed Billy's ankles with one hand and dragged his legs over the edge of the trunk. He slipped the gun into a back pocket, then grabbed Billy's shirt and pulled, leveraging him the rest of the way out of the trunk. Earl stepped back as Billy settled himself against the edge of the trunk.

"Hoo, boy! You ain't in bad shape—I'll give you that—but you are one heavy son-of-a-beehive." Earl sniffed. His face wrinkled up in disgust. "You smell bad, too. You piss yourself in there?"

Billy wobbled. Earl held his shoulder to keep him from falling. Earl's hand was big and warm and felt almost friendly. Billy looked Earl straight in the eyes, vocalizing a muffled request that even Earl could figure out.

Earl put a finger to his lips. "I can understand how you might be a bit upset with me, even disappointed. I take partial responsibility for getting you into this fix, but it won't do you no good out here to carry on and holler. I'll just have to do unpleasant things to you. If you promise to be civil and keep your voice down, I'll take the tape off your mouth. *Comprende, amigo*?"

Billy nodded.

Earl put his fingers on one edge of the tape. "These things are best done quickly," he said and ripped the tape from Billy's mouth in one pull.

"Tastes like ass." Billy's voice was dry and rough. He spit on the ground.

"Well, that's something I do not have first-hand knowledge about," said Earl, "so I'll rely on your experience on the subject."

Billy looked around and saw that he was back in the compound within the fence.

"Why am I here?" Billy twisted at the waist and shoulders to look around and made himself dizzy. "What the fuck did you do to me?"

"Taser," said Earl. "Lit you up like a Christmas tree. Wanna see it?"

Billy shook his head without taking his eyes off Earl.

Earl made a point of taking in the scenery and air. "You'll feel better in an hour or two. Now we're gonna wait for the others. Lovely spot, ain't it?" Wonderment shone on his face. "Pretty and peaceful."

"Waiting for who?"

"Why, waiting on a friend of yours from Boston, that's who. Should be here in less than an hour. John and Tyler should be here any minute."

"Friend from Boston? Who?" said Billy, sitting a little straighter.

Earl snorted a laugh. "That's what I said. What's wrong with your ears?"

"Who—"

"Who? Who? You an owl?" Earl looked pleased with himself. "Come on. Makes no sense waiting out here for the sun to heat up. Let's go inside and wait there."

"Wait for...?"

"Now, against my better judgment, because I

don't want to carry you, I'm going to cut the tape and free up your legs so you can walk. If you try anything funny, like making a run for it, I'll taped you back up and drag you by the hair. We clear?"

Billy did not move.

Earl took out a pocket knife and opened it. It had a different color handle than the one Brianna had given Billy. "You behave now." Earl bent and grabbed one of Billy's legs. The blade sliced through the tape in a single motion. "C'mon now," Earl straightened, closed the knife and slipped it back into a pocket. "Let's go wait in the office and get us a cold beer. I'm buying."

37

B illy sat on the same couch as before, with the addition of a wooden chair placed in front of him to serve as a table for a can of Coors. His wrists now were handcuffed in front, a courtesy along with the chair provided by Earl. Earl looped a long bicycle security cable between the cuffs and a recessed tie-down D-ring screwed into the floor just under the front edge of the couch. A large Master Lock joined the two ends of the cable. Billy's legs remained free, but he wasn't going anywhere yet.

Earl was stretched out in John's recliner. His gun, Billy's car keys and another set of keys, a pack of Camels, a metal ashtray, and a can of Coors Light were on a side table next to him. His rifle lay flat on the floor by his feet. He finished the beer, then bent down and placed the can upright on the floor. He stood up, raised a foot and stomped the can, then tossed the flatted disk like a Frisbee into a wastebasket next to the desk. He fished a Zippo lighter out of his pocket and with a well-practiced double-snap, opened the lid and snapped the wheel, igniting the flame. He lit a cigarette and closed the lid with another snap, then returned the lighter to his pocket. He plopped back into the recliner, a smug grin across his face. On top of the world.

He glanced at his wristwatch, then slapped both hands on the recliner's armrests. "Looks like we still got time to kill. The TV's in the bedroom, but we got a stereo in the living room. Want to listen to some music?"

Billy turned and looked out the window. Only his car was in the parking area. The sky was blue with fluffy gray clouds backlit by the sun. He saw a plane emerge from a cloud and wished he was on it. This could not be happening. But it was.

"No? Then what do you want to do?" Earl pointed at the can on the chair with the hand holding the cigarette. A thick stream of smoke snaked through the air like a pale blue ribbon. "Go ahead," he said. "Drink your beer. There's plenty more in the 'fridge."

Billy shook his head.

Earl looked down and scraped the edge of his boot against floor. "You want to hear how all this came about."

Billy nodded.

Earl settled into his story. "We called this Boston feller up, Kyle. You know him?"

Billy said, "Not personally."

"We talked to him. Well, I didn't actually do the talking. Tyler did the talking on the phone."

"Why?"

"Well, Tyler put a lot of time into this and he's got a better manner of speaking, so I don't mind—"

"No, I meant why did you guys call him?"

"Good Lord, Billy. I'm genuinely starting to feel sorry for you. We called him about you and the money, of course."

Billy forgot to breath for a few seconds. "What about me and the money?"

"Twenty grand." Billy looked confused and Earl sounded defensive. "I told Tyler to ask for a hundred grand, but this Kyle fellow jewed us down."

Billy thought about it. "He's paying you twenty grand for me? Alive?"

Earl looked at Billy with contempt. "Don't go getting any ideas. He was clear about you being able to walk and talk, but didn't say nothing about being banged up, so don't push your luck."

Billy was quiet. If they asked for a hundred thousand and settled for twenty grand, then Earl didn't know about the three million Billy and Doc stole.

Earl misinterpreted Billy's silence. His expression softened. "Come on, Billy-boy. Don't pout." Billy detected a degree of embarrassment in Earl's voice. "It ain't like this is personal or nothin,' though I can see how you might get the impression." He shook a finger at Billy. "Me and you, we ain't never been that close."

Billy sat up. "So, let me get this straight. You kidnap me to sell to some guy you never met from

Boston for twenty grand?"

"Kidnap! Now that's a strong word. I'm just helping you get back with old friends. They're just paying me for my trouble."

"How's Brianna fit in?"

Earl shook his head. "Relax. Your girlfriend don't know nothing about what's going on here. I tried asking, but she didn't say nothing about anything. But I could tell she was hiding something. She's smart, but not that smart, if you catch my drift."

"No, I don't." Billy's mind raced. "So, how'd you end up calling this guy from Boston about me?"

"Now, this'll impress you." Earl rubbed his beard. "Tyler fixes Brianna's laptop, see? He done it a couple of times before. Goes to her place and *upgraded* it." Earl emphasized the word with a nod.

"Yeah, so?"

"Well, I don't know if you noticed, but Ty's kinda keen on Brianna. He put one of them keyboard tracking spy app-thingies in her computer. You know what that is? It's so's he can check on what she's looking at online, see? Not that I personally approve of his spying on her, but it's pretty damn clever. And paid off, wouldn't you say?" He looked at Billy with satisfaction. "You know where I'm going with this, don't you?"

Billy didn't hide his surprise or anger. "You're a bastard. You know that?"

Earl snorted. "That's how he found out about you being interested in that dancer lady that got killed in that drug deal. Somebody used Brianna's computer, and I'm guessing it was you, to look the whole mess up on the internet. So, we figured you might be involved in that deal, maybe even it was you that killed the poor lady. This guy, Kyle, confirmed it when we called to check it out.

"That's all?" It slipped out of Billy's mouth.

"Ain't that enough? Jesus, you got balls. What more you got?"

Now Billy was sure Earl didn't know about the stolen money. Billy did the only thing he could do. He lied.

"Look, I don't know anything about robbing and murdering some dancer or whatever you're talking about."

"That's your story and you're sticking to it?"

They were silent for a while, then Billy spoke. "What will you tell her when I'm gone?"

"Huh?"

"What are you going to tell Brianna about what happened?" Earl looked confused. "About why I'm not here, Earl."

"Hadn't thought about it." Earl shrugged. "We'll make something up. She'll get over it."

"What ever happened to Southern hospitality?"

Earl chuckled and dropped his cigarette into an ashtray on the table. "We're still pretty big on hospitality. It just don't apply to uninvited guests." Earl got out of the recliner and picked up the gun from the table. He stepped up to Billy and smacked it flat against Billy's face. Then he pressed the barrel against Billy's forehead.

Billy jerked his head back. Earl pressed harder. Billy looked past Earl and the gun. He focused on smoke from the cigarette in the ashtray streaming in a remarkably straight line toward the ceiling. It calmed him. Earl wasn't about to shoot him and forfeit the twenty grand. He was sure of that at least. Pretty sure.

Laughter burst from Earl's mouth. "Easy-peasy," he said and backed himself into the recliner. He placed the gun back on the table and scratched his belly. "Got to take it easy on you. Don't want you pissing your pants and ruining the furniture, college boy."

"I never went to college."

"Huh." Earl shrugged. "Well then maybe you should have applied yourself better."

Billy almost agreed with him. Instead, he picked up the can with both hands and wet his lips. The beer was already warm.

Earl pointed at Billy. "This guy Kyle must have been pretty sweet on that dancer to get so upset with you. Is that what happened?"

Billy hesitated. "Didn't you ask?"

"Sure we asked, but he wouldn't say much. Not too friendly a fellow, I'd say. Not friendly at all. You're in a whole heap of trouble."

"It's got nothing to do with her. I stole money from him, a lot."

Earl's eyes grew.

"A lot." Billy repeated, waiting while Earl took his time crushing out the cigarette that was smoldering in the ashtray. "A lot more than twenty grand. A lot more than a hundred grand."

Earl lit another cigarette and blew the smoke out his nose before speaking. "Yeah? Exactly how much we talking about? And where is this money? Does Brianna know about it?"

"No, she knows nothing about it," Billy lied. "I hid it good. I'll split it with you if you let me go."

"How much?"

"Over a million," said Billy.

"You!" Earl snorted a laugh. "That a fact?"

"It is."

"Well, then it's a deal. You tell me where you hid it, and I'll go find it and then let you go."

Billy shook cuffs and cable. "Get this off me and we'll go together."

Earl shook his head. "Oh, sure thing! Hell, there ain't no money. Look at you. You drive a piece of shit car and don't even have a decent job!"

"Your share would be half."

Earl took a moment. "Half of nothin'."

"Over a half a million for you."

Earl sat forward on the chair. "Twenty grand against the word of a loser? Bird in the hand, worth two in the bush." He leaned back and rubbed his chin. Billy could see he was thinking about it. He pointed a finger at Billy.

"Okay. Tell me why the hell you're here if you got all that money? How come you're not living in

Paris or London or some fancy place like that? Huh? It makes no sense what you're saying." Earl looked around the room, then back at Billy. "You got nothing but stupid, that's all you got."

Billy took a deep breath, not yet ready to quit.

Earl wagged the finger at Billy. "It's all on you, chained here like a dog."

Billy shivered. Earl's smile widened.

"No deal, Billy, boy, but nice try."

Billy dropped his head only half-feigning resignation, and spoke in a low voice. He couldn't give up.

"So, how's this going to work? You going to buy me a plane ticket to Boston?"

Earl laughed. "Somebody's driving down to give us the money and take you back with him."

"Who? The boss, Kyle?"

"See? I knew you knew these guys. Nah. He's sending somebody who works for him. Name's Russ. He's bringing the money."

Billy recognized the name. What did Doc say Tiffany told him about Russ? The guy is Moe's muscle, a scary dude who was an ex-cop and Navy SEAL. Billy ran with it. He sat up and leaned toward Earl, forcing new energy into his voice.
"Shit, Earl. Do you know what you've done?"

"Yeah, sure. I made us twenty grand and rid myself of your sorry ass. It's a damn clever plan."

"For a hundred grand the risk might be worth it. But ten? For murder?"

"Who said anything about murder?"

"Think the State of Florida will let you choose between lethal injection and hanging? Firing squad is an option here, I hear. Your lawyer should check into that."

"Whoa, there! What you talking about? I ain't murdering nobody, least I don't expect to today." The threat was absent from his voice and something new was in its place. Billy though he heard doubt.

"Kidnapping and murder is federal. The FBI will—"

"Hey, I got nothing to do with what they do with you later. You end up dead later, it don't concern me at all. Ain't my business."

"You may not have to worry about a trial, anyway. If Kyle told you he wanted me alive, it won't be me they'll kill when his team get here."

"Team?" Earl grinned, but his nostrils flared. "What the hell you talkin' about?"

"You said they're sending Russ, right?"

Earl's eyes were big. "Yeah?"

"I know all about him. He used to be a cop. *And* a Navy SEAL." He had Earl's attention. He leaned back and kept himself from smiling. "This guy can snap your neck with one hand before you see him coming. He's their enforcer, their hitman."

"You don't say?" Earl sounded more concerned than skeptical.

"He's a killer is what I'm saying. That's what he does for them. He cleans up messes, takes care of loose ends, and he's good at it. They don't send him on errands delivering cash and fetching runaways.

He's coming to take me back, sure, but he's sure as hell not leaving any witnesses behind. They'll kill you and Tyler and John and anybody else who's here and can identify him. And he'll keep the twenty grand for himself as a bonus, that is, if he's even bringing the money."

"Well, damn it," said Earl smiling and rising to stand. "Now you're finally showing balls." He paced the floor, head down as if he was looking for something he dropped. "Well, damn it," he repeated. He stopped, looked at Billy and snorted. "Hell, I might have been born at night, but..., nah. This guy will pay up. Otherwise, it don't make sense his boss jewin' us down for nothing—"

"I stole his money."

"—going through all this trouble, then attracting attention from the police killing a bunch of locals because we *might* talk. It don't make any sense is all I'm saying." Earl squinted, dismissing Billy. "Nah. Safer to pay up and everybody goes their own way. And anyway...." Earl spread his arms and laughed to the air. "We're at the compound. We got every contingency covered."

Billy's shoulders slumped. Earl caught it. "Nice try." Earl snorted. "You think you're smarter than the rest of us, but you New York City Jew boys are sneaky bastards. And save your breath. I know you're from Boston. Close enough."

"I'm not Jewish."

"You sure? We thought you look like a kike." Earl acted disappointed. "Well, what are you, Italian?" He leaned over Billy as if to slap him on the back, but instead punched him hard in the side of his neck.

38

Billy collapsed to one side and almost slid off the couch, the cable keeping him from falling further. He lay there for a few seconds expecting more. Earl stood over him waiting, as if Billy was a bug and all Earl had to do was step on him. Billy kept his head down and slid his butt back into the couch. He stayed still. He said nothing. But he wasn't ready to give up. He waited until Earl returned to the recliner. When he finally spoke, Billy could hear the pain in his voice. "Where's Tyler? Thought you two were joined at the hip."

Earl ignored Billy.

"And John? He lets you do all the work?"

Earl's smile was halfway back. "You don't have to concern yourself...." As he considered his words, the smile waned. "Like I already told you, it's a damn clever plan."

"Look. I know all about these guys. I know how they think."

"So you say."

"Listen! This is about you as much as me. This guy, Russ, is definitely not going to walk away and worry about you ratting him out if things go south later... ah, no offense."

"Offense taken! I never snitched on nobody."

"You think Russ knows or even cares? He's a cop. He knows you'll get pinched sooner or later. When you're looking at real jail time or worse, you'll give him up in a heartbeat for a deal. Anybody would."

"Not me. I don't snitch," said Earl, but his voice lacked conviction. His eyes shifted left. He wasn't smiling anymore. There was something there. Billy took it as a minor victory.

Billy pressed on, making it up as he went. "Guys like Russ don't leave loose ends. Look how fast he's coming down to get me. He'll bring other guys from their gang."

"Gang," repeated Earl with a smirk, but his confidence rang hollow.

"Crime organization, whatever you want to call it. *Soldiers* is what they call themselves." Billy saw that in some old movies, and the look in Earl's eyes told him Earl had seen the same movies. If he could get the cuffs off, get to the table, get the gun or the rifle.... "Maybe a van full of soldiers. You picture it! They practice this kind of thing together all the time. The plan is to get me and kill you."

"Let them try." The defiance was back. Damnit.

"I know these people. You can't beat them.

Nobody can. They roll right over you and take what they want. Why do you think I ran?"

"Because you're stupid and weak, that's why," said Earl, rising from the chair, his eyes still on Billy's. "And you're alone. You got no organization, no community to watch your back. Makes a whole lot of difference, being a part of something bigger than yourself."

He took a step toward the couch, and Billy recoiled, but Earl went still as they both heard whirring and squeaking which indicated the gate was opening. Then they heard what sounded like an oversized lawnmower outside.

Earl looked out the window. "Finally." He looked relieved and then at his watch. "Well, thanks for the entertaining conversation. I'll pass on your offer of Monopoly money to John. He'll get a good laugh out of it." He looked over Billy's shoulder out the window. "And thanks for the warning." Billy turned and watched the VW pull up next to his Honda. "Even if your friend's intentions ain't honorable, like I said, we got it covered." Earl's smile grew nasty. "We'll see whose balls get caught in a trap."

"I gotta take a leak, Earl." Billy gestured with his chin toward the bathroom.

Earl smiled like he was in on the joke. "Do I look like an idiot to you?"

"Ask me something harder." Billy remembered the last time he heard that and bit his lip.

Earl's smile softened. "Funny man." He looked relaxed. "Just squeeze your knees together, sweetheart. Won't be but a minute or two longer and you're Boston's problem again."

They both watched as John emerged from the passenger side of the VW.

"Looks like the party's ready to start." He looked down at Billy, his face and tone all business. "Wait here. Don't try nothing stupid. You got no place to go." Earl holstered the gun, then collected his cigarettes and the keys and dropped them in his pockets. He picked up his rifle off the floor and walked out the door without looking back.

Billy pulled at the cable, but he knew it was hopeless. Earl was right. He'd reached the end of the line. He was going back. He was fucked.

A car door slammed. Billy twisted around and looked out the window, watching as the militiamen prepared.

Tyler stood by the driver's side of the VW wearing wraparound shades and a camouflage ball cap with an orange "F" on the front. His silver gun was holstered on his right hip. Earl walked up to him, said something, and handed Tyler the keys to the Honda. John, on the other side of the car, gun in a belt holster in the small of his back, reached into the back seat of the VW and brought out a slim rifle with a forward lens so large Billy would have found it comical in any other situation.

John spoke to Earl. Billy couldn't make out what they were saying, but wondered if John would believe the story about Russ or the money. That might stall them or it could be just as bad as being handed over to Russ. He saw no way out of this.

Tyler walked around the Honda inspecting the car like a potential buyer, raising the hood and checking the engine.

Earl watched as John drew an arc with his finger in the air from the gate to a small hill beyond the trees on the opposite side of the lot. Earl nodded and watched as John walked off toward the hill carrying the sniper rifle.

Earl called Tyler and waved him over. Tyler lowered the hood, folded his arms and leaned against the Honda. Earl called again, sounding angry this time. Tyler gave Earl the finger, then turned his back on him. Earl turned to the window, saw Billy watching, then stomped over to Tyler.

Billy turned away and tugged again at the bike cable. If he could get free, Billy planned to slip out the back door by the kitchen, but he had no idea what to do next. There was an eight-foot fence, a large open clearing, and about a quarter-mile dirt road between him and the highway, say a half mile total distance. He was handcuffed, didn't have his car keys, and Earl and Tyler blocked the gate. Even if he could get past them and the fence and onto the dirt road, they knew the area better than he did and would track him down before he got far. They'd never let him get away. Plus, John was somewhere out there with a scope and rifle. Billy let go of the bike cable along with his hopes for escape.

He sensed a low rumble and looked out the window. A black Escalade entered the clearing from the dirt road and the woods, but instead of crossing the clearing and driving through the gate, it turned immediately to park under the shade of trees close to the road.

Billy thought, if it's now or never, then I guess it's never.

The driver's door swung open. And a large black man, Billy assumed Russ, stepped out and walked around to the front of the Escalade. He wore a striped dress shirt, sleeves rolled half way up, black slacks, dark sneakers, and a ball cap. Billy watched Earl and Tyler watch the man walked across the clearing and stopped halfway to the gate. Tyler said something to Earl who barked a laugh without taking his eyes off Russ.

Earl slapped Tyler on the back and started walking toward Russ. He was carrying his rifle. Tyler followed him. Billy wasn't sure who to root for. Russ was not the cavalry sent to rescue him.

39

Concepcion Jesus Maldonado lay prone in a tangle of vines under the shadow of a huge oak decorated with Spanish moss. The tree was about ten feet from the clearing, its canopy of leaves shading the Escalade parked under it. The ground was warm and moist. He had been careful to avoid anything that looked remotely like poison sumac. The ants seemed to ignore him, but he was on the lookout for spiders.

A narrow break in the underbrush to the right of the Escalade gave him a clear view of the action. Russ towered over the two rednecks. Through the scope on CJ's AK-74M, they seemed mere inches away.

By design, Russ stood at a 45-degree angle so CJ would have clear line-of-sight on the other two. They were too far away for him to hear what was being said, but to CJ the older one seemed as phony as a three-dollar bill. He did most of the talking, beaming a wide-ass grin, while the kid watched Russ like a hawk, laughing now at something the old guy said. CJ could see the edge of a Kevlar vest peeking out from the top of the older man's shirt. He centered the crosshairs between the man's eyes for practice.

CJ had seen the guy with the sniper rifle enter the woods on the other side of the clearing before Russ drove up. There was no way to warn Russ that his suspicions were right. But Russ wasn't stupid. He'd know. Using the scope, CJ had examined the ground the sniper would likely have covered. Across the clearing and halfway up a hill, no more than two hundred feet or so away was a particularly dense stand of trees and bushes. A good vantage point if you had the right weapon. CJ concentrated on the spot for a good thirty seconds before he was rewarded with a glint of reflected sunlight. Through the leaves, he could make out the contour of the man's body and the barrel of a rifle, a straight line pointing at the men in the clearing.

CJ congratulated himself and committed the spot to memory. It was a good location. Still, he felt his own spot was the better choice—closer to the action for better accuracy and faster reaction time.

He returned his attention to the men in the middle of the clearing. He saw only Russ and the older grizzly one. He jerked away from the scope and found the kid had passed the gate and was heading for the log cabin.

CJ scratched his right ankle with the toe of his left boot and prayed that it was only his imagination and not a chigger digging into his skin under the elastic of his sock. Earlier, he'd made Russ stop at a Circle-K and bought a little green bottle of camphor-phenol, knowing the inevitability of encountering a vast kingdom of bugs in the woods.

His jeans felt thick in the heat and humidity. The long-sleeve camouflage shirt Russ gave him was okay, but the Kevlar vest beneath it another story—stiff enough to restrict movement, forcing him into a less relaxed and less optimal posture. His only movement was occasionally wiping streams of sweat dripping into his eyes. I knew I forgot something, he thought. Headband. Next time. Next time.

Four days earlier, he and Russ had made the drive from Boston in two days, almost a day early. Russ followed the directions Tyler provided to the turnoff, but instead of turning down the dirt road, Russ turned around and drove back a quarter mile. He pulled off the main road, parking the Escalade under a clump of trees. This, he told CJ, would be their secondary rendezvous point if things went to shit. Russ grabbed a pair of binoculars and a bottle of water.

He and CJ walked to the turnoff and down the dirt road until they caught their first glance of the fence and compound. "This is our primary rendezvous spot. Look around. Find a landmark you will remember." Russ waited until CJ was done memorizing the location. "As soon as you hear me start the car, slip away and meet me here. Don't expect me to wait for you."

They left the dirt road and hiked into the woods, making their way slowly toward the fence. When Russ thought they were close enough, he scanned the compound through the glasses from behind some massive tree.

"Looks deserted," he whispered, handing the binoculars to CJ, "but someone might be inside. Stay invisible. I'm supposed to drive up to the fence, but I'm not gonna do that. Too close to that sentry tower. Safer to meet out in the open, where you can keep close tabs on me and him. Look there." He pointed to where the dirt road from the highway met the clearing. "Tomorrow, I'll turn the car around and park it right there, pointing the front wheels at the road so all I'll have to do is hit the gas when it's over."

"Where do you want me?"

Russ was silent while he examined the terrain. Finally, he pointed to a spot at the edge of the trees close to where he planned to park the Escalade. "There! That'll do the trick." They moved like shadows to the spot. It had a view through the trees of the clearing. "I'll park it right here. This'll be good to hide, close enough to give you a good view and get off a clean shot if it's called for. This work for you?"

CJ looked in all directions. "Yeah, this'll work," he said.

Russ reached out and gripped CJ's arm. "Listen closely to me. If I raise my hand over my head, either hand, doesn't have to be both of them, you cut that cracker down and anybody with him beside me and Billy. Don't wait for me to start shooting. Stay cool —don't lose control—but work fast and drop everyone but Billy and me if I give you the signal. You got that?"

"Yeah, sure. I got it." Russ kept staring at CJ until he was sure he got it.

They jogged back to the highway. Neither spoke until they were in the Escalade headed toward Gainesville to find a motel.

"I'll leave the money in the car so he has to walk with me when I turn my back to the place. If there's a second or third guy there, they're not likely to try something with one of their own so close."

"Makes sense."

"Remember, once I start the engine, make a beeline for that rendezvous point. I'll slow down, but don't wait for me to stop. Just jump in. Now this is critical—I can't wait for you. We're sitting ducks in their backyard. If I don't see you there, I'll wait at the secondary rendezvous point by the bend on the highway. I'll give you just two minutes, that's all. If the shit hits the fan and you miss me, call my cell and we'll figure something out."

"Got it."

"Make sure it's charged up and on mute. Your wife been calling?"

CJ shook his head. "She knows I'm working.

She won't call unless she goes into labor, but she ain't due for another two weeks. We're cool."

Russ looked hard at CJ. "The purpose of this whole thing... it's all for nothing if we don't take Billy alive and get him to tell us where the money is. Right?"

"Sure."

"So, move your ass and don't expect me to come back looking for you. This ain't the Marines. You understand what I'm saying? I'll do what I can, but in the end, we're each on our own."

"Don't worry about me, Mom," said CJ. "I won't miss my ride."

Russ stared at CJ for a long time before he spoke. "From your lips to God's ear. That's what Moe would've said."

40

First impressions count. The three got busy sizing up each other as they stood in the middle of the clearing, about five feet of sun-baked ground between them. The older guy was holding an M16, the teenager a silver semiautomatic pistol holstered on his hip. Looked like a Colt to Russ. And then there was a sniper somewhere out there to consider. Russ saw them look at his face and the black gun and holster showing on his hip. Mostly, at his face.

The big guy had a gut but broad shoulders and big arms. He moved slowly but looked like he could handle himself in a fight if it didn't go on for too long. The kid was tall and wiry, trying to stand tough with a dumb grin on his face. He kept shifting his feet which worried Russ. Nervous type. Probably impulsive. Possibly reckless.

Earl looked up at the tall black stranger and was impressed. He looked like he could take your best punch and still knock you down. A fucking

Iron Man. This guy's physique and posture screamed military, just like Billy said. Earl sucked in his gut without thinking. And an ex-cop, too. Probably crooked. Definitely prepared for a fight. He noticed under his crisp blue shirt, Russ wore a Kevlar vest. In addition to the gun on his right hip, Earl figured Russ wore a small caliber revolver in a holster strapped to an ankle, just like the cops on TV.

Earl guess wasn't far off. Russ, a formidable opponent in any situation, was armed for bear. His primary weapon was the big Sig Sauer holstered on his right hip, loaded with seven hollow-point .357 cartridges. And while he wore a small revolver holstered to an ankle for backup, that gun was not like the ones depicted by cops on television. His five-shot S&W J-frame was chambered for hefty .357 rounds and loaded with three different types of ammunition. What Tyler and Earl didn't suspect was Russ also carried a small SOG in a short black sheath attached to his belt where his left hand rested. In close combat, the razor-sharp 3.5-inch double-edged knife could strike faster than any gun. It didn't require aiming or chambering a round.

"Well, I'll be damned." Earl smiled. "So, you're Russ?"

Russ nodded. "You Tyler?"

Earl cocked his head at Tyler without taking his eyes off Russ. "That's Ty. I'm Earl." He looked Russ up and down. Neither man offered a hand. "You're way too pretty to be from around here."

"Way too dark, you mean," Tyler smirked.

Earl saw Russ's eyes go hard and found pleasure in it even as he backhanded Tyler on the arm. His smile remained. "What'd I tell you about making our visitor uncomfortable?"

"Nothin'..." said Tyler.

"I thought you agreed we'd come alone," Russ said.

"That was me talking... to your boss," said Tyler.

"Tyler, here, he don't count," said Earl. "He's a kid."

"Couldn't find a babysitter?" asked Russ.

Earl suppressed a laugh. "Just ignore him. I do."

"Where's our guy?"

"Where's our money?"

"When he's in my car, you'll get your money."

Earl's eyes wandered. "Fair enough," he said, then told Tyler to make himself useful. Tyler hustled back through the gate, then slowed to a walk as he entered the cabin.

Russ thought some small talk might help. "He give you any trouble?" he asked Earl.

"Naw, he's a good kid," answered Earl. "Does what he's told, usually."

"I mean Billy."

"Oh." Earl chuckled. "Naw, he's got a mouth on him but not much else." Earl's expression changed. "Said he stole money from your boss?"

Russ took it in stride. "You think this clown is smart enough to steal from us? I wouldn't believe anything that came out of his mouth."

"Uh-huh," said Earl, using his best poker face.

"We think he and his friend might have killed a lady working for us. We just want to talk to him and get to the bottom of it."

"Seems like a lot of travel and trouble just to talk."

Russ waited a beat for effect. "She was a close friend, if you catch my drift."

Billy appeared in the doorway, head bowed. His hands were cuffed in front. Tyler shoved him forward and walked behind him, Tyler's hand resting on his holstered gun.

"Tell your kid to take his hand off his gun," Russ said. "If he keeps doing that, I'll spank him."

Earl laughed. "Yeah, well, I'd like to see you try." Tyler's hand stayed on his gun.

Russ scratched the back of his head, ready to give CJ the signal. "Whatever you're thinking, son," he said to Tyler, "don't fuck this up for everybody."

"Ty, you stay right as you are," said Earl. "Mister, we showed you Billy. Now where's our money?"

Russ ignored the question and looked sideways at Billy. "Seems you got yourself in a bind, Billy Bear."

"Billy Bear!" Tyler repeated like a taunting six-year-old. "Billy Bear! Billy Bear!"

Billy met Russ's gaze. "Listen, man. I didn't—"

"Save it." He squinted at Earl. "Let's you and me and your little sidekick get something straight. I brought a few friends of my own to watch my back."

Tyler looked left and right, scanning the woods, but Earl didn't break eye contact with Russ. His smile remained casual. "Just what I expected. You planning to rip us off or something?"

"Just insurance, that's all. Don't try to sell me a story you don't have the same."

Tyler bounced on his toes and looked at Earl. Earl's expression gave nothing away. He didn't have to.

"That's what I thought. So now that we're both motivated to follow the rules, here's what we're going to do. The two of us are going to walk this piece of crap to my car, then I'll hand you an envelope with the money, $20,000 in hundreds. I'll wait while you count it. Then I'll get in my car and drive away and you can pop open a beer and watch the game."

"You give Ty the money. I'll wait here," Earl said.

"All right," said Russ. He looked at Tyler. "You go first, kid. We'll follow you."

"Wait a damn minute," said Earl. "Tyler! Don't let him walk off with my best cuffs. They're my Police Edition. Use your key."

"Viperteks?" guessed Russ.

"Yeah." Earl said, surprise leaking into his voice.

Tyler fished a small key out of his front pocket. "Give me your hands," he said. Billy raised his arms and Tyler unlocked the cuffs. Before anyone knew it, Russ had out a pair of his own handcuffs and slapped them on Billy's outstretched wrists with a well-practiced motion.

He *was* a cop, thought Earl, adjusting his stance. "Ty. Go get our money."

Tyler led the way, Billy between him and Russ. As they approached the Escalade, Tyler said, "Platinum model, ain't it? This year's?"

Russ was becoming less patient with this kid by the second.

"Limo tint... nice," said Tyler, stretching out the word *nice*. "Mint condition from what I can see through the dust on it. Wheels look excellent. What's the mileage?"

Russ ignored the yapping. He needed to close the deal and put some distance between him and these amateurs before they did something stupid.

41

Math might have been Tyler's strong suit but money was his motivation. He was thinking about both. Asking for a hundred grand was Tyler's idea, but Earl was a pussy and gave up too fast.

After all, the plan was his idea, not Earl's. The work and risk were worth more than his split of the twenty grand. John said that sixteen was going toward the mortgage on the Compound and funding recruitment parties, and that Earl and Tyler could keep two thousand each, which Tyler had to admit was decent considering they all hung out at the Compound. But Tyler couldn't shake the feeling they were missing out. He needed real cash if he was ever going to move out of his mother's house and get his own place.

This top-of-the-line Escalade seemed like a second chance, the opportunity Tyler had been waiting for, driven right to his doorstep. It looked loaded. Off the top of his head, he figured parts would pull in at least thirty, thirty-five grand. The silver-spoke chrome wheels alone would fetch $2,500 in Jacksonville. Easier still, he could sell the car intact in Jacksonville for $50-60 grand, doing nothing more than switching the VIN plate and driving a couple hours. An even, three-way split would put $20 grand in his pocket on top of the grand he got for Billy.

Once Earl and John saw how easy it was to sell the car, he was pretty sure they would be fine with his move. And he considered shooting Russ and Billy a bonus. Nobody would go asking about a drifter and some black stranger, especially when no bodies turned up. Everybody knows 'gators swallow people whole and don't leave leftovers.

The only fly in the ointment was the sniper the black guy said he brought along. Even if there was one, with his McMillan TAC-50 John could pick the shooter's nose hairs off once he saw the muzzle flash. That is, if the shooter didn't shit his pants and run when he saw his guy go down. What'd be the point hanging around, out-numbered and out-gunned? If I'd known about this here Escalade beforehand, Tyler thought, Earl and John might have been able to help instead of me doing all the work.

Making enough to get his own place wasn't Tyler's only concern. Getting Billy out of the way was another benefit Tyler was counting on. He Tyler forward to telling Brianna that he heard that Billy split town without saying goodbye to anybody. Just took off, like some drifter without roots.

Wouldn't actually be a lie. Tyler thought he might have to console Brianna, give her a shoulder to cry on.

Tyler knew if he didn't act in the next minute, it would be one more opportunity lost.

42

They were almost to the Escalade when Billy leaned in and whispered to Russ. "They got a guy with a rifle in the woods. I saw him." Russ didn't even bother to look at Billy.

"We got it covered," was all he said. He did not try to lower his voice.

We? Billy thought? Who's *we*? But of course, Russ would have his own shooter. These guys were professionals. Which was the problem, because Billy knew once he led Russ and his companions to the safe deposit box—and he knew he would eventually—he was as good as dead. He wished he could tell Brianna and Doc what happened, but he knew he was out of time. The best he could hope for was it would be quick.

His legs began to shake. He stumbled and felt the ground giving away. He fought to stay upright and resist the urge to run into the woods, flag down a car somewhere—but he knew he wouldn't get ten steps. He came so far and now this, he thought as he struggled to put one foot in front of the other. Out of the frying pan....

Russ opened the back door and grabbed Billy's arm, startling him. Billy jumped so hard he almost bolted. Russ's eyes met Billy's. It was as if he was reading Billy's mind.

"Don't do anything stupid. Get in."

Tyler watched with amusement as Billy climbed onto the rear seat with difficulty, unable to steady himself with his hands. Russ noticed Tyler's grin was back.

Just one more thing to do. Russ kept his voice soft and casual. "Let's get your money, kid." Russ gestured toward the rear of the car. "It's in the back."

Tyler followed him to the rear of the vehicle. Russ pressed a button on the car's key fob. The tailgate swung up and open. The interior was clean and tidy, an encouraging sign to Tyler that the owner took care of the car. Russ leaned in and pulled out a manila envelope from under a blanket and held it out to Tyler. "Pleasure doing business with you," he said as the hatch closed. "Have a nice day."

"Hold on, hold on" said Tyler. The envelope was sealed. He ripped the top off and pulled out two stacks of one hundred $100 bills secured with a white bank strap stamped with *$10,000*. Russ thought Tyler looked disappointed. "This all of it?"

Russ looked down with pity. "You think I shorted you ten bucks for candy and condoms? Go ahead, kid. Count it quick. I'm in a hurry."

Tyler held the money in one hand, the empty

envelope in the other. Russ held the key fob in his right hand and waited, glancing once into the woods in the direction of the road and thinking about slowing down for CJ. When he looked back at Tyler, he noticed the hid staring back at him, not counting bills.

"What's the matter? You can count, can't you?" Russ said.

"Up yours! I count fine," spat Tyler.

Russ detected something in that response, the same mix of humiliation and challenge, the same impotent bravado he'd heard a thousand times before from teenagers he'd stopped and frisked in Roxbury and Dorchester. It usually meant nothing, but this wasn't his beat, and he wasn't dealing with some Mark Wahlberg-wannabee. He was on this kid's turf, and this kid had a gun....

The envelope and cash dropped to the ground as Tyler began to pull his gun from the holster. Even at that moment, Russ was impressed with the kid's speed.

Russ let the key fob fall from his hand, but knew he wouldn't draw his own gun in time. He played the hand he'd been dealt. In a single motion, the SOG was in his left hand and struck out. But even as the razor-sharp blade sliced Tyler's forearm, Russ knew he was milliseconds too late.

43

Tyler squeezed off a shot as the knife sliced the underside of his forearm. A white-hot pain threw his aim off. The 9mm slug missed Russ's chest and vest, but passed through his upper right arm. Russ spun and fell. The SOG flew out of his hand, bounced off the Escalade, and sailed into the trees.

"Tyler! What the fahhhh—" Earl ran toward the Escalade as he fumbled with the safety on his M16.

Russ looked up at Tyler through blurry eyes. Blood flowed like water from a busted pipe from a slit in the kid's forearm. His gun was now in his left hand and pointed at Russ, but he wasn't looking at Russ. Instead, the kid was looking back toward Earl and shouting his name.

Lying on his right side, unable to move his right arm or reach the gun holstered beneath him, one part of Russ wondered where the hell CJ was. Another part of his brain already had him reaching for the backup gun on his left ankle.

"He cut me, Earl! I'm bleeding really bad!" As he looked back at Russ, Tyler registered three flashes of white light and felt the impact before he heard the shots.

Russ fired the backup gun from the ground with his left hand. In the three middle chambers, Russ had decent accuracy and stopping power with .38 caliber hollow points. In the last chamber, he loaded a .357 Magnum Speer 158-gram UHP that could stop a car engine with a kick that matched. But with a panic situation in mind, the first chamber held a shell cartridge loaded with #10 shot, similar to a shotgun shell.

That first shot propelled an 81-gram cluster of hundreds of half-grain lead pellets through the air at 1000 feet per second. Such a low mass couldn't penetrate Tyler's Kevlar vest, but they pepper the kid's legs, groin, arms, neck and face with "rat-shot." One pellet hit Tyler in the eye. That's all it took.

Tyler felt like he'd walked into a fireball. Hammer-like impacts to his groin, chest and face competed for attention, but rising above it all was a singular pain in his eye. He dropped his gun and stumbled backwards, hands to his face as Russ shot him again. Russ aimed for Tyler's head, but the hollow point plowed a half-inch wide path through Tyler's raised forearm and tore a hole into his jaw. The third hollow hit him in the neck, ending his suffering.

A rain of bullets hit the side of the Escalade,

kicking up dirt and smashing metal and glass. Russ rolled away from the fire and saw Earl running toward him, the barrel of the M16 flashing. Russ fired his last two rounds at Earl as Earl walked fire up into Russ, hitting both his legs. The impacts threw Russ back against the rear wheel of the Escalade.

The automatic fire stopped.

Russ couldn't open his eyes. He tried calling to CJ for help, but his voice wouldn't work. Blood from a wound to his left thigh flowed into the dirt. He didn't try to stop it. Thirty-seconds later, it stopped on its own.

44

Some thirty feet into the woods, CJ had eyes on the old man and Russ, but the Escalade blocked his view of the kid. He could hear that the kid was acting up, but CJ wasn't worried until he heard a shot and saw Russ spin to the side. Then he saw the old man running and firing toward Russ. CJ tracked the old man but before he could get him in his crosshairs, the M16 began to strafe the Escalade. A few bullets overshot and hit the tree next to CJ, forcing him to roll out of the way for cover. He heard three, then two more shots from the other side of the Escalade, then silence. He crawled back on hands and knees and looked for but couldn't see anyone. CJ belly-crawled further and saw the old man face down on the ground. He still couldn't see Russ or the kid.

"Russ? Hey, man, you okay?" CJ heard the fear in his own voice.

He crouched out from the woods into the open. Out of the corner of his eye, he sensed more than saw a flash from the trees halfway up the hill on the other side of the clearing, a good 200 feet away. The bullet struck a tree behind CJ. He dropped and sank back into the underbrush then crawled leftward with the Escalade as cover.

"Russ! Russ!" No response.

CJ peeked over the hood. Another flash. Another bullet. This time hitting the rear of the Escalade where he had been hiding.

CJ's visual memory was excellent. In one continual sweep of the rifle's scope, he found the spot on the hill where he'd seen the flashes and emptied an entire clip at it, then ducked back behind the Escalade where he swapped out the empty clip for a full one. He crawled on his stomach to the back of the Escalade and took up a position under the rear wheel to wait. Through his scope the distance seemed as close as courtside at a Celtics game. Patience rewarded him. Another flash appeared from the hill as a bullet smashed into the hood. Through the scope, CJ zeroed in on an unnaturally straight line in the brush—the top half of a hunting blind. He centered the crosshairs below it, and before he pulled the trigger, another flash appeared, the bullet striking the dirt inches from him. He pushed panic aside, aimed between the two flashes and emptied his clip. He waited and was rewarded with silence. There was no return fire.

CJ shimmied out from behind the Escalade and ran in a crouch into the woods. He reloaded and watched through the scope for another flash.

There were no more flashes.

He raced through the trees back to the Escalade, certain Russ and Billy were badly hurt or dead, but he was not driven by sentimentality. It was necessity. He needed the keys to the Escalade to get away from here. That's when he saw Billy in the clearing, his back to CJ.

CJ swung his rifle toward Billy and crept forward.

45

R ifle fire pushed through the void in Earl's head, followed by daylight. He felt something gritty in his mouth. It tasted like dirt, and he realized he was lying face down in it. He turned his head to spit, dislodging a tiny stone wedged between his teeth.

He took a deep breath to clear his head, but pain in his belly made him stop short. He rolled far enough onto his side to slide a hand down over his chest and abdomen and groin, afraid to look. Everything felt tender, but dry and intact. He sighed in relief and tried to make sense of what happened.

The money must have been wrong. Earl saw Tyler drop the stack of bills, draw his gun and shoot Russ. Russ fell, but Tyler started yelling and dropped his gun. He must have taken his eyes off Russ. That's when the bastard shot the poor kid.

Earl remembered grabbing his M16 and running, firing at Russ as he went. That son-of-a-bitch got a couple of shots off. Earl remembered the impact low in the vest.

He cursed not Russ but Tyler. All he had to do was.... Another rifle exchange scattered Earl's thought. He had to focus. This wasn't over and his head was still in a fog.

From the gunshots and their echoes in the woods, Earl determined he was between two rifles firing at each other. John was on the hill. The other rifle sounded like it was coming from somewhere near the Escalade. No doubt Russ's man. Earl realized he would have run right into Russ' sniper. He felt lucky in a way that Russ stopped him.

He also felt certain Russ's sniper was toast. John could hit a target over 1,700 yards with his TAC-50, and he knew these woods like the back of his hand. Earl estimated John and the sniper were just a couple hundred feet apart. Just a matter of time before the other guy runs out of ammo or reveals himself.

But until then Earl was out in the open and vulnerable. He had to retrieve his weapon and find cover before Russ's sniper sighted him. He tipped onto his side and tried to get up on his knees. His chest and stomach lit up like a bonfire. He found the breath to scream before his legs folded under him. He rolled onto his back and took inventory. There was a ragged hole ripped in his shirt and a tear in the front of the vest where a squashed bronze bullet rested. The Kevlar stopped the big slug from punching through to his stomach. That was the good news.

He lifted up the bottom edge of the vest. Blood saturated his undershirt. He pulled the shirt up and was relieved to see no bullet wound, but instead a palm-sized purple mark weeping blood under his left bottom rib. He probed the area with his fingers. Electric shocks ran through his insides. At minimum he had a broken rib, but that would have to wait. Right now, he needed to recover his weapon and find cover. He still felt lucky. If Russ's sniper had hit him, his bullet would have gone through the vest and Earl. Maybe the sniper was overwhelmed by the automatic fire from the M16, or maybe the Escalade blocked his view. Either way, Earl had to get moving.

His M16 was on the ground just a couple of feet away. He crawled toward it one painful inch at a time, keeping as flat as he could. When he got to it at last, he hugged it like a lost child and lay still in the embrace. He needed a moment to rest before finding cover. He checked the magazine and found it was almost empty. He had ammunition in the office, but that might as well be on the moon.

He'd made some progress toward the Escalade and Tyler when five rapid shots punched the air from the woods to the left of the Escalade. Russ's guy must be shooting an automatic. The rifle wouldn't be as powerful or accurate as John's bolt-action TAC-50, good news for John as Earl estimated the distance between John and the shooter was a couple hundred feet. But with less than fifty between Earl and the shooter, range wasn't as important as rate of fire, which was bad news for Earl. He sped up, using his elbows, keeping the Escalade between him and the sniper, ignoring the pain in his belly as he dragged himself forward.

When he stopped to catch his breath, Earl cried out when he saw Tyler lying in the brush close to some trees. He recognized Russ looking like pile of rags crumpled against the back tire of the Escalade. Both bodies blended into the surroundings.

Earl realized he hadn't heard rifles exchange in the last couple of minutes. Maybe Russ's shooter was on the move, changing positions deeper in the woods. Earl knew he had to find cover fast, but now it was hard to feel his legs.

He didn't see or hear the jeep until it slid to a stop in a small cloud of dust a few feet from him.

46

Brianna leaped out of the jeep and crouched on the ground next to Earl. She pressed her hand on his shoulder, causing him to grunt.

"Earl! Earl! What's happened? You shot?" Earl was squinting up at her, but couldn't seem to raise his head.

He pointed at his abdomen. "Vest stopped it," he whispered.

"Jesus! What happened?" She quickly scanned left and right, but saw no one, missing Tyler and Russ on the ground. She pointed at the Escalade. "Is that them? Did they shoot you?" She shook Earl's arm. "Where are they now? Earl!"

She saw he was fading.

She shook his arm again. "Where's Billy? He's not answering his cell, but I know he's here. His car's over there." But Earl only shifted his eyes away from her.

She stood and took out her phone and dialed.

"Wait!" Earl managed to croak out. "What are

you doing?"

"I'm calling 911. You need an ambulance. And the cops."

"No, no, woman. Don't..." he said, choking on panic. "Help me to your jeep. Drive to town. Hospital. No cops." He clutched his side with one hand and propped himself up with the other into a sitting position. "No cops... no cops."

Brianna slipped her phone back in her pocket and squatted next to Earl. "You must be all right," she said shaking her head. "As stubborn as ever." She looked at his shirt. "You look like shit, but I don't see much blood." She lifted the shirt.

A large, flattened bullet clung to the outside of the vest. Somewhere in the back of her mind she knew how much damage a round that size travelling at supersonic speeds would cause. She heard stories from those in combat about the injuries soldiers sustained from bullets that failed to breach their vests. Tissue and organs were pulverized. Ribs shattered. Shards of bone spun through lungs and viscera, shredding organs like the liver, spleen and sections of intestine. She knew Earl would be dead in minutes.

"Help me up," he wheezed. He raised an arm.

Brianna stood up and looked down on him. She nudged his leg with her sneaker to get him to look at her. "Tell me where Billy is. Tell me now." She knew there wasn't much time. "And don't tell me you don't know."

"I don't know." Earl shook his head and turned

away. "His car was here ... when I got here. But haven't seen him ... anywhere."

She put a foot down on his shoulder. "Bull."

Earl looked indignant. "What the hell? I'm hurt!"

"Billy wouldn't have come here on his own."

"I swear I don't—"

"Where're John and Tyler?" She put more weight onto her foot, her voice hardened. "They in on this, too?"

He put his hand on his stomach. "Jesus! Are you crazy, woman? That hurts!"

Brianna stepped back and watched as Earl use both hands to lift himself a few inches off the ground, but he was too weak to get any higher. He gave up and fell onto his back.

She bent down and reached out a hand. He raised his arm for her to help lift him, but instead she picked up the M16. She made sure Earl was watching while she checked that the safety was off and the bolt was in the forward position, indicating a round was in the chamber. She stood tall and pointed the weapon right between his eyes.

"Where the fuck is Billy, Earl."

47

At the first shot, Billy slipped off the back seat onto the floor. He flattened himself and covered his head with his cuffed hands as best he could. He thought it was the end and screamed something primitive and unintelligible when automatic fire slammed into the car body and shattered the windows. Two loud shots ended the barrage.

He was covered with beads of glass. His head and hands shook and his ears felt stuffed with cotton. He thought he heard a voice call out. He forced himself upright to peek through bottom of a shattered side window. Everything outside looked alien —too bright and too quiet. Overhanging branches from the trees blocked his view of parts of the clearing, but he saw no one and had a moment of glee thinking they might have left him behind or all be dead. He pulled the door handle and pushed the door open, being careful not to cut himself on the glass.

Even before his foot hit the ground, Billy saw Russ crumpled against the rear tire, his clothes and the hard brown ground soaked with blood. At the front of the Escalade Tyler was lying face down in the grass and weeds. They were both dead and already looking like part of the landscape. Tyler's hat, two stacks of money and a silver gun lay nearby.

Russ's big Sig Sauer was visible in his shoulder holster. Without hesitation, Billy crouched beside him and removed the gun. Brianna taught him how to check the safety, but Billy didn't see one. He was checking Russ's pockets for the key to the handcuffs when he heard a man's voice from the clearing. It sounded like Earl. Billy stood up, Russ's gun in his right hand. It was heavy and his hands were cuffed so he held his wrist in his left hand.

Then he heard Brianna's voice. He was sure of it! He ran out to into the clearing and saw her pointing a rifle down at Earl, a grim expression on her face. He called out her name. She looked up and found him, her expression instantly changing to relief. She smiled wild and waved as she called his name.

He saw the smile vanish as she pointed behind him, shouting his name again but this time something was wrong.

48

CJ was close, the butt of his rifle up against his hip, the barrel pointed at Billy's back. Billy was staring at a jeep and a woman CJ didn't recognized. She was standing over the old man on the ground, the one that shot up the Escalade and Russ. It looked like Russ got him.

She was holding the old man's M16.

Billy shouted the woman's name, "Brianna," startling CJ so much he almost pulled the trigger. The woman looked up and called Billy by name. She waved, then saw CJ closing in on him.

"Billy! Behind you," she shouted.

Get Billy alive, was what Russ said. He had to move fast. With no time to aim, he swung the barrel toward the woman and shot from the hip. She toppled without making a sound next to the old man.

Billy spun around to the source of the shot and locked eyes with CJ.

CJ found Billy's expression of shock comical until he saw Russ's Sig Sauer in his cuffed hands.

It was pointed at him, while CJ's rifle was pointed away from Billy toward the center of the clearing. CJ knew Billy would shoot if CJ so much as moved his rifle a fraction of an inch.

CJ wanted to take Billy alive. It meant twenty-five grand, but it was more than just the money.

CJ let the barrel drop toward the ground as he pivoted sideways to make himself a smaller target. He put on a practiced smile. He was a bouncer and knew how to de-escalate a situation. And if not, he was still the better shot, had the better weapon, and wasn't handcuffed.

"Hey, Billy," he said. "My name is CJ. I'm here to help."

Billy's whole body shivered, like he was cold. He said nothing.

CJ took a half step forward as he nodded at the gun in Billy's hand.

"That Russ's gun? It's got a hair trigger, you know that? Be careful with it. I don't want either of us to get hurt."

He moved his left foot a half step forward.

Billy's shaking increased. He kept the gun pointed at CJ. "You... shot her."

"Me? From back here? I don't think that was me." He shook his head. "That would make me a pretty good shot. Look...." CJ took a step as he held out his free hand, palm out as if he was appealing for calm. "Let's just both of us stay cool, brother. Hear what I have to say." CJ took another step, positioning himself to grab the gun from Billy's cuffed hands.

Billy shifted from foot to foot and turned his head a little, as if he wanted to check on the woman in the clearing, but couldn't take his eyes off CJ.

"Let's you and me go out there and make sure the lady is okay. She might be bleeding and we need to help her. All I want is for us to get the hell away in one piece. You with me?"

CJ lifted his right foot just as his cell phone vibrated audibly in his pocket. He stiffened, the smile vanishing from his face.

Billy pulled the trigger. He kept pulling until the magazine was empty and the bolt slid forward. He looked at what used to be Concepcion Jesus Maldonado, bouncer, husband and father, then dropped the gun and ran out into the clearing to Brianna.

49

Billy hadn't made it halfway to Brianna when he saw someone emerge from the trees on the opposite side of the clearing. John was limping but moving fast, carrying the long rifle with the big scope. Billy turned on his heels and was already running back into the woods when John cocked the rifle and raised the scope to his eye. Billy knew his best option would be to keep running, that he could outrun John judging from the limp, but he couldn't leave Brianna behind without knowing. He grabbed CJ's rifle and hid behind the Escalade for cover.

John kept coming toward him.

"You son-of-a-bitch," John yelled. "You're a son-of-a-bitch. You know that?"

Billy rested the AK on the hood, pushed his shoulder into the stock, and brought his cuffed hands up to the trigger to steady the rifle. He centered the scope and fired. The rifle was louder and kicked harder than Brianna's M4. The recoil tore the scope from his eye. It took what seemed forever to reposition the rifle. Through the scope, he saw John bent low but still coming at him. John raised his rifle and Billy ducked as a bullet smashed into the Escalade. When he looked up again, John was reloading. This time, Billy aimed lower, at John's crotch, and pulled the trigger. The recoil was the same. When Billy looked, John was still advancing, holding the rifle waist-high.

"Your shooting still sucks," he laughed.

Billy crawled under the Escalade and planted his elbows in the soil. He aimed at one of John's knees and pulled the trigger. He banged his head on the car with the recoil, but when he looked again, John was halfway across the clearing and still limping toward him.

Billy aimed at the ground in front of John. He prepared himself for the noise and the recoil. He pulled the trigger. Nothing happened. He pulled the trigger again. And again. Empty. Billy slithered backwards in a panic, eyes glued to the legs moving toward him. The back of his belt caught on something in the undercarriage and for a moment Billy was stuck. Then he heard a shot and saw John's rifle drop to the ground, his legs crumble. John's face fell into view, his eyes looking directly toward Billy's. Billy held his breath while he waited, but John never moved, never closed his eyes.

Billy crawled backwards until he was out from under the car, then made his way crouching around the front, still clutching the empty rifle for comfort. John still hadn't moved. Billy started walking, then dropped the rifle and ran toward Brianna, lying on her back next to Earl. When he got close, she raised an arm and gave him a faint wave.

"Oh, God. Thank God. You're alive," he panted, slipping his arms around her shoulders and lifting her to a sitting position. She cried out. "You're hurt!" Blood dripped from a graze on her right arm. Earl's M16 lay on the ground next to her other side.

She flashed a crooked smile. "Not bad for shooting lefty," she said.

PART THREE

THE SUMMER

50

It took Doc five days to get to the west coast in his Mustang, almost twice as long as he expected. A flat tire at night in the desert west of Phoenix ended up costing him two days. His spare was worthless and the tow truck that rescued him would go only as far as Quartzite. The garage didn't open until morning so Doc checked into a motel. The garage didn't carry snow tires so Doc had to replace all four tires. It was 5:00pm by the time the car was ready. Doc stayed an extra night, caught up on his sleep, and left around noon the following day for Los Angeles.

He got off I-10 in Westwood Village and instinctively headed west toward the ocean, passing through Brentwood to Santa Monica along San Vicente Boulevard, four lanes wide with only one traffic light and a large grassy median populated by Coral trees and joggers. San Vicente ended humbly at a stoplight at Ocean Avenue. While waiting for the light to turn green, Doc watched as directly ahead the remnants of a blood-orange sun lowered itself into the Pacific. He turned left onto Ocean Ave and drove a couple of blocks when he saw the Georgian, an old Victorian-style hotel painted white with blue trim with a deep wrap-around porch that overlooked the ocean. It seemed to Doc to be the right place for him to end the drive and begin the journey.

After a good night's sleep, Doc showered and shaved, then got into his jeans and a blue work shirt. He rolled up his sleeves and looked at himself in the mirror. Clearly, he'd have to shop for some clothes more suitable for the California climate. He took $1500 in cash from the weekender, relocked the bag, then took it with him down to the lobby.

Doc asked at the front desk for the manager. After a minute, a woman appeared wearing a blue sports coat with *The Georgian* embroidered above the pocket. She wore a small badge that said, *B. Smith, Manager*. She asked if everything was okay.

Doc was casual and friendly. "Sure. Things are fine. I'm enjoying myself here." Then he lifted up the weekender. "Do you have lock boxes in the hotel vault for guests? I can't fit my bag in my room safe," he said.

She pointed to a corner of the registration desk. "The concierge can check your bag for you."

Doc adopted an intimate, regretful tone. "You see, it took me years to collect these family photos and documents, get them notarized and sealed. They are irreplaceable, important evidence in a lawsuit my mother is engaged in."

The manager cocked her head but wanted more. Doc leaned into her. "Reparations," he whispered.

"Oh, I see," she nodded. "In that case, your guest room number?" She wrote the number on a ticket, tore off the top part, and handed it to Doc. He held up the bag for her as she tied the rest of the ticket to the handle with a string. "You can present the ticket to anyone at the desk to retrieve your bag," she said. "We'll keep it in the vault for you." She reached out with her hand to take the bag from him.

Doc held onto the handle and let the bag drop to his side. "Thank you," said Doc. He held out a $20 bill in his other hand. "I was hoping to be able to place the bag in a lock box myself, if that's all right." He tilted his head. "Chain of evidence, you understand."

She hesitated, then took the bill from his hand. "Oh! Thank you. I will have to see some identification, though. A driver's license will suffice."

Showing ID was no longer an issue for Doc. He used his license when he checked-in. He took out his wallet and held out his license for her to see.

She glanced at it. "Thank you," she said. "This way."

She led him behind the reception desk through a doorway into a large office area. People at several small desks were talking on phones or typing on computers. At the far end of the room was a large rectangular metal vault door, open to reveal a closed day gate blocking entry into the vault. She used a key to open the gate. They walked past about a dozen suitcases with tags in the small anteroom before entering the interior of the vault.

Doc guessed there were about 100 safe deposit boxes of three difference sizes lining the far wall and two long walls of the interior of the vault. Keys hung from one of the pair of locks in the doors of boxes not yet assigned. About half of the boxes were already in use.

The largest boxes were positioned low on the wall adjacent to the floor. Ms. Smith led Doc to a large safe deposit box at the bottom of the far wall. A key hung from one of the two locks. She took a ring of guard keys from her jacket pocket, selected one, stooped down and placed the key in the vacant lock. She turned both keys and opened the door, then pulled out the empty container box.

"Right here is fine," he said. He took the box from her and placed it on the floor. He opened the lid, placed the weekender into the box, and closed the lid, then slid the box himself back through the open door. Ms. Smith closed the door to the box and turned both keys, locking the door. She retrieved her key on the keyring, put the keyring in her pocket, and handed the other key to Doc.

She pointed at the key in his hand as she spoke. "The box number, *126*, is printed on the key. If you lose it, we'll have to charge you for a locksmith to open the box and to make a new key and lock. That won't be cheap so don't lose it."

"Got it," said Doc. "Thanks." He put the key in his front pocket and gave it a pat.

"Just show your ID to anyone at the desk when you're ready to get your bag," she said. "They'll alert me or the Assistant Manager to escort you into the vault."

He walked out of the lobby, the ticket and key shoved deep into his pocket.

He found a donut shop a few blocks from the hotel where he bought coffee and three newspapers, then searched the classified for apartments. *The Santa Monica Astro* listed only places for sale. *The Daily News* and *The View* together listed only a half dozen places. None looked promising.

Doc sipped his coffee and thought about it. He'd stay at The Georgian for as long as it took for him to find an apartment. The rules had changed. He was in no rush.

There was an ad in the *Astro* for the West Los Angeles Guitar Gallery on Pico Blvd, just a couple of blocks away. Guitar Gallery was part of a national chain and a superstore that mostly sold guitars and amps, but a good place to get some sense of the local music scene. Doc finished his coffee and headed for the store. It took only a couple of minutes.

He walked through the clamor and commotion of notes and near-misses emitted from customers trying out guitars and keyboards. The Musicians' Bulletin Board was on a back wall. He read through flyers, index cards and scraps of paper listing schedules for local venues, ads for music lessons and notices from bands looking for musicians and singers. There was only one group looking for a drummer and that was for a surf band. Doc wrote the number down anyway, just in case.

He was almost out the door, writing off the effort as a waste of time, when he heard someone starting up on an acoustic drum kit. The drum sound had impact and resonance. The drummer's style was fast and clean, the technique mature and confident. Each riff had a clever hook. Doc was intrigued so entered the tiny drum section and was surprised to see a teenage girl, maybe 14, playing a used set on display, a vintage 1965 Ludwig six-piece kit in black oyster pearl—same wrap as Ringo's.

The kit was priced high, more for a collector than a working musician, but that didn't bother him. Not anymore. Doc slowly circled the kit as the kid continued to play. Despite a few scratches and some pitting on the chrome, the kit looked and sounded like the drum set he always wanted. All eight cymbals were classic Avedis Zildjian. The 22-inch ride in particular was thick and heavy, a little slow on the attack and long on the decay, and likely started out as half a set of symphonic orchestra cymbals that some kid stole from his high school. The hi-hats and crash cymbals though were thin and still sounded crisp. The rides and crashes blended overtones and crested like waves at the beach.

The kid stopped playing and left the pair of

sticks on the big floor tom. Doc picked them up—7A's, too thin and light for his hands. He found a pair of 2As with plastic tips on the counter and took his place on the drummer's throne. He twirled the sticks to find the sweet spot, then launched into familiar routines and fills, sampling each drum and cymbal in varying combinations. He couldn't stop smiling.

He hadn't found a place to live, but as the saying goes, love keeps little company with logic. He negotiated with the manager, a funny and warm fellow, Jack Daguio, who after hearing Doc just moved to town, accepted a grand in cash down to hold the kit for a week while Doc looked for a job and place to live. Jack, Doc learned, was from Honolulu, the same age as Doc, and a drummer himself. The two men connected immediately.

Jack handed Doc the receipt for the deposit. "Ever sell?"

"Why? You got something available?" said Doc.

"Could be, could be," said Jack. "What else do you play? Our stock is mostly new guitars and amps. We don't move a lot of drums here and corporate's not looking to expand." He looked a little guilty. "Guitars take up less floorspace."

"I know my way around electric guitars and synth keyboards. I play some six-string and a little bass. I'm pretty decent on blues harp."

Jack rubbed his chin. "I could start you part-time, minimum wage, no bennies," he said, "and see how you work out. After a couple of weeks, I could upgrade you to full-time with a raise and bennies. You could make a few bucks while you look around for a band gig. Might even connect with somebody here. Sound like something you'd be interested in?"

"Will my employee discount apply to the Ludwig kit?" Doc asked.

Jack laughed and shook his head, "No discounts on used gear, but if you stay on, I'll find a way to cut you a little slack." They shook on it, agreeing Doc would start Monday.

"Any suggestions on where I can find an apartment nearby? I like this part of town."

"What did I already tell you? This is working out." He told Doc about friends with a studio apartment available nearby on the ocean, both amateur musicians Jack knew well. "She sings and plays piano. He's plays bass. I've been playing with the both of them on and off for years." Jack raised his eyebrows. "They're a bit picky and the place ain't cheap. It's in Malibu."

"I might be able to swing it. They have a problem with drummers?"

"Not if you use practice heads and cymbals." Jack smiled. "I got a used set that'll go nicely with the Ludwig kit. I can let you have it for a song."

Doc laughed. "Man, you don't quit, do you?" He held his hand out. "Give me their address. I'll check it out now."

Jack wrote the address and directions on his business card. He handed the card to Doc, saying he would call ahead and let them know he was coming.

Doc drove up Ocean Avenue and down Pacific Coast Highway. It took almost 20 minutes to drive the four miles, but he was getting use to the traffic. It wasn't that hard to find. Homes were built on the beach side, but because of concerns about erosion and safety, few homes were built across the street under the cliffs on the east side of PCH.

The houses were on large lots to show off more of the beach and ocean. Some were modern mansions while others were small ranch-style houses from an earlier era. A few looked run-down, waiting for the lot to be sold and cleared to make room for new construction. Although the beach was public, this far north it was rocky, certainly picturesque but not as welcoming to swimmers as further south. Except for the flow of traffic on PCH, home owners here had an expectation of privacy.

The directions on Jack's card lead Doc to a modest bungalow on an oversized lot with plenty of vacant beach on both sides. The house looked old, tiny and isolated. He checked the address on the card. There didn't seem to be an apartment attached.

There was no driveway so Doc parked behind an old Lincoln on the gravel shoulder and rang the bell. Fred and Dorothy Wilburn greeted him together and invited him in. They were expecting him, Dorothy said, explaining Jack had called. Doc felt less anxious having already been introduced by Jack, but felt even better when he saw Dorothy was

African American.

Doc followed them into the living room to sit and talk. A black baby grand by an east facing window practically dominated the room. The lid was open, indicating that the piano was probably played daily. Towering behind the piano against the wall stood a dark maple double bass in a padded wood stand, its bow resting against the wall.

Doc chatted with Dorothy about the piano, a Steinway, as Fred brought glasses and a pitcher of lemonade on a tray from the kitchen. "When Jack said you played bass, I assumed an electric bass guitar" he said to Fred.

Fred said he had a Fender Jazzman bass guitar and Bassman amp "'somewhere," but he hardly played it anymore. "This beauty," he said, gesturing with his glass toward the double bass, "was made in Romania by Alexandru Ozon, a master luthier." He winked at his Dorothy. "My second love." She rolled her eyes.

"Did Jack tell you that's how we met?" she asked Doc, who simply shook his head. "We had a gig and our regular bass player couldn't make it. Jack was on drums and brought Fred to sit-in."

"She was making eyes at me all night."

She heard it before. "You wish."

The three talked more about music, then Dorothy asked what brought Doc to Los Angeles. He was prepared for the question and told them a half truth. Doc always wanted to move to southern California, but felt obligated to live close to his mother who was elderly. She died recently and he ended up selling her house for a big profit. Dorothy patted Doc on the arm. "You were a good son," she said. Doc looked at the floor to avoid her eyes.

She turned to Fred and they exchanged a silent signal. "Well, let's show you the apartment," said Fred. He slapped his leg and stood. They took Doc back out the front door and around to the garage.

Or what had been the garage. The apartment was a converted two-car garage attached to the north side of the house. It was quiet inside, insulated from road noise. It had a large front room with a galley kitchen by the door and a bedroom at the back with a bathroom and shower. Windows to the north and west provided views of the ocean. An area in front of the sliding glass door in the back was the right size to accommodate his new Ludwig kit.

When he opened the sliding door, a sea breeze greeted him like an old friend. He stepped out onto a wooden deck. A stone fire pit in the center of the deck marked the unofficial border between the tenant's and the owners' sides. On Doc's side were two chaises and a little round red plastic table. A thin wood railing ran along the edge of the deck low enough not to obscure the ocean view. At the Wilburn's end, a steep planked stairway with a landing halfway led down 30 feet to a rocky stretch of the public beach below. The view of the ocean was magnificent.

Standing there on the deck, Doc filled his

lungs with the salt air. No one said a word. Doc was already sold on the place. He hoped they were as certain about him.

They descend the steps to the beach as Dorothy explained that people rarely swam or sunbathed here because the beach was so rocky, but it was pretty, especially at sunset.

Supporting the deck from below were three huge circular concrete pilings sheltering a collapsed beach umbrella, some folding chairs, an empty ice chest and a bin full of beach towels. Chained to a piling was the Wilburn's six-man inflatable dinghy, complete with oars and a small half-horsepower engine. Fred even showed Doc where they hid the key to the lock. Dorothy said they use the dinghy sometimes to join friends on their boats rather than drive down to the marina.

Doc commented on how peaceful the place was. "The privacy works both ways," said Fred. "I get worried leaving the house empty for a few days when Dorothy and I drive down to San Diego. We got an alarm system, but having a tenant here, one we can trust, helps make the place look not so vulnerable. You know what I mean, right?"

"I'll probably end up spending most of my evenings right here on the deck," said Doc. "Can't think of a prettier place to be."

They went over the rental agreement and other details, like parking space and trash pickup, at the Wilburn's kitchen table. Fred made coffee and brought out pastries from the refrigerator. Doc offered to pay six month's rent in advance. He explained he just got to town and hadn't established a bank account yet, but could pay them with cash within a couple of hours. As Doc anticipated, the Wilburn's were practically giddy at the thought of cash, which they wouldn't have to declare.

They signed a one-year lease and shook hands. The only caveat was for Doc not to play drums "too late into the night, even with those practice heads Jack'll try to sell you." Doc told them it wouldn't be a problem.

They walked him out to his car.

"Is that a '78?" asked Fred.

"Guilty," responded Doc. He wasn't sure what was coming.

"That was Mustang's worst year. You made it out here in that?"

Doc decided to get ahead of the conversation. "I'm looking for a new car."

Fred was a dog with a bone. "You could have afforded to buy yourself a decent car, son. Why—?"

"Fred!" said Dorothy. "Leave your nose out of his business."

"I'm just trying to understand—"

"It was my mother's car," said Doc. "When she died, I just couldn't... you know."

Dorothy gave Fred a look.

"But now I'm ready for another car." Doc was desperate to change the subject.

"Practical or sporty?" asked Dorothy. "You should get something that's fun to drive out here."

"Sporty," said Doc. Why not?

"My friend, Marsha, lives in Brentwood. She's selling her sports car, a BMW, but it's a stick. Do you drive a manual?"

"Dorothy, this car is a manual," said Fred, trying to make a comeback.

Marsha was selling her BMW Z3 roadster. Doc checked it out the next day. It was a 1997 painted old-school British racing green with a light brown convertible top. The interior was a matching brown in leather. The mileage was under 30,000 and the car was in mint condition. Marsha told Doc she loved the car but grew tired sitting in traffic with her foot on the clutch. She was looking for the same model as an automatic.

Doc had to suppress a groan the first time he bent down to squeeze in behind the wheel, but a test drive sealed the deal. The following day he drove to the DMV where he passed his California driver's test, registered the Z3, and ordered a vanity license plate, *LNGGDBY*, after his favorite book, set in Los Angeles. He sold the Mustang for $100 four days later to one of the other salesmen at the Guitar Gallery.

The vanity plate on his new car was a statement Doc had to make. For many prisoners their book was the Bible, but Doc's guiding light was *The Long Goodbye*, a book he read while working in the prison library.

Many claimed to interpret the Bible word-for-word, but Doc understood what is written between the lines is often as or more important than the printed words themselves. While beautifully written, the story beneath Raymond Chandler's detective novel told of friendship and betrayal, how even people meeting by chance can make a difference to each other. After all, friends, spouses and lovers all start out as strangers.

Doc saw his world in those pages. Most convicts he met had no one but themselves to blame for their mistakes, but they never got a break at the moment they needed it most. Everyone should have the option to reach for the stars, but to people without means, poverty and bigotry are forces as powerful as gravity. Offering to help at the right moment can make all the difference. Chandler's story inspired Doc to reclaim some part of his former self and forge his own path out of the wreck his life had become.

Doc wasn't sure when it happened, but driving the little roadster back to his apartment by the ocean, he knew, somehow, he was on the right path now.

51

It was a slow Wednesday. Doc was thinking about lunch while demonstrating a vibraphone to a customer who was never going to buy. He snapped to attention when he heard a familiar voice call his name. He turned around and there were Billy and Brianna. "I'll be damned," said Doc. He put the mallets down on the metal keys.

The customer picked them up. "Okay if I try it?"

"Be my guest," said Doc without looking back. He hopped over and hugged Billy first, then Brianna, like it had been years, not months. "I'll be damned," he repeated. "You made it. When did you get in?" He dropped his voice and the smile. "Everything okay? Who knows you're here?"

"Nobody, Bro. Just us. Drove the whole way in her Jeep." Billy said with a nod to Brianna.

"Then I know you did all the driving," Doc said to Brianna. "Billy can't drive a stick."

"I can now," he said, putting an arm around

Brianna "This lady's a better teacher than you, Doc. And, she saved my life."

Doc's smile almost evaporated. "Yeah? Something I should know about?"

"We're good now," said Billy. "No worries. I'll tell you about it later."

Brianna told him they arrived a week ago and began looking for him right away, visiting music stores in the area. They're also looking for an apartment.

"We're here to stay," she said, then asked, "You ever join a band?"

He shook his head with a sheepish grin. "Played some but nothing worth mentioning." He turned to Billy. "But I bought a couple of great kits."

"A couple?"

"Yeah, you'll have to see them. Where you guys staying now?"

"At the Sandbar in Santa Monica."

"You guys might as well stay with me while you look for a place. It'll be tight, if you don't mind. I got a small studio, but it's on the beach and got a nice deck. No neighbors aside from the landlord and they're nice people. And there's beer in the fridge. We got a lot of catching up to do."

"Wait till you hear what we've been through," said Billy. "We got a lot to talk about."

"I bet. Tell you what," Doc said, looking at the time. He remembered his customer but he was gone. "It's been slow. Maybe Jack will let me off. You can follow me back to my place. Wait until you see my new car." He looked them both up and down. He could hardly contain himself. "Christ! I can't tell you how good it is to see you guys."

They followed Doc in the Jeep back to his apartment. Brianna in particular loved the place. Billy stood by the sliding glass door with Doc, admiring the drums. "This is my practice set, too vintage for gigs." He pointed at the large chrome-on-brass snare drum. "I take that heavy mother with me to play. I got a small three-piece Tama kit in green pearl, 20-inch kick drum. Jack lets me keep at the store but, honestly, other than sitting in a little, I haven't gigged in a while."

"This one is nice," said Billy. "How old?"

"1965. Here, let me show you something."

Billy stepped back. Doc lifted off the tom-toms and the mount from the top of the bass drum and put them on the couch. He took the pedal off and laid the bass drum down on the floor.

Brianna came over. "What are you doing?" She put an arm around Billy as they watched Doc removed the tension rods on the exposed front side. He lifted the wooden rim and white opaque resonance head off the drum, exposing the interior. He stepped back to give them a better view.

Brianna broke the silence. "Doesn't that affect the sound?" asked Brianna.

"Not the way he plays," joked Billy.

Stacks of $100 bills filled the filled the drum.

"Actually, all that paper deadens the resonance and makes for a perfect thud."

"I bet it sounds like a million bucks," said Billy.

52

Doc introduced Billy and Brianna to Fred and Dorothy who, over more lemonade and Fred's chocolate chip cookies, passed along the number of their realtor to Brianna. Brianna hadn't seen or heard a Steinway baby grand up close so at her request, Dorothy played a classical piece by Chopin and sang and played, "Yesterday" by The Beatles. That evening, Doc built a small fire in the pit and sat with Billy and Brianna on the deck, sharing Chinese takeout with chopsticks on paper plates. They drank beer from the cooler as they watched the sun set and Billy and Brianna told Doc what went down after he'd left Gainesville.

Brianna showed Doc the scar on her right arm from CJ's bullet.

"Christ! You're lucky to be alive."

"Tell me about it," said Billy. "We both thought we were goners."

"And lucky to have made it here. This is such a cool place." She turned to Billy. "I love the ocean, the air. Everything feels right."

She finished the last of her Strawberry Blonde Ale and placed the empty on the deck next to her feet. "I feel responsible for what happened," she said, more to Doc than Billy, but avoiding their eyes. "I got too used to things around me, even when I knew something wasn't right about it. I knew those guys for a long time. We had laughs and I thought they were friends, but... they...." She shook her head at her feet. "No, I just ignored the signs. It's so obvious now. After they tried...." She took a deep breath of ocean air and looked at Billy. "When it all fell apart and I didn't know which way to go, Billy said 'Let's go to California and find Doc.' I'm glad we did."

Billy gave her shoulder a squeeze. "Hey, you saved my bacon. And we're still together and safe now." He looked at Doc. "I'm just sorry to drop all this stuff on you like this. What an adventure, huh?"

The only sound was from waves breaking on the beach. Doc put down his chopsticks and dug into the cooler.

"I used to think I should go it alone, swim or sink all by myself, but now I know, even if I could make it on my own, a solitary life ain't all that worth it," he said as he rummaged through the ice. "Things are better when you share them with people you care about."

"People are a multiplier," said Brianna.

"A what?" asked Billy.

"Something that intensifies something," she answered.

"Like drinking!" joked Billy.

Doc laughed and pulled out a Boomtown Beer. He took a long drink before he handed the bottle to Billy who swigged and then passed it to Brianna. She drank and handed the bottle back to Doc. He leaned forward, his expression dead serious in the flickering yellow firelight, extinguishing the smiles on Billy's and Brianna's faces. "We're in this together, now, the three of us. We got to watch each other's back."

Billy and Brianna nodded in silent agreement. Doc put the bottle down on the deck and leaned back into his chaise, his posture relaxed.

"*Woe*! Sorry. Didn't mean to get so heavy there."

"It's okay, Doc," said Brianna. She put a hand on Billy's arm. "We understand."

Doc sat up and addressed them both. "Have you thought more about what you're going to do with your money?"

Billy looked at Brianna. "Your money, your decision," she said. He looked at Doc.

"What are you thinking?" Billy said.

"An investment," said Doc, "an investment in a dream."

And then he told them about his dream.

After a while the fire burned out and the air became chilly. Billy and Brianna drove back to their hotel to check out and get the rest of their things. They left their backpack with Billy's share of the money in Doc's closet. They stayed five more days, sleeping on the couch, enjoying the beach and the peace, until they found an apartment in Venice on Ozone Avenue, a half-block from the beach and between Doc's place and the Guitar Gallery. Billy rented a safe deposit box at a bank to store most of his share, while putting a few thousand in checking and savings accounts. Doc followed up by getting his own safe deposit box at the same bank to store the cash hidden in his bass drum.

All Brianna's Jeep needed after the long trip was a wash and an oil change, but Billy needed a car. A day after they moved into their new apartment, Billy found an ad for a white Toyota Tacoma with a short bed for sale on Craigslist.

The day was sunny and getting warm. On the way to Westwood Village to meet the seller and see the truck, Billy took Teddy's wallet out of his jacket pocket and held it up.

"What's that?" she asked.

"It's somebody's wallet I found. I thought maybe I could use his ID if we buy the car, so I don't have to use my real name." She looked doubtful. "What do you think?" he asked.

"Naw, you don't have to do that," she said. "Anyway, there'll be some kind of official form you'll have to sign, a temporary transfer form or something, that is a legal document just like in Florida. If you sign somebody else's name, that could be forgery."

"You think so? I was just trying—"

You're going to have to use your real name anyway when you register the truck."

"Oh, yeah, I guess...."

"Unless...." He waited for her to complete her thought. "Unless I buy the truck for you and register it in my name. You won't have to put your name on anything. Maybe it's a little paranoid, but...."

"No, I like it. Let's do that." Billy put the wallet back in his jacket pocket. "Smart *and* beautiful. Thanks!"

Billy bought the truck for cash and headed back to their new apartment, Brianna leading in the Jeep. The day was heating up so Billy slipped off his jacket, rolled it up and stuffed it behind the driver's seat. Their apartment had no garage, but street parking was restricted to residents so Billy found a space on the street one house down from theirs.

About a week later, someone broke into his truck at night. Brianna put in an insurance claim. The next day, the insurance company adjuster, Ken Law, examined the door and doorframe closely, running his fingers along the edges.

"See here?" he said, pointing at a spot by the driver's door. "The doorframe is dented and bent just a little. Can you see that?" Billy looked closely where he was pointing but couldn't see anything wrong. "You bought this truck used, right? Well, what the previous owner didn't tell you was it was broken into before."

"She didn't mention that, Mr. Law," said Brianna.

"Call me, Ken, please. Well, I wouldn't expect that she would tell you. They should, but the seller doesn't have to."

"That doesn't sound fair," said Billy.

"I see this a lot," he said. "What the thieves do is they shove a thin crowbar in between the door and the frame and slowly separate the door from the frame, just enough to pop the bolt out of the box in the strike plate. Whoever repaired the damage painted over it, but didn't try to straighten out the frame." He pointed at a spot along the frame. Billy and Brianna bent down for a closer look. "The doorframe is mis-aligned here. All whoever broke in had to do was bump the door here and it opens." He demonstrated by pushing his hip into the door panel. They all hear a *click* and the door swung open a few inches. "I hope they didn't get anything valuable."

They stole Billy's nylon jacket, his new sunglasses and the contents of the glove box, which included the truck manual and a map of L.A. Teddy's wallet was in the jacket, but Billy didn't care about that. He missed the sunglasses the most. The next day they installed alarms in both of their vehicles. It seemed their neighborhood was not as safe as they thought.

After a few days sitting on the beach watching the ocean, swimmers and boats, they both agreed sailing looked like fun. They signed up for an eight-week course at Duffy's Sailboat Charters in Marina del Rey. It wasn't easy, but they earned their certificates from the American Sailing Association. Billy bought a 25-year old sailboat within the week, moving the cash from the safe deposit box into his checking account. The Beneteau 331 was a 34-foot sloop with a 35 HP Volvo diesel inboard motor. Billy paid $17,900 in cash to the couple that ran the business, Joe and Penny Duffy.

They christened the boat *Red Wind*, which is what Billy called the rust-colored smog they could see some days hovering over the beach. They docked their new boat in Marina del Rey along with Duffy's small fleet of sailboats. Brianna and Billy wanted to try fishing, so Penny helped them pick out some gear. A few weeks later, Billy and Brianna sailed with them on *Red Wind* to Catalina Island, giving Billy and Brianna the opportunity to try out their new sailing skills under expert supervision. They passed. Brianna felt she was living in a dream and Billy was just starting to forget his nightmare.

53

The CITGO sign burned red, white and blue, a patriotic Boston landmark. Locals knew the sign represented a Venezuelan oil conglomerate and had nothing to do with Old Glory, but that didn't matter. For decades, the red triangular eye in the middle of the giant white square at the top of 660 Beacon Street watched tirelessly over the inhabitants of Kenmore Square. When a game was being played down the street at Fenway, the sign's eye could be seen peering over the top of the Green Monster as if to check on the Sox's progress. The blood reds, ocean blues and cloud-like whites came from LEDs installed in 2005, replacing neon tubes first used in 1965. People from all over town looked on the sign like the face of an old friend.

Kyle watched the rich colors dance across the sign in the cold and crisp winter air. He took a sip from a bottle of Sam Adams without looking away. He wasn't particularly fond of Sam Adams but it was on sale.

"Carolyn, you want a beer?" he said to her back.

Without turning around, she held up her mug of coffee to show him she was fine.

They sat in silence on the fire escape. They were five blocks west of the CITGO sign and four stories above Beacon Street. Kyle subleased the one-bedroom walkup six weeks earlier from a friend who spent the winter in Florida. It was a considerable step-down in size and quality from his modern three-bedroom condo in Newton. That place had a wide balcony made of redwood furnished with chaise lounges and tables and a small refrigerator stocked with imported beers. The view was of tree-covered hills, the leaves changing with the seasons. The place also had a mortgage he could no longer afford. It was at that point that Katie had enough and left.

He toasted the CITGO sign then fought the urge to drop the empty bottle onto the sidewalk below.

The fire escape under them was an 80-year-old black scaffold of rusty round metal bars. They accessed it by crawling through the bedroom window. The owner warned Kyle to prop the window open when he went out on the fire escape because the window tended to slid shut on its own. Carolyn always carried an apartment key just in case.

Kyle leaned against the exterior brownstone wall by the window, left leg stretched out straight, still aching from the skiing accident almost a year ago. An open envelope rested on his lap. He took a moment away from the sign and his thoughts to admire the way Carolyn's soft red leather motorcycle jacket followed the shape of her shoulders and tapered at her waist.

They met at the gym. He noticed the attractive young Asian woman stepping onto the treadmill next to his. He was pleased when she asked him for help adjusting the settings on the machine. He showed her how to select a program and difficulty level. It really wasn't that hard. She explained this was her first time at this gym. She just moved from Canada for a job that fell through and was using a free voucher to try out the gym. He told her he was trying to get out of his contract and they both got a laugh out of it. Things moved quickly after that, and with all the bad happening to him, he was grateful for her and the comfort she brought him.

Carolyn Jesse Kasaka sat on the edge of the grating drinking black coffee from an ugly brown ceramic mug. She'd wrapped her long black hair in an effortless updo with a few loose tendrils pulled behind her ear to settle on her shoulders. Clad in skinny black jeans, her legs dangled between the vertical railings, hanging down toward the street below. The distant sound of traffic played in the background. Neither of them spoke.

Three hours earlier he was in the kitchen stirring pasta in a rolling boil when Carolyn answered a knock at the door.

"Hey, Shelly," said Carolyn. She raised her voice a notch. "Hey, Kyle. It's your sister." Carolyn held the door open for her. "Come on in." Peggy followed Carolyn into the kitchen.

"Hey, brother." Peggy waved even though they stood only about six feet apart.

"Hey, sis. What's up?"

Kyle and his sister rarely saw each other. His first thought was she was in a jam and he, broke, was in no position to help. Plus, he and Carolyn only made enough pasta for two.

Peggy held up an envelope.

"What's that? Another bill?" asked Kyle.

"It's a certified letter from the Los Angeles Police Department, I had to sign for it."

"What do they want with you?" Kyle asked, genuinely concern.

"It's not for me," she said, pointing to the front of the envelope. "It's addressed to Leonard Theodore. Hall."

Kyle stopped stirring. He looked at his sister for an explanation.

"It came the other day. I almost threw it out. He was such a P.O.S. But I thought you might know where he was living and send it to him. You know, if you want to. I don't know." She shook her head and spoke to them both. "I don't care. He must have been living with me when he renewed his license so he used my address." She held up the envelope. "I opened it already."

Water spilled over onto the stovetop. Kyle

gave the pasta a stir and turned the heat down.

Carolyn grabbed the envelope from Peggy's hand. "Here, let me take a look," she said.

More water spilled. Kyle kept stirring. "What's it say, Carolyn?"

Carolyn took out the letter. "It's a couple of pages, dated almost a week ago. The letterhead says it's from the *Public Communications Group, Los Angeles Police Department.*" She started to read the letter to herself, then remembered her manners. Without taking her eyes off the letter, she asked Peggy, "You want to stay for supper?"

"Sure," said Peggy. "Smells good. Spaghetti and meatballs?"

"Penne," she said, continuing to read.

"Wicked! Your favorite, little brother." She went to the fridge and took out a beer. "I'll heat up the sauce. Is it in the cupboard?"

"Middle shelf. Help yourself to a beer," Carolyn mumbled. She finished reading and handed the letter to Kyle. She took over pasta stirring duty but kept an eye on Kyle as he sat at the table and read:

Dear Mr. Leonard Theodore Hall:

Attached is a photocopy of a Massachusetts driver's license retrieved by officers as part of a cache of stolen property recovered from an individual allegedly involved in a vehicle burglary ring. We believe the driver's license may belong to you.

On November 12 this year, Police were called to a retail clothing store in the Brentwood

Gardens Mall and arrested a juvenile shoplifting subject apprehended by mall security. In her possession were several driver's licenses, including one we believe may belong to you. When questioned, the subject stated you gave her the license, but she was unable to provide any credible explanation to support her claim.

Our Auto Burglary Task Force (California Penal Code 459) would appreciate any information you can provide to us regarding your license and if it was stolen, the date, time of day, place, and other details you deem may help us in our investigation. Please contact me directly by phone, email or mail using the information at the top of this letter. The actual physical license will be released back to you at the conclusion of the investigation.

Most Angelenos are law-abiding citizens who welcome visitors. I am sorry if you were a victim of a crime while here. Your experience should not discourage you from visiting Los Angeles again soon.

Very truly yours,
RICHARD W. BECKER, Police Commander
Commanding Officer
Community Affairs Group

After dinner, Peggy helped clean up then left to visit her friends, Ronnie and Norton, in J.P.

"I'm making coffee," Carolyn said as she slipped a pod in the coffee maker. "You want?"

"No," he said, deep in thought. She gave him a strange look. They both were too quiet.

While she waited for the water to boil, Kyle grabbed a jacket from the closet. He took a bottle of beer from the fridge, then headed for the bedroom. She heard him open the window. By the time the coffee was ready, she had her coat on. The bedroom was cold. She grabbed a paperback off the night-stand and put it down on the sill under the open window. She followed him out to the fire escape.

"You're letting out all the heat," she said. "Give me a hand."

"You got your key, too?" She ignored him.

Kyle lifted one arm. Together, one arm each, they closed the window on the book, leaving a small gap at the bottom of the frame.

She stood over him holding the mug. Steam rose into the night air.

"How do you know the guy in the letter?"

"Teddy? He used to work for me, that's all."

"Are you going to do something about it?" she asked, but Kyle raised the bottle to his lips and stared at the CITGO sign. He finished the beer, then rested the empty bottle between two bars left to him so it wouldn't roll off the platform.

"Do you care?" she asked. He was holding the envelope in his hand but not looking at it.

"Don't know yet. No, not really. Why should I?"

She sat down by the railing, slipping her legs through the opening with her back to Kyle. Neither she nor Kyle said another word until they went back into the apartment.

His life was shit. He lost his club, his condo, his savings and his dreams, even his friends, and he had no protection, no connections since the Russians took out Moe. He heard they considered the debt settled, but that didn't make him feel much better.

Christina, Lexi's friend, told him the two thieves' first names, or at least a name and a nickname. The big white dude was "Billy" and the older black guy was "Doc." These were the guys that caused him all his troubles. That's all he knew about them until Peggy handed him the envelope. Now he knew at least one of them was in L.A., maybe both. Kyle figured that was the only way Teddy's license would end up in there. They wouldn't leave the money behind so there was a better than even chance the money was in L.A, too. It was a gamble, but the stakes were high—it was in fact the whole pot on the table—and he was at the end of his rope. It had to take the shot.

The letter said the "Auto Burglary Task Force" was involved, which probably meant the license was stolen out of a car, some type of vehicle. Kyle figured if this juvie could tell him where she got the license, where the car was parked, he'd have a street and maybe an address for these guys. The lead had potential and that's all the encouragement Kyle needed. He'd played worse odds in the past and come out ahead. Tonight, he'd give Carolyn some song and dance, then fly out to L.A. and track the bastards down. He'd hurt them enough to make them hand over the money. Then he'd have to kill them if he wanted to keep himself safe. They were stone-killers. But that wasn't the only reason. He *wanted* to kill them.

54

Carolyn Jesse Kasaka swung her legs as she sipped coffee and watched traffic below. She kept her back to Kyle to prevent him from seeing her smile.

When Tiffany told her about Teddy making the deposits, Jesse worked out the details of the plan. It was short, simple and let others take the risks. She and Tiffany were supposed to be safe no matter what happened.

Once Tiffany showed up in New York with the money, Jesse planned for them to relax and celebrate New Year's Day together. The next day when the banks opened at 9:00, they would deposit most of the money into the seven accounts Jesse set up at five different banks. They'd have lunch if they were hungry, then take a cab to the airport and use cash to buy tickets for flights to Heathrow that evening. The banks would report the large deposits to the IRS, each well over the $10,000 limit, but that didn't matter. By the time the feds responded, the funds would have been withdrawn from the London banks. She and Tiffany and the $2.9 million would be gone.

Carolyn Jesse Kasaka sipped from her cup, unconcerned that the coffee already cooled. She revisited the horror she felt almost a year ago during the first hours of New Year's Day when the plan started falling apart. The memories transported her from Kenmore Square to Times Square, from sitting on a fire escape four stories over Beacon Street to looking out a hotel window fourteen stories above Broadway.

The last text Tiffany sent Jesse was right after Tiffany had counted the money. There was a million more than they planned, almost three million! Jesse had let out a shriek of delight and danced around the hotel room and jumped on the bed until she flopped down breathless. Then... she heard nothing more from Tiffany. The drive from Boston to New York should have taken Tiffany four hours, five tops. Jesse waited thirty minutes before texting Tiffany to see if she was on her way, but got no response. She texted again ten minutes later, but... nothing. She called and panic welled up in her when the call went straight to voicemail without first ringing. Tiffany, or somebody else, had turned off her phone.

Sitting on the fire escape separated by eleven months and 200 miles, Jesse felt shame for first thinking Tiffany ran out on her. Jesse understood it was a lot of money and people are weak, but she knew Tiffany. They were friends, they were partners, and they were lovers. Together they were invincible and with that realization came respect and the fear of disappointing the other. No way Tiffany double-crossed her. Otherwise, why would she have texted her updates? Everything was going as planned. No, it must be a dead battery or God-forbid an accident! All Jesse could do was wait. She sat on the bed and tried to watch TV.

After a full day of hearing nothing, Jesse took a flight to Boston. It was January 2nd. They should have already deposited cash at the banks and be on their way to Kennedy. She took an Uber from Logan to Tiffany's building. She had a key to the apartment but walked past the door when she saw the yellow police tape. Having nowhere else to go, Jesse got a room at the Park Plaza. That evening she went to The Improper Bostonian to have a drink at the bar and learn what she could. She had never been there before, so needed time to find someone she could talk to. It was almost midnight by the time a bartender told her. The rumor was one of the dancers was murdered in her apartment on New Year's Eve, a drug deal or something. Through the gossip and speculation, Jesse pictured what really happened to Tiff and the money.

Jesse never met the two tools Tiffany picked for the job, but Tiffany told her everything she knew about them. Billy's full name was William Kaye, no middle name, and Doc's last name was Hayes. Tiffany could never get Doc's first name out of him or Billy. It was like a game between them and at the time didn't matter. She knew all about their sad plans post robbery. Fleeing to Hawaii was a pathetic fantasy Tiffany planted in Billy's empty brain just to keep him in line. On the other hand, Doc's goal of going to Phoenix for his asthma or something sounded genuine enough. Jesse knew with the money they had now, Doc and Billy could go anywhere.

But Jesse couldn't just walk away. She spent too much, sacrificed too much and so much was at stake. She bled money to set this up and was almost broke. The first step for her was to figure out where Billy and Doc were. They stole her money and they murdered Tiffany. That would cost them more than just money. It will cost them their lives.

She was certain if anyone learned where they went, it would be Kyle. He was the person at the center of this. She had about a month before she would max out her cards, then she would be out of options. She found an old, inexpensive hotel on Farrington Avenue not far from the club that would help her stretch her remaining funds.

Jesse learned a few things about Kyle that Tiffany hadn't shared, including Kyle's workout schedule. She sidled up to him at his gym by dressing the part and chatting him up at an adjacent treadmill. Twice they went for drinks after working out. They saw a movie in Kenmore Square one afternoon, and then went to her hotel room before he headed back home. He never mentioned Katie. When Moe disappeared and the Russians took over the club, his world fell apart. He lost his income, his condo and his girlfriend all within a week. Jesse let him stay with her until he found a place he could afford, a short-term sublet from an acquaintance on Beacon St. As expected, he returned the favor and invited her to move in with him.

After a few weeks Kyle worked up to telling Jesse a little about the robbery, the mob, and Moe. It brought her no closer to the money. She was almost out of funds and patience when Kyle told her they found Billy in Florida. When she learned Billy got away, she gave herself one more month before she'd have to give up and crash at her mother's house until she could save up enough to start the search again. Then, today, Peggy showed up with the letter and now their best guess puts the men and the money in L.A., maybe Brentwood.

Jesse smiled at the traffic below. Persistence, brains and luck. She was back in business.

She used her phone to book a 5:10 am non-stop to LAX for the next day on American. She used another app on her phone to reserve an Uber for 3:00 am to Logan. Before they go to bed tonight, she'll tell Kyle she received a text from her sister: Her mother was sick and in hospital so she has to fly to Toronto straight away. Kyle won't care. He'll probably book a flight for himself late in the day or at night, spend the day packing, and plan to sleep on the plane, getting to L.A. in the morning refreshed. By then she'd have been in L.A. for almost a day.

She had a full name and now a city so an eight-hour-plus lead should be enough with the information she had and he didn't. She didn't know for certain how Kyle would work it, but could guess. Using the information from the letter, he could learn the girl's identify from the security guard or from a sales person at the mall where the girl was arrested, maybe even read the police report, track her down, and get her to tell him what the car looked like and where it was parked when she stole the license. He could stakeout the street or scour the area looking for the car, then wait for Billy or Doc to show up. If that's the way he went at it, it could take him days and still yield nothing. She considered that approach desperate and a waste of time. If that's what he did, the worst estimate gave her a head start of a day if she were lucky. And she was always lucky.

PART FOUR

THE FALL

55

J esse wrapped her hair in a towel as she stepped
out of the shower. It felt good getting clean after
sitting on a plane for five hours even if it had
been first class. You can only do so much with those
little hot towels. She grabbed a second bath towel
and wrapped it around her body. The traffic report
was on the TV. Just like the weather, the traffic never
changed. Same as yesterday. Same as the last time
she was in L.A. And they'd be the same tomorrow.

Still, she loved the view. From the balcony
she could see Venice Boardwalk and a bike path that
curved back and forth between the Boardwalk and
the beach as though it couldn't make up its mind.
People were cycling and skating on roller blades,
more interested in the ride than a destination.

She fell back onto the bed, opened the towel
around her body, and let herself air dry while allowing herself a moment to reflect. She closed her
eyes against the background noise of the TV, but
no peace came. Instead her mind raced through

her new plan for moving the money. She'd buy three small cardboard moving boxes, packing material and gift paper at Home Depot, wrap the cash in sheets of bubble plastic, then cover each bundle with gift paper and a ribbon. The "gifts" would go into the moving boxes that she'd FedEx to her mother's house in Vancouver. She'd tell her mother they were Christmas gifts for some of her friends and not to open them, just leave them in the closet of her old bedroom until she arrived a few days later. She'd warn Mom not to tell anyone about the gifts or her visiting for the holidays. That would spoil the surprise! Jesse reminded herself to pick up something for Mom in the airport—a Lakers jersey should do the trick—just to keep her quiet. Vancouver wasn't London and Canada wasn't Europe, but from the safety of her mother's house Jesse would have time to make whatever arrangements she needed.

If Tiffany was here, she'd be out on the balcony or down by the pool right now sunning herself. Tiffany.... Tears filled Jesse's eyes. She told herself she felt tired, not weak, and focused on the people she needed to go through to get the money. She squeezed her eyes shut, forcing the last of the tears to run down the sides of her face and onto the pillow as sorrow and loss turned to white hot anger.

She sat up and re-wrapped the towel around her body, then grabbed her laptop from her carry-on and slid it onto the little desk in the corner. She unwound the towel from her hair and spread it on the chair, then sat at the desk and opened the laptop.

There were over 353 William Kaye's living in the United States. Examining them all would be foolish, wasting her limited time and money and be useless if he ran to Canada or Mexico or anywhere else. But now she and Kyle knew Billy was somewhere in L.A., which had about eighteen million people in the metro area. It could take him days or weeks, but Kyle could eventually track down Billy and the money. Jesse chewed her lip. She was aware this was a race. She hadn't gotten where she was without using her head.

People Finder was an app she'd used in the past. She knew it was a gamble that Billy still used his real name, but it was a pretty safe bet. Creating a new permanent identity wasn't as simple as in the movies, especially these days. These amateurs wouldn't know how to change identities without leaving breadcrumbs and it was unlikely they knew the kind of people who did know. Now that she had a general location, finding Billy might be as easy as looking his name up online in the phone book. *People Finder* made it easier than that.

The app came up with only 17 William Kaye's without middle names living in southern California. Five were in the L.A. area, two along the coast. Who wouldn't want to live close to the ocean, especially if you hated the cold and had three million dollars burning a hole in your pocket? The one living in Seal Beach was a 69-year-old widowed bus driver who had lived in Long Beach for most of his life.

The other one was her Boston Billy. She was sure of it. He was 27, living in Venice on Ozone Avenue. He'd lived there for just a couple of months. The one name associated with his was Brianna Steiner, 28. She had lived in Gainesville, Florida, but now had the same address. Bingo. Billy brought a girlfriend with him from Florida! Two vehicles were registered in her name. One of them must be for Billy, making her feel even more confident she found the right guy. Just in case, she scanned information about the other 15 names, but none fit as well as the Billy from Venice.

She found a ballpoint pen in the drawer and wrote the address down on a piece of hotel stationery, then checked Google Maps. It was so close she could walk there! She logged off and closed the laptop with a bang. She ran her fingers through her hair. It was still wet.

The girlfriend was a minor complication but Jesse knew how to turn that into an advantage. She worked in clubs and dealt with the private lives of men married or involved with other women. She could turn up the heat and be subtle or direct, whatever the situation called for, and still make it work. It had never been a problem.

She pulled out her cell and dialed. She patted down her hair with her free hand waiting for the other end to pick up.

"Tommy! Jess. Yeah, hi…. Good. You? No, L.A. Yeah…. It's great! I'll have to fill you in later. I'm pressed for time, and it looks like I'll need you to FedEx the item.... Yeah, you got a pen?" She read the address of the hotel from the letterhead on the stationery. "Repeat it back." She listened, then said, "Yep, that's it. It's got to be next day delivery, don't forget. It gets here in time, there'll be a bonus for you... I promise a big one.... I don't know exactly, but a few days, for sure. I'll take care of you, don't worry. You know we're always good to.... Yeah? Well, what kind of inventory problem?"

She listened, frowning. "Thomas. You know what I'm like. This is not what we agreed on. I trained with the... with it for a reason." She threw the pen down on the desk and it bounced up and fell onto the rug. She bent down and picked it up and started clicking the pen over and over. "Well, how similar?" Click-click-click-click. She listened, her anger dissipating but not disappearing. Click-click-click-click. "Well, that doesn't sound so.... I'm desperate for something."

She put the pen down on the desk and took her time choosing the words. "I appreciate what you can send me, Tommy. I'm disappointed, sure, but... it won't be a problem as long as I get it early tomorrow.... Good. Fantastic. Yes, I'll try. Tommy, I-I really, really appreciate this. You're the only one I trust to.... Okay. Yeah. You, too."

Jesse disconnected and put the phone down on the desk, then stood up and scratched her head furiously with both hands. She looked up at the ceiling and screamed her favorite obscenity, then sat down on the bed.

Tom was an old friend from Canada she'd met when she worked at Justine's Men's Club in Toronto. One source of his income was selling handguns. She'd never handled a gun until he taught her to shoot a Ruger LC9S Pro, a small semiautomatic 9mm with a crisp trigger and a seven-round capacity. The pistol fit her hand like a glove. It was exhilarating to hold such a tiny object, point it at something thirty feet away, and with a slight pull of a finger have it kick and see the target disintegrate. So uncomplicated compared to dance or Taekwondo. Took no time at all. No wonder guns were so popular in America.

That was the gun she'd paid for, the gun he was to send if or when she called. It was unacceptable that he'd sold it to someone else. She'd never seen this substitute he was talking about, let alone practiced with it. He said the Glock 43 was the same size as the Ruger and the magazine held six rounds, not seven, but that made the gun lighter to hold. To add insult to injury, it was two hundred bucks more. Screw it. The money wouldn't matter soon, and difference wouldn't either. Load it and point like you mean it, that's all there was to it. And when the time came, it would be the same pull on the trigger.

The fact that she'd never met Billy or Doc was a good thing. But Tiffany told her both of them were strong and could put up a fight. Billy worked out and knew some martial arts, or at least said he did. Doc kept in shape and had learned to box to defend himself in prison. I bet he did, she smirked. And then there was Kyle to consider. She'd seen him up close. He was old but fit, despite his ski injury. She admired that about him, the benefits of a lifetime of discipline.

Jesse was confident. She was a runner and studied dance and Taekwondo since she was little, then graduated to Krav Maga when her world got rough. She could defend herself in most situations. Still, she knew men who simply refused to be threatened by a woman. But she knew from experience there were few things more intimidating than looking down the barrel of a loaded gun. It simplified everything. She made a gun with her fingers and shot all three of the bastards. Pop, Pop. Pop.

She needed that gun.

56

Billy was in his underwear, his new paunch showing, as he walked barefoot into the kitchen. Brianna sat at the table by the large window, dressed for work and reading The Los Angeles Times on her phone. On the table sat a carton of milk, her coffee cup, a spoon and an empty cereal bowl. Through the open window, Billy thought he could hear the surf.

"I smell coffee," he said rubbing his face. "Want to make eggs?"

"None for me, thanks," she answered, side-stepping his request. "There's still coffee. I got to leave in a minute. Penny said the auxiliary on the *Atticus* blew white smoke on the way back from Catalina yesterday. Joe's going to show me how he'd work it."

"White smoke? That mean they picked a new pope?"

She gave him a look, but he missed it, as he reached up for his cup on a high shelf in the cupboard. His body looked soft. She bit her lip and almost shook her head. He was letting himself go.

"Means the combustion chamber isn't getting hot enough. Could be just a clogged filter or water got in the fuel, but it might be something worse. Joe's showing me how to find the problem and fix it." She went back to the paper. "Says here 10% chance of rain tonight."

For the past six weeks, Brianna had worked part-time at Duffy's Marina & Charter in Marina Del Rey. She made a decent hourly wage repairing and maintaining the auxiliary motors on the eight sailboats in their fleet. She got the job when the Duffy's mechanic, Pete, a blond local with artless tattoos and a laid-back attitude, announced he was leaving the next day to go to Ensenada for a month and surf with friends. Joe fired him. A Navy vet, Joe was impressed with Brianna's experience in the Reserves repairing diesel engines on helicopters. He needed a good mechanic asap and offered to show her the ropes.

Billy poured himself a cup and sat down next to her at the table. "Don't you know how to fix that stuff from working on Apache helicopters?" She watched him scratch his head then give her a cock-eyed smile.

She loved the smile and considered whether his question was just dumb or he was putting her on. She gave him the benefit of the doubt. "Yeah. There are similarities. But it doesn't exactly translate. Not all diesels are made the same and they sure don't work the same way. Helicopter engines are unique. So are sailboat auxiliaries. This one's a Westerbeke W10 Two, a two-cylinder diesel they don't make anymore."

Billy was reading the back of the Cheerio's box. "Hmm," he said.

Brianna returned to her phone. He dumped Cheerios and milk into his bowl. "If they don't make the engine anymore, then why don't he just buy a new motor? It's probably just going to break down again, anyway."

He was listening, she thought, and looked right at him. "Maybe, but why throw something away if it's still got life in it?"

Billy shrugged. "I guess," he said through a mouthful of Cheerios. "You're like giving it a second chance."

"Yeah." She like that thought and smiled. "It's fun, too, like doing a jigsaw puzzle."

"I hate puzzles. What's the point?"

"'Cause it's a challenge. Okay? Using my wits to keep the little old-time motors working. The T 700 on the Apache—you needed a computer to figure them out."

"But if you got it wrong, they fell out of the sky and splat!" He moved his spoon up and down. A drop of milk slipped off and landed on the table as if to demonstrate his point.

"Yeah, there's that. With these little auxiliary suckers, if they don't work you raise the sail and get where you're going an hour or two later, that's all."

"Less stress," concluded Billy. "More peaceful, too."

"That they are," Brianna looked concerned. "How'd you sleep?" Billy shrugged. She patted his arm. "You need me to make you some eggs, sweetheart?"

He scooped more Cheerios into his mouth and shook his head. "I'm not that hungry anymore." He stared out the window. "Looks like another nice day."

"It's southern California. You going into work this afternoon?"

Billy shrugged. Doc had gotten him a part-time job at the Guitar Gallery but Billy was less than enthused about selling. "I guess. See how I'm doing later. I'm feeling kinda low right now. I'm going to sit out on the beach for a while."

Billy had gotten into the habit of carrying a chaise down to the beach and dozing off to the sound of the waves.

"You still thinking about joining a gym?" She kept her tone neutral. She didn't want an argument. "You used to enjoy working out." She almost added, *and staying in shape.*

"Yeah, I'm thinking about it."

Brianna looked at her watch. "It's already ten." She got up and rinsed out her bowl and spoon and left them on the counter to dry. "Don't forget. Dinner tonight with Doc. What do you want to bring?"

"Anything. Everything. He's such a bad cook.

Why don't we tell him we'll bring Mexican?"

Brianna said, "Sure. Check with him first. It's his place. And tomorrow night, you boys are on your own." She headed for the doorway, speaking over her shoulder. "We won't be getting back until late the next day, maybe around 5:00pm."

"Excited?"

She stopped and turned around to look at him. "Yeah, I am," she admitted. "Only been to Catalina that one time on *Red Wind* and that was just for the day. And we'll be staying overnight at the Dolphin Resort and Spa!"

"Fancy!"

"The charters from Minneapolis wanted to stay someplace nice, so Penny booked them there and got a deal on a room for us to stay, too."

"She knows her business, I'll give her that."

"Tonight, we'll be taking watches. Two hours on and two off. Me first."

"So, you better fix that engine right."

"We're not taking *Atticus*. We're taking *Reliance*. A 45-foot ketch. Newer. I'm not worried about her. I'm worried about me and how I'll do."

"You'll do fine. Just point and steer."

"Ha. Ha. As *if*! Love you, Billy Bear! See you tonight."

57

Kyle slept three hours of the six-hour flight, arriving at LAX the next morning. He retrieved his bag from the overhead, then waited at the curb under the blue Rental Car Shuttles sign. He got off at Hawaiian Bros. Car Rentals, and rented a purple Ford Taurus. The interior smelled like mothballs sprayed with Lysol. The GPS in the car led him north on the 10 to the 405 and onto Wilshire Boulevard. It took almost fifteen minutes to drive the mile-and-a-half to the San Vicente Organic Food Market where he left the car.

He walked one block east to Brentwood Gardens, an upscale three-story outdoor mall, where the girl was arrested on November 12, according to the letter from the police. He checked the directory by the escalator, narrowing his search down to four stores that catered to teenage fashion.

He started at the street level, identifying himself as a writer doing an article on "kids who commit crimes" and asking each manager if they had experienced any recent incidents of shoplifting. The first store, *Pink*, was empty except for inventory and the manager who looked bored. He was dressed in a crisp work shirt and distressed jeans and said they caught a shoplifter, but it turned out to be on the wrong day. The managers of the two stores on the second floor both reported that thefts were noticed after the fact and no one was arrested. He took the stairs to the top level and walked west to the last store, already planning what to do next if this didn't yield results. *Terri Lenox* was printed in a stylized script on the large front window.

A simple chime rang when he passed through the doorway. A shoe gazing rock track played from ceiling speakers. The store was stocked with colorful women's clothing. In a far corner, two girls were inspecting blouses hanging from rods on the far wall. A woman with short blond hair wearing a sleeveless navy-blue floral print dress stood alone in front of the register. Kyle figured her for late 30s in the time it took for her to turn his way.

"May I help you?"

"Hi, are you the manager?"

He could see her sizing him up and determining he wasn't here to buy. "Yes, I'm the manager," she said extending her hand. "Lynn. I own the store." They shook hands. She glanced toward the two girls before returning to Kyle.

"I'm sorry to bother you. If you're busy, I can come back."

She looked him over a second time. She

smiled with her lips but not her eyes. He could sense her deciding to get it over with. Fine with him. "How may I help you?"

"I'll get right to it. My name is Larry Chambers. I'm writing an article about kids and crime. I'm looking for some information. That's all. If you got a minute...." He let the request hang.

She kept an eye on the customers. "Sure, what can I tell you, Larry."

"Some kid tried to shoplift here two weeks ago, a young girl."

"Can you be more specific?"

"November 12. The police arrested her."

"Oh, yeah. You should talk to Stephen, the mall guard. He's off today."

"Do you know her name, or where the police took her?"

"Why?" she asked. "You working for her lawyer? You want me to help her?"

"I don't even know her." There was a long moment when neither of them said anything. Kyle became aware again of the music coming from the speakers in the ceiling. The chime rang twice. They turned toward the door together and watched as the two girls walked out empty-handed. The store was deserted now except for Kyle and Lynn.

He took out his wallet and fished out five $20s. "What's her name? Where'd they take her?" He offered her the bills.

Kyle wasn't surprised when she snatched the money from his hand. She slipped behind the counter and pulled out a folder. "Her name is Eva Maldonado and they took her to the Brentwood Precinct just down the street." She took a sheet of paper out of the folder and held it up for him to see. It was a photocopy of an official-looking form filled out with typing and writing. "For another hundred, I'll give you my copy of the police report."

58

Billy was happy for Brianna. She loved her job. He was less excited about sailing. He liked being on the ocean, but sailing was a lot of work, and secretly he longed for one of those twin-engine cabin cruisers he saw moored in the marina. Something with comfortable seats and a fridge and TV. He could afford one, of course, but he wasn't sure how Brianna would react.

He also wasn't comfortable with work. Doc had a profound love for music, but Billy only had a guitar to impress women. When Doc got Billy a sales job in the guitar section at the Guitar Gallery, it meant nothing special to Billy. He might as well have been selling shoes. He worked two afternoons a week, enough to keep up the appearance that he worked. He rarely initiated a sale.

Billy spent most of his free mornings working on his tan by the ocean. His favorite spot was on Venice Beach, a half-block from their apartment. In addition to a chaise and towel, he usually brought a couple of cans of beer with him, concealed in the towel, and kept them cold and out of sight by burying them in the sand directly under the chaise. He sipped on his breakfast beer and watch the ocean as he eyed the procession of female joggers, tourists and sun worshippers on the beach between Santa Monica Pier to the north and Venice Pier to the south.

She may have saved his life back in Gainesville, but Billy still resented Brianna for drawing him into danger in the first place. That anger didn't go away even though Billy was in love with her. The woman had spirit, passion, intelligence and beauty and clearly loved him, too. But as the newness receded and infatuation waned, boredom and restless began to fill the void. It felt natural to fall back on old habits. He didn't think about it all that much.

Venice Beach was nothing like Wollaston Beach back in Boston where he'd hung out in the summer to meet girls. The ocean there was rough and cold, even when the weather was warm. On a nice day, the sky could be gray, the water almost black, the sand mixed with sharp rocks and shells and sometimes broken glass.

But here the sand was pale, clean and smooth. A city crew drove vehicles that combed debris from the beach every few days. The water was cool, peaceful and the color of a baby's blue eyes. It looked like a postcard.

A breeze passed over his skin like a soft hand massaging his tired muscles. A few tiny grains of sand rolled and danced across his bare torso. He sipped from his second beer, then placed it under the chaise, not bothering to screw it into the sand. The sound of waves hitting the beach grew louder, and Billy relaxed from the inside out. He drifted off.

"How ya doing?"

Billy opened his eyes and saw an olive-skin brunette in an electric green two-piece smiling down at him. She smelled of sweat and coconut.

"Hi, yourself," he said, returning the smile. They exchanged five words and two smiles in seven seconds. That's all it took. He remembered to suck in his stomach. She removed her sunglasses and looked down on him, shielding her eyes from the sun with a hand. His smile held her attention while he picked her apart and took in the details: she was Asian, maybe five-six. Maybe thirty. Nice arms and legs, a cross-trainer, maybe a dancer or a runner who lifts. Straight jet-black hair tied back in a ponytail with bangs covering her forehead. High cheekbones. Small nose. Dimples. Nice mouth and lips. Teeth bleached, but that was par out here. Long neck. Sturdy shoulders. Nice cleavage and totally flawless skin without a mark or tattoo showing. She stood still long enough, posing almost, then turned as if checking the surf, but giving him the opportunity to view her backside, stretching her arms up and arching her back with grace, like some kind of dancer. He took in the whole show. He was sure they never met before, but something about her was familiar. Isn't that how it usually goes, he thought. He relaxed, then sucked his stomach back in again.

He took off his shades as a reciprocal gesture, sat up on one arm and remembered to restrain himself so as not to appear to leer, which of course was exactly what he was doing. He offered his hand. Her grip was firm, her skin soft and cool.

"You're not that tanned for someone from around here." From his expression, she added, "Sorry, did I embarrass you?"

"No, it's just... I sort of just moved out here." His tongue felt thick. Maybe he it was the beer or he was just tired.

"How long ago?"

"Ah, a couple, couple of months ago."

"Okay...." She laughed once. "Where from?"

"Back east." He wasn't about to be specific this time. "You?"

"I've moved about a lot, been around here and there."

It was subtle but he caught it. "You sound Canadian."

Her smile vanished for a split second, then bounced back. "Yeah! You got me." Now it was her turn to seem embarrassed. It made him feel comfortable.

"Where in Canada?"

"Toronto," she blurted. Damn! "You're good at this." She rewarded him by pointing at the can of beer in the sand under the chaise and asking for a sip. Billy passed the can to her. She threw her head back as she took a long pull, then handed it back and slipped her shades over her eyes. She shrugged. "American beer... at least it's wet."

Billy forced a laugh.

"We'll I got to get going," she said and turned as if to resume running, but waited, viewing the ocean and giving him time.

"Hey, ah..." she heard him say. She suppressed a smile.

"Tell you what," she said, turning. "This is my first time out here and I'm headed home in a few days. I don't know anybody and doubt I'll have the chance to come back," she said, studying his eyes. "How about I buy you a decent drink, not domestic beer." She waited but he didn't respond. She could see him thinking it over, weighing the risks and possibilities. All he needed was a push. "Just a drink. You can fill me in on the local color, what I should see and do. Otherwise, I'll end up at Disneyland or Universal with a million kids and their parents. You can save me from that sad fate."

Billy looked out at the ocean.

"What, are you married or something?" she said pointedly.

"Me? No." His eyes met hers but his eyes looked weak to her. "I can't right now. I gotta work. How's tomorrow night? I'll buy you dinner."

You got to know which buttons to push: sit up, roll over, fetch, beg. "You sure tonight won't work?"

"No." He was adamant.

She nodded, confident there still was time.

Her voice stayed casual. "Then, sure, tomorrow night." She held out her hand. "Here, give me your phone."

He entered his code to unlock his cell and passed it to her. He watched as she poked at the screen, entering the number of the disposable pre-paid phone she bought at the airport. "You're texting me," she said. "I'll reply and we'll have each other's numbers." She handed him his phone. "How about 5:00 tomorrow under the Santa Monica Pier sign? You can show me the Pier and we can check out the carousel, watch the sun set, then grab a bite. I'm sure there's a good restaurant nearby."

"You know about the carousel?" He chuckled.

Her eyes narrowed but he missed it. She covered it with a shrug. "Read about it in a brochure at the hotel." All she needed to do was to give him the look and he was happy. "See you tomorrow under the sign at 5:00." She turned and walked a few steps south down the beach toward Marina Del Rey.

"Wait a minute! What's your name?"

She heard him but made like she didn't, quickening her stride into a run. She didn't look back, knowing he was watching her. Let him wonder. She knew he'd be there.

Billy put on his Ray-Bans and peeked over the top. He snapped a mental picture of her runner's butt in his memory, then concentrated on her receding figure, her ponytail bouncing left and right from shoulder to shoulder with the rhythm of her stride. She looked strong, her movements were smooth. Definitely a dancer, he thought. He drifted off, remembering he liked dancers, while forcing down the image of Tiffany on the floor, her face covered by towels and blood.

59

They built the Brentwood Hotel near the intersection of the 405 and 10. The cylindrical building resembled the old Capitol Records offices in Hollywood but its shape reminded Kyle of a stack of pancakes. His room was wedged-shape like a piece of pie, which made sense once he thought about it. He called room service and ordered a BLT and coffee, then showered and changed by the time the food arrived.

He wolfed down the sandwich then sat at a desk under a flat screen TV mounted on the wall. He opened the drawer and found a too-skinny pen and a thin pad of paper, both inscribed with the name of the hotel. Using his cell, he found the number for, then called the Los Angeles County Department of Corrections, telling a series of receptionists and clerks he was a concerned neighbor who needed to talk to Eva Maldonado's parole officer. He finally spoke with Jodi Ansel, Eva's Parole Officer. Doing his best to sound like a sympathetic soul, Kyle called himself "Glenn Caron" and said he lived two houses over from Eva's family.

"I watched her grow up only to get mixed up with the wrong crowd," he told Ms. Ansel. "Late last night, I was sitting in my living room watching TV and heard kids talking real loud outside in the street. Then I heard glass breaking and when I went to the window, I saw the driver's door to my car was open. There were four kids in the street standing next to my car. One of them was holding my backpack I left on the back floor."

"What was in the backpack?" she asked automatically.

"A paperback book and some tax papers, stuff for my accountant."

"Uh-huh."

"I opened the window and yelled but they walked away. Didn't even try to run."

"Did you notify the police? That's how these things should be handled, Mr. Caron."

"I was going to, but then I think maybe these are Eva's friends, the boys she hangs out with. If I have to testify against them, I don't want them to take it out on her or her mom. Her mother seems like a very nice lady."

"Let's not get ahead of ourselves, Mr. Caron. I understand your concern, but—"

"Look, Ms. Ansel, all I want is my stuff back. Insurance will cover the broken driver's window. I don't care about the book, but the papers have personal information I don't want floating around, like my social security number. All I'm asking is the next time you see Eva ask her if she knows anything about it. You don't have to tell her I called. If you think she has nothing to do with it, I'll do as you said and report it to the police. But if she's involved, I'll want to give her a chance to return my papers. They can keep the backpack and the book."

"Well, sir, that's pretty generous of you, I guess, but it's been my experience that these kids never admit to something if they don't have to. I mean, lying is the least of it. I admire, sir, what you're trying to do here—"

"Thank you."

"Giving her a chance, not that.... Listen, I don't think it will help, but.... She knows you?"

"Ah, maybe just to say hello, on the street."

"What about asking her mother?"

"Same thing. She seems really nice."

"This happened last night?"

"Yes, mam."

"Well ... okay. I will ask Ms. Maldonado about it."

"Thank you! I really appreciate it. When—"

"Why don't you call me.... Let me look at the schedule.... Here she is.... She's supposed to see me this afternoon, so call me back between 3:00 and 3:30, no later 'cause I'm out the door by 4:00. I got to catch a bus."

"Yes. Sure, I'll do that. Ah, so her appointment today? I'm asking because I'm worried that the kids will come back and...."

"I'm seeing her at 2:00. It's important to make these kids be punctual. That's my last appointment for the day... the last hour's paperwork and a briefing, so call a little after 3:00 but before 3:30. Sound good to you?"

"Perfect. Thanks so much, Ms. Ansel."

"Hang on a minute. You have my direct extension?"

Got it right here," he said, then crumpled up the paper with the number and dropped it into the waste paper basket next to the desk. "Thank you for your help and have a nice day."

60

It took less than an hour to get to a section of downtown dominated by empty stores, iron window grates and fences trimmed in razor wire. Kyle parked the rental in the first lot he saw and walked one block past a row of tall, soot-stained granite office buildings. He stopped in front of 1605 Eastlake Avenue, the location of The Los Angeles County Department of Juvenile Correction's mid-city office and the seventh-floor office of Ms. Jodi Ansel, Senior County Parole Office Supervisor. He crossed the street and entered the Lost Angel Coffee Shoppe where he bought a coffee and a Danish, and sat at a table by the window with a good view of the entrance to 1605.

He watched people enter and leave the building while he waited for his coffee to cool. He was not comfortable. The chair was small and hard. The table wobbled. Both chair and table were glazed with a sticky semitransparent grime that also covered the window. Kyle hoped it was from the smog. He wished for time to move faster.

Five minutes before 2:00pm, two teenage girls dressed in dark jeans and identical blue jerseys with Dodgers logos walked into 1605. Both were about medium height, had straight dark hair and looked 15 or 16. Three minutes later, one of the pair descended the stairs and disappeared down the street. Kyle ignored her and figured the other girl was the one with the 2:00 appointment, Eva Maldonado.

With nothing to do but wait, Kyle turned to his coffee and Danish. The cup and saucer as well as the plate were porcelain with a pleasant matching pattern, impressive for a dive like this. He lifted his cup and smelled cinnamon and coffee, two of his favorite aromas, but stopped when his nose detected the faint stench of bleach. He put the cup down and examined the cherry Danish on his plate. It looked more like it came out of a 3D printer than an oven, but he was hungry so took a bite. It was dry and tasteless, more like powder than pastry. The jelly filling had the color and consistency of coagulated blood. He dropped the pastry back onto the plate. He instinctively needed to wash the taste and texture off his tongue and reached for his coffee, but stopped before the cup touched his lips. An imprint of red lipstick on the rim survived the cursory rinse it must have received since the previous customer last drank from it, a woman, Kyle hoped. He shifted the cup to his left hand and, already acclimated to the bleach smell, sipped from the opposite side to wash down the powder and blood. The coffee itself was weak with a faint aftertaste of soap. He drank more anyway. In for a penny. Back pain had kept him from sleeping much the night before, so he planned to keep the caffeine coming and who knows... the bleach might kill of any germs he picked up from this place.

Other than finding a bad place for an afternoon snack, he was making progress. He was looking forward to the reward and the revenge. He was even thinking about forgoing returning to Boston altogether, buying a car and driving to Mexico. Customs didn't worry as much about what you were taking out of the States as what you were bringing in. He could deposit his cash in a bank in Mexico, then buy a first-class ticket to... anywhere. He thought again about Portugal.

Kyle watched through the window as the second girl descend the steps. He looked at his watch. Twenty minutes had passed. She had to be Eva.

He dropped a ten on the table and hurried out into the street. A car slowed, the driver cursing as Kyle crossed the intersection diagonally to approach the girl from behind. He got close enough to read the name on the back of her jersey, *Hernandez*, and the number, *14*.

Across the street, a scattering of people. On his side, a solitary man was walking toward them. Kyle let him pass, then looked behind. No one else was nearby. They were approaching a chain link fence enclosing a parking lot.

"Eva," Kyle called out, his voice natural and controlled. He was almost close enough to catch her if she bolted.

Eva kept walking, but turned her head toward Kyle, giving him a defiant look.

"*Cual es tu pinche pedo?*"

Kyle didn't have a clue what she'd said. He walked up beside her and kept his voice natural.

"Hey, you're Eva Maldonado, aren't you?"

She did not slow down. Her face was a practiced expression of defiance and anger. "Whatever you're selling, I don't want, old man. Go away or I'll scream."

Kyle held his hand high enough so she could see what he had been holding. The creases between her eyes disappeared when she saw the hundred-dollar bill. She kept walking but slowed her pace.

"All I want is information. This is yours for answering a couple of questions and then I'll go away. That's it. I swear I won't bother you again. Just two questions and the hundred is yours. That's all I want. I mean, Jesus, you're just a kid."

"I'm not a kid. I'm eighteen." Her voice shook a little but still defiant. Her eyes showed no fear but flickered between his and the money.

"Sure you are." She watched him put the bill back in his pocket.

He glanced left and right and saw someone down the block walking in their direction. "We got a deal or not?"

Her large brown eyes searched Kyle's. He noticed she wore blue eye shadow and pale pink lipstick. Her jaw was set, her expression, determined. She adjusted the strap of her bag on her shoulder. "'kay," she said nodding. "What's your question."

Kyle motioned for her to stand closer to the fence and got to the point.

He took out the photocopy of Teddy's license and showed it to her. "You got bagged for shoplifting and they took this driver's license off you...." He gave her time to think. She studied Kyle face.

"What about it?"

"Where'd you get the license, from a parked car?" She nodded. "Where was the car parked? That's all I want to know and the hundred is yours."

"Excuse me, young lady. Are you all right?"

A woman appeared holding a tote bag in one hand and leash in the other. At the other end of the leash was a harness worn by a small boy. The kid bent down, picked up something from the sidewalk and put it in his mouth. The woman didn't notice. She was addressing Eva but looking at Kyle.

Eva stepped up. "*Si, dona*. My mother is sick and I'm on my way to get her medicine." She held a palm toward Kyle. "*Tio* Miguel brought me the money and is driving me back to Mama's." She kept her hand out, working the angle.

"She's a good niece," smile Kyle, leaving his hands in his pockets.

The woman's eyes turned on Kyle. Her nostrils flared. "You should be ashamed of yourself. She's a child." She looked down at Eva. "*Puta*," she spat. The woman tugged at the leash and continued down the block, the child following behind.

Kyle turned to Eva, her large brown eyes almost soft, still holding her palm out for the $100 bill.

"Money first," she said.

Kyle brought the hand with the hundred around, but held it beyond reach. "Don't bullshit me, kid." His face was granite.

The defiant expression was back but she conceded. "Okay, but you better pay up."

Kyle's eyes burned into hers.

"It wasn't a car. I got the wallet out of a pickup truck, a little one, parked in Venice, on Ozone Avenue, a block from the beach, um, north side of the street."

"Ozone Avenue... in Venice, a block from the beach." He tilted his head and frowned. "You sure about that? I was hoping we could do business, but if you're wasting my time with some bullshit—"

Eva's laugh was cold. "I'm telling you the truth, old man. Me and my friends look in the windows and if there's no blinking alarm light, we try the doors. This truck had some junk on the seat and in the glove box. But there was a black jacket behind the driver's seat that Paul kept. He's my boyfriend. All he did was push hard on the door and it opened. That works sometimes. The wallet was in a pocket in the jacket. No cash, but a credit card Paul kept. He gave me the ID 'cause I said I knew a guy who I thought would pay fifty bucks for it, but the guy he didn't have any money." She barked a short laugh. "*Estúpida.*"

Kyle didn't care about any of that. "A little pickup truck, you said?"

Eva narrowed her eyes. Kyle could see wheels turning, almost causing him to smile. He liked this kid.

"Yeah, a Toyota, the little one you see around everywhere. It's called... a Tacoma. That's the model. No backseat. A short bed. Good for tooling around and to move stuff."

"What color?"

"It was dark and the streetlights they're yellow, but it looked white to me."

"Looked white?"

"Was white. I'm sure of it."

"A white Toyota Tacoma pickup, short bed." Kyle pictured the truck. "Ozone Street, you said?"

"No. Ozone Avenue. Your memory is bad. You should write things down," she admonished him.

"Ozone Ave. A block from the beach," he repeated.

"Really like half-a-block. North side of the street. In front of a gray house that had a bunch of apartments in it. On the right side of the street, that's the north side, because the ocean is always west. The houses on that street don't have garages so the people who live there park on the street."

Kyle found that encouraging. He folded the hundred in half and pointed it at Eva. Her hand struck like a snake and the bill disappeared into a front pocket on her jeans. He knew he had her when he produced another hundred and her eyes grew even larger.

"Now I need another favor." He saw that defiant look again, but she smiled when he asked, "Where can I get a gun?"

61

Brianna was rinsing off when the shower door opened a crack, startling her. She saw Billy's shining eyes peeking in, bright and playful, ready to tease.

"Mornin' gorgeous."

"Mornin' yourself, Billy Bear!" She squinted through the soap in her eyes and saw he was dressed for work. "Turning over a new leaf?"

"Huh?"

"You headed for work already?"

"Oh. Yeah. Kind of. Me and Doc are having an early lunch, then he's off and I'm working the afternoon."

"I thought you guys were getting together tonight."

"Yeah, maybe. I might call it an early night and stay home... now that I'll have the place to myself for the evening. Relax with a beer and watch a game. We were up late last night, weren't we?"

"Sounds like you're getting too old to keep

up." She turned the water off. "Hand me a towel, will you?"

"Too old, huh!" His hand reached for her hip.

She stepped back and laughed. "You'll get water on the floor!" He pulled back. She grabbed the handle and yanked the door closed.

He shouted through the glass. "A little water never hurt anybody."

"Towel!" Her voice echoed from behind the glass.

The door opened enough for him to hand her a towel. "You have fun on your midnight cruise without me."

"It's not for fun. I'm working!"

"Whatever you call it, you be careful. Have fun, but measure twice before you cut—"

"That advice is for carpenters."

"—and listen to Penny. She knows what she's doing."

Billy moved back, giving her room to step out and onto the bathmat. She used part of the towel to dry her hair. "Remember, we're staying at the Dolphin Inn. My cell should work from there. I'll call you when we get to the hotel."

"Text me, in case I'm already in bed," he said. "I'll text you back as soon as I can."

She put her hand on his forehead and brushed back his hair. "You feeling okay?" she asked.

"Yeah. Yeah. I'm a little run down, that's all. I'll hit the sack early tonight... a cold or something, that's all." He turned and headed for the doorway. "I better get going."

There was concern in her voice. "I love you," she said.

He looked her in the eyes. "Yeah. Love you, too," he said and meant it. He disappeared around the corner. After a minute she heard the front door close.

Billy checked his watch as he stepped off the porch onto the flagstones leading to the sidewalk. It was a little past 11:00 and Doc's morning shift ended at 11:30, plenty of time to get to the Guitar Gallery.

By the time he got to his truck, Billy re-affirmed his decision not to tell Doc about the woman from the beach. It won't sit right with him, Billy thought, but that's Doc. What did she say, she was leaving town in a week? Whatever happens, Billy told himself, nothing will come of it. As he drove off to the sound of Tom Petty, he thought how things sometimes appear out of nowhere and make up your mind for you.

He waved hello at an elderly couple walking their dog as he drove north uphill and away from the beach. He took a left onto Ocean Avenue and headed east consumed with thoughts about the evening to come. He did not see the maroon Ford Taurus with rental plates in his rearview mirror.

Kyle followed the white truck until it pulled into

an open-air mall and parked in a space opposite a music superstore. He parked two rows over and waited. He smiled with satisfaction when Billy came out of the store with a black man, shorter than Billy, and clearly the older of the two, just like Teddy described. They got into the white truck. "Hello, Billy. Hello Doctor," said Kyle to himself. He felt like it was Christmas morning.

He followed the truck six blocks to a Mexican restaurant. Billy parked in the front lot. Kyle found a space further down the street. He adjusted his rearview mirror and watched them enter the restaurant. Doc led the way, Billy looking at him. Kyle figured Doc was the one in charge. Good to know.

If Doc was the brains of the outfit, he wouldn't let the money get too far from his sight. It was probably stashed at his place. Kyle decided to follow Doc home. If he lived alone and away from nosy neighbors, then Kyle would move on him right away.

There also was the issue of the gun. What he had was a Smith & Wesson J-frame, an old but reliable revolver loaded with six .22 LR cartridges. Kyle preferred something bigger, especially if he had to stop a crazed Billy from charging. But not this little guy. A .22 would stop Doc in his tracks. There was also the option of using a .22 to wound him to speed up the conversation should Doc be reluctant to talk. All Kyle had to do was make sure he left a bullet to finish the job when it no longer mattered what Doc had to say.

62

Billy parked at a meter on the west side of Ocean Avenue close to the California Incline. He walked south down the path that ran along the edge of the cliff overlooking PCH, Santa Monica Beach and the Pacific Ocean. He paced himself, not wanting to sweat, and figured it should take him ten minutes to get to the Santa Monica Pier. He had walked this way before with Brianna.

He weaved past people jogging, on skates or bikes, just strolling or standing admiring the sun setting over the ocean. Up ahead, Billy saw an old man with gray stubble leaning on the white rail fence separating the path and the edge of the cliff. He wore an old tan suit with wide lapels and a tan fedora, and held a tiny dog in his arms. As Billy approached, he heard the man talking to his dog, "It all ends here, the largest open space on the planet." Billy stopped, wondering if the man were about to climb over the fence and jump. The man turned to Billy and said, "Right here, where you're standing, is the Terminus, the end of sunlight on the American mainland, the finish line for the Manifest Destiny, the western boundary of the American Dream, the Hotel California." Billy's eyes followed the old man's fingers as he pointed out to the ocean. "Drink it in, boy," the man wheezed. "Taste the smog, the sweat, the salt, the stuff of dreams... it's all over now."

"Have a nice day," Billy said and resumed walking, leaving the man and dog in the fading orange light of the setting sun.

A short time later he stood beneath the arch of the Pier curving over his head like a damaged rainbow. Billy expected to see her waiting, but she wasn't there. He checked his phone for the time. He was six minutes late, and she wasn't here. He started to pace. Maybe she came and left.

He wore dark blue jeans and the black flowered shirt Brianna had bought him, which he now regretted wearing. His white undershirt peeked out over the open top and his hair was perfect, but he was anxious. He asked himself why he was here. He didn't like the answer.

Now she was seven minutes late. She wasn't coming. In a small space in the back of his mind, he felt disappointment and relief. A man to the left was fishing off the pier and a barefoot teenage couple walked past with skateboards. Beyond them, a woman walked a large dog on a leash down the center of the pier. Things began to feel pleasantly surreal.

Then he saw her, coming from the north, looking out at the sea as if she owned it. Her hair hung past her shoulders, loose and long, thick and black and almost straight but for one gentle wave against the side of her face. It bounced a little as she walked and made him forget his guilt. She wore all silk: a black jacket, black slacks, and a plain white blouse. The stuff of dreams indeed. When she got close, her eyes commanded his attention. Her perfectly shaped, lightly glossed lips opened and he waited for that voice.

"Hope I didn't keep you waiting long." she said. Her voice was as hypnotic as her eyes.

"Uh...no, just long enough. You look great!" He succeeded at tamping down the eagerness he felt. "You, ah...what do you want to do first?"

As she looked around surveying the scene, he noticed the small fire opal droplet hanging from a thin gold chain at the base of her throat. It reminded him of a necklace he'd bought Tiffany a lifetime ago. He pushed the memory away, but the betrayal stabbed at him, opening up a raw wound that stained the moment.

"Want to walk around, then grab something to eat?" he asked to bring himself back to the here and now. He pointed across the street. "Ivy by the Shore is over there. I think you'd like that."

"I'd like to see the Pier first, walk to the end and back, then go eat."

"Yeah, sure."

"Then we'll see what happens."

"Excellent," he proclaimed. He licked his lips. "Ah, this is a little embarrassing, but I forgot to ask you your name. I'm Billy."

"I'm Jesse."

He took her by the arm and they walked down the road onto the Pier. They entered the Hippodrome and stood by as Carousel riders rushed to mount a favored horse or resigned themselves to a sleigh or the rabbit or goat. The bell rang, music started up and the carousel began to spin.

If she noticed Billy staring at her, she didn't react. They watched laughing children ride the colorful wooden creatures.

"You want a ride?" Billy asked.

She didn't, so they left the Hippodrome and crossed the Pier to the edge. She leaned against the railing. The sun had set but the horizon was still visible. She turned around, her back against the railing, and studied the people walking past with ice cream cones and cotton candy.

Billy watched her watching the crowd. Mixed in with scent of fried fish and cotton candy was something else... gardenias. Her perfume, delicate yet heady. It made him think of the way paradise would smell. Hawaii, that long-ago dream..... He turned back to the ocean. The sky was starless.

She broke the silence, startling him. "Let's see if we can get a table."

She took his hand and led him off the Pier. They crossed the street and walked a half-block north to the restaurant with not a word spoken between them.

She thought about luring him back to her hotel, but that was risky. His place was obviously out since he lived with someone. She wondered what he'd told her about tonight, certainly not the truth. His shoulders were huge and his neck and wrists thick. She felt the heft of his hand in hers and imagined for an instant what damage he could do if he felt trapped or panicked. He moved with athletic grace, and like Tiffany had said, he'd had some martial arts training. An image drifted in of him holding her beyond her reach, impervious to her fists and nails, lifting her off the floor, his grip crushing her throat. Her Tai Kwan Do brown belt wouldn't matter once 250 pounds of trained muscle got his hands on her that way. Better to confront him in public where he'd be more likely to behave. Might as well have a nice meal at an expensive restaurant, too. She wouldn't be paying the bill.

The fresh air felt good so she asked for a table on the patio under the baby blue awning. They'd be less likely to be overheard in the open air.

Billy sat across from her studying his menu. She glanced at the menu and at him, wondering if he or his girlfriend picked out his clothes. When the waiter returned, they each ordered a gimlet and crab cakes to share for an appetizer. For the main course they ordered a seafood platter for two that arrived with grilled lobster, scallops, shrimp, more crab cakes and calamari.

She waited until they finished eating and Billy's belly was full of food and drink. He was working on his third gimlet and was in the middle of some empty speech meant to impress her when she changed his life.

She hadn't touched her drink, but took a sip now for effect, shut her eye halfway and gave him her Mona Lisa smile. She held out her glass as though she were about to make a toast. Once his eyes locked on hers, she announced, "You know, Billy, it's no accident we met on the beach like that."

"You mean, it was fate?" he laughed.

Jesus! She blinked, fighting the urge to laugh herself. Instead, she dropped her smile and the bomb. "No, I'm afraid it wasn't fate, you murdering son-of-a-bitch. It was Tiffany."

63

She watched the blood and confidence drain from his face. She found humor in the way his jaw dropped as he changed from slick to shocked. He tried to recover, cocking his head as if he didn't quite hear her right and expecting her to explain the joke. When she didn't respond, he slumped forward, elbows on the table, gripping his hair. She thought of Sampson and Delilah.

"Wh-who?" he stuttered.

She shook her head, dripping with disappointment. "Man up," she commanded.

He slowly looked up, his eyes narrowed. She didn't hide her satisfaction with herself. She knew how to control this dog. Maintaining eye contact, she raised her eyebrows and put an index finger to her lips. She leaned closer, their faces inches apart. "Sweetheart," she said. "I know all about you and Doc. I know what you did in Boston, the three million you stole and then killed Tiffany. I even know about Florida and Brianna."

Billy shot up, the legs of his chair scrapping the floor, his napkin floating off his lap.

"Sit down," she hissed. He didn't move. He looked lost. She lowered her voice but her eyes stayed on his. "Don't be an idiot. Calm down and listen. We can work something out." Her voice softened. "Come on, sit down and finish your drink."

He slowly sat back down, staring at her. But didn't touch his glass.

She leaned back. "Don't be a fool and force my hand. I could have called the cops already, but I haven't. You're smart enough to figure out why."

"I have a pretty good idea," Billy sat back and crossed his arms.

"Good. Now listen. Tiffany was my friend. When I found out what happened, there was nothing I'd have liked better than to see you dead." She lowered her eyes for split second. "But that's ancient history. I can't change the past, much as I'd like to, right?" She paused. "But what I can do is get my share. After all, it was my plan in the first place." She wasn't sure he'd fall for the line, but it didn't matter as long as he played along. She widened her eyes and tried to sound sincere. "Only fair, right? What do you think? Sound reasonable to you?"

She could see hope in Billy's eyes. Now to reel him in. She softened her tone even more. "Look, we both know the take was almost three million so give me an even million for the expense and trouble you put me through. That leaves you and Doc almost a million each. And you know I won't risk losing my share by going to the cops. Everybody gets to keep their original share and stay happy. Makes sense to me. Make sense to you?"

She waited. Billy's head bobbed. She took it to mean he agreed. "So, you're *that* Jesse..." he said.

"Tiffany talked about me?" She wanted to know.

"No, she didn't. Doc saw your text message." She noticed his expression was different. He sounded different. It took her a moment to realize he had calmed down a bit because he felt some control. It unnerved her a little and she became defensive. She couldn't keep the edge out of her voice.

"So, do you agree to the deal or not?"

Billy stared at her but said nothing.

She snapped her fingers twice. "Hey, Earth calling Billy! Are you listening to what I said?"

The woman at the adjacent table was watching them. Jesse mouthed something obscene in her direction. The woman turned back to her table.

"I hear you," said Billy.

"So you're onboard?"

"I, I got to talk to Doc, first."

"In time, Billy. I'm asking if you agree." Think for yourself!"

"Okay, a third." He looked away and then turned back to her and said, "For the record, you and Tiffany weren't going to split the cash with us, were you? But yeah. Okay. What choice do I got?"

She searched his eyes. He was either beat or bullshitting. He might be ready to hand over the money or he might try to kill her first chance he got. She couldn't tell which. Maybe both. It didn't matter as long as he led her to the money.

She'd torture them if she had to, but once she had the money, she'd get it over with. She never killed anyone, but she had the gun and three million reasons to use it. These two loose ends deserved dying, anyway. And if the opportunity presented itself, Kyle, too.

"Where's the money? You got it in your apartment in Venice, right? I know you kept the cash close by. Don't try giving me a story about it being in a bank or something. Then I'll have to consult your sweetie to make sure you aren't trying to double-cross me."

Billy didn't react outwardly to the threat. He didn't move. He said nothing. She thought he was scrambling to come up with some deception, some lie, but that wasn't it. The bank was precisely where the money was, although not in an account, but in safe deposit boxes. The idea this woman would even talk to Brianna was like a kick in the gut. He felt paralyzed. He didn't know what to do.

She knew something was wrong. He was taking too much time, but she wouldn't let him up for air.

"Hey," she said, reaching into her purse. "If I even think the first words out of your mouth are bullshit, I'm making the calls right now." She wagged her cell phone at him. "All I got to do is press 9-1-1 and you'll get nothing but jail time. The cops can't touch me. I've done nothing they care about. It's your word against mine and who will believe you? Brianna?" She sneered. "Not after hearing what you've been up to with me. Do it my way and she and the cops will never know, and you and your buddy end up with more money than you'd make in a lifetime."

He spoke in a whisper. "Put the damn phone away," he said.

"First, tell me, Billy Kaye from Boston, Massachusetts, where the hell is the money?"

"The money... it's at Doc's place." It was all he could think of, remembering how Doc hid his money when they first arrived. And he knew he needed Doc's help. Doc would know what to do. "It's at Doc's place."

"All of it? Your share, too?"

He nodded.

She looked at him with disdain. "You think I'm that stupid?"

"Ask me something...." Billy stopped himself. "I don't know what you mean."

"You're shitting me?" she asked, her pitch rising. "You let him hold your share?"

"I trust him." Billy looked down at the table and rearranged his silverware. "We've been... it's hard to explain."

It's not the move I'd make, she thought, but then again, I'm not dealing with a rocket scientist. She glanced at the time before putting the phone back in her purse. Okay. She had what she needed.

"Pay the waiter. We're leaving for Doc's. I'll take my share and then I'm gone forever. You'll never hear from me again. That's a fair deal considering you killed my girlfriend, don't you think?"

The word girlfriend sunk in. Their eyes locked. Billy was silent.

"Come on, Billy-baby! Don't pout. You got yourself into this thing for what, four-five grand?"

"I did it for Tiffany. We were—you were her girlfriend? As in ...?"

"Spare me." She resisted the urge to slap him. "You were in love and going to Hawaii to work in a bar together. Who do you think came up with that line of bullshit?"

She still couldn't tell if he was giving up or getting ready to fight. She dropped it back a notch.

"Come on, Billy. It wasn't personal. You seem like an okay guy. She just played you, that's all, and I'm taking over her hand. Nothing's changed except you and Doc get to keep two million instead of nothing. You know you wouldn't have made a dime without me and Tiffany. Right? Right?"

"Maybe. I guess." He looked half-convinced.

"You're damn right I'm right. You'd still be unloading boxes from trucks if it weren't for us. It's a win-win. So, let's go get my share and get on with our lives." She waited to see if he fell for this line.

Billy took out his wallet and left money on the table. "Let's go."

She still couldn't tell if he was onboard or buying time, but the outcome would be the same either way. "You know where Doc is now?"

"Yeah. He's at home. We were supposed to hang out at his place tonight."

"Alone?"

"Yeah, him and me."

"Jesus!" She rolled her eyes. "No, I'm asking if he's alone now."

Billy seemed to take it in stride. "Yeah. That's what I said. He's alone."

She needed her car to get away with the money. She wanted the cops to find Billy's truck parked at Doc's. Otherwise, there would be questions about how he got there when they found the bodies.

"Gimme your cell." She held her hand out. He handed it to her. She turned it off and dropped it in her purse.

"I'm parked across the street from you. You drive to Doc's and I'll follow. You know what'll happen if you lose me, even by accident."

He nodded.

"And don't think you can get me alone and get rough. If I don't check in with my friends tonight, they'll call the L.A. cops and say you abducted me. Then they'll drop a letter in the mail that I wrote for the cops in Boston telling them all about you and Doc killing Tiffany." It was all a lie but it would give Billy something to think about. And when Kyle got to Doc's place—and she was confident he would eventually—he'd find them both dead and the money gone. Then once the bodies were discovered, the cops would assume Kyle saw them last and had done it. Two birds, one stone.

She was ready to leave but still had one more question.

"Which one of you shot her?"

"What?" Billy's eyes widened. She was talking about Tiffany. "While I was knocked out from whatever shit she put in my drink, she pulled a gun on Doc and he was defending himself. And me. He was defending me, too. That's how it happened. It was self-defense."

"Self-defense, huh?"

"Doc wouldn't shoot anyone. He's a good guy. She didn't give him a choice."

"So, you think you guys are the victims here?" She picked up his gimlet and finished it for him, then put the empty glass down on the table with a smack. "Grow a pair, Billy. Even coincidences have consequences."

She stood up and gestured for him to do the same.

"Come on. Let's go see the doctor."

64

Doc opened an 18-ounce bottle of his favorite beer—Sam Smith Oatmeal Stout. He walked from the fridge past the flat screen and couch and turned off the lights as he stepped out the sliding glass door to his side of the deck. He left the door open to allow the sea air in. The deck was all his tonight and concealed in darkness. The entire house was dark. Fred and Dorothy had driven down to Seal Beach to stay with friends and hit up a jazz club or two. They didn't expect to be back until the next evening. And Billy backed out of coming over claiming a headache, which was unusual. So tonight, the deck, the view and the sound of the surf belonged to Doc alone. He was fine with that.

He stood by the edge of the deck, resting his beer on the railing, watching the tide go out as the sun closed in on the ocean. When the sun finally kissed the horizon, he turned back to his lounge chair and rested his half-empty bottle on the small round plastic table. He took his time arranging kindling and logs in the fire pit, then picked up the butane fire starter. He held the trigger and applied the long blue flame to the kindling. The dried wood wheezed and crackled as fire wrapped itself around the logs.

He stretched out on the chaise with a rolled-up beach towel to support his neck. A cool breeze competed with the heat from the fire in perfect two-part harmony. He reached over and picked up the bottle and got ready for the show.

It did not disappoint. Orange and purple clouds shrouded the blood-red disc. The afterglow remained, deepening the color. Eventually, the abandoned clouds lost the light, and the ocean grew an inky black while the darkening sky and sea merged until the horizon disappeared. Although no moon shone that night, light from the city spilled into the sky, obscured the stars. Doc searched for some anyway.

A sudden gust off the ocean stoked the fire as orange and yellow flames grew taller and black embers billowed to reveal blushing red interiors. Flakes of incandescent yellow swirled upwards carried by the warm currents only to blink out, their ashes scattered by the same gust that had encouraged their escape. The sound of retreating waves crashing onto the beach below blended with the steady hum of tires on the highway behind the house. He drifted off and dreamed of music and sunshine and lost loves.

"Wakey-wakey."

Doc felt a sharp pain explode behind his eyes. His head jerked back into the towel, and for an instant he thought he'd fallen asleep at the wheel and was in a car crash. He heard cloth rip and buttons pop as somebody pulled on his shirt, yanking him up to a sitting position. Doc put a hand to his face and felt raw skin. His fingers felt wet and sticky and dripped with blood.

"Where's the fucking money, asshole?"

Sharp pain again, this time from the left side of his head. Blood ran into his eyes and all he could see was the silhouette of a man hovering over him, about to hit him with the butt of a gun. Doc lifted his arms to block the blow, but the man let go of Doc's shirt and shoved him back into the chaise.

When Doc looked up, he saw a gun pointing at him. The man, his back to the fire, his face in shadow, said, "Where's the fucking money? Don't make me ask again or I'll split your head open."

"Who the fuck are you?" ask Doc, trying to swing his legs off the chaise and stand up.

"Don't you fucking move." The man's voice was full of rage. "Keep your hands up and stay right there on your back and tell me where the fucking money is."

"Okay, okay," said Doc. The pain was starting to subside, but there was no point trying to bluff. "It's in the house." Doc touched his head. It hurt and felt hot. The skin was torn and tender and he was still bleeding. "Can I sit up at least? I'm fucking choking here." Doc slowly sat up on the edge of the chaise, still holding his hands on his head, trying to make himself look more hurt than he was. He could hear the man breathing heavily. Then his eyes finally focused and he saw the man clearly. It was Kyle, owner of the strip joint in Boston. He wasn't totally surprised.

"You. How'd you find me?"

"Never the fuck mind how I found you," said Kyle. "Take me to my money. Now!"

"Okay, take it easy. I'm gonna stand up now so I can show you," he said. He rocked back and forth on the chaise as if to gain momentum, but on the second rock backwards, he reached back and picked up a log from the stack by the fire pit. He swung it down toward Kyle's arm with the gun.

Doc missed. Still pointing the gun at him, Kyle kicked Doc's knee. Doc fell back over the chaise and against the fire pit, but scrambled up and away from the flames, scattering hot embers into the air. Kyle stepped back to avoid them. As he did, Doc scooped up the butane fire starter, pressed the trigger and swung the long blue flame at Kyle, striking his hand. Kyle shouted in pain, dropped the gun, and stumbled backwards toward the ocean. Doc ran at him pushing the blue flame into Kyle's face. Kyle twisted his head but the flame scorched his ear and neck and the collar of his shirt.

Kyle knocked the fire starter out of Doc's hand as Doc hit him in the face with a solid left that hardly had an effect. Kyle swung a leg around and kicked Doc in the hip, then kicked him in the stomach. Doc folded and landed on his butt, facing the ocean. Kyle towered over him.

Doc fought to breathe as he watched Kyle pick up the log. He tried to stand but was too slow. Kyle lifted the log over his head, about to bring it down on Doc. Doc cringed and raised his arms to deflect the blow, but it never came. Kyle seemed frozen in position as Doc registered the sound of a gunshot.

"What are you...?" Kyle's expression went from rage to shock. He dropped the log and placed a hand on the center of his chest. A black stain bubbled past his fingers and spread into a large circle. Kyle fell like a chopped tree, bouncing once before settling on the wooden deck.

65

Doc rolled onto his side to look in the direction of the shot. It was hard to see, but Doc recognized Billy in the dark, standing on the deck by the open doorway. A woman Doc thought at first was Brianna stood next to him. She held a gun in one hand and a flashlight in the other.

"Thanks," Doc said to her. She turned the flashlight on and shined the light in Doc's eyes. He raised his hand to block the light.

"Over there," he heard the woman say to Billy. "Move!" It wasn't Brianna's voice.

Billy walked over to Doc and offered a hand to help him up.

"Don't touch him! And you, don't get up." She stepped toward them, gun pointed at Billy. "Stay right where you are, both of you. Don't move if you don't want to get shot."

Doc realized he didn't know this woman. He saw the purse hanging on a strap from her shoulder, then noticed she and Billy were dressed up as if on a date. He turned to Billy but Billy averted Doc's eyes.

The beam of light traveled from Doc to Kyle. Doc followed the light and saw Kyle on his back, half his face burnt, gasping for breath. Doc watched in fascination as wisps of smoke rose from Kyle's skin and hair and curled upward. The dark stain covering most his shirt became red in the bright light, but the puddle of blood on the deck next to him was black in the yellow light of the fire. Blood dripped down between the slats of wood onto the sand below.

Billy looked like he was about to piss himself. Doc caught his eye and nodded at Kyle's gun on the floor by Billy's feet, but Jesse caught the motion.

"Don't," was all she said.

Doc raised his hands behind his head in surrender.

She kicked Kyle's gun and sent it spinning to the other side of the deck.

Kyle groaned. His head moved. He opened one eye.

Jesse turned to look at him, her gun now on Doc.

"Kyle." Her voice was ice. She took a step back to avoid getting blood on her shoes. Kyle lifted his head to look at her. His lips moved as he tried to speak. Finally, he whispered, "Carolyn?" His head fell back with a thud. He blinked once at the sky. Then the wheezing stopped.

Doc and Billy were staring at Kyle's motionless face. Jesse aimed the beam back at Doc's eyes. He blocked the light with his arm.

"I know you got the money here. You got one minute to hand it over or I'll shoot you both and look for it myself. This place just ain't that big."

"She told me she was just gonna take Tiffany's share," Billy said as if it were a fact.

Doc looked at Billy, then turned to Jesse and acted a little embarrassed for Billy. "Really?"

"Please," she said. "He's your friend."

"Lady, who are you?" asked Doc.

"All you need to know—"

"Jesse," said Billy. "She's Tiffany's friend, Jesse."

"Jesse?" Doc paused. "Oh, that Jesse." He looked toward Kyle. "Were you his friend, too?"

"I'm holding the gun here," she said. "You really looking to piss me off?"

"Don't argue with her," Billy said. "She knows everything."

"What you should be focusing on," she directed to Doc, "is this gun I'm holding pointing at you." She waited for him to look at her. "Now, tell me where the money is as if your life depended on it, because it does." She lifted the gun pointed it at Doc's face. "I know it's here. Billy already told me."

Good move, Billy, thought Doc. I can work with that. He looked past the gun and the light. "It's in a safe, a floor safe. Billy doesn't know the combination, only I do. Shoot either of us and I promise you won't get a cent."

"Right. Not a cent." Billy felt obligated to add in.

"We can all walk away from this in one piece. I mean, everybody but this guy here you just shot." Doc cocked his head at Kyle.

"Fine. Give me the money and we all walk away."

"Okay. Just don't shoot us. That okay with you, Billy?"

"Whatever you say, Doc."

She nodded and motioned with the gun. "Get up. I see the money in sixty seconds and no one gets shot."

Doc guessed the opposite was true. Billy helped him to his feet.

"You." She held the gun on Doc. "You're the one that shot Tiffany?"

She waited for a response but Doc didn't move.

"All right," she said and closed her eyes for a half-a-second. She took a deep breath. "The money's inside, right?" she asked. Doc nodded. "You first, then Billy. Hurry the fuck up," she said.

Billy followed Doc into the apartment. Jesse stood in the doorway holding the gun and flashlight on them.

"Turn on a light."

"The switch is by the door, to your right," said Doc.

She stepped into the room. Without taking her eyes or the gun off them, she found the wall switch with the back of her hand, then dropped the flashlight and turned on the ceiling lights. She slid the glass door closed. The two men waited while she took in the room.

"What are you paying for this place?"

"3200 a month." Doc still had his hands up.

"Jesus," she said. "The money," she said. "Where's—"

"It's right here." Doc pointed at the drums.

"The money's in the drums?" she said.

"It's under the drums in the floor safe. I got to move the drums first."

"All right." She kept the gun and her eyes on Doc but spoke to Billy. "Help him move it."

Doc tapped his cheek twice with his fingers as he spoke to Billy. "Grab the seat and the hi hat and lay them on the couch." Doc could see Billy's eyes widen. "Go ahead. It's all right."

Billy moved the pieces as Doc went around to the front of the drums and loosened the clamps on the front head. As Billy approached the couch, Jesse took a step back to keep an eye on what they both were doing.

"The snare, Billy," Doc said pointing at the metal drum. "Get the snare," he said, adding, "Careful with it. Two-ten."

Doc stole a look at Jesse. She didn't blink.

Billy returned to the drum kit. He lifted the chrome snare off the stand and carried it in both hands toward the couch. Jesse moved back against the sliding door to put more distance between her and Billy and the metal drum he carried.

Doc wrapped both hands around the stand

supporting the 22-inch Zildjian ride cymbal. He held it horizontal to the ground like half a barbell. He turned in Jesse's direction.

"What do you want us to do with the body out on the deck?" Doc asked.

"Huh?" She turned to Doc. Billy swung the heavy shell of the metal drum into the side of her head.

66

The first strike surprised and stunned her. Billy hit her a second time, throwing her off-balance. Doc held the cymbal stand like a lance and charged into her, using the large brass cymbal as a shield, ramming it into the gun in her hand. She got off three quick shots before they forced her into the glass door. The shots were loud and smoke filled the small room, but the cymbal's solid bronze sloped surface deflected the first two bullets to the ceiling and the wall. The third bullet bounced off the cymbal past her into the sliding door, shattering the glass into a thousand little beads.

Jesse fell backwards through the broken glass, tripping over the threshold and landing on the deck. She fired two more times, but they went high. Then the bolt shot out and everyone knew she fired the last bullet.

She threw the empty gun at Doc. He knocked it away with the cymbal. A part of his mind noted a crack in the cymbal from one of the bullets.

Doc dropped his shield and weapon and went for her. Billy got there first, swinging the snare back for the coup de grâce. Jesse's legs swung up and forward and she leaped to a standing position, straight arming Billy in the jaw. Billy ran into the punch, compounding its impact and throwing him backwards. Doc was almost on her when she swung her purse by the strap, hitting him in the face. Billy threw the drum at her. She dropped her purse and caught the drum, then threw the drum at Doc. He blocked it with his arms as she kicked once at his groin. She missed.

Billy ran behind her and had her in a bear hug, lifting her as she elbowed him and kicked the air. Doc punched her stomach but she kicked him in the chest with both feet, pushing him backwards. She reached behind her head and boxed Billy's ears, loosening his grip on her.

Twisting free and pivoting on one foot, she raised her leg and kicked Billy in the stomach sending him onto his butt. She and Doc traded punches until Billy got up and tackled her from behind. They bounced and rolled around the deck, a six limbed beast until Doc heard the railing crack. He watched helplessly as Billy and Jesse disappeared off the edge of the deck.

Doc picked up Kyle's gun and leaped down the steps to find Billy in a daze lying on top of Jesse.

"Billy! Get up," whispered Doc. "You okay?"

The night was dark, the sky and ocean black.

Doc looked up and down the beach but saw no one. Billy, breathing loudly, rolled off Jesse and lay on his back.

Jesse was motionless on her stomach, half-covered with sand. Doc kneeled down and pulled her face out of the sand. Her eyes were closed and she was bleeding from her forehead where she landed on a fist-sized rock.

Doc stood and checked the beach again. No lights. No people that he could see. He shook Billy by the shoulder. "Can you walk? Are you okay?" Billy nodded and sat back on his heels. "Think so," he said. "Is she...?"

"Forget her. Push the dead guy over the deck and toss him down here. Fast! And bring her gun and pocketbook, too."

"What?" Billy looked drunk. "Shove him over the railing?"

"You want to carry him down the stairs? Just do it!"

For a split-second Doc wasn't sure what Billy was going to do before he spoke up.

"She told me she had a friend and if she didn't call him, they'd—"

Doc was firm. "Too late now. Anyway, it was probably B.S. We did the same thing to Teddy. This lady had no friends, not anyone she could trust, and I'm sure she wasn't planning to share the money with anyone. Once we take care of these bodies, there won't be anything to connect us with any of this. Now throw the guy down here and bring the gun and purse. Now!"

Billy got up and climbed the steps to the deck. When Doc looked back at Jesse, he saw her eyes were open. He didn't hesitate.

He straddled her back and pushed on the back of her head with both hands, shoving her nose and mouth back into the sand. She arched her back and tried to lift her head, but she was too damaged, too weak to fight. Her arms and legs flailed for almost half a minute before she went still. It was another 30-seconds before he released the pressure on the back of her head, when Kyle's body crashed down on the beach from the deck above. Billy rushed down the stairs. He handed the gun and pocketbook to Doc.

"I already got back my cellphone. She took it." Billy looked at Jesse's body. "She's dead, huh?"

"She's dead." That's all he'd ever tell Billy. "Empty their pockets. I'll get the dinghy. We're dumping the bodies in the ocean."

"We're dumping them out in the ocean?"

"I am. And the guns. And that purse."

"Won't they wash back up?"

"Maybe, but not for sure and probably not together. If we're lucky, there won't be enough left to identify them or link them to us."

Billy went through their pockets and her purse, taking their wallets and car keys, while Doc unlocked the dinghy and dragged it close to the bodies. They moved both bodies into the dinghy, then tossed in both guns and the purse. Together they dragged the dinghy into the water until it floated, rocking gently in the outgoing tide. Doc held the bow while giving Billy final instructions.

"Burn their wallets in the firepit. Don't keep anything."

"What—"

"While that's burning, sweep up the glass, bag it and throw it in the trash. You know where the broom is?"

"Yeah."

"Then wash the blood off the deck with the hose. Do the best you can. I'll clean myself later."

"What about the door and the railing? We messed things up good."

Doc was mostly talking to himself. "I'll call an emergency glass door guy first thing in the morning, and I can fix the railing myself good enough before Fred and Dorothy get back the next day." He checked up and down the beach and saw no one. "We're pushing our luck standing here. We'll dig out the bullets from the ceiling and wall and spackle the holes with toothpaste when I get back. There's time for that." He looked at Billy. "What are you supposed to be doing right now?"

"Burn their IDs. Wash the blood off."

"Toss the ashes from the fire off the deck onto the beach, then come down here and kick up the sand to mix it up." He thought for a second. "Put the drums back together. What else? When's Brianna coming back?"

Billy looked at his watch. "Around dinner

time. What about their cars?"

"Yeah.... When I get back, in a few hours at the most, we'll drive them into L.A. and leave them with the keys in the ignition. Somebody will take them. Did we forget anything? You can tell me later what the hell you were doing with Jesse... Carolyn... whatever her name is, was."

Time slowed and the two men stared at each other in silence. Doc suspected what Billy had been up to with the woman, but that was a discussion for some other time. "You don't want to involve Brianna in any of this, right? You want to protect her, in case something goes wrong?"

"Yeah, I do," he answered.

"Well, something has gone wrong, so say nothing to her," warned Doc. He stepped into the dinghy, avoiding the bodies, sat in the middle and grabbed the oars. "I'll row out a distance before starting the engine in case somebody can hear it." Billy pushed the dinghy over short breaking waves until the oars grabbed water. Billy gave the dinghy one last shove, then ran across the sand and up the stairs to the deck.

PART FIVE

A NEW YEAR

67

Doc wanted the sign to have a retro, blue neon-look. The others agreed. It read, Doc's Drum Shop. It had been a used bookstore on Pico Boulevard, two-and-a-half blocks from the ocean. Fred and Dorothy hooked them up with the landlord. Jack helped with the inventory.

Used guitars and old-school amps surrounded Doc's vintage Ludwig kit in the huge front window that always seemed to need washing from finger-prints and smog. His show kit's large Zildjian ride cymbal now sported a groove and a triangular piece missing where cracks were excised. Both defects were caused by bullets fired from a gun, but even though customers frequently asked, Doc never told them what really caused the cracks.

A recessed doorway from the street led right into the large showroom. Electric and acoustic gui-tars, bass guitars, 12-strings, ukuleles, mandolins—there was even a bouzouki and an oud—all used, hung on the left wall, sharing space here and there with autographed photos of local bands and signed concert and charity posters from nearby venues. Keyboards and electronic drum kits connected to amplifiers populated the center of the floor. On the right side, a pair of conga drums and some frame drums from Africa and the Middle East shared space with conventional drum sets complete with cymbals and hardware. In the back right corner was a sound-treated room with stacks of cymbals on multilevel stands and pairs of wooden- and plastic-tipped sticks resting nearby. Guitar picks, cables and drumsticks were available to anyone who wanted to give an instrument a try, making the place popular with musicians, wannabes, and school kids. Shelves and glass showcases along the wall by the front window contained sticks, strings, pedals and other accessories and the lone cash register.

All the way in the back, a hallway led to a practice room with sound-treated walls and a pair of synth drum kits facing each other where Doc gave lessons, sometimes free to kids from the neighborhood. Further down the hallway were doors to a bathroom and the office with a couch for taking naps after lunch.

The store was open from 10:00 to 5:00 Monday through Friday and 10:00 to 3:00 on Saturdays. Doc taught students for a half-hour each before the store opened on Saturdays and late in the afternoon during the week. Billy did not have to show up to open until 10:00, but he was usually there by 9:30.

He was supposed to wash the front window every morning, but usually forgot unless Doc reminded him, which Doc did less often because Billy was never one for details. He left streaks on the glass which seemed to bother Doc more than Billy. The store was big but quiet enough most days for the two to manage, but Brianna helped out on Saturdays and for special events.

It was Brianna who encouraged the friends to invest the money in Doc's dream. It was now or never. Life clearly didn't offer many second chances, and she figured Doc and Billy just about used up their share of them. Since the place had been a bookstore with a lot of open space, Billy, Doc and Brianna were able to do most of the renovation themselves, cutting costs and making it a more personal project.

Brianna also came up with the plan how to finance the startup costs legally and leave a legitimate paper trail. Doc and Billy had made some safe investments according to their original plan, but Brianna suggested buying a sailboat that needed work. She overhauled the engine and electrical system while Doc and Billy painted and repaired the exterior and deck. They sold the refurbished boat through Duffy's Marina, making a decent profit and paying Joe a small commission. As soon as one boat was finished, they bought another and restarted the process. Making money wasn't the only objective; laundering it was, too. By the time the fifth boat sold they had cleared enough money to cover startup costs for the store, including the first and last month's rent, initial inventory and insurance.

Doc and Billy never told Brianna about what happened that night at Doc's apartment or on the beach, but from time to time, it was heavy on their minds, particularly for Billy. For a while, Doc looked out to sea during the day from the spot where blood had dripped from the deck and wondered if the currents and sharks worked in their favor or if the bodies would someday wash up on the beach. It was months before he could bring himself to sit out on the deck at night and enjoy the view and a fire in the fire pit.

Billy spent most of his time at the store or with Brianna. Images of Jesse and her pony tail kept Billy away from his morning routine at the beach. Some nights he still dreamed of the bedroom in the foster home, the one with the blond headboard and the big oak and the pool in the backyard, the safe bedroom he only imagined in a loving home that never really existed, and each time he woke, he would roll over and find Brianna and let the goodness of his world come back in.

It was Saturday afternoon, a slow time for sales in the musical instrument business. Billy was still at lunch with Brianna, leaving Doc alone to manage the shop. Doc sat on a stool behind a glass showcase making the most of the quiet, searching the laptop for local venues to see who was playing when and where.

He was certain the man in the ball cap and shades looking at the guitars and drums in the front window was just killing time with no intention of entering. But enter he did. He took his time checking out the layout of the store as though he was planning to buy the place. Backlit by the storefront window, it was hard to see his face.

"May I help you?" Doc finally asked.

"Nice place you got here." The man pointed at the guitars hanging against the wall. "Lot of shapes and color in those guitars. How long you been in business?" He took off his sunglasses and approached Doc.

Shapes and colors? Clearly this guy wasn't a musician. The way he said "guitar" and "here," dropping the "r", made another thing clear. The man was from Boston. Late sixties, maybe older, pale skin, red nose, thinning gray hair in need of a trim. His polo shirt was a little heavy for the climate and tight around the belly, but it was the black leather Reeboks below his wrinkled chinos that nailed it. The guy was a Boston cop.

No jacket and his shirt was tucked in. He looked unarmed to Doc.

"Looking for something specific?" Doc waited a beat. "But something tells me you're not interested in an American Strat."

"An American what?"

"Exactly. How can I help you, officer?"

The man smiled broadly. "Am I that obvious?"

"You know you are. You can't help yourself. Tell me what you want and I'll see what I can do."

"You're Alonzo Hayes, aren't you?"

Doc came around the counter.

"People call me Doc. And you are?"

The man held out his hand. Doc shook it. The man carried the faint smell of cigarettes and Aqua Velva. "Bob Wertz. Detective with the Boston Police, or at least I was. Retired now, out here with my wife visiting our daughter and her husband. They just had twin baby girls. Looks like we'll be out here visiting from time to time."

"Congratulations," said Doc. He pointed at the closest drum kit on the floor. "May I suggest that green and black 4-piece Tama kit with Zildjian cymbals? Tama is having a sale and Zildjians are the only cymbals we carry."

Wertz gave a short laugh. So far, he was playing Good Cop. "No, thanks. I don't think their mother is quite ready for that yet." He glanced back at the drums. "Do girls really play drums?"

"Some of the best."

"You're kidding me."

"Nope."

"What about...." He searched for the word. "You know, muscles, arm strength?"

"They hit plenty hard, but drums aren't about how hard you hit. It's about skill, speed, technique, taste and timing."

"Timing's everything, don't you think?" said

Wertz.

Doc said nothing and waited. Wertz turned back to him with a frozen grin. "You got kids, Alonzo? You got a daughter?"

"You want to tell me what you're here for, Bob? I mean, you're not exactly looking to buy."

"Well, I guess I'm losing my touch. Let's just say I was in the neighborhood and thought I'd get a close up look at the man who got away with a pile of mob money and shooting Cynthia Marcus."

Doc swallowed. Wertz noticed. "Who's Cynthia Marcus?"

"You probably knew her as Tiffany, an exotic dancer at one of your hangouts—The Improper Bostonian. You remember. Somebody shot her around the time you stopped showing up for work and disappeared. And I noticed you didn't ask about the money."

"What money?" Doc sounded calm but impatient. "Look, Bob Wertz, retired cop from Boston, if that's who you are and not some squirrelly nutcase trying to bust my chops so he can get out of the sun, let's get this straight. I run a legitimate business. I played a little drums in Boston and don't remember the name of every stripper I met or every club I worked. I never owned a gun, never shot nobody, and know nothing about mob money. So, unless you're planning to buy something, let's not waste each other's time. Get back to your granddaughters and let me get back to work."

Wertz waited until Doc finished, then

dropped the smile. "You don't recognize me, do you Alonzo?"

It dawned on Doc why this cop looked so familiar.

The words came out slowly. "Yeah ... I do now." Doc took a step closer. Wertz didn't budge. "You were one of the cops from UMass that framed me. You testified against me at the trial."

The muscles around Wertz's eyes softened. What Doc saw in his face was shame.

"No, I didn't frame you." He sounded hoarse and cleared his throat. "I made a mistake. I was a security guard back then."

"That's it? You made a mistake?"

"A bad call. I listened to the wrong people. It was a different time, Alonzo, a difficult time."

"Stop calling me Alonzo. We aren't friends."

"True enough. I didn't come here to make friends, but you know how it works, especially back then. Once the lawyers took over, it was out of my hands. I was a guard and, yeah, I backed up the cop's testimony. That's the way it was done, the way it's still done. Hell, the only difference is that today everyone knows the system is broken. Back then, when you were low on the totem pole, you did what you were told."

"Did what you were told ...," repeated Doc. A voice in the back of Doc's head started to shout, but Doc ignored it.

"When you were convicted, I thought I did the right thing and that was the end of it, but it never felt right. Some cases never feel right, but you get used to it. Not this one."

Doc's face felt hot. He clenched his fists. "What are you doing here, Bob?"

Wertz shrugged. "I was on the Cynthia Marcus case. My last case as detective. Maybe I wouldn't have ID'd you, but I remembered you from... before."

"So what, now you're looking for a shake down? I had nothing to do—"

"No, not that. More like a chance to... square a debt."

"Square a debt? What the hell are you talking about?"

"Look. I'm a grandfather who doesn't give a rat's ass about strip clubs, low-life gangsters or their money. They all can kill each other for all I care. I'm just letting you know...."

Wertz took a deep breath and looked out into the street through the front window, then looked down at the floor. When he looked up at Doc, he was bent over as though he was carrying something heavy on his back.

"All these years dealing with human garbage, it gets to you." He took another deep breath, then swallowed while Doc waited. "But what I know is that you weren't a part of that until I helped put you there... until I went along with what they did to you... what I helped to do to you. I've carried that around long enough. I'm tired. It's been poisoning me, and I'm afraid it's poisoning people I love, my wife, my daughter, my granddaughters... so now I'm going to do the right thing so maybe that will help."

"Do the right thing? Now?" Doc sneered. "I don't need your help now."

"Not help you. Help me." He looked around the store. "I just wanted to meet you and say...."

Doc waited. "Say what?"

He stood upright and took a big breath, but said nothing. Instead, he flapped his arms in defeat. "I got to get going and meet my wife. She's shopping for baby stuff."

He lifted his right hand toward Doc and dropped it just as fast, then turned and walked to the door. He turned back to Doc. "When Allie and Nikki, that's the twins, when the girls get a little older, I'll bring them down and pick out musical instruments for them." He smiled the half-smile again. "Anything but drums."

"No. Don't." Doc shook his head. "Don't come here again, Bob."

It took a moment, but Wertz responded with a nod. He put his sunglasses back on, turned then raised a hand in half of a wave as he walked out the door. Doc stared at the doorway for a long time. He'd never look out the doorway again without wondering when Bob Wertz was coming back.

Doc decided to call it a day and close early. He shut the lid of the laptop and called Billy to let him know not to bother coming in. He locked up the store, and as he passed the alley next to the store, he saw a bearded figure in dirty gray clothes, a homeless man, maybe thirty, sitting on a broad piece of cardboard, his back against the wall. Doc had seen him in the neighborhood before, but never paid him much attention. Their eyes met and Doc walked toward him. The man sat up, ready to bolt, but Doc already had a hundred dollar bill in his outstretched hand. He leaned over and handed it to the man, then pointed toward the front of the store.

"How would you like a job every morning washing the front window of my store here?" Doc asked.

THE END

AUTHOR'S NOTE

ACKNOWLEDGMENTS

My interest in crime fiction began as a boy working in my father's store. Boylston Jewelry was a small 400-square foot one-person shop just off Washington Street and the infamous Boston Combat Zone. Dad's store was flanked on one side by Joe & Nemo's where I chomped on paper-thin hamburgers while staring at the words "LOVE" and "HATE" tattooed on the knuckles of the cook's hands. On the other side of my father's store was the infamous Gilded Cage which by that time devolved from burlesque and jazz acts into a strip club and center for B-girl activities. Diagonally across Washington Street was the Pilgrim Theatre where the marque proudly displayed the titles of two new porn films weekly, expanding my youthful interests and vocabulary.

Dad's customers and friends represented most every ethnicity and background. I met professors, doctors and lawyers, politicians, cops and police detectives, insurance investigators, laborers, Boston Brahmin WASPs and the maids who traveled from Ireland to work in their homes, members of the clergy, actors from the theater and local TV, standup comics, jazz and classical musicians, grocers, bookies, *makhers, mamzers, kibitzers, kvetschs, gonifs, gazlins, shikers, schmoozers, shnorers, shimazls and alter kakers*. Everyone had a story to tell. Dad treated them all with respect and compassion while still earning an honest living.

My father's perspective on people did not come easy. He was street smart, having been homeless himself for a time as a child in Boston's West End. He grew up with a severe hearing loss so trained himself not only to lip- and speech-read, but to be an astute observer of behavior. He could infer people's intent and motivation as though he were telepathic, a useful talent in retail but also in life.

He used these skills in the two worlds he inhabited. During the day he worked in his store and when he got home was a loving parent to us kids and loving husband to my equally loving mother, Ruthie. At night, he played alto sax with small jazz combos in clubs all over town late into the morning. He enjoyed both worlds. He was tough and confident and protected himself and his family, but at the same time demonstrated empathy for others, especially the vulnerable. He wasn't afraid to show he cared. He was fearless, but also a mensch, and I picked up what I could from his example.

I remember one afternoon a pink Caddie pulled up in front of the store (a no parking zone; even Dad couldn't park there). The big burley driver got out, opened the back door and two tall, identically dressed women—mother and daughter—got out and entered the store. They both had their hair up in beehive arrangements and wore identical pastel colored satin dresses. The *shtarker*, Yiddish for thug, stood by the door so no other customers could enter—he was obviously their bodyguard, too— while my father waited on the women. After a short while they picked out matching St. Christopher medals, telling Dad to send it to their home. They left without paying.

I immediately asked Dad who they were. He said they were the wife and daughter of a gangster who ran a large crime organization in town. My father explained that, a few years earlier, a man came into his store in the middle of the afternoon, opened the cash register and grabbed a fistful of $20 bills. When Dad challenged him, the *gonif* (thief) leaned to the side and pulled up his jacket to show a gun holstered on his hip. He told Dad he would be back next week and left. When Dad described the man to a beat cop, he was told there was nothing that could be done. Complaining to the police would only result in trouble from the mob, explained the cop. Dad then spoke to a customer with whom he occasionally had a drink next store at the Cage and who worked for the same organization. That man told Dad either learn to live with it or risk talking with the mob boss. The boss, he explained, was the only one who could do anything about it. Dad made an appointment to see the boss at his office the next day.

Soon after Dad entered the building and identified himself, a man in a suit, who turned out to be the boss's bodyguard, escorted Dad to the boss's office. Dad introduced himself and thanked the boss for his time. Both men listened without reaction as Dad explained that he owned a small shop and was trying to make a living to take care of his wife and three children and his wife's elderly parents and that he couldn't do that if someone was taking money from the register. The boss acknowledged that the man who stole Dad's money worked for him and told my Father he understood Dad's problem. "I'll talk to him and he won't bother you anymore," the boss said, "but you understand, I expect a favor in return."

Dad said, "I'm just a salesman. I don't want to hurt anyone." Dad said the boss and the bodyguard found that funny and laughed.

"Relax, Mr. Katz. Nothing at all like that," the boss said. "I'm going to send my wife and daughter to see you at your store. All I ask is that you take care of them."

Dad agreed. The next day, the man who took the money walked into the store, all smiles, and addressed my father by his first name. "I didn't know you knew the boss," he said. "You don't have to worry about anything anymore. Just let me know if anybody bothers you and I'll take care of him."

I interrupted my father to ask, "Did he give you the money back?"

"No-o-o," Dad said, shaking his head. "That was never going to happen." Dad said about a week after that, the wife and daughter showed up, picked out some modest earrings, and Dad mailed the pieces to them. "They come every year, for the past four years, and pick something out and I mail it to them."

"That's it?" I asked.

"Sometimes I have to engrave something, but that's it."

"So, it's like you're paying for protection," I said to Dad.

"Oh, I don't give it to them for no," Dad said. "I include a bill in the package." Then he added, "For cost."

"Does he pay it?"

"Mails me a check," said Dad. "He admires my chutzpah."

So, my first acknowledgment is to my Dad, William Katz, for teaching me see each person as an individual worth getting know, no matter who they are or what they do. Without that ability, I never would have written this book.

Writing fiction is a fun and imaginative process, but requires a set of skills I did not possess until I studied under Seth Harwood, author, teacher and friend. His support, guidance, novels and short stories remain an inspiration to me. I will always be in his debt for the doors he opened.

As important were the contributions of author and good friend, Penny Myers Duffy, who shared with me years of lively back-and-forth about the nuts and bolts of writing. Penny's detailed edit of this manuscript and her valuable suggestions helped me mold the telling of Doc and Billy's adventure into a coherent narrative that I hope appeals to a wide range of readers as a story of two very real people.

I am fortunate to be surrounded by a talented community of creative and caring friends. Joe Duffy, Michael Kimbarow, and former bandmates, Glenn Kelly, Mark Caron and Chris Code, provided valuable feedback effecting the clarity of the narrative and direction of the story. I'm also grateful to fellow drummer, Tony Strivens, for providing copy editing and continuity services.

I'm deeply appreciative to author, screenwriter, humanitarian and friend, Larry Chambers, who corresponded with me over many years about the nature of screenwriting and storytelling and whose life's adventures inspired some of the more noble aspects of the characters in this book. Friends Fred Wilburn, Jim Moulé, Rich Becker, Mark Wright, Tom Jennings, Kevin Kearns, Mick McNeil, Phil Loverso, Chick LaPointe, Terry Wertz, and Peggy Morrison all read various drafts of this manuscript or related works and provided valuable feedback and discussion. I am forever grateful for their time and effort. It was Kevin who first pointed out to me there is something ironic in a book entitled *Every Dog* written by an author with the last name of *Katz*. I would be remiss not to thank my sister, Michele, and our late brother, Leonard, who were always supportive, always encouraging in my writing and practically every other pursuit. There are many other people who read my short stories and encouraged me to write this novel. I am grateful to them all.

Finally, I thank my late wife, Lynn Gilbert Johnson Katz, for introducing me to film noir and classic and contemporary crime literature. I was 20 years old when Lynn and her mother, Marion, took me to a theater one evening to see a double-feature revival of *The Maltese Falcon* and *The Big Sleep*, introducing me to the works of Dashiell Hammett and Raymond Chandler. To this day, Chandler's *The Long Goodbye* remains my favorite novel and serves as an ideal for me to work toward. I know my reach exceeds my grasp, but I don't know any other way to write, and Lynn was there, encouraging me every step of the way. Lynn was loving, fun, creative and exciting, initiating many of our personal adventures, some that worked their way into this tale in one form or another. She was always supportive, always encouraging me to tell my stories. She was my favorite critic and coach and my best friend.

Emerald eyes, this book is for you.

Rich Katz
Scottsdale, Arizona, October 2019

Made in the USA
Las Vegas, NV
15 December 2020

13323344R00254